Donna Douglas is the *Sunday Times* bestselling author of The Nightingale Girls series and The Nurses of Steeple Street series. She began writing stories on top of the coal shed in a south London back yard when she was a child, but has since graduated to a spare room at her home in York, where she lives with her husband and family.

A Mother's Journey

Donna DOUGLAS

ORION

First published in Great Britain in 2020 by Orion Fiction,
an imprint of The Orion Publishing Group Ltd
Carmelite House, 50 Victoria Embankment,
London EC4Y 0DZ

An Hachette UK company

1 3 5 7 9 10 8 6 4 2

A CIP catalogue record for this book is
available from the British Library.

ISBN (Paperback) 978 1 4091 9089 9
ISBN (eBook) 978 1 4091 9090 5

Typeset by Input Data Services Ltd, Somerset

Printed and bound in Great Britain by Clays Ltd, Elcograf S.p.A.

www.orionbooks.co.uk

To my wonderful family –
Ken, Harriet, Lewis and Seb.

Chapter One

1940

It was Big May Maguire who saw her first.

It was a bright, sunny Thursday afternoon at the end of June, the day after the Luftwaffe dropped their bombs on King George's Dock. Heat reflected off the cobbles of Jubilee Row, making the air shimmer. Front doors and windows were thrown open, and children sat in huddles on the kerb, too hot even to play.

May was working alongside Beattie Scuttle, braiding a net together. They often worked outside when it was fine, to save all the hemp dust getting in the house but also because it meant they could exchange gossip and keep an eye on what was going on in the street.

May's daughter Iris, who lived next door to Beattie, was on her hands and knees, donkey stoning her front step in a desultory fashion. From time to time she stopped to wipe away the perspiration that trickled down her face.

This afternoon, as May and Beattie handled their twine, needles and spools, they were discussing what they would do when Hitler's troops invaded.

'It's only a matter of time, Pop reckons,' May said. 'Now France has fallen, he says we'll be next. I'm surprised they haven't landed already.'

'I'll be ready for 'em,' said Beattie, not looking up from her work. 'I've got all my bankbooks and papers in my handbag and a bag packed under the bed, ready to go.'

I

'Go where, though?' Iris sat back on her heels, pushing a stray lock of damp dark hair back under her headscarf. 'Archie! Keep an eye on your sister,' she called out to her eight-year-old son, who was playing with his cousins at the top of the road.

'Our Lil says I can stay with her in Stockport.'

May glanced at her daughter. Her slight smile told her they were thinking the same thing.

'And you reckon you'll be safe over there?' Iris said.

'What are you talking about, Iris?' May turned on her in mock outrage. 'Of course she'll be safe. It's Stockport, in't it? Jerry will never think of going over there.'

'You're right, Ma,' Iris joined in. 'I mean, how will they ever find it? Especially with all the street signs taken down?'

Beattie looked from one to the other, very cross. 'I might have known you two would make fun,' she snapped, as May and Iris roared with laughter. 'Go on, then, since you've got all the answers as usual.' She paused to rub away a splinter in her thumb from the coarse sisal twine. 'What are *you* going to do when the invasion comes, May Maguire?'

'I'm not leaving Hull, that's for sure.' Hessle Road was the only home May knew. She had grown up overlooking the fish docks, seeing the tall masts of the trawlers from her bedroom window. Her father and her brothers had been fishermen, as were her husband and her sons.

And Jubilee Row had been her home for all her married life. She had first set up home at number sixteen as a young bride, forty years ago. Her children and their families had settled here, too. Her grandchildren now played on the cobbled street, just as her own five bains once had. When the Germans finally came, at least they would face them together.

'It's all right for you,' Beattie said. 'You've got a husband to

2

protect you. God only knows what those Germans will do to a poor widow like me . . .'

May cackled. Beattie was nearing sixty and as scrawny as an old chicken. 'You should be so lucky, Beattie Scuttle!'

Beattie looked offended. 'You can laugh, but I'm telling you, you hear all sorts—'

But May was no longer listening to her. Her gaze had shifted past Beattie, towards the top of the street.

A young woman was coming down the street towards them, staggering under the weight of a heavy suitcase that was nearly as big as she was. Her slight figure was huddled in a heavy black overcoat, in spite of the heat. Brown curls poked out from under a black felt hat.

'Who's this, I wonder?' May said.

Beattie glanced up from her work. Iris stopped her scrubbing and the three of them paused to watch the girl dragging her suitcase down the street. She was young – barely twenty, May would have guessed. Although the frown between her brows and the grim set of her mouth made her look older.

'She must be mafted in that big coat,' May said.

'She in't local,' Beattie Scuttle declared. 'I can tell you that now.'

As if to prove her point, the young woman paused on the other side of the road and took out a scrap of paper from her pocket. She studied it for a moment, then looked up and down the terrace, scanning the line of front doors.

'Are you lost, lass?' May called across to her.

The young woman looked up, startled, as if she had been roused from a dream. At first she did not reply, then she called back:

'I'm looking for number ten.'

Beattie was right, she wasn't local. Her accent was from

3

further north – York, or Harrogate perhaps. But that coat was too shabby for Harrogate.

'That's the one, with the polished brass knocker.' Beattie pointed it out. 'But you'll get no answer if you knock.'

'Thank you.' The girl put the scrap of paper back in her coat pocket.

'What's your business there?' Beattie called out.

The girl regarded her with a cool expression. 'That's my business,' she replied, then picked up her suitcase and began dragging it down the street.

Beattie turned to May, her pale eyes bulging with indignation. 'Did you hear that? I was only trying to be friendly.'

Big May laughed. 'You were being nosey, as usual.'

Beattie ignored her and threw a scowling look back at the young woman. 'She in't going to get far in this street with that attitude, I'm telling you that.'

'I wonder if she's visiting?' May said.

Beattie raised her brows. 'Now who's being nosey?' She shook her head. 'I doubt it. Since when did *she* ever get visitors?' She nodded towards number ten.

'That lass is a widow,' Iris said quietly.

May and Beattie both turned to look at her. 'Oh, aye?' Beattie said. 'And what makes you say that?'

'I can just tell.'

Of course you can, May thought. Iris had lost her own husband Arthur not a year since. Even though she made a good show of getting on with her life for the sake of her three children, May could still see the raw pain of grief behind her daughter's smile. It was only natural that Iris would recognise another woman's suffering.

'Happen she's moving in?' Beattie's voice broke through her reverie. 'Those upstairs rooms have been standing empty six months since.'

4

May Maguire turned her gaze to number ten, the only house on the street whose front door remained firmly closed, in spite of the heat. Thick lace curtains shrouded the windows.

'God help her if she is,' she said.

Chapter Two

Edie Copeland was aware of the three women watching her every step as she dragged her suitcase up the cramped stub of terraced houses. One was as tall and broad as a man, the other thin as a whip, both dressed in faded flowery pinnies, their heads wrapped in scarves. They were working together on some kind of heavy net that hung from a rail over a window frame. But the flat wooden needles were idle in their hands and Edie could feel their stares burning between her shoulder blades.

She should not have been so sharp, she thought. This was her new home, her new start. She was supposed to be fitting in, making friends not enemies. But her secrets had made her guarded, wary.

She reached the front door of number ten and turned to look back at the women, ready to give them a smile. But they abruptly turned away from her, going back to their work with disgruntled expressions. Only the younger woman gazed back at her with a sympathetic little smile before she turned and went on with her scrubbing.

Edie put down her suitcase and paused for a moment to massage the life back into her cramped, sore fingers. As she did, a flash of movement behind the lace curtains caught the corner of her eye. But when Edie looked again, it was gone.

She fumbled in her pocket for the key the landlady had given her. But before she could find it the front door suddenly opened and a voice from the shadows within said sharply, 'Come in, then, if you're coming. And take off your shoes, I've just done this floor.'

Edie dragged her suitcase over the front step and found herself in a narrow, tiled hallway. The overpowering smell of carbolic soap and furniture polish made her eyes water.

An elderly woman stood before her, very upright, her narrow shoulders pushed back. She bristled with severity, from her old-fashioned tweed skirt and twinset to her grey-ing hair, scraped back so tightly it drew her skin taut over her bony face. Her pale-blue eyes fixed on Edie through thick, horn-rimmed spectacles.

She did not look too friendly, but Edie was determined to win her over. She smiled and held out her hand. 'You must be Mrs Huggins? I'm Edie—'

'I know who you are.' The woman pointed to Edie's feet. 'Shoes,' she barked.

Edie bent to unbuckle her shoes, aware of the woman watching her. So this was the famous Patience Huggins, she thought.

Mrs Sandacre the landlady had warned Edie about her when she handed over the keys. 'They've been renting the downstairs rooms since my aunt owned the house,' she had said. 'He's a nice old soul, but she – well, let's just say she can be a bit – difficult.'

But that didn't concern Edie. After twelve years of living with her stepmother Rose, she could put up with anything.

Besides, beggars couldn't be choosers. She was lucky to find anywhere she could afford.

She was about to take off her coat, then saw the way Mrs Huggins was scrutinising her and thought better of it. In-stead she picked up her shoes in one hand and her suitcase in the other and headed for the stairs.

7

'By rights, this passageway is ours, seeing as it's on the ground floor,' Patience Huggins said, following her down the hall. 'You'll have to use it to go to and from your rooms, of course, but I'd appreciate it if you didn't dawdle, or make a mess. And be careful of the paintwork—'

'I'll do my best.' Edie turned and found herself nose to nose with the old woman. Patience Huggins obviously meant to follow her up the stairs.

'I think I can find my own way,' she said.

'Oh, but I—'

'Thank you for your help,' Edie cut her off firmly. 'I'll let you know if I need anything.'

Another bad impression I've made, she thought as she dragged her suitcase up the stairs, bumping it up each step, still aware of Mrs Huggins watching her from below. But this time she didn't care. After living with her stepmother she could recognise a bully when she saw one. And she was determined not to put up with it again.

Besides, she longed to explore her new home on her own. It was the first time Edie had seen the lodgings. She had been so desperate to find somewhere to live, she had taken the rooms as soon as Mrs Sandacre offered them to her, without even bothering to view them.

Now she was surprised at how small her new home was. Just two rooms: a cramped little kitchen at the top of the stairs, then a larger bedroom-cum-parlour at the front overlooking the street. As Edie opened the door, an overwhelming odour of musty damp and old age wafted out to greet her.

She pulled back the limp curtains and opened the sash window. Dusty beams of sunlight fell on the threadbare rug, the dark wooden bed, the chest of drawers and the two worn armchairs flanking the tiny fireplace. The wallpaper was yellowed with age, its faded flowers barely visible. Even with the June sun streaming through the glass, it all seemed dark, unloved and unwelcoming.

Edie lay back on the bed. The lumpy horsehair mattress barely yielded under her weight.

She suddenly felt bone weary, her limbs too leaden to move. She knew she should get started on her unpacking, but she did not have the strength.

She stared up at the ceiling. The plasterwork was yellowing, crazed with cracks. As Edie watched, some tiny black bugs emerged from one of the cracks and made their way unsteadily towards the light fitting. Outside, in the street, seagulls wheeled shrieking past her window and a distant factory hooter sounded.

So this was it. Her new start.

Oh Edie. What have you done?

She always was too impulsive for her own good. Perhaps she should have stayed in York, found a place to live there. At least she knew the city, she had friends there. Here she knew no one.

This was Rob's city, the place he had called home. Edie had never even visited. Rob had promised to bring her here, but there had not been time before he went away.

Now he would never show her around. She was all alone.

No, she corrected herself. Not all alone. She slipped her hand inside her coat, feeling the slight swell under her cotton summer dress.

How long before she started showing, she wondered. At the moment it was her secret, but in a couple of months she would not be able to hide it under her coat so easily. Everyone would know.

And what then?

Perhaps she should have been honest with the landlady, told her she was expecting. But then Mrs Sandacre would not have let the rooms to her, and she desperately needed a place to live.

She's going to find out sooner or later, a small, insistent voice needled at the back of her mind. *You can't hide it forever. Especially not with that nosey old woman downstairs . . .*

Edie pushed the thought away. That was a worry for tomorrow. She had enough on her mind for now, without looking for anything else.

Like how to make ends meet. She had very little money, except for a few pounds she had managed to save in the post office. She had enough to pay her rent and bills for a couple of months, but after that . . .

Irresponsible, that's what you are. How on earth do you think you can bring up a baby?

Her stepmother's sharp words rang in her ears, unleashing a wave of despair. Rose was right. It was irresponsible to take on lodgings she could barely afford in a city where she knew no one. Edie had no job, no friends, nothing familiar to cling to, and a desperately uncertain future ahead of her.

You'll make a mess of it, you mark my words. And you needn't think you can come crawling back here when you do. If you ask me, the best thing you can do for that child is to get rid of it . . .

Edie sat up sharply. This wouldn't do. She had to keep going, to stop herself thinking, otherwise she would be lost.

This was her new start, and she had to make it work. She simply had no other choice.

She hauled her suitcase on to the bed, unfastened the clasps and threw it open.

She did not have very much with her. She had pawned most of her good clothes. She hung up the few things she had in the wardrobe, trying not to notice the smell of damp wood and mothballs that assailed her as soon as she opened the doors.

At the bottom of the suitcase was a small wooden jewellery box. Edie had no jewellery to speak of, except for her wedding ring, but the box contained her treasures, as she called them.

Don't open it, a small voice whispered inside her head. Edie picked up the box and went to put it in a drawer but at the last minute she couldn't resist lifting the lid to look inside.

Immediately the dull gleam of Rob's pocket watch caught her eye. It had arrived three days ago, sent from a military hospital by one of his injured comrades. One of the lucky ones who had made it home from Dunkirk three weeks earlier.

Rob would have wanted you to have this, he had written. *He loved you with all his heart.*

Her fingers closed round the watch tightly, as if she could somehow feel the warmth of him through the engraved metal.

Underneath the watch was a newspaper clipping from the *Hull Daily Mail.* Rob's friend had sent that, too. Edie felt a tiny jolt at the blurry photograph of her darling Rob, smiling and handsome in his RAF uniform, underneath the headline, 'More Hull War Casualties'.

Casualties. It made it sound as if Rob was laid up in hospital somewhere, waiting to come home, instead of lost over France.

Edie smoothed out the clipping in her lap, smiling at the photograph. She did not need to read the words, she already knew them by heart:

The death on active service has been notified of Flight-Sgt Robert Copeland, aged 25 of Gypsyville. He leaves behind a wife.

Not just a wife, Edie thought, her hand resting on her belly again. Rob had been so looking forward to being a father. His joy had overcome all Edie's fears and misgivings.

How she wished he was here now to reassure her that everything would be all right.

As she placed the watch back into the box her fingers found the seashell her father had brought her back from Scarborough. She was ten years old and had been looking forward to going on the day trip for ages. But at the last minute Rose had decided she had been naughty and had to stay at home as punishment. Her father had pleaded Edie's case, but as usual, Rose had got her way.

Edie put the shell back in the box with the clipping and Rob's watch, snapping the lid shut. There was no point in dwelling on memories, good or bad. She had to keep looking forward, or else she would give up.

She was about to close the suitcase when she spotted the envelope tucked down the side. Edie took it out, read her name written on it in her father's handwriting, and her heart leapt. It had only been a few hours, but she already missed him dreadfully. Their parting had been so sudden, so harsh, there had been so much she wanted to say to him. But it was difficult with Rose standing there, watching them with her narrowed, jealous gaze as usual.

But her father had cared enough to smuggle a letter to her. Edie ripped it open, her hands shaking in anticipation. She couldn't wait to read it, to feel warmed and reassured, to know he still loved her, that in spite of Rose's best efforts he would always be there for her . . .

Inside was a five-pound note and a scrap of paper hastily scrawled with just two words:

I'm sorry.

The words slapped her in the face. Edie looked down at the money in her hand. She knew it was his way of saying goodbye.

She stuffed it back into the envelope and threw it in a

drawer. Stiff pride made her want to send it straight back to him, to hurt him as she felt hurt. But deep down she knew pride was a luxury she could no longer afford.

Edie took a deep, steadying breath. She couldn't afford to give in to self-pity. She had made a promise to Rob to make a home for them, and she meant to keep it.

'Find a place for us,' he had said to her. 'Somewhere we can be together, the three of us. Then when all this is over I'll come home to you, I promise.'

She pressed her hand to her belly. 'It's just the two of us now,' she said aloud to the empty room. Rob might not be able to keep his promise, but she still meant to keep hers.

Chapter Three

'It won't do,' Patience said, scrubbing at a grease spot on the wooden counter. 'I don't know what Mrs Sandacre was thinking of, I really don't. Horace, are you listening to me?'

'Yes, dear.' Her husband's weary voice came from behind his newspaper.

'I mean, we know nothing about her,' she went back to her cleaning. Her shoulder ached from scrubbing, but she was too agitated to stop. 'Who is she? Where has she come from?'

'Happen you might know a bit more about her if you hadn't bitten off her head the minute she walked in,' Horace mumbled from behind the newspaper.

Patience balled up the cloth in her hands and fought the urge to throw it at him. At least it might get his attention. There was no talking to Horace these days. If he wasn't reading the news in the paper, he was fiddling with the wireless, trying to find the news broadcasts. He even listened to the German stations giving out the names of the captured soldiers every night.

'And she's so young. She looks – lively.'

'It might be nice to have a bit of life about the place,' Horace said mildly.

'A bit of life?' The tightness in her throat made her voice shrill. 'A bit of life? I hope you're still saying that when she's throwing parties, having strangers tramping up and down the stairs, through our hall, in our back yard—'

She looked past the brown-taped windows to the back yard. *Her* yard. It wasn't right.

'Give the girl a chance, Patience. You've said yourself, you know nowt about her yet.'

'I know trouble when I see it,' Patience said darkly. 'And that girl's trouble, believe me.' She turned back from the window. 'You'll have to talk to Mrs Sandacre, anyway,' she said.

'What do you want me to say?'

'Tell her we don't want her here!'

'And why should she listen to us?'

'Because – because we've been good tenants for nearly forty years.'

'I shouldn't think that will make any difference.' Horace folded up his newspaper and nodded towards the stove. 'Summat's boiling over.'

Patience snatched up the bubbling pan of cabbage before it spilled and swung it over to the sink to drain. Infuriating as it was, she knew Horace was probably right. Things had been very different when Mr Sandacre owned the house. He would never have stood for any riff-raff. He had breeding. Not like his widow, renting out rooms to all and sundry.

Patience carefully transferred the drained vegetables to a china serving dish. It wasn't her very best china, but even though there were only the two of them she still liked to do things properly.

'That's not the point. Mrs Sandacre should have asked us.'

'It's her house, she can do as she likes.'

'That's as may be. But it's our home.'

'It in't like we haven't shared it before.'

'That was different. Miss Hodges was refined.'

Miss Hodges had been quiet, inoffensive and respectable.

She knew how to keep herself to herself. Patience hadn't even noticed when the old dear had quietly expired in bed just before Christmas.

Patience dumped the china dish down in the middle of the table. 'So when will you talk to Mrs Sandacre?' she asked, as she watched Horace ladling cabbage on to his plate. 'I think you should go down to the rent office tomorrow. It needs to be sorted out before the weekend—'

'No.'

She looked up sharply. 'What do you mean – no?'

'What I say. I in't doing it, Patience.'

Patience stared across the table at her husband as he calmly picked up his knife and fork and started eating.

'But you must!' she said.

'Why?'

'Because – because I don't want her here!'

Horace took a moment before he spoke. He looked back across the table at her, his jaw moving back and forth as he chewed his food.

'I do a lot for you, as you know,' he said finally. 'But I won't see a young girl put out on the street just because you've decided you don't like the look of her.' He shook his head. 'If you want to talk to Mrs Sandacre, you'll have to go and see her yourself.'

Patience's gaze dropped to her plate. 'You know I can't do that,' she said quietly.

'I don't know why.' He pointed towards the hall with his fork. 'There's the front door. All you have to do is go through it.'

They faced each other across the table, and Patience saw the mute challenge in his eyes. She pushed her plate away and stood up abruptly.

'Aren't you eating?' Horace asked.

'I'll put it in the oven and have it later.' She seized the Vim and doused the sink in a thick cloud.

And so it began, she thought. Edie Copeland had only been here half an hour, and she was already causing trouble. Horace would never have spoken to her like that usually. He understood how she felt, that her home was her sanctuary, the only place she truly felt safe.

'There's something about her,' she muttered. 'You see if I'm not right.'

Chapter Four

The first week of July came and went and there was no sign of the Nazi invasion everyone had feared. The air-raid sirens that had moaned over the city night after night fell silent, as did the anti-aircraft guns in Costello Playing Field. Meanwhile, according to the newspapers, the Spitfires were doing their best to keep the Luftwaffe from the skies.

Sam Scuttle was digging a hole in his mother Beattie's back garden. Iris watched him over the fence as she pegged out her washing next door. He had only been working since that morning but he was already waist deep, his vest stained with dirt, skin slick with sweat as he flung spadefuls of earth on to an ever-growing heap behind him.

'Burying a body, Sam?' Iris called out to him.

He paused, looking up at her with a grin. His sandy hair clung damply to his perspiring face.

'Nowt so exciting,' he called back. 'Ma wants an Anderson shelter.'

'The public shelter on the corner not good enough for her, then?'

'It's good enough for her, all right. But it's our Charlie she worries about.' Sam leant on his spade. 'Ma has a terrible job getting him out of the house when the sirens go off. He can't stand the noise.'

Iris nodded, understanding. Charlie Scuttle had been best pals with her older brother Jimmy. They had gone off to war together as a pair of happy-go-lucky sixteen year olds twenty-four years before. They had both returned home sadder and wiser. But while Jimmy had got on with his life, going back to work on the trawlers, getting married and having a family, poor Charlie had returned a terrified, mute husk of the young man he once was. Even now, more than twenty years later, he was a constant worry to poor Beattie.

But at least she had her younger son to help her. Sam was thirty years old, the same age as Iris. But unlike the other trawlermen in Jubilee Row, who had all gone off to join the Royal Naval Patrol Service when the war began, Sam had chosen to stay at home and signed up with the Auxiliary Fire Service.

He had never married, either, although Iris could not imagine him being short of offers. She let her gaze stray briefly down to his bare arms and shoulders, his muscles rippling under the gleaming golden skin. He was handsome enough to catch any girl's eye.

'I could build one for you, if you like?'

Iris looked up sharply at him, feeling guilty for staring. What was she thinking?

'I'm sorry?'

'A shelter.' Sam smiled, his sea-green eyes crinkling. If he'd noticed her watching him he did not show it.

'Oh no, I'd never hear the last of it from my mum if I did.' Iris shook her head. 'She likes us all in the communal shelter together. She reckons that way we'll all go together.'

'That's one way of looking at it, I suppose.'

'But you're right, I should do something with the garden.' Iris gazed around at the small, scrubby patch of ground. The sun had scorched and withered all the plants, leaving bald, baked earth. 'Arthur was the one with the green fingers, not me.'

He was always out there, rain or shine, tending his plants. Iris hadn't had the heart to touch it since he'd died.

'I could dig it over for you,' Sam said. 'I know I wouldn't do as good a job as your Arthur, but I could have a go? Happen you could grow some vegetables?'

'That's what Pop says I should do,' Iris said. 'He's offered to fettle it, but he's busy on his allotment this time of year.'

'Then let me help.'

Iris shook her head. 'I wouldn't want to put you to any trouble.' She nodded towards the hole. 'Besides, it looks as if you've got enough to do.'

Sam looked down at the spade in his hands. 'It will soon be finished,' he said. 'I don't mind helping out.'

'What's going on here, then?'

Iris' sister-in-law Dolly appeared at the back gate, flanked by her two young sons. The eldest, nine-year-old George, was staggering under the weight of a wireless battery accumulator which he carried in his arms.

'How long do I have to carry this?' he grumbled.

'Until I tell you not to,' Dolly snapped.

'But I want to go and play!'

'I want never gets.' Dolly cuffed her son around the ear. She was as petite and pretty as a china doll, with her pink lips, wide blue eyes and perfectly styled blonde curls. But as Iris knew, looks could be deceiving. And they certainly were in Dolly Maguire's case.

'What are you two talking about?' she wanted to know, looking from one to the other.

'None of your business.' Iris changed the subject, looking at the accumulator in George's arms. 'You off to Shelby's with that?'

Dolly nodded. 'Mum's orders. I thought you might fancy walking up to Anlaby Road with me?'

'Aye, I would. I could get mine refilled while I'm at it. Wait there while I fetch it. We can stick them both in the pram.'

Kitty, her baby, was in the middle of her morning nap. She barely stirred as Iris tucked the battery accumulator under the blanket at her feet. By the time she had pushed the pram out of the back door into the yard, the boys had disappeared, Sam had gone back to his digging and Dolly was leaning on the back fence, watching him. Iris knew instantly from her sister-in-law's smile that Dolly was flirting with him. She might be happily married to Iris' brother Jack, but that didn't stop her practising her charms on any man she met.

She turned her smile on Iris when she appeared.

'Ready?' she asked.

Iris nodded, glancing at Sam. He had his head down, his back turned to her. 'Help me get your battery in the pram.'

As they set off, Dolly turned and called back over her shoulder, 'I'll be seeing you, Sam. Remember what I said, won't you?'

Sam made no reply, but as he turned his head Iris thought she could see him blushing.

'What were you saying to him?' she wanted to know as soon as they were through the gate into the ten foot that ran along the backs of the houses.

'Nothing.' Dolly shrugged her slim shoulders, a maddening gleam in her blue eyes.

'Were you flirting with him?'

'Would anyone blame me if I was?' Dolly sighed. 'I get so lonely with my Jack away on the minesweepers for months on end . . .'

Iris gasped in shock. 'Dolly Maguire!'

Dolly laughed. 'Oh, Iris, your face! As if I'd ever do that to my Jack.' She shook her head. 'Anyway, Sam Scuttle in't interested in an old married woman like me.'

Iris looked sideways at her friend. Married she might be, but Dolly was still by far the best-looking girl in Jubilee Row. She turned heads wherever she went and she knew it.

Although she would have to go a long way to do better than Jack Maguire. Iris was devoted to her handsome older brother. They were the closest in age, with just two years between them, and Iris could not have been more thrilled when he married her good friend Dolly.

'He was telling me he'd offered to do your garden for you,' Dolly said.

'That's right.'

'You should let him help you.'

'I said I'd get Pop to help.'

'Yes, but that in't the point!'

Iris stared at her. 'What are you talking about?'

'Nowt.' They continued in silence for a while, then Dolly said, 'Do you like him?'

'What kind of question is that? Of course I like him.' She had known Sam Scuttle since they were children at school together. Later on, he had worked on the trawlers with her husband. It was Sam who had jumped into the icy Arctic waters to try to save Arthur the night he went overboard. 'He's been very good to me and the bains since Arthur died.'

'I daresay he has,' Dolly said.

Iris sent her a sidelong look. Sometimes her sister-in-law could be utterly incomprehensible.

Chapter Five

But before Iris could ask what Dolly meant, they arrived at Shelby's Ironmongers shop on the corner of Anlaby Road and Bean Street.

It wasn't a big shop by any means, and to Iris it always seemed to be bursting at the seams. Every shelf and inch of floor space in the cool, shadowy interior was crammed with enamel kitchenware, pans, kettles, brushes, light fittings and cardboard boxes full of nails, nuts and bolts and various other bits and pieces. Galvanised zinc tubs, dolly sticks, washboards and mangles were stacked against the walls, and brooms and mops hung from hooks in the ceiling.

Charlie Scuttle was halfway up a ladder stacking boxes on one of the top shelves, supervised by Joyce Shelby, the owner's wife. When she saw Dolly and Iris, she came towards them, wiping her hands on her brown apron.

'Good morning.' Joyce was in her late thirties, but her permanently furrowed brow and the lines etched around her washed-out blue eyes made her look much older. She had a nervous, almost apologetic manner about her. Even her voice came out in a thin, breathy thread, as if she was hesitant about being heard.

'Morning, Joyce. We've brought the accumulators to be filled.' Dolly went to lift the heavy batteries from underneath Kitty's blanket, but Joyce put out her hand to stop her.

'Don't go straining yourself. Charlie can do it.' Joyce

turned to summon Charlie down from the ladder. 'Take these through to Mr Shelby in the workshop, if you please.'

Charlie edged towards them with his usual curious side-long gait, his head down and his shoulder hunched towards them, as if shielding himself from a blow. He was as tall as his younger brother with the same sandy hair and sea-green eyes, but there any similarity ended. Where Sam Scuttle was well built and handsome, Charlie's face was gaunt, his gaze downcast. His clothes hung loosely from his painfully thin, bent frame.

'A terrible shame,' Iris' mother always said, with a mournful shake of her head. She could remember a time when Charlie was as full of life and mischief as her own son Jimmy. Looking at him now, his long limbs as awkward and disjointed as a broken puppet's, Iris could hardly believe it.

'Good morning, Charlie.' Of course Dolly couldn't resist turning on her charm, even for Charlie. The poor man gaped in confusion at her bright smile and fluttering eyelashes for a moment, then turned bright red and shuffled away quickly, a battery tucked under each arm.

'Poor soul,' Dolly whispered. 'It makes you wonder whether he would have been better off not coming home at all, doesn't it?'

'You'd better not let his mother hear you talking like that,' Iris warned. Beattie Scuttle was devoted to her son, and had spent the last twenty years caring for him.

'But it's no life for him, is it?' Dolly insisted. 'What must it be like, being so slow-witted?'

'Charlie isn't slow-witted. He's just nervous,' Iris said.

Joyce said nothing, but she stared hard at Dolly, her mouth pressed in a firm line, as if to stop herself speaking up.

The next minute her expression cleared and she bent down to pick up the rattle Kitty had just thrown out of her pram.

'She's growing so fast, in't she? How old is she now?' she asked.

'Just turned a year.'

Joyce sighed. 'She's bonny.'

'She can be a little devil sometimes. Can't you, Kitty?' Iris smiled down at her baby daughter. Kitty grinned back mischievously, waving the rattle in her plump little fist. Then she hurled the toy again, sending it skittering across the floor. 'You see what I mean?' Iris sighed.

Joyce smiled. 'My Alan was just the same when he was a bain.' She bent down to pick up the toy. As she reached out, Iris caught a glimpse of her bony wrist. She glanced at Dolly to see if she had noticed, but her sister-in-law was examining a display of brushes twirling above her on strings hung from the ceiling. When Iris looked back, Joyce was already standing upright, her cuff slid back into place.

'Was that all you wanted?' she asked.

'Mum wants some clothes pegs,' Dolly said. 'She'll go mad if I forget.'

'Let's see . . . I think we've got a box of them somewhere waiting to be put out . . .'

Joyce disappeared behind the counter, only to emerge a moment later with a small cardboard box in her hands.

'Here we are,' she said. 'How many do you need?'

'A dozen should do.' Dolly gazed around at the cluttered shelves. 'Honestly, I don't know how you find anything in this place.'

Joyce gave a little smile. 'I've been in this shop for nearly twenty years. I should know my way around it by now.'

As Joyce was handing over the clothes pegs, the bell over the door jingled and a young woman walked in. Iris recognised her straight away.

'That's the lass that moved into number ten last week,'

she whispered to Dolly. 'You know, the one I was telling you about?'

'Is it now?' Dolly regarded her with interest.

As if she knew she was being watched, the girl turned and caught Iris' eye. Iris hesitated, remembering how she had snapped at Beattie Scuttle four days earlier. But this time the girl gave Iris a quick, tentative smile.

'Can I help you, love?' Joyce asked.

The girl glanced questioningly back at Iris and Dolly. 'Are you—?'

'Oh, don't mind us,' Dolly said airily, waving her towards the counter. 'We're just waiting, in't we, Iris?'

The girl produced a list from her pocket and began reading it out to Joyce. Iris busied herself fussing over Kitty, while Dolly listened in shamelessly.

The list seemed endless. 'Borax, carbolic soap, Lysol, Reckitt's Blue ...' the girl read out, while Joyce darted back and forth, fetching packets from shelves and unearthing boxes from dusty corners of the shop.

'Sounds like someone's going to be busy?' Dolly remarked loudly.

The girl darted a quick sidelong look at her. 'There's a lot to do.'

'Aye, I daresay Miss Hodges' place could do with a spring clean after all these years. I'll bet it reeks of damp and moth-balls, doesn't it?'

'Miss Hodges' place? In Jubilee Row?'

Even in the dim light of the shop, Iris could see Joyce Shelby's face grow pale. Her voice sounded even fainter than usual.

'That's right,' the girl said. 'Do you know it?'

Iris caught Dolly's eye. She lifted her eyebrow but said nothing.

'I – er . . .' Joyce looked lost for a moment, then she changed the subject. 'Was there anything else you wanted?'

The girl seemed to hesitate, looking back over her shoulder at Dolly and Iris.

'Spit it out, lass,' Dolly said with a grin.

The girl turned back to Joyce. 'I – was wondering,' she said in a low voice, 'if you need any help in the shop?'

Joyce looked startled. 'You're looking for a job?'

'I could do anything,' the girl went on quickly. 'Work behind the counter, clean up the shop, stack shelves, do deliveries . . .'

Iris caught Dolly's eye again. She felt embarrassed to be eavesdropping, but Dolly was listening avidly.

A flush rose in Joyce's pale cheeks. 'Well, I don't know.' Her gaze darted about the shop. 'I'd have to ask my husband—'

'Ask me what?'

Reg Shelby appeared in the doorway that led to the work-shop, carrying the battery accumulators. Iris immediately felt her skin crawl with dislike. Reg was in his early forties and very full of himself, dark and handsome in a swaggering, over-confident way.

Joyce's mouth opened and closed for a moment, as if even her whisper was lost. Iris suddenly thought of the ring of dark bruises she had glimpsed on her wrist earlier.

'Ask me what?' Reg repeated, an impatient edge to his voice.

The young woman turned to him. 'I was looking for a job,' she said in a cool, level voice.

Reg shook his head. 'Then you'll have to look elsewhere. We don't need anyone.'

'Are you sure?' Joyce found her voice at last. 'It might be good to have an extra pair of hands around the place, espe-cially when Charlie's so busy in the workshop—'

Reg held up his hand, silencing her. 'I run this business, Joyce, not you,' he said. 'We can't keep taking on charity cases. We're already wasting enough money, taking on Charlie Scuttle.'

It was hard to know who turned a deeper shade of red, Joyce or the young woman at the counter. Iris could almost feel the mortification radiating off both of them.

But Reg seemed oblivious as he turned his back on Joyce and the young woman and went over to dump the batteries at Dolly's feet.

'That'll be one and sixpence each,' he said.

'One and sixpence?' Dolly repeated, scandalised. 'It was only a shilling last week!'

'I can't help it if prices go up, can I?' Reg held out his hand for the money.

Dolly glared at him for a moment, then looked at Iris. She shrugged helplessly back.

'I suppose I'll have to pay it, won't I?' Dolly rummaged through her purse. 'But I've a good mind to take them down to the garage next time,' she grumbled.

'Suit yourself. There's plenty of customers that will pay my prices, even if you don't.'

'I wouldn't bet on it.' Dolly handed over the coins grudgingly. She did not even bother to flirt with Reg, Iris noticed.

As they left, Dolly called back to the young girl, 'I daresay we'll see you in Jubilee Row. Good luck with cleaning up Miss Hodges' place.'

Iris saw Reg Shelby's eyes narrow for a fraction of a second. His glance flicked to the young girl standing at the counter, then to Joyce and back again. Iris could almost see the cogs whirring in his devious brain.

'You said that on purpose,' she accused Dolly as they emerged from the shop into the bright July day.

Her sister-in-law flicked her blonde curls in a careless gesture. 'I'm sure I don't know what you mean,' she replied.

Iris shook her head. Dolly Maguire could never resist making mischief.

Chapter Six

Reg Shelby peered out through the glass, a smirk on his face.

'They'll be back,' he said. 'They moan about the price every week, but they always come back.'

Edie did not speak. She was still burning with rage over the comment he had made to her, casually dismissing her as a charity case.

She stared at him, his brown overall straining over his broad back. He might have been well built once, but now his powerful muscles were clearly turning to fat.

'That'll be two pounds five shillings.' Mrs Shelby's whispering voice distracted her. Edie turned round and caught the other woman's gaze across the polished wooden counter. Her pale blue eyes were full of silent apology.

Edie dug through her purse and took out the money. There wasn't much left. She had spent all night sitting up, a blanket pulled around her shoulders, obsessively adding up columns of figures, wondering how she could make ends meet. But no matter how hard she tried or how much she thought she could do without, the stark reality was that she needed to earn some more money, and quickly. She had been hopelessly naive about how much it would cost to live by herself. She could just about manage to pay her rent and bills if she was very careful, but there was so much more to think about. She needed to brighten up her depressing, dirty little rooms, to turn them into a home. And she would soon have to think about buying things for the baby. When she had registered at the clinic on Coltman Street the previous day, the midwife had presented her with a dizzying list of what she would need, from towelling nappies to blankets, a cot and a pram, not to mention all the clothes the baby would need. Edie had stuffed the piece of paper in her pocket, too frightened to read it properly in case it sent her spiralling into despair.

Not only that, the midwife had taken one look at Edie and declared that she was too thin and needed malt and vitamin supplements at a cost of ten shillings. Edie had nodded and accepted the prescription, then slipped out of the clinic when the midwife wasn't looking.

She had spent all morning traipsing up and down the length of Anlaby Road, asking in every shop and business whether they needed help. She had bought the *Hull Daily Mail* and circled various job advertisements. Many of them were live-in jobs or on the other side of the city, but Edie was quickly beginning to realise that beggars could not be choosers.

She thought of the five-pound note her father had given her, still tucked away in her suitcase. No matter how desperately broke she was, she could not bring herself to spend it. Her pride would not allow it.

Edie was waiting for Joyce to finish writing out her receipt when Reg Shelby turned to face her.

'Is it right, what I heard? You live in Jubilee Row?'

Edie looked back at him. He might have been handsome once, but like his body, his face was now soft and fleshy. His mouth was full, almost too feminine, while his grey eyes were as hard as flint.

'That's right.'

'And you live at Patience Huggins' place?'

Edie lifted her chin. 'We share it,' she corrected him firmly.

31

Reg Shelby cackled. 'Oh, I like that! I'll bet Patience Huggins doesn't see it that way. She'll be in charge, if I know her.'

'Then you don't know me, do you?' Edie replied.

Reg's smile grew wider. 'Did you hear that, Joyce? Sounds like Mrs Huggins might have met her match at last.'

Out of the corner of her eye Edie saw Joyce's hand still as she wrote out the receipt, but she said nothing.

'Do you know Mrs Huggins, then?'

'Oh, we know her all right. We know her very well. In't that right, Joyce?'

'Your receipt.' Joyce's voice was calm, but her hand was shaking as she held out the piece of paper.

'You'll be sure to mention us to Patience, won't you?' Reg called after Edie as she left the shop. 'Tell her Reg and Joyce Shelby send their regards.'

Edie glanced back at Reg's blandly smiling face, then at Joyce. The other woman did not meet her eye.

* * *

The two women from the shop were loitering on the pavement outside when Edie came out a moment later. She could hear the blonde woman's lively, chattering voice as soon as she opened the door.

They did not stop their conversation when Edie appeared, and it was almost as if they had not noticed her. But as she went to pass them the dark-haired one suddenly said, 'Did I hear you say you were looking for work?'

Edie looked over her shoulder at her. The woman was a head taller than her, about thirty years old and more striking than pretty, with her jet-black hair, pale skin and warm, brown eyes.

She thought about telling her to mind her own business, then thought better of it. 'I am,' she said.

'Pickering's are taking on girls for braiding nets at St Andrew's Dock, if you're interested?'

Edie looked from her to her friend. 'But I've no experience,' she said. 'I don't know the first thing about net braiding.'

'You'll soon learn,' the blonde woman said. 'And once you know how, you'll have a trade for life.'

'How much does it pay?'

'It's piece work, but you should earn two or three quid a week.'

Edie thought about it. Even two pounds a week would be enough to cover her rent and all her bills.

Her hand started automatically towards her belly, then dropped to her side when she saw the women looking. Another month or two and there would be no hiding it. But at least by then she might have been able to get some more money together, enough to buy some things for the baby.

'Who do I see about it?' she asked.

'Go down to St Andrew's Dock and talk to Big May, the forewoman,' the dark-haired woman said. 'Tell her Iris sent you. She'll sort you out.'

'Thank you, I will.'

'Are you going back to Jubilee Row?' the blonde woman asked. 'You can walk back with us.'

'I can't,' Edie said. 'I've got another errand to run in town first.'

The blonde woman looked disappointed. 'That's a shame. We were looking forward to having a chat, weren't we, Iris?'

'I'm sure we'll have another chance, once she starts working with us,' her friend said as she swung the pram round to head up Bean Street. As she turned, Edie caught a glimpse of a plump, happy-looking baby with a wide, gummy smile and a shock of jet black hair.

As Edie watched them walking away she called out, 'Wait. Do you really think I stand a chance of getting a job?'

'You will if I put in a good word for you.' The dark-haired woman looked back over her shoulder at her and winked. 'Big May Maguire's my mother!'

* * *

Edie was still smiling to herself as she walked into the city. She had a job! Well, as good as, anyway. All she had to do was convince this Big May to take her on, and then all her troubles would be over.

For now.

There were others lurking on the horizon, but Edie could not allow herself to think about those yet.

The city of Hull basked in the warm July sunshine. It was a bigger, much more imposing place than York. The streets were wider than the ancient, winding lanes and snickelways Edie was used to, and the buildings seemed far grander, with their spires and domes and ornate columns. There were statues on high plinths, and broad squares, and vast department stores with striped awnings that took up nearly a whole street. Edie wandered around, awestruck. She had never seen anything like it.

This was the place Rob had called home. Before he met Edie, he had walked these same streets, gazed into the same shop windows as she was now.

She wished she had known him then. They had met when he was stationed at an RAF base just outside York, and they had not been together long enough for her to visit his home. Now, as she wandered through the city, Edie tried to imagine that Rob was beside her, pointing out the landmarks. The tower of the Prudential Building, the Dome Ballroom at the top of Hammonds department store where he used to go dancing . . .

Being here made her feel closer to him. Sometimes it felt as if their romance had all been a dream. And sometimes Edie feared that it might slip away like a dream too, if she didn't hold on to it with both hands.

But coming to Hull had not been easy for her. Even though her family had turned their backs on her, she had still given up a job that she loved and her friends when she left the city. A pang of longing went through her at the thought of the other girls on the fuse-filling line at Rowntrees and the fun they used to have. The Saturday night sixpenny factory dances, cycling out to Strensall to visit the barracks, flirting with handsome Canadian pilots at Betty's . . .

There had been times over the past few days when Edie had despaired that she had made the right decision. When Patience Huggins came thudding up the stairs with yet another of her petty complaints; when she woke up to the sight of dreary, yellowing walls and the skittering of mice behind the floorboards; when she had taken the old velvet curtains down to wash them and they had fallen into shreds in her hands . . .

Edie shook her head, forcing the thought away. At least she could do something about that particular problem. That was why she had come into town, to look for some cheap blackout fabric to make new curtains. She did not know the first thing about sewing, but she was sure it could not be too difficult to hem some fabric and get it to hang straight.

She managed to find some blackout material, and a cheap offcut of cheerful flowery fabric to go with it, in Thornton Varley's. But as she was coming out of the store with her purchases tucked under her arm, a display of paint tins close to the hardware department caught her eye.

I want you to paint it blue.

Suddenly she was transported back to a sunny day in May, just before Rob left. They had taken a picnic down the Ouse to Bishopthorpe and were lazing on the river bank, watching the boats drift by. Edie could still remember the tickle of the long grass against her bare legs, and the warmth of the sun on her face. They had just spotted the bright blue flash of a kingfisher darting on the opposite bank when Rob suddenly said, 'I want you to paint the baby's nursery that colour.'

The comment was so sudden and unexpected, Edie laughed. 'And what if it's a girl?'

'It won't be. You're going to have a boy. And he's going to have a blue nursery.' He twisted to look at her, his face turned up to hers. 'Promise me?' he said.

Rob never stopped smiling, but this time there was such a strange intensity in his face, it almost frightened her.

Had he known, she wondered? Had he seen what his future held, that he would never hold his child in his arms?

'I promise,' Edie had said. 'Anyway,' she'd added, 'with any luck you'll be home in time to paint the nursery yourself!'

Rob had said nothing to that. Instead he had reached for her hand, turning it over to kiss her palm.

'Everything will be all right in the end,' he'd said.

She looked again at the display of paint. It was a sign, she thought. Rob was telling her he was with her, urging her to make good on her promise to him.

She thought about her meagre savings, dwindling further with every day that passed. Buying paint seemed like such an extravagance when there was so much more she and the baby needed. She remembered the midwife's stern warning when she had handed over the prescription earlier that morning.

'You need to take care of yourself, Mrs Copeland. This won't do at all.'

She looked back at the paint, and once again she heard Rob's words.

Everything will be all right.

She would get the job, she told herself. Iris had already said it was as good as hers. And once she was earning, she would not have to worry about money, at least not for a while.

Rob was right, she thought. Everything would be all right in the end.

Chapter Seven

After Edie had finished her shopping, she headed back east, towards Hessle Road.

Hessle Road, or 'Road, as the locals called it, was a long, bustling thoroughfare that ran east along the river from the city to the village of Hessle. On one side were the fish docks, a string of quays, wholesalers' warehouses, chandlers, filleting sheds and netting lofts along the banks of the mighty Humber. To the north of the docks lay a network of narrow streets and terraces that housed the fishermen, the dock workers and their families.

Jubilee Row was one such terrace, tucked in off Gillett Street, which ran between Hessle Road and West Dock Street. It was a short stub of twenty houses, with a grocer's shop on one corner, and a high brick wall at the far end. Number ten was halfway along on the right-hand side. It stood out from its neighbours with its thick lace curtains, spotless doorstep and polished brasswork, a testament to Patience Huggins' formidable housekeeping skills.

Patience Huggins had very high standards, as Edie was beginning to find out. She certainly never seemed to stop pointing out Edie's faults. She only had to walk across her kitchen floor before she heard the dull thump of Patience's broom handle on the ceiling below her, warning her to keep quiet. In the four days Edie had been living there, Patience had objected to her singing, to her hanging out washing in the yard – 'Only when I'm not using the line, and you need to ask my permission first. Oh, and don't think you're going to be tramping through my kitchen to get to the back yard. You'll have to go by the ten foot round the back' – and even to her standing on the doorstep – 'Can't you see I've just finishing donkey stoning it?'

Edie had started to challenge herself, to see how many paces she could manage between the front door and the stairs before Patience appeared and told her off about something.

This time she was loitering in the hall, dusting down the skirting boards, when Edie walked in.

'Shut the door, you'll let the dust blow in,' was her blunt greeting as Edie stepped into the hall.

Edie stifled a sigh. 'Good afternoon to you, too, Mrs Huggins,' she muttered under her breath.

'I don't see what's good about it.' Patience Huggins put down her duster and turned to look at her, her arms folded across her chest. Her narrowed gaze immediately moved to the basket Edie was carrying. 'Been shopping again, I see?'

She made it sound as if Edie went on a spree every day.

'Just some things to cheer up my rooms, Mrs Huggins,' she replied through gritted teeth.

'Cheering up? I don't see as anything needs cheering up.'

Edie looked at the old woman's face, her downturned mouth set in lines of permanent disapproval. 'No,' she said. 'I daresay you wouldn't.'

'And what's that?' Mrs Huggins nodded to the tin of paint Edie was cradling.

What does it look like? 'It's paint, Mrs Huggins.'

'And what do you intend to do with it?'

'What do you think?'

Patience's pale blue eyes bulged behind her horn-rimmed spectacles. 'Does Mrs Sandacre know about this?'

'I'm sure she won't mind me brightening the place up.' Edie looked around the hall. 'I could give yours a coat of paint too, while I'm at it?' she offered.

It was worth it to see the look on Patience Huggins' face. 'You'll do no such thing!' she spluttered. 'And I'll be having a word with Mrs Sandacre about this, too. This is my home, and I like it just the way it is, thank you very much!'

Edie watched her striding off down the hall, then she remembered something.

'Mrs Huggins?' she called out.

'What?'

'I nearly forgot. Reg and Joyce Shelby send their regards.'

Patience stopped dead. Even from the other end of the hall, Edie could see her flinch, her features locked in an expression that was somewhere between fear and horror.

'Mrs—' Edie started to say. But the next moment she had disappeared, slamming the kitchen door with a resounding crash behind her.

* * *

Patience was cleaning the brass again, a sure sign she was in a state. She had been at it for over an hour, a forest of candlesticks and ornaments spread out on the kitchen table in front of her. Horace Huggins watched her polishing away as if her life depended on it.

'I wish you'd calm down,' he said. 'It was just a comment. The lass meant nothing by it.'

'Then why would she say it?' Patience kept her head down, rubbing away furiously at an invisible spot on a candlestick. She would wear a hole in it soon, if she wasn't careful.

'You do realise this is what Reg Shelby wanted, don't you?' Horace said gently. 'To get you all upset.'

40

'Yes, well, I can't help that, can I?' Patience stopped polishing, her duster crumpled tightly in her fist. 'Oh Horace, I can't stop thinking about what she said. "Reg and Joyce Shelby send their regards." Like he was – mocking me. I can just imagine him saying it, too, with that horrible smirk on his face ...' She shook her head. 'You know, I'd hoped I'd never hear that man's name in this house again.'

'So did I,' Horace said quietly.

For a moment their eyes met, then Patience went back to her polishing. 'I wonder what else he said to her,' she murmured.

'What do you mean?'

'Do you think he told her what happened?'

Horace shook his head. 'I doubt it. I shouldn't think the lass would have said owt if she'd known.'

'I don't know about that.'

'She's not unkind, love. No matter what you might think of her.'

Horace watched his wife's thin hands working away at the brass. She had been cleaning when he first saw her, polishing silver in the butler's pantry at Crompton House. Horace Huggins had watched her through the window as he went about his weeding in the kitchen garden. She seemed so conscientious, her head bent low over her work. It wasn't until later, when he had got to know her properly, that Horace realised that imposing order on her surroundings was Patience's way of dealing with her inner turmoil.

'Anyway,' he said, 'what if he did say something? It's not as if it's a secret. And if she didn't hear it from him, there's bound to be someone round here who'll tell her.'

'I know.' When Patience looked up at him, he could see tears brimming in her eyes. 'Why did she have to come?' she said, her voice choked. 'I feel as if I haven't had a minute's peace since she arrived ...'

As if to prove her point, at that moment the muffled sound of Edie's singing drifted through the ceiling.

'I can't bear it,' she said, her mouth quivering. 'I don't feel safe, not any more. She's changing everything, Horace, and I don't like it.'

'I know, love.' Horace longed to take her in his arms, but Patience snatched up her duster and started rubbing away at the brass again.

Poor Patience, he knew she could be a trial at times, but no one else seemed to understand that she was a sensitive soul under all that bluster. It just took a while to get past all those prickly defences she put up.

Unfortunately, not many people took the trouble.

'Mrs Sandacre should be told,' Patience muttered under her breath.

Horace frowned in confusion. 'About Reg Shelby?'

'About the paint!' Patience snapped. 'She should know what's going on, before the girl's allowed to ruin the place.'

Horace thought it would be impossible to ruin Miss Hodges' damp, dark little flat, but he decided not to argue. Sometimes it was better to let Patience go on and on until she tired herself out, like a passing storm.

But other times, her rage did not pass. It went round and round in her head, buzzing angrily like a trapped wasp, getting louder and louder.

Unfortunately for Edie Copeland, she seemed to have got stuck in Patience's head.

'Mrs Sandacre needs to be told,' she insisted, as Horace picked up the newspaper. 'You'll have to go and see her, Horace. I know you've refused in the past, but this time you'll have to do something.'

Horace pretended not to hear her, concentrating instead on the headlines in the *Hull Daily Mail*. The oil tanks at Salt

End refinery had taken another hit from a German bomber. It had been chased off by three Spitfires but not before it had set one of the tanks alight.

'Are you listening to me, Horace Huggins?'

Horace put down his newspaper with a sigh. He would not get any peace until this matter was sorted out.

He wished it hadn't come to this. Damn Reg Shelby! Hadn't that man done enough to ruin his family already? It was thanks to him that Patience's world had shrunk so much that she could barely step outside her own front door. He was the one to blame for this, even though it was poor Edie Copeland who was being punished for it.

'Come on, love, don't get yourself in such a state. It's only a pot of paint, after all. At least the lass is taking an interest, trying to brighten the place up.'

'She's changing everything . . .' Patience whimpered, her lip trembling.

'Things change, Patience. That's the way of the world.' He reached for her hand, covering it with his. Her bones were as fine as a bird's under the papery skin. 'Why don't you stop mithering about it and try to get to know the lass? I reckon you might even get to like her, if you give her a chance . . .'

'I will not!' Patience snatched her hand from his. 'I'm telling you now, Horace, I'm not putting up with it. And if Mrs Sandacre won't get rid of her, then I'll just have to find a way to do it myself!'

Horace looked into his wife's tense, determined face and sighed. As he knew only too well, there was no arguing with Patience Huggins when she had decided she was right.

Chapter Eight

'You will take her on, won't you?' Iris asked anxiously.

It was teatime at the Maguires' house, and as usual the small kitchen was crowded. Dolly and Iris stood shoulder to shoulder at the stone sink, scrubbing mud off the potatoes and carrots Pop had brought home from the allotment the previous day. May's eldest daughter Florence, who had just come home from work, was laying the table. Meanwhile Dolly and Iris' children ran to and fro in the yard, their whooping laughter carrying through the open back door.

Big May considered the matter as she rolled out the pastry for the pie she was making.

'I'm not sure she'd fit in,' she said. 'She seemed like a sharp little thing to me.' But at the same time, she couldn't help smiling at the memory of Beattie Scuttle's face when Edie Copeland told her in no uncertain terms to mind her own business.

'She's all right once you get to know her,' Dolly said.

'She needs help,' Iris added. 'But I reckon she's too proud to ask for it.'

'I heard from Viv Pearce at the corner shop that she lost her husband at Dunkirk,' Dolly said. 'Barely a month widowed, can you imagine?'

Big May glanced at Iris. Her youngest daughter was busy scrubbing away at a potato, her head down, dark hair falling about her face. She took after her, not just in looks but in

44

manner, too. They were both good at getting on with things, taking life's blows as they came and trying to make the best of anything that came their way.

But Big May knew how much her husband Arthur's death had affected Iris. And while she was proud of her daughter for being so stoical and managing so well, she did sometimes wonder if it would have been better if she had been able to ask for help.

She went back to rolling her pastry. It didn't stick together the same with so little fat in it. But she couldn't waste her rations.

'I feel sorry for the lass, of course. But can she do the job? I'd far rather have someone with a bit of experience.'

But those girls were hard to find. When the war started, the trawlers had all gone to Fleetwood and Milford Haven, so there was no need of nets. The lofts had closed down and most of the girls had either got married, joined the forces or gone to work in the cod liver oil factory on Hedon Road.

Then, in the past few months, Pickering's had started to produce camouflage nets for the War Department, and May and the other braiders that remained on Hessle Road had been called back to work.

'I'm sure she'll be a quick learner,' Iris said. 'She seemed keen.'

'She seemed desperate,' Dolly added. 'You should have seen her face when Reg Shelby turned her down.'

'That was the best thing that could have happened to her, I reckon,' May said grimly. 'I wouldn't work for Reg Shelby for all the tea in China. Beattie reckons he bullies her Charlie something rotten.'

'He bullies his wife something rotten, too,' Iris muttered.

'That's none of our business,' May said shortly.

'What's this? Your mother saying something in't her business? Surely I must be in the wrong house?'

Pop stood in the back doorway, dressed in his shabby old work clothes, his cap pushed to the back of his head.

May turned on him straight away. 'And you needn't think you're coming in here like that, Pop Maguire. You can go out in the yard and have a wash. Dolly, fetch him a bucket of water.'

'You see what I mean?' Pop addressed his daughters. 'I've not set foot in the door and she's already started on me.' He looked down at himself. 'What's wrong with me, anyway?'

'Can't you smell yourself? You stink of horses. And those boots! God only knows what you've been treading in.'

Pop winked at Dolly as she handed him a tin bucket of water. 'What sort of greeting is that for a hard-working man, eh? I get a warmer welcome off my Bertha than I do my own missus.'

'Happen you should go and have your tea in the stable with her, then,' May snapped. She had never forgiven him for naming that wretched horse after her mother. He smirked every time he said it.

'And miss your happy, smiling face, my love?' Pop took off his cap and polished his balding head with the flat of his hand. He had grown stout in his old age and several of his teeth had gone, along with his hair. But he still had the same youthful twinkle in his eye.

'I'll give you a happy, smiling face,' May growled. 'What have I got to be happy about, married to you these forty-odd years? And you can keep your hands off me, an' all,' she backed away as Pop advanced on her, his arms held out. 'Get away from me, Pop Maguire, or I swear I'll—' Her warning was lost as Pop grappled her into an embrace.

May pushed him off, trying hard not to laugh. He had been greeting her the same way since the day they married. Except back in those days he had been on the trawlers, only returning home every three weeks. It was a relief to her that he had stopped going to sea, although she knew he missed it. He now worked as a carrier on the railway, hauling goods from the yards in his horse and rully.

He carried the bucket out into the yard. May watched him pulling off his boots, his grandchildren gathered around him. There were Dolly's two boys, George and Freddie, and Iris' eight year old, Archie. Little Lucy, four years old and not nearly as tall as her brother and cousins, was at the back as usual, standing on tiptoes to try to get a look-in. Meanwhile, baby Kitty pottered unsteadily around the yard on her chubby little legs.

May smiled contentedly as she went back to preparing the meal. This was just how she liked it, all her family around her. She was only sorry her sons couldn't be there, too.

She couldn't let herself dwell on the lads too much, in case the panic gripped her and she let her brave face slip.

May had just put the pie in the oven when Pop came back in. 'Better now?' he said, displaying his pink, newly scrubbed hands.

'They'll do,' May said grudgingly.

'Good. Happen I can read my paper in peace.'

He sat down in his usual worn old armchair in the corner, opened his newspaper and then searched around for his spectacles. May watched him patting his pockets for a moment until Florence went over and retrieved them from the mantelpiece.

'They're here, Pop,' she said, handing them to him.

'Thanks, love.' Pop smiled gratefully up at his eldest daughter.

Iris and Dolly finished chopping the vegetables and May tipped them into the pan, ready to boil.

'So do you think you'll give her a job, Ma?' Dolly asked.

'I've told you, it depends. She'll be no use to anyone if she's all fingers and thumbs.' May paused, remembering the forlorn little figure in a heavy coat, dragging her suitcase down the street on the day she had arrived. 'But I daresay we'll find a use for her,' she added.

Dolly and Iris smiled at each other, as if they had always known this would be her answer.

'You know Ma,' Florence muttered. 'She can never resist a waif or a stray.'

May glared at her. She hated to admit it to herself, but she could not find it in her heart to love her eldest daughter, not like she did her three sons, or Iris, or even her daughters-in-law.

She felt badly about it. She had tried, but they were too different.

May blamed Pop for that. Florence was his favourite, he'd encouraged her schooling and reading when he should have been encouraging her to find herself a husband. Now she was too sharp and clever and set in her ways for any man. At thirty-eight, she was an old maid, still living at home and acting as if she was better than everyone else, just because she worked for the corporation at the Guildhall and not down the docks like the rest of the women in Jubilee Row.

Luckily, Dolly decided to change the subject. 'Did you hear, Sam Scuttle's building an Anderson shelter for Beattie in their back garden?' she said.

May sniffed. 'I did hear summat about it. She thinks she's too good for the likes of us now.'

'It's for Charlie,' Iris said.

'He asked if Iris wanted one too, but she said no,' Dolly said.

May caught her daughter-in-law's eye across the kitchen. 'Happen it might be a good idea if you did have one?' she said, going back to her pastry.

Iris looked over her shoulder at her. 'I thought you liked us all in the communal shelter?'

'I do, but it might be as well to have somewhere closer, just to be on the safe side. You can't be too careful with the bains, can you?'

'You'd be better off turning it over to vegetables,' Pop said. 'I could give you a hand, if you like?'

May glared at him in frustration, but he did not meet her eye. 'She's better off with a shelter,' she insisted.

'I'll think about it,' Iris shrugged.

She put down her knife and went out into the yard to summon the children for tea. As soon as she had gone, Pop turned to May, peering at her over the top of his glasses.

'What was that all about?' he asked.

'Can't you tell?' Florence sourly put in, before May could reply. 'Mum's matchmaking again.'

'So what if I am?' May defended herself, picking up a cloth to wipe her hands. 'It would be nice to see Iris happy again. And Sam's a nice lad.'

'You can be happy without a man, you know,' Florence said.

'And you'd know all about that, wouldn't you?'

May knew immediately it was the wrong thing to say as soon as she saw her daughter's face fall. But she couldn't keep tip-toeing around her. For heaven's sake, it had been more than twenty years since she'd lost her sweetheart. And it wasn't as if she was the only girl whose man didn't come home from the Great War. But while everyone else just got on with it and found someone else, Florence had gone on pining.

A tense hush fell over the room. Over by the sink, Dolly held herself rigid, her blue eyes flicking between May and Florence and back again. Even May held her breath.

Florence's lips twitched, as if she wanted to speak but could not find the words. Then she turned on her heel and left the room, slamming the door behind her.

'You've done it now,' Pop said quietly.

'Me?' May swung round to Pop. 'This is all your doing.'

He looked at her over the edge of his newspaper. 'How do you work that out?'

'You should never have encouraged her to stay on at school. Now she reckons she knows it all.'

'Oh, no,' Pop shook his head. 'She gets *that* from her mother.'

Chapter Nine

'Show me your hands.'

Edie held out her hands and Big May Maguire grasped them, pulling them towards her and turning them over to inspect them.

She was an imposing woman. She stood at least a foot taller than Edie, with a broad, strong frame. Her greying hair was cut in a short, practical style around her square-jawed face. Even the way she looked at Edie was intimidating, her dark eyes shrewdly assessing, as if she could see right into her soul.

Edie dropped her gaze. The last thing she wanted was for Big May to notice the purple grooves of sleeplessness under her eyes, or to look closely at her face and see how, under the artful dabs of rouge, her skin was as grey as ashes.

Last night she had tried to take the midwife's advice and eat properly. But even as she prepared the salad she felt her stomach recoiling. And when she broke the shell of the hard-boiled egg, the smell was enough to send her running for a bowl to be sick.

And that was how she had been all night. By the morning, she felt like a wrung-out rag, desperately weary, her body aching for sleep. She would have gladly stayed in bed, but she could not miss her chance of this job. Instead she had crawled out of bed, washed and dressed and powdered her face. But even though she had washed carefully and brushed her teeth with powder, she could still smell the faint whiff of vomit and stale sweat clinging to her, making her stomach churn.

She only hoped Big May did not notice it too.

'I hear you've no experience?' she was saying.

Edie glanced over her shoulder at Iris. She nodded encouragingly back.

'I'm a quick learner,' she said.

Big May released Edie's fingers.

'Ladies' hands,' she dismissed with a snort. 'What work were you doing before?'

'I started off in the card box mill at Rowntrees. Then when the war started I was moved on to fuse filling.'

'The card box mill, eh?' May's mouth twisted. 'I daresay you'll find this work a lot harder than putting pretty ribbons on chocolate boxes, I can tell you.'

'It can't be any harder than making bombs,' Edie said, her voice rising over the women's laughter.

Big May looked grudgingly impressed. 'I see you know how to stand up for yourself, and that's something you'll need in this place. But you'll have to do something about those hands,' she said. 'You're best off soaking them in methylated spirits every night until they're like mine.' She turned up her hands to show Edie the thick calluses striped across her palms. 'Now, let me show you around.'

The netting loft was a vast room, with a sloping roof and a line of open windows that looked out over the Humber.

'We keep them open all weathers to get rid of the hemp dust,' Big May explained.

Four long tables ran the length of the room, with around a dozen women sitting down each side, facing each other. The nets they were working on were draped between them, over a long stand down the centre of the table.

The women worked feverishly, their hands moving with such speed that Edie's eyes could hardly keep up with them.

'You'll be as quick as them one day,' May said. 'But you'll start as a needle filler while you learn. You'll have to be quick at that too, mind. This lot won't want you hanging about.'

'No, we won't,' one of the older women muttered. 'Time's money in this place.'

She eyed Edie narrowly as she said it, but her hands carried on her rapid work. Her fingers were bent and gnarled with arthritis.

'You've met Beattie Scuttle?' There was a smile on Big May's face when she said it.

'Aye,' Beattie answered for her. 'We've met all right.'

'I'm not sure—' Edie began, then she remembered Beattie and Big May watching her from across the street on the day she had arrived. She had been sharp with Beattie, and from the scowl on the old woman's face she clearly had not forgiven her for it.

'I'm sure you and Beattie will be the best of friends before long. In't that right, Beattie?' Big May grinned. Beattie scowled again and went back to her work.

May led Edie to the other side of the loft, where half a dozen women were threading strips of muddy-coloured hessian through the nets to make camouflage.

'You'll need to buy your own needles,' she said. 'Four dozen should do you to start off with. Of course, you might want more once you really get going, but four dozen should be enough for now.'

'And how much do they cost?' Edie asked nervously.

'About two bob a dozen. You can get them from Tom Capes on West Dock Avenue. Dolly and Iris can show you where to go. Right, now I think I've shown you everything . . .' May looked around. 'Come and sit down, and I'll get one of the girls to get you started.'

Edie followed her, her heart sinking. Eight shillings! Her meagre household budget would not stretch to that.

Panic mingled with nausea, rising up in her throat. She tasted burning bile on her tongue and looked around desperately.

'Is everything all right, ducks?' May was watching her curiously. 'Only you've gone a bit pale.'

Edie took a long, steadying breath. The hemp dust clung to her throat but she did not dare cough in case she was sick again. 'Yes. Yes, thank you.'

'I expect you're making her nervous, Mum!' Iris called out.

'Here, come and sit here, by me.' Dolly budged along the long bench to make room for her on the end. 'I'll show you what to do. Here's your needle . . .'

She presented Edie with a flat piece of wood about ten inches long by an inch wide, with a point at one end. 'You take the twine and wind it round the lug, like this . . .'

Edie soon forgot about feeling sick as she tried to follow Dolly's instructions on how to braid. Her first attempts were slow and clumsy. The rough sisal twine cut into her fingers, and the tiny fibres stuck in her skin like splinters, but Edie refused to let the pain show. She could feel the other women at the table watching her with knowing grins, and she didn't want them to think she wasn't up to the job. Especially not Big May, who was watching her most keenly of all.

'See what I mean about toughening up your hands?' May said.

'You'll get used to it,' Dolly told Edie. 'My fingers were covered in sticking plasters when I started.'

'Stop gossiping and hurry up!' Beattie tutted from the

other end of the table. 'Honestly, what kind of a needle filler have you landed us with, May Maguire?'

Gradually, Edie got into the swing of winding the twine around the lugs. Her palms were soon blistered and throbbing with pain, but she couldn't afford to pause because there was always someone calling for a filled needle.

The women chatted and sang as they worked. It reminded Edie of the Rowntrees works, and for the first time since she had arrived in the city she began to feel truly at home.

Big May worked alongside them on her own net, stopping every so often to check the women's finished work with her yardstick.

'How do you like living with Patience Huggins, then?' Beattie asked Edie after a while.

'It's all right.'

'All right, she says!' Beattie shook her head. 'You must be a saint, that's all I can say. I wouldn't last five minutes.'

'Nor me,' Dolly giggled.

'I daresay you have to mind your Ps and Qs, eh?' Beattie said to Edie. 'Very proper, is Mrs Huggins. She likes things done just so.'

'It's all those years in service,' Big May said. 'It's taught her to be a cut above the rest of us.'

'Or so she likes to think,' Beattie scoffed. 'But as far as I'm concerned, a few years emptying chamber pots for the gentry doesn't make anyone a lady!'

Edie looked from one to the other, the conversation going back and forth as fast as their wooden needles worked. She didn't want to get involved in their gossip, but she didn't want to look stand-offish, either. Especially not with Big May watching her.

'I wouldn't know about that,' she said. 'Mrs Huggins likes to keep herself to herself.'

'I'll say she does!' Beattie cackled. 'We've barely seen her in twenty years.'

'The only time I ever see her is when she's hanging out her washing or scrubbing her front step,' Dolly said.

'I saw her posting a letter on the corner once,' Iris put in. 'But that must have been a couple of years since.'

'She never goes out,' May said to Edie. 'She gets that poor husband of hers to run all her errands for her.'

Edie looked from one to the other. It hadn't occurred to her before, but they were right. She had been living in Jubilee Row for nearly a week and she had not seen Patience Huggins venture further than the back yard in all that time.

'Why?' she asked.

The other women exchanged meaningful looks.

'Ah, well. That's the thing, you see,' Big May said. 'No one really knows.'

'Of course we know!' Beattie scoffed. 'It's on account of that falling-out she had with her daughter.'

'We don't know for sure,' Big May corrected her. 'Besides, it hardly makes sense, does it? You don't lock yourself away for twenty years just because you fall out with your daughter, do you?'

'Mum would never come out of the house if that was true!' Iris joked, earning herself a glare from Big May at the other end of the table.

'Well, I know what I know,' Beattie said. 'You can think what you like, May Maguire, but it's obvious to me. She hides herself away because she's too scared to come face to face with her.'

Edie looked from one to the other. 'You're saying Mrs Huggins has a daughter?' she said.

'Oh, aye,' Big May said. 'She's got a daughter, all right.'

56

'And does she live local?'

The other women looked at each other, grinning. 'Aye, she's local,' Iris said.

'And I'll tell you summat else,' Dolly added. 'You've already met her!'

Chapter Ten

'Joyce Shelby?' Edie said. 'Joyce Shelby is Patience Huggins' daughter?'

'That's right,' Beattie nodded. 'Although you'd never know it, since they've not spoken these last twenty years.'

'Not since she ran off with a tinker!' Dolly said.

'I don't blame her,' Beattie said. 'I'd probably run away from home too, with a mother like that.'

'Tinker Reg, we called him,' May's voice cut across them. 'He used to cycle round the streets on his bike with a contraption on it for sharpening knives, with pots and pans hanging off the back. They made a terrific clanking and clattering as he went, you could hear him coming for miles.'

'Shame Patience Huggins didn't hear him coming for her daughter!' Dolly chuckled.

May sent her a silencing look, but Edie could tell she was trying not to smile. 'Poor Joyce. She used to go to school with our Florence. They were friends, but Patience Huggins didn't like her mixing with the other children in the street. Joyce used to tell Florence how her mother kept her at her books all the time. She wanted her to better herself.'

'And then she met Tinker Reg!' Iris said.

'Patience Huggins only had herself to blame for that,' May said. 'If she'd let the lass see a bit of life, happen she wouldn't have fallen for the first lad to show her any interest. Although he was a handsome young man, I'll give him that,' she conceded. 'I can't say I'm surprised he turned Joyce's head.'

'What did Mrs Huggins say when she found out?' Edie said.

'She was beside herself, as you might imagine,' May said. 'She tried to stop Joyce from seeing him, but of course that only made her even more keen. Next thing, they'd eloped together.'

'No!'

'Isn't it romantic?' Dolly said.

'It's downright daft, if you ask me,' May glared at her daughter-in-law. 'She broke her mother's heart. And no mother deserves that, not even Patience Huggins.'

'What did Patience do when she found out?' Edie asked.

'Ah, you see, that was where she made her second mistake.' May looked down, braiding furiously. Needles, spools and twine flew fast in her hands. 'She should have let them get on with it. I mean, what's done is done, in't it? It might have been hard for her, but if she'd just given them her blessing, it might have all turned out different.'

'Would you have given your blessing if he'd eloped with our Florence?' Iris asked her with a grin.

'I would have clapped my hands, believe me,' May replied grimly, and the other women laughed.

'But she didn't give them her blessing?' Edie said.

May shook her head. 'She disowned her on the spot. I think Joyce was expecting it all to die down, but she didn't know her mother. Patience Huggins bears a grudge, all right. She wouldn't have anything to do with Joyce when she came home, and she hasn't spoken to her since. She didn't even go to see her when her grandson Alan was born, if you can believe it.'

'She's never seen the lad,' Beattie said. 'He's turned eighteen now and she's had nothing to do with him or her daughter in all that time.'

'It's all wrong to my mind,' May declared firmly. 'Families should stick together through thick and thin. If you in't got your family, what have you got?'

Edie had a brief image of her father, standing silently by as she left the house for the last time. Her last memory had been of him on the doorstep with Rose and her two sons by his side.

Once again, her stomach roiled and the sickness rose up, scorching the back of her tongue.

'The funny thing is, Reg did all right for himself in the end.' May's voice sounded distant, as if it was coming from the end of a long tunnel. 'He's got the shop, and a good business repairing cycles. They're not short of money.'

'It's a pity he doesn't pass any of it on to my Charlie,' Beattie grumbled. 'My lad works his fingers to the bone and gets a pittance for it.'

'That's Reg Shelby all over, in't it?' May said. 'Mean in every way.'

'In any case, you'd think Patience Huggins would be happy her daughter married such a good businessman,' Iris said.

'I reckon she'd sooner Joyce married a bank manager, or a headmaster,' May said. 'Reg Shelby was never going to be good enough for her, no matter how much money he's got.'

'If you ask me it's pride,' Dolly said. 'Mrs Huggins is too proud to admit she was wrong about him.'

'What kind of pride would keep a mother from her own child?' May said. 'Talk about cutting off your own nose to spite your face. She must be a very sad and lonely woman, that's all I can say.'

Just then there was a shout from the street below. One of

the girls at the far end of the table looked up at the clock on the wall.

'That's my Alec,' she beamed. 'Regular as clockwork.' She glanced at May, who nodded back.

Edie watched as two of the girls left the bench and ran to the window. They lowered down a length of twine and pulled it up a few moments later. On the end was a packet of Woodbines.

'Time to take a break,' Dolly said to Edie.

The girls shared out the cigarettes among a few of their friends. Some of the others got up from their benches and walked around the loft to stretch their legs, rolling their shoulders to ease the tense muscles.

Edie tried to join in, although the smell of the cigarette smoke made her queasy. She never used to mind it, but ever since she fell pregnant, it seemed as if every aroma had become more pungent. Sitting there on the other end of the table, her lips pressed together, it was all she could do not to heave.

It was too much to hope Big May would not notice.

'Are you sure you're all right?' she asked. 'You're as white as a sheet.'

'Here,' Dolly waved the cigarette she had been sharing with Iris under Edie's nose. 'Have some of this. You'll feel better.'

Edie caught a whiff of the smoke and felt her stomach rise in protest. Before she knew what she was doing, she was on her feet and pushing past Big May, shoving her roughly aside as she made a desperate dash for the lavatory.

She got there just in time. Afterwards, she sat back on her heels, spent and exhausted. Her stomach felt as if it had been turned inside out. She quickly pulled herself together and washed her face, but when she looked in the mirror, a ghost stared back at her. Her eyes were wide and red-rimmed in her ashen face, her hair clinging damply to her cheeks.

She could not go out and face them, but she knew she had to do it. By the time she returned to the loft, all the girls were back at their nets and Big May was waiting for her.

'Everything all right?' she asked.

'Yes.' Edie looked down at her shoes, unable to meet the other woman's eye. 'I – I think it must have been something I ate.'

'Aye, I daresay it was.' Big May sounded so sympathetic, for a moment Edie was almost tempted to tell her the truth. But she needed this job too badly for that.

She went to return to her table, but Big May stopped her.

'No,' she said. 'I reckon we can manage without you today.'

Edie stared up at her in dismay, but then Big May added, 'Come back again tomorrow, when you're feeling better.'

Edie looked past her solid bulk to the tables, where the girls were hard at work. 'But I'm sure I'll be all right—'

'Come back tomorrow,' Big May repeated firmly. She looked down at Edie and her dark eyes softened. 'Don't look so frightened, lass. There'll be a job waiting for you.'

'Can we have the rest of the day off too?' Dolly asked.

'What do you think?' Big May turned to her, her grim expression back in place. 'Get on with your work. Them nets won't braid themselves!'

'More's the pity,' Dolly muttered, with a wink at Edie.

* * *

Tell her Joyce and Reg Shelby send their regards.

The words haunted Edie as she trudged back to Jubilee Row.

Poor Patience. No wonder she had been so stricken when Edie mentioned their names. She remembered Reg Shelby's smirking face as he had said those words. She should have known then that something wasn't right.

As if things weren't difficult enough between her and Patience Huggins already, now she had gone and made them ten times worse.

The house was silent when Edie let herself in. She paused for a moment in the hall, listening. At the far end of the hall the kitchen door was closed, but she could hear the faint strains of a wireless coming from behind the parlour door to her right.

Edie took a deep breath. The sooner this was all sorted out, the better. Before she could think twice about it, she hurried over to the parlour door and knocked.

She heard the wireless being turned down, and the sound of a whispered conversation from within. A moment later, the door opened and Horace Huggins stood there.

He smiled at her, his kindly old face full of concern. 'Everything all right, love?'

'Yes, thank you. I just wondered if I could have a word with Mrs Huggins?'

She half expected him to close the door in her face. But instead he said, 'Of course. Come in,' and stood back to let her into the room.

Edie had never seen inside the Hugginses' parlour before, and what she saw amazed her. She would never have pictured Patience Huggins as the fanciful type, but the small front room was crammed from floor to ceiling with frills and fancy gewgaws. No surface seemed to go undecorated, from the gilt-framed paintings covering the embossed wallpaper, to the chenille-covered table and the intricately embroidered, lace-trimmed antimacassars that bedecked the brocade armchairs. Staffordshire china dogs vied for space on the crowded mantelpiece with delicate porcelain shepherdesses, gleaming brass candlesticks and colourful Venetian glass.

Patience was standing in front of the fireplace, her spine as rigid as a poker. She stared at Edie, her pale eyes full of suspicion behind her spectacles.

'Yes?' she snapped. 'What do you want?'

'I'm sorry to disturb you.' Edie looked at the half-mended shirt which lay abandoned on the armchair.

'Would you like a cup of tea, ducks?' Horace offered. 'It's just brewed.'

'I—'

'She doesn't want tea, she's not stopping,' Patience snapped before Edie had a chance to reply. 'Well?' she said. 'Say what you came to say.'

As Edie looked at the other woman's cold, unforgiving eyes she began to regret the impulse that had made her knock on the Hugginses' door.

Her gaze strayed to a heavy, old-fashioned, dark-wood dresser, intricately carved with flowers and leaves and twisting vines, on which was displayed an array of blue-and-white Wedgewood pottery.

There was one missing. The gap struck her as odd in a room where everything else was so carefully arranged.

'I'm waiting,' Patience prompted her.

Edie turned back to face her. 'I wanted to say I'm sorry,' she said.

Patience's eyes flickered with surprise. 'What?'

'I swear I didn't know who Reg Shelby was.' She saw the other woman flinch at the sound of his name. 'I would never have said anything if I had. I didn't mean to upset you, honestly.'

There was a long silence. Patience coloured slightly but

didn't utter a word. In the end, it was her husband who spoke for her.

'Thank you, my dear. We appreciate that, don't we, Patience?'

Patience said nothing, her gaze turned stubbornly towards the window.

The silence stretched, becoming unbearable.

'Well, I've said what I came to say, anyway,' Edie murmured.

As she started towards the door, Horace said, 'Are you sure you wouldn't like a cup of tea?'

'No, thank you.' Edie glanced over at Patience. She had her back to her now, facing the dresser. Without thinking, Edie said, 'It's a shame about the missing one.'

Patience twisted round to face her. 'What?'

'The missing plate.' Edie nodded towards the dresser. 'It spoils the look of it, don't you think? You should get another one.'

Patience glanced towards the dresser and for a moment she seemed lost in thought. 'Some things can't be replaced,' she said tautly.

Chapter Eleven

'It was good of the lass to apologise, wasn't it?' Horace said. 'I told you she meant no harm.'

Patience did not reply. She was staring at the space on the dresser shelf. It had been there for so long, she had stopped noticing it. Even when she was dusting she barely looked at it these days.

'She's right, though,' her husband's voice broke into her thoughts. 'It's about time we replaced that plate.'

'No,' Patience said. 'I want to leave it as it is.'

'Why, love? It spoils the look of it.'

'To remind me.'

Horace sighed. 'You don't need a missing plate to do that, surely?'

He was right. Patience had lost more than a plate that day, and the memory of it would stay with her forever.

It had been Joyce's twenty-first birthday, and Patience had prepared a special tea for her. As it was such a special occasion, she had even used her best china, from the set she kept on the dresser. She could not wait for Joyce to come home and see what an effort she had made for her. But her happiness dissolved like mist when her daughter walked in holding hands with Reg Shelby.

Joyce looked nervous, as well she might. Patience thought she had put an end to all that nonsense six months earlier, when Joyce had come to her all bright-eyed, declaring she had fallen in love. With a pot mender, of all people! Of course, Patience had dismissed it and forbidden her from seeing him again, and as far as she was concerned, that was that.

But she had underestimated Reg Shelby. Because here he was, standing in her parlour, smoking and letting his ash tip on the hearth as if he owned the place. The arrogance of him still made Patience's hackles rise.

'What's he doing here?' she demanded.

Reg's smile widened. 'Now, then, Mrs Huggins,' he said. 'That's no way to speak to your son-in-law.'

The world seemed to tilt on its axis and Patience put out a hand to steady herself.

'Reg!' Joyce hissed. 'We agreed I'd tell them.'

'Sorry, love,' Reg smirked. 'It just came out.'

Horace found his voice before Patience found hers. He looked from Joyce to Reg and back again. 'Would someone mind telling me what's going on?' he said gruffly.

Joyce opened her mouth to speak, but Reg got in first. 'We went down to the registry office this morning.' He couldn't have looked more pleased with himself if he had tried. 'We're husband and wife. In't we, love?'

He looked at Joyce, but she could only stare at the floor, her face glowing red.

'Is this right, Joyce?' Horace sounded hurt.

'It can't be.' Patience found her voice at last. 'It's the most ridiculous thing I've ever heard.' She turned to Reg. 'I suppose this was all your idea?'

She couldn't blame Joyce. She was young and naive, she had led a sheltered life. Of course she had lost her head over the first man to show her a bit of attention.

But Reg Shelby was older, he knew his way around the world. He had set his sights on her daughter and he was cunning and clever and manipulative enough to do anything.

'Actually, I was the one who wanted to get married,' Joyce said.

Patience flicked her a contemptuous look. 'Only because he put the thought in your head. Can't you see he's trying to turn you against us?'

'Seems to me like you're managing that all by yourself,' Reg murmured.

Patience glared at him. 'I wasn't speaking to you.'

'Well, that's nice, I must say.' Reg turned to Joyce. 'Well, say summat. Or are you just going to let her talk to your husband like that?'

'Don't, Mother, please,' Joyce begged quietly. 'Don't ruin everything.'

'Me ruin everything? That's rich, coming from the girl who has just thrown away any chance of bettering herself!' Patience looked down her nose at her daughter. 'I suppose you know you can kiss goodbye to your future now?'

'My future is with Reg.'

Joyce reached for his hand. The sight of their fingers entwined sent hot anger scalding through Patience's veins.

'So you want to throw away your life on a tinker, is that it?'

Reg's jaw tightened, his grey eyes turning to flint. 'It's better than being an old snob,' he hit back.

Patience looked at her daughter, but Joyce said nothing. She could feel her slipping away but she wasn't going to break down and beg. She would never give Reg Shelby the satisfaction, even though her heart was tearing in two.

She straightened up, pulling herself together with effort. 'We can get this sorted out,' she said briskly. 'We'll go down to the registry office first thing in the morning. I'm sure there must be a way to get you out of this . . .'

'You don't understand,' Joyce said. 'I don't want to get out of it. I love Reg.'

'But I forbid it. We forbid it, don't we?' Patience turned to Horace, who stood back, silently watching the scene.

'You can't. I'm over twenty-one now, I can do as I like. You can't tell me what to do any more.'

'We'll soon see about that.' Patience turned to her husband. 'What have you got to say about this?'

'There's not much to say, as far as I can see,' Horace said quietly. 'Not much to be done about it, either.'

'Father's right,' Joyce said. 'There's nothing to be done about it. We only came to let you know, and to ask for your blessing.'

'My blessing!' Patience stared at her, aghast. 'As if I'd give my blessing for you to marry him!'

'But it's what I want.'

'You don't know what you want,' Patience insisted.

'You're only saying that because it's not what you want!' Joyce turned to her, her face full of appeal. 'Why won't you understand, Mother? I don't want to be a schoolteacher. I'm tired of trying to please you, to live up to what you want me to be. I'm tired of trying not to disappoint you.'

Patience frowned. 'I don't understand—'

'Don't you? You think I don't know what a nuisance I was to you, from the minute I was born? You never wanted me, you never wanted to be a mother. All you ever wanted was to look after your precious prison Governor and his family, and having me meant you had to give that up. I don't think you ever forgave me for it, did you?'

'I—'

'I'm not saying you weren't a good mother. I mean, I never went without. Your pride wouldn't let you do that. I always had to go to school well fed and nicely turned out. But there was a price to pay for it. I had to be the perfect daughter. I wasn't allowed to complain, or cry, or make a mess. And I tried, Mother, I really did. I studied hard at school, I didn't make friends because you thought the other children were too common, I trained to be a schoolteacher because it was what you wanted. I spent years trying to please you, to be the daughter you wanted. But now I've met someone who loves me the way I am. And I love him, too.'

All Patience could do was stare. She had never seen Joyce so angry as she was that day. She had always been such a sweet girl, quiet to the point of shyness. She scarcely recognised the creature she saw before her now, her face full of spite.

Patience wanted to tell Joyce that what she had said wasn't true, that she had only wanted the best for her. If she pushed her, it was because she did not want her to follow the same path she had, to spend her life skivvying and cleaning up after other people.

But the words would not come.

Horace sought to calm things down. 'Can't you do something?' he appealed to Reg. 'Let's sort this out, man to man.'

But Reg only shrugged his shoulders. 'Joyce has a right to say what she feels,' was all he said. 'Happen she should have said it years ago.' There was a malicious gleam in his eye, as if he was enjoying the situation far more than he should.

'She wouldn't have said it at all if it hadn't been for you,' Patience accused. 'You're the one putting these ideas in her head—'

'For God's sake, why don't you listen to me? The only one who has ever tried to put ideas in my head is you!'

Joyce picked up one of the plates and hurled it to the floor. It hit the ground with a resounding crash, shattering on the patterned tiles.

There was a shocked silence as they all stared down at the fragments scattered at their feet. Even Joyce looked dismayed at what she had done.

'Oops,' said Reg.

Patience fell to her knees, gathering up the china shards in her apron. Her best plate. The Governor's wife had given her the set as a wedding present. It had sat on the dresser and Patience lovingly dusted each piece and admired them but hardly ever used them because the set was so precious to her.

'I'm sorry,' Joyce whispered. 'Mother—'

'Go.' The word came out as a low growl, deep in Patience's throat. 'Go and never come back.'

'Mother?' Joyce turned pale. 'You don't mean that.'

'Of course she doesn't mean it,' Horace put in swiftly. 'You don't, do you, Patience?'

Patience was silent, staring down at the fragments in her hands. Joyce could not have hurt her more if she had taken one of the sharp shards and driven it into her heart.

'I reckon she does, love.' Reg ground out his cigarette in Patience's aspidistra plant and went to comfort his trembling wife. 'You can see it now, can't you? She cares more about a bit of broken crockery than she does her own daughter.'

His arms went around Joyce, but his eyes met Patience's over the top of her head. There was no mistaking the triumph glinting there.

Even then, she could have done something. If only she had said something, told Joyce that it didn't matter, that she loved her, then perhaps it might have all turned out differently. She could feel Horace watching her, silently urging her to say the right thing.

But pride held back the words.

'If you leave this house with that man, I never want to see you again,' she said. 'You've made your bed, now you must lie in it.'

And that was it. Joyce left with Reg, and she had never set foot in the house again.

They had not seen each other since.

Horace had done his best to make peace between them, but Patience refused to budge. As far as she was concerned, she was the injured party.

'If she wants to apologise, let her come here,' was all she would say.

Horace had been to visit Joyce, and Patience hoped that he might have been able to talk some sense into her. But he came back with a look of sorrowful resignation on his face.

'Seems as if what's done is done,' he said. 'We'll just have to get used to it, Patience. Our Joyce is a married woman now. But I had a word with Reg Shelby, and he seems to have his head screwed on all right. You never know, he might make her happy ...'

'I don't care.' Patience shook her head. 'While she's married to that man, she's no daughter of mine.'

And she had been as good as her word. Patience had seen Joyce on the street from time to time, but they always crossed the road to avoid each other. When Reg Shelby opened his shop Patience stopped going up to Anlaby Road because she couldn't bear to see it. In the end just the thought of coming face to face with Joyce filled her with so much anxiety that she stopped venturing out entirely, until the three rooms and back yard in Jubilee Row became her whole world.

Horace still visited Joyce, but he rarely spoke to Patience about her, and she was too proud to ask.

But that didn't stop her thinking about her. That was why she kept the missing plate, to remind herself of what Joyce had done to her. She needed the pain to stay strong, lest she forget and allow herself to weaken.

And that would never do.

Chapter Twelve

There was a letter from Alan in the morning post. Joyce smiled to herself as she picked up the letters from the door-mat and saw his handwriting on one of the envelopes. It was just what she needed to take her mind off the headache that stabbed at her temples.

She slipped the letter into her apron pocket and set about preparing Reg's breakfast of sausages, grilled tomatoes and mushrooms. She was especially pleased with herself for get-ting hold of the sausages, even though it had meant a long queue at the butcher's.

But Reg's face fell with disappointment when she put his plate in front of him.

'No bacon?' he said.

Joyce shook her head. 'I won't be able to get any more till Saturday.'

'I miss my bacon and eggs every morning.'

'I know, love. But I'll see if I can sort out something nice for tea.'

Joyce sat down and poured herself a cup of tea. She took Alan's letter from her pocket and placed it on the table. Reg looked sidelong at it.

'Another one?' he said, through a mouthful of food. 'He can't be doing much training, if he's got time to write long letters to his mother all the time!'

'We're lucky if we get one letter a week,' Joyce said, tearing open the envelope with her thumbnail. 'Besides, I like hearing all his news, don't you?'

Reg forked more food into his mouth and said nothing. Joyce took out the letter. Just two sheets of paper this time, she noticed with disappointment. When he'd first gone down to Tidworth he was so homesick his letters had run to several pages.

'Dear Mum and Dad,' she started to read out loud. 'Thank you for the kind gift of cigarettes that arrived yesterday. I've shared them out with the other lads in my hut and very welcome they were, too. I'm not smoking so much myself on account of having a sore throat. I sleep at the end of the hut opposite the door, so a draught rattles around all night. And we did a six-mile route march yesterday in the rain, which didn't help matters . . .'

'Listen to him complain!' Reg muttered. 'And there was me, thinking the Army would make a man of him!'

'The poor lad's feeling ill,' Joyce defended him. 'I hope it doesn't get any worse. Every time he gets a cold it goes to his chest.'

'Happen you should go down there with some goose grease and brown paper?' Reg sneered. 'I'm sure his commanding officer wouldn't mind him getting a visit from his mother.'

Joyce ignored him and returned to the letter. 'He reckons the food hasn't improved. Apparently this morning's porridge tasted of yesterday's kippers, and their tea tasted of the prunes they'd had for lunch . . .'

She smiled to herself. That wouldn't go down too well with her son. Alan had always loved his food, although he was a lanky lad with not an inch of spare flesh on him.

'He should be thankful for what he can get,' Reg said.

Joyce looked at her husband, hunched over his plate, shovelling sausage into his mouth, but said nothing.

She went on reading. 'He says he's started drilling with the guns they'll be using when ...' She stopped, her voice betraying her.

'For heaven's sake, woman. It's only a drill. No one's going to be shooting at him.' Reg waved his fork at her across the table. 'You'd best buck up your ideas before the real trouble starts.'

Joyce shuddered. 'Don't. I can't bear to think about it.'

'It won't be long now. He could be sent anywhere.'

'You sound as if you're looking forward to him going.'

'The lad's got to do his duty, there's no getting away from it.' Reg took a slurp of his tea and stood up. 'Right, I'm going down to get started on those bicycles.'

Joyce looked down at her empty plate, summoning up the courage to speak. 'I can't open up. I've got some shopping to do first thing.'

'What shopping? I thought you went yesterday?'

'I have to go every day, Reg. You never know when they'll be getting different things in, and I wouldn't want to miss out.'

He towered over her, his hands on his hips. 'And what about our shop?'

'I was thinking, happen you could mind it while Charlie was in the workshop—'

'Oh, you were thinking, were you? Telling me what to do now?'

'No, Reg, honestly, I wasn't—'

'Anyway, I can't spare you,' Reg cut her off. 'If you must go, it'll have to be after we close up.'

'Yes, but the shelves will be empty—'

'Joyce, I won't argue with you.' Reg frowned across the table at her. 'I in't losing money just so you can go gallivanting off to the shops and spend all morning gossiping with your friends.'

What friends? Joyce thought, but she said nothing.

By the time breakfast was finished, Charlie Scuttle was knocking on the workshop door. Reg glanced at the clock, then unhurriedly went on with his breakfast.

'Aren't you going to let him in?' Joyce ventured.

'He's five minutes early. He can wait.'

'But it's raining—'

'Then he'll get wet, won't he?' Reg chewed noisily. 'Teach him to keep better time.'

Joyce looked anxiously towards the rain streaming down the kitchen window pane. Charlie would be soaked to the skin by the time Reg went down to unlock the door.

'It just seems a shame for him to be standing out there when he could be working,' she mused. Then, seeing Reg's ears prick up, she added, 'And that's five minutes you won't be paying him for.'

As usual, appealing to her husband's greed did the trick. When Charlie knocked again a few seconds later, Reg set down his knife and fork with a clatter.

'I s'pose I'd better go and let the daft beggar in,' he sighed loudly. 'I'll not get any peace otherwise.'

Joyce listened to his heavy footsteps receding down the stairs, then sat down at the kitchen table among the dirty breakfast dishes and read Alan's letter again. This time she allowed herself a few more minutes to read it properly, relishing the sight of her son's familiar scrawl on the paper. Listening to his words in her head, it was almost as if he was still there, sitting across the table from her, laughing and joking.

She missed him so much. His physical presence in the house, the sound of his voice, just being able to look after him. Her boy. Her baby.

Reg always said she smothered him. 'He needs to toughen

up,' he would say. 'How will he ever learn to be a man while you're fussing over him all the time?'

Reg had been fending for himself since he was scarcely more than a boy, and he thought his son should do the same. He had wanted Alan to follow in his footsteps, to leave school as soon as he could and start working alongside him in the workshop.

'He'll be taking over the business one day, so why shouldn't he start now?' he had reasoned.

Joyce would have preferred him to go on to university after school. She felt as if her son was meant for better things than mending bicycles. She had tried to explain that to Reg, but he had gone into one of his tempers and she hadn't dared speak of it again.

But then the war broke out, and Alan had gone off to enlist. Now Joyce wished he was there, in the workshop with his father. At least he would be safe.

* * *

On the dot of nine, Joyce drew the bolt on the door to the ironmonger's shop and opened up. Outside, the rain was still lashing down, leaving the usually busy shopping thorough-fare on Anlaby Road quite empty, apart from a few intrepid women heading for the Co-op, wielding their empty shopping baskets as they went in search of food to put in them.

Joyce closed the door on the grey day with a smile. She loved it when the shop was busy, but she also enjoyed the peace and quiet when it wasn't. Especially as it meant she could catch up on her reading. She always kept a book behind the counter to keep herself occupied.

It was the only chance she had to get stuck into her read-ing. Reg had never learned to read properly himself, and it irritated him that Joyce enjoyed it so much, so she preferred to wait until she was alone.

But today she had her knitting with her. She was halfway through making a pair of socks for Alan, but now she thought she might abandon them and start on a scarf for him instead, after what he had said about his sore throat and draughty sleeping conditions.

She had just got comfortable on her stool behind the counter and started on shaping the heel when the bell over the door jangled and Ruby Maguire walked in.

As she stood for a moment on the mat, shaking the rain off her coat, Joyce quickly stuffed her knitting back into her work bag.

'Please don't stop your work on my account.' Ruby approached the counter. She looked smart in her green WVS uniform, although the felt hat pulled low on her red head was rather soggy from the rain. 'What are you making?' she nodded towards the open work bag.

'Just some socks for our Alan.'

'May I see?'

Joyce took out her knitting reluctantly and showed it to her. 'They're not perfect,' she said. 'I had to unravel an old cardigan of mine for the wool, so the stitching is a bit uneven . . .'

'You're too modest, Joyce,' Ruby said. 'This is beautiful work. We could do with knitters like you at the WVS.'

Joyce felt herself blushing. 'I don't know about that,' she mumbled, staring down at the work in her hands.

'I mean it,' Ruby said. 'We need women to knit socks and jumpers for the Serviceman's Comforts Fund. We meet at the centre on Ferensway on a Thursday and a Saturday afternoon. You should come along one day. You'd be most welcome.'

Joyce looked away as she put the knitting back in the bag. Ruby Maguire could be very persuasive when she wanted to be. She was forty years old, the same age as Joyce, and married to Big May Maguire's eldest son Jimmy. She was one of those very capable women, the kind who always got stuck in and got things done and made it all look effortless. No one was surprised when she joined the Women's Voluntary Service just after the war broke out. Now she was in her element, organising fundraising events, selling raffle tickets and arranging talks in everything from First Aid to Ration Book Cookery. She had recently been manning a refreshments stall at Paragon Station for the soldiers returning from Dunkirk.

Joyce admired her, but she was also a little intimidated by her. She could never imagine herself doing half the things Ruby did.

There was no doubt she was after something today. Joyce could see the determined glint in her green eyes.

Sure enough, Joyce had scarcely had time to put her knitting back in the bag before Ruby said, 'I'm collecting for the aluminium salvage drive. I wondered if you had any old pots and pans you could spare?'

'I – I'm not sure . . .'

'It's for our Forces. To build Spitfires. I thought you'd be bound to have something here.' Ruby looked around meaningfully at the shelves, crammed with all manner of ironmongery. 'They don't have to be brand new. We'll take anything.'

Joyce thought for a moment. 'We do have some old stock down in the cellar. It's badly dented so we can't sell it. Would that do?'

Ruby smiled. 'It sounds like just what we need.'

'What's all this?'

Joyce jumped at the sound of Reg's booming voice. He stood in the doorway to the workshop, his arms folded across his barrel chest. For a big man, he could move as lightly and silently as a cat when he wanted to.

'Good morning,' Ruby Maguire greeted him brightly. 'Joyce and I were just discussing pots and pans for the WVS aluminium drive. She seemed to think you might have something for us?'

'Did she now?' Reg was smiling, but Joyce cringed at the look in his eye. 'We've got pots and pans, all right,' he gestured towards the teetering piles on the shelves around him. 'And you're welcome to them, as many as you like.'

Ruby's face lit up. 'Really? That's very generous of you—'

'Not at all,' Reg said. 'We are a shop, after all. If we've got it, you can buy it.'

'Oh. I see.' A flush rose in Ruby's cheeks. 'I don't think you understand, we were looking for a donation . . .'

'You're the one who doesn't understand, Mrs Maguire. I'm running a business here, we don't give handouts to all and sundry.'

'But Joyce said—'

'Joyce spoke out of turn.' Reg sent her a glaring look. Joyce closed her eyes and silently prayed for the ground to open up and swallow her.

There was a long silence, then Ruby cleared her throat. 'Well, I'll be on my way, then.' She turned to Joyce. 'I'll be seeing you, Joyce. Let me know if you change your mind about the knitting, won't you?'

'Can you believe her cheek?' Reg peered through the streaming shop window, watching Ruby as she made her way down the street through the rain. 'Who does she think she is, marching around demanding this and that?'

'She's only trying to do her bit, the same as everyone else,' Joyce said quietly.

'She's a bloody busybody! And you had no business promising her anything, either.' He wagged a warning finger at her.

'If I find out you've been giving my stock away I won't be best pleased about it, d'you hear me?'

'Yes, Reg.'

'And what was all that about knitting?'

'Nothing.'

Reg's eyes narrowed. 'I hope she hasn't got you working for her?' he said. 'Because I don't think I could stand listening to those needles clicking away night after night.'

'No,' Joyce murmured. 'No, of course not. I know you don't like it.'

Reg came towards her. Joyce automatically flinched as his hand came towards her cheek. But this time it was only a caress.

'You're lucky I'm here to look after you, otherwise everyone would be taking advantage of you,' he said. 'You do know that, don't you?'

'I – I know.'

Joyce held herself rigid as his fingers stroked her face, then closed around her chin, tipping her face back until her eyes met his.

'I love you, Joyce.' He made it sound like a threat.

The next moment he had released her. 'By the way, I've got a nice surprise for you,' he said.

'Oh yes? What's that, then?' Joyce put her hand up to her face where his fingers had pinched her chin.

'I had a word with a pal of mine earlier on. He's bringing half a pound of bacon in for us this afternoon. And a few eggs, too, if he can get hold of them.'

Joyce stared at him. 'Where did he get them from?'

Reg tapped the side of his nose. 'Ask no questions and you'll be told no lies. Let's just say he knows a few people.'

'You mean the black market?' Joyce bit her lip.

'I told you, ask no questions. Now, I'd best get back to work. Those bicycles won't repair themselves, will they? Oh, and before I forget – mark up those matches by a halfpenny, too,' he said as an afterthought. 'My pal reckons they're in short supply, so folk will be bound to pay more for them.'

Chapter Thirteen

'This is a stirrup pump. As you can see, it consists of two parts – the pump itself, and the nozzle, which is on the end of this length of hose . . .'

The ARP warden's voice was lost in the crowded school hall.

'The pump goes into a bucket, like so, and is held in place by putting one foot on this bracket at the bottom . . .'

Edie tugged at the collar of her summer dress to fan herself. It was so hot and stuffy in the hall, she could scarcely breathe. People were growing restless, fidgeting and whispering among themselves. Behind her, Edie could hear the rhythmic click of Big May Maguire's knitting needles, while Pop snored gently beside her.

Only the children seemed at all interested in the fire safety demonstration. They sat cross-legged in a row at the front, watching avidly.

'Look at them,' Dolly whispered next to her. 'They just want to see summat burst into flames.'

'Aye,' Iris said, shifting baby Kitty in her arms. 'It'll be me if it gets any more mafting in here!'

Edie shifted in her seat and wiped the perspiration from the back of her neck. The heat was making her feel decidedly woozy.

'You all right, ducks?' Big May prodded her between the shoulder blades.

'Just a bit uncomfortable, that's all.'

'In't we all?' Dolly muttered.

But at the front of the hall, the ARP warden seemed oblivious to the restless atmosphere as he carried on with his demonstration.

'It takes at least two people to operate a stirrup pump,' he said. 'One to pump water from the bucket, while the second operates the nozzle. Ideally, there should be a third to replenish the water supplies with a spare bucket.' He handed the hose to Florence Maguire, who was assisting him. She looked very severe in her blue ARP uniform. 'The operator of the pump should always stay outside the room.'

'Well, that's nice, I must say!' Big May called out. 'You mean to tell me you're sending our Florence in to fight the fire while you stay nice and safe outside? What a hero you are, Harry Pearce!'

Florence glared at her mother from the platform.

'Remember to always point the water at the fire and not the bomb . . .' Harry worked the pump, his arms moving up and down while Florence stood on the other side of the stage, waving the hose at an imaginary fire.

'Put your back into it, Harry!' someone in the audience called out.

'Someone tell him there's no water in that bucket!' someone else shouted.

'There's no fire, neither. This is a swizz.'

'A stirrup pump . . . can pump one and a half gallons of water a minute . . .' Harry puffed, his face red with exertion. His spectacles slid down his sweating nose and he pushed them back up again. 'It can take . . . up to six gallons . . . to extinguish a single incendiary device . . .'

'Careful, Harry, you'll give yourself a heart attack if you carry on like that!'

Edie glanced across the aisle to where Sam Scuttle was rocking with laughter beside his mother and brother Charlie. He caught her eye and grinned. Edie smiled back. In the two weeks she had been working at the netting loft, she had seen a lot of Sam. He often dropped in to see Beattie. Handsome as he was, he was very popular with the other girls.

Behind her, Big May sighed. 'And to think, I'm missing Joe Loss and his Orchestra on the wireless for this!'

'Hush, woman. You might learn summat,' Pop growled back.

'What would you know? You've slept through most of it!'

'Shh! Listen to our Florence.'

Edie waited for Big May's temper to explode, but she grumpily returned to her knitting. In the two weeks she had known the family, Edie had come to realise that Pop, mild-mannered as he might seem, was the only one who could control his wife.

The doors at the back of the room suddenly flew open and a woman entered, ushering a small boy in front of her. She was well-built, with a bold, ruddy face and an untidy mop of corn-coloured hair.

Everyone turned to look at her, including the warden on the stage.

'Sorry I'm late,' she called out in a loud, coarse voice, waving her hand at him. 'You carry on, love. Don't mind me.'

The boy turned to her. 'Can I go down the front with the other lads, Ma?'

'Go on, then. Just don't get too close or make a nuisance of yourself. And don't set off any bombs, either!' she called after him as he hurried to join his friends at the front of the hall.

There was another commotion as the woman went to find a seat. As she squeezed her ample body down the row in front, she caught Dolly's eye and grinned.

'All right, Doll? Long time, no see.'

'Now then, Bessie. I thought you were over in Fleetwood?'

'I've had to come home for a while. Mum's poorly and there's no one to look after our Ronnie.'

The woman's gaze snagged on Iris and she nodded. 'Hello, Iris.'

'Bessie.'

At the front of the hall, Florence cleared her throat.

'If we can get on with the rest of the demonstration?' she called out, throwing a pointed glance at Bessie, who was now wiggling into her seat, disturbing the two women on either side of her.

A hush fell as Harry Pearce returned to the stage carrying a rather ominous-looking box.

'This looks interesting,' Big May commented from the rear.

'A great danger to the home and workplace will come from incendiary devices,' Harry explained. 'Incendiaries are not designed to penetrate the ground. Instead they are intended to create large conflagrations, to damage property and also to light up a target area for subsequent aircraft carrying high explosives.'

'Dirty Jerries,' Pop muttered.

Harry Pearce nodded to Florence, who rifled through the box and took out a short, stumpy-looking item, which she handed to him. An awed hush fell over the room. At the front, the children all craned forward to get a better look.

'He's going to set off the bomb,' Dolly said. 'Look!'

Harry placed the device down in the middle of the platform and set it off. It immediately burned with a blindingly bright light, causing a brief commotion in the audience.

On the other side of the hall, Charlie Scuttle sprang to his feet and let out a yell of fear.

'It's all right, lad, I'm with you. There's nowt to worry about,' Sam patted his arm, pulling him gently back into his seat. 'It's just a whizz-bang, that's all. Look, he's got it all under control.'

'Never pour water on an incendiary or it will explode,' the ARP warden was saying from the stage. 'The best way to deal with it is to put it out with sand.'

Florence approached with a square sand bucket in one hand and a shovel in the other, which she handed to him.

'Lay the bucket on its back and shovel out all the sand to cover the device,' Harry said. 'Then scoop up the incendiary with the shovel, put it back into the bucket and dispose of it.'

He handed the bucket with the bomb in it to Florence, who took it off the stage. A moment later, clouds of smoke could be seen, billowing from the wings.

'That can't be right, surely?' Pop muttered. The smoke grew thicker. A moment later, Florence staggered back on to the platform, coughing and spluttering. Harry took off his spectacles and wiped his streaming eyes with a handkerchief.

'I'm fetching the bains.' Dolly hurried to the front of the hall to collect the children, while all around them the audience started to cough as the smoke drifted out from the stage. As the cloud began to envelop them, Harry rushed off stage and returned a moment later with the incendiary, still burning fiercely in the bucket.

Charlie Scuttle screamed with terror, blundered to his feet and started to fight his way out of the row.

'Charlie, wait!' Sam tried to block his way but his brother had already fled, wrenching open the doors to escape into the night.

Sam went to follow him but Beattie was already there, taking charge.

'I'll go after him. I'm the only one who can calm him down when he's like this. You sort this mess out.' She jerked her head towards the stage, where Harry Pearce and Florence were both blundering about in the smoke.

'Ooh, this is better than the wireless!' May grinned, settling back in her seat as Sam strode towards the stage and disappeared into the smoke.

'Get more sand,' Edie heard him shouting. 'No, more than that. Hell's teeth, man, have you never done this before? No, give it to me, you haven't got a bloody clue! Go and open some windows, if you want to make yourselves useful!'

Finally, the device was put out and the smoke began to clear. Harry and Florence emerged sheepishly, amid much coughing, choking and laughter from the audience.

As Sam was revealed by the thinning smoke, a shovel in one hand and a bucket in the other, the audience burst into spontaneous applause. He grinned and made a mocking little bow.

'Look at him,' Iris laughed. 'He can't resist making a show of himself.'

When the excitement was over, Edie followed Dolly and Iris into the warm summer evening. The sun was setting, streaking the sky with violet and deep salmon pink.

It was a relief to feel the cool air on her face again. Edie sat down on the low wall outside the school, her face upturned, breathing in deeply.

'Are you sure you're all right, love?' Dolly asked her.

'I'm fine. Just a bit dizzy, that's all.'

'I'm not surprised. It were mafting in that hall.'

'Look who it is!' Iris pointed to where Sam Scuttle was striding towards them, brushing down his clothes. Iris and Dolly's boys immediately rushed to him, little Lucy toddling behind.

'You did a good job in there, lad,' Pop said, slapping him on the shoulder.

'Thank you, Mr Maguire.'

'Don't encourage him, Pop,' Iris said. 'He works for the Auxiliary Fire Service. It's no surprise he knows how to put out a fire.'

Sam pulled a face. 'And there was me, hoping you might think I was a hero!'

'Not a chance,' Iris said. 'I know you too well, Sam Scuttle. Is your Charlie all right?'

'I daresay Ma will manage to calm him down.'

'Poor Charlie.'

'Aye.' Sam shook his head.

Just then the blonde woman, Bessie, strode past them with her son in tow. She waved to Dolly as she passed. Edie watched as the blackout swallowed her up.

'Who was that?' she asked.

'Bessie Weir. We grew up in Wassand Terrace together. She's a herring girl. She travels all over the country, working in the factories, splitting and smoking herrings to make kippers,' Dolly explained, when Edie looked blank. 'She gave it up when she got married, but she had to go back after her husband died.'

'And is that her son?'

Dolly nodded. 'Her mother looks after him while she's away.'

'Why doesn't Iris like her?'

'What are you on about?' Dolly frowned at her.

Edie looked at Iris. She was still talking to Sam Scuttle, but a corner of her gaze followed Bessie's swaying walk down the street. 'They could barely bring themselves to speak to each other earlier on.'

'No, you've got it wrong. There's no bad blood between

Iris and Bessie. I would know about it if there was.' Dolly lowered her voice. 'Besides, they've got a lot in common. Ted Weir was washed overboard in the same storm that killed Iris' Arthur. They were best pals, and they died together,' she sighed. 'Terrible, in't it?'

But Edie was no longer listening to her. Something was happening to her, a strange fluttering sensation, like a butterfly trapped deep inside her.

She pressed her hand to the curve of her belly, more pronounced now but still concealed under the folds of her summer dress. Nothing happened. She began to think she might have imagined it, but then it started again.

'Edie?'

She looked up to see Dolly watching her curiously. 'You sure you're all right?'

Edie stared back at her, her hands still pressed against the fluttering life in her abdomen.

My baby's moving!

It was all she could do not to cry out the words. Her joy bubbled up inside her and suddenly she wanted to scream it out, to tell everyone how strange and wonderful it was.

My baby's moving. He's real. This is real.

Her pure elation gave way almost immediately to plunging sadness. She had no one to share the moment with. It should have been the happiest, most exciting time of her life, and she could not tell anyone. She had no friends, no family.

No Rob.

It wasn't fair. He should have been here. He should be resting his hand on the curve of her belly, grinning with wonder when he felt that tiny stirring against his fingers.

And this little one inside her should be celebrated, welcomed, not treated like a shameful secret.

She thought about her father. She could write to him. He was the only one she could tell. And even after everything that had happened, surely he would want to know about his own grandchild?

Even if he didn't, even if she never posted the letter, Edie needed to tell someone, or else she would go mad.

Dolly peered at her. 'Edie, love. Are you crying?'

Edie took a deep breath. 'It must be the smoke making my eyes water,' was all she could allow herself to say.

Chapter Fourteen

The WVS centre was buzzing with activity on Saturday afternoon when Big May turned up for her usual knitting circle.

As well as the usual knitters, there was a sewing party on one side of the room, while on the far side of the hall more women were busy sorting through a heap of old clothes for salvage. The whirr of the sewing machines mingled with the clink of teacups and the sound of lively conversation and laughter.

Beattie Scuttle had saved her usual spot beside May. She was already knitting, her needles flying despite her bent, arthritic fingers. She did not look up from her work as May settled herself next to her.

'You're late,' she said.

'The buses were terrible up 'Road.' May looked around. 'It's busy today.'

'Aye. All your lot are in, I see.'

Beattie nodded towards the clothes salvage section, where Dolly and Iris were busy sorting through the pile of donations that had just come in. Beside them, May's eldest granddaughter Ada was going through the newspapers in the paper salvage area, bullied into it by her mother Ruby, no doubt. Not that she was doing much work, May noticed. She was spending more time flicking through the old newspapers than sorting them.

There was a new face, too. Edie Copeland was with Dolly and Iris, going through the old clothes.

'Don't you see enough of us lot at work?' May called out to her. Edie grinned back.

'I daresay she fancied the company,' Beattie muttered, her eyes fixed on her knitting. 'It can't be much fun, stuck in that house with Patience Huggins.'

'I daresay you're right.' Big May settled herself and took her own knitting out of her work bag, a pair of socks in oiled wool supplied especially by the Admiralty.

'They're coming on nicely,' Beattie remarked.

'I want to finish them today.' The sooner she made them, the sooner they would be off to someone who needed them. She liked to think of a sailor feeling thankful for their warmth as he stood on the deck of a ship in the cold, grey sea, lashed by icy winds.

Her thoughts strayed to her three boys. The eldest two, Jimmy and Jack, were on the minesweepers while her youngest, John, had joined the Merchant Navy, much to the amusement of his older brothers.

They were never far from May's mind. She had worried about them enough when they were on the trawlers, but being the daughter and the wife of a trawlerman, she had grown up accepting it was a hard, dangerous life.

But now, as well as the icy swell of the Arctic seas, they faced the terrible menace of the German planes or the dreaded U-Boats that lurked deep beneath the surface of the waves. And then there were the mines. The sweepers were supposed to clear them, but it only took one magnetic mine to attach itself to the iron hull of a ship, and . . .

She pushed the thought away. If she allowed herself to dwell on it, she would surely go mad.

She turned her attention instead to her granddaughter.

Ada was reading aloud from an old copy of the *Hull Daily Mail* she had retrieved from the paper collection box.

Of course, being a bride-to-be herself, she had gone straight to page three, where the wedding reports were written up.

'Miss Phyllis Barker, only daughter of Chief Inspector T. H. Barker, of the Hull Fire Brigade, and Mrs Barker was married on Saturday at Christ Church, Hull, to Mr Thomas Clarence Southwick, second son of Mr and Mrs E. Southwick, of Beverley,' she read out. 'Given away by her father, the bride wore a picture gown of shell-pink lace, with a tulle headdress, and her bouquet was of pink carnations and lilies of the valley. She was attended by Miss Edna Stevenson and Miss Robinson, who carried blue irises with their gowns of turquoise and mauve and matching headdresses . . .'

'Turquoise and mauve?' Over in the clothes salvage area, Iris pulled a face. 'That sounds awful. What do you reckon, Doll?'

'Happen she doesn't like her bridesmaids?' Dolly pulled out a pair of trousers, examined them closely then tossed them to one side.

Ada went back to the newspaper. 'The ceremony was conducted by the Rev. H. J. Mundy, and A. Kitson was the organist,' she read. 'The honeymoon is being spent in Bridlington, and the bride travelled in a two-piece of dusty pink, with navy-blue accessories.'

She put down the newspaper. 'I wonder if my wedding will get written up in the newspaper?'

'I doubt it,' Iris said. 'Only fancy people get their weddings in the paper.'

'Mine wasn't,' Dolly said.

'I'm not surprised,' Beattie said in a low voice. 'It all happened a bit quick, as I recall.'

'At least our Jack did the right thing by her,' May hissed back.

'Only just in time.' Beattie fixed her gaze on her knitting, ignoring the look May was giving her.

'I'm surprised yours didn't get in the paper,' Dolly said to Iris. 'You and your Arthur made such a lovely couple.'

Iris did not look up from the clothes she was sorting. 'Who wants to read about a trawlerman's daughter getting wed at Hessle Mission?' she said quietly.

'What about your wedding, Edie?' Dolly asked.

Edie Copeland looked up sharply. 'Mine?'

'Did you have a big white dress?' Ada's face lit up. 'I've always wanted a big dress from Elsie Battle on Paragon Street. That's where all the society brides go.'

Big May sucked in a breath as she went about her knitting. She doubted if her son Jimmy's Navy wages would stretch to society prices.

'I didn't wear anything special,' Edie said.

Ada looked disappointed. 'So it wasn't a big wedding?'

'There wasn't time, what with Rob being posted . . .'

Edie's voice trailed off. Poor girl, May thought. What with her and Iris, there seemed to be painful memories everywhere.

Not that Dolly seemed to notice. 'How did the two of you meet?' she wanted to know.

Big May winced at the question, but Edie did not seem to mind. A smile curved her lips as she said, 'It wasn't exactly romantic. I took in his washing!'

The other girls gathered around her avidly. Even Beattie Scuttle put down her knitting to listen.

'There was a scheme at Rowntrees,' Edie explained. 'Bundles of dirty washing would arrive from the local barracks and the air bases, and we'd take them home, wash and iron them and bring them back. The overlooker made sure that each girl had the same serviceman's washing every week. Mine was from Flight Sergeant Copeland, stationed out at Church Fenton.' She looked wistful as she said the name. 'After a few weeks, some of the other girls started leaving notes in the bundles and waiting for replies. Some even stuffed in cigarettes or sweets from the factory. There were quite a few love letters passed, as time went on.'

'Did you write any love letters?' Iris asked.

Edie shook her head. 'I never thought about it,' she said. 'But one day, I opened the washing and there was a note inside for me. He thanked me for doing his washing, and hoped that one day we might meet.'

'What did you write back?' Dolly asked.

'I didn't,' Edie said. 'I ignored it. But then another note came the following week, and the one after that. I never replied to them, but I started to look forward to his letters. They were always so full of fun and stories.'

'But you must have given in eventually?' Iris said.

'Of course she gave in,' Dolly said. 'She married him, didn't she? Oh, Edie.' She looked at her friend pityingly. 'Only you could start a romance off by scrubbing a man's socks!'

Edie grinned. Her face glowed when she talked about her husband, May thought. Poor bain, she must have loved him so much.

'Well, I never. Look who's just arrived.' Beattie distracted her, nodding towards the entrance. Big May twisted round to see Joyce Shelby standing in the doorway, looking lost and bewildered. She stared around her, clutching a shopping basket in each hand so tightly, her knuckles were white.

'Now then, Joyce. What are you doing here?' Beattie called out to her. Joyce jumped like a startled rabbit at the sound of her name. But before she could reply, May's daughter-in-law Ruby came bustling over.

'Joyce?'

'I'm not stopping,' the words rushed out of Joyce's mouth. 'I just came to give you these.' She thrust the shopping baskets at her. 'For the Spitfires?'

Big May watched as Ruby took a battered pan from one of the baskets. Her daughter-in-law had told her about the short shrift she had received from Reg Shelby a few days earlier.

'They're all right, aren't they?' Joyce's face was anxious.

'Yes. Yes, they're perfect,' Ruby said. 'But I thought—'

'They're old stock,' Joyce muttered. 'He won't miss them.' A mottled flush spread up her throat.

'Thank you, anyway.' Ruby picked up the baskets. 'I'll just take them through to the back. Why don't you stop for a cup of tea, while you're here? It's the least we can do, since you've been so generous.'

'Aye, come and sit by us,' Big May called out to her.

Joyce shook her head. 'I can't. Reg will be expecting me back. I told him I was only going down to the Co-op . . .' Her gaze trailed around the room as she spoke, and there was no mistaking the look of longing on her face.

'I'm sure he can spare you for five minutes?' May said kindly.

Her words seemed to jolt Joyce back to reality. 'I – I can't,' she said. 'I have to go.'

'What about your baskets?' Ruby called after her, but Joyce had already fled, slamming the door behind her.

Chapter Fifteen

The first thing Joyce heard when she returned was the sound of Reg shouting from his workshop.

She smoothed down her hair, quickly put on her apron and went to investigate, fumbling her apron strings with nervous fingers.

The workshop was a single-storey building, a lean-to attached to the shop. The big wooden doors to the street were thrown open and sunlight illuminated the long workbench, littered with heavy-looking tools. Bicycles in various states of repair lined the walls. Sawdust covered the concrete floor and a smell of fresh paint and sawn wood hung in the air.

Reg was at the workbench, sawing a plank of wood and muttering to himself.

'I'll teach you to cheat me, you lazy good-for-nothing,' he was saying. 'Trying to rob me when I pay your wages!'

'What's going on?' Joyce looked around the empty workshop. 'Who are you talking to?'

'Him.' Reg nodded towards the door that led down to the cellar.

'Who—?' Joyce started to say, then stopped at the faint sound of whimpering that came from inside.

'Reg, no! You didn't?' She stared back at her husband in shock.

'He forgot to charge a customer,' Reg muttered, and carried

on with his sawing. 'They would have got off without paying if I hadn't caught on in time.'

'You can't lock him in.' Joyce was already at the cellar door, rattling the handle. It was firmly locked. 'You know he hates the dark.'

'He should have thought of that before he tried to take money out of my pocket then, shouldn't he?' Reg glared at the cellar door.

'He can't help it, he gets confused when he has to deal with customers.' Joyce looked about her. 'Where's the key?'

'He's staying there till he learns his lesson.'

'For pity's sake, Reg! Take it out of his wages if you must, but don't leave him in there,' Joyce begged.

'And who are you to give me orders?'

Joyce recognised the dangerous glint in Reg's eye and realised she had overstepped the mark.

'I'm not,' she chose her words carefully. 'I'm just worried for you, that's all. If his brother gets to hear about this . . .'

Reg hesitated, his gaze flicking to the locked door. He might have no fears about bullying her or Charlie, but Sam Scuttle was another matter.

'I daresay he's had enough time to think on what he's done.' He took the bunch of keys from his back pocket and tossed them to her. 'Here, since you're so worried about him.'

Joyce hurried to the door and unlocked it, her fingers trembling. There was no movement from inside.

The smell of musty damp hit her as she peered into the darkness. 'Charlie?'

A soft whimpering came from the gloom.

Reg sighed angrily. 'Listen to him. It's pathetic. Imagine a grown man being frightened of the dark!'

You would be too, if you'd been buried alive.

Joyce stepped cautiously to the top of the cellar steps.

'Charlie? It's me. Mrs Shelby. You're safe, ducks. Just come to my voice.'

She reached out, into the gloom. At first there was no response and then, suddenly, a clammy hand clutched hers, the fingers biting into hers so tightly, it made her gasp.

'That's it, Charlie,' she coaxed him gently. 'Come to me. You're safe.'

He emerged, blinking, into the gloom, his face slick with sweat, eyes bulging. There were streaks of blood down his cheeks and forearms where he had torn at his face and body in panic.

She looked at Reg but he had gone back to his work, apparently unconcerned.

'Come through to the kitchen,' she said to Charlie. 'I'll bathe these wounds for you.'

Reg did not even look up as she led Charlie, still trembling, out of the workshop.

In the kitchen, Joyce sat him down and made him a cup of hot tea. She added three sugars from her own ration to it, not caring that she usually saved it for Reg. Charlie deserved it far more than her husband, she decided.

She fetched the first-aid box and a bowl of warm water, then set about bathing the livid scratches on his face and arms.

'I'm sorry,' she said. 'He doesn't mean to do it, his temper just gets the better of him sometimes ...'

She looked up and her eyes met Charlie's. He was gazing back at her with such understanding, Joyce had to look away again.

How much does he know? she wondered. Just because he was mute didn't mean he couldn't see or hear what was happening around him.

She blushed deeply at the thought.

Charlie sat, docile as a child, while she applied antiseptic to the deepest scratches. Poor Charlie. Joyce remembered him when he was a young man, as tall and strong and handsome as his brother. She wasn't allowed to mix with the Maguires or the Scuttles when she was growing up, but she remembered watching Charlie from her window, striding down Jubilee Row with his best pal Jimmy Maguire, laughing and joking together. They had been apprentices on the trawlers since they were bains, working on the same crew as Jimmy's father.

And then the war had come along and taken everything from Charlie.

Joyce thought about her Alan, and prayed he wouldn't come home from the war as scarred as Charlie Scuttle.

'I saw your mother earlier on,' Joyce said, as she dabbed a wound on his cheek. 'At the WVS centre.' She felt safe telling him; Charlie was the one person in the world who would never give away her secrets. 'They all looked as if they were having a nice time, knitting and chatting together. It must be wonderful to be part of something like that, don't you think?'

Charlie smiled back at her blandly. Joyce shook her head.

'Hark at me!' she laughed. 'As if you're interested in knitting!'

As she leaned over to apply more antiseptic to his cheek, Reg suddenly appeared in the doorway.

'What are you laughing about?' he demanded.

Joyce tensed at the sound of his voice, the antiseptic bottle nearly falling from her hand. She looked at Charlie and saw her own fear mirrored in his green eyes.

'N-nothing,' she stammered.

'Laughing about nothing. You're as daft as he is.' Reg nodded to Charlie. 'It's time you went back to work.'

Charlie did not move. His gaze was still fixed on Joyce.

'Well? What are you waiting for?' Reg barked. 'She doesn't give the orders round here. I do.'

Still Charlie did not move. Joyce gave him the briefest of nods and he darted away, sidling quickly past Reg to escape to the workshop.

Reg watched the door close behind him, then turned back to Joyce. 'Got him well trained, haven't you?' he sneered. 'Proper little lap dog, he is.'

'I don't know what you mean.' Joyce's hands were trembling as she packed away the first-aid box. All the time she watched Reg out of the corner of her eye. He stood at the kitchen window, rocking back and forth on his heels, jingling the coins in his pockets. Over the years she had learned to read his moods, and this one made her wary.

'Had a nice time shopping?' he asked.

It sounded like an idle question, but Joyce knew there was no such thing for Reg. 'Yes, thank you.'

'What did you buy?'

'Nothing, in the end. I'd heard there was some corned beef on sale at the Co-op, but when I got there it was only pilchards left, and I know you don't like them ...' She was gabbling, but she couldn't stop herself.

'That's a shame,' Reg said. Then, just as Joyce let out the breath she had been holding, he said, 'Where are the pots and pans?'

Joyce felt the blood rush to her feet. 'What?'

'The pots and pans we had in the cellar. When I put Charlie down there I noticed they were gone.' He turned to face her. He was smiling, his tone pleasant. 'Where are they, Joyce?'

'I – I don't know.' Her mouth was suddenly as dry as sand. 'I suppose they must have been moved ...'

'Oh, they've been moved, all right. There was a clean patch in the dust where they'd been. So they must have just been taken.' His smile faded. 'I'll ask you again. Where are they, Joyce?'

Joyce could hear her heartbeat crashing in her ears. She stared at Reg, torn between a lie and the truth. She didn't know which would be worse for her.

'They were old stock, Reg,' she pleaded. 'You said yourself they were too damaged to sell. They were only cluttering the place up—'

The stinging slap to her face silenced her, knocking her off balance.

'Don't ever go behind my back again,' Reg grated, his voice low and threatening.

Joyce pressed her hand to her throbbing cheek and braced herself for another blow. But the next moment Reg turned on his heel and left.

She stood for a moment, still trembling with shock. Then, slowly, she sank down on to the kitchen chair and opened up the first-aid box.

She only hoped the bruises would not show too badly this time.

Chapter Sixteen

'Are you there, Nellie?'

Nellie Weaver's boyfriend Alec called out from the street below, signalling the start of the girls' break time. Big May gave the nod and Nellie and her friend Maureen hurried to the window to let down the twine for their cigarettes.

Edie shifted her position on the hard wooden bench, trying to ease her aching back. Even with all the windows open, the room seemed hot and airless, and the swirling fug of hemp dust made it difficult to breathe.

'Not taking a break, Edie?' Big May called over to her as all the other girls gathered around to share out the Woodbines Alec had delivered.

'I'll carry on, if you don't mind.' Edie picked up her needle and went back to her work. 'I just want to get this net finished.'

'Mind you don't make us all look bad!' Dolly called out.

'Not much chance of that!' said Edie.

After four weeks in the netting loft, Edie had finally been put on to braiding. She was getting quicker, but she was still nowhere near as fast as the other women. Big May seemed pleased with her progress, but Edie was aware that she needed to work fast if she was going to make any money.

As it was, she still had to save enough to buy her own set of needles. Dolly had kindly lent her some to start her off, but Edie was aware she couldn't keep them forever.

Sweat ran down her face and she wiped it away with her

hand, wincing with pain as the salty perspiration stung the raw, blistered skin on her palms. She had been soaking her hands in methylated spirits every day since she'd started work in the netting loft, but they were still horribly sore.

She felt the familiar lurch in her belly and smiled to herself. The baby was making its presence felt more and more every day. And every tiny flutter and prod made her feel less alone.

She looked around at the other girls, laughing and chattering together, and wished once again that she could tell them. But it had to be her secret, at least for now.

At least her father knew. In a moment of weakness, Edie had given in to the impulse to write to him. It had been over a week and she still hadn't had a reply, but she felt happier knowing she had shared her good news with someone at least.

'Right, back to work, girls,' Big May's voice rang out across the loft. As the girls stubbed out their cigarettes and went back to their places, May came over to Edie.

'How are you getting on, lass?' she asked.

'All right, I think.'

'Let's have a look.' Big May produced her yardstick as Edie spread the net out for her to inspect.

As she sat back to let May examine her work, the blood rushed to her head and the world began to spin.

Not now, please! Edie took a gulp of air, swallowing down the sudden queasiness. May's soapy scent seemed to fill her throat, sickly and overpowering.

'It's good,' May was saying. 'But you've missed a loop here, d'you see? That'll need putting right.'

Edie peered at the work and tried to force her eyes to focus, but the net shimmered like a heat haze in front of her.

'You go and work on my net while I sort this out,' May said.

Edie started to her feet, but her legs wouldn't hold her.

The wooden needle fell from her hands with a clatter as she gripped the table to hold herself up.

'Edie?' Dolly's voice sounded faint, as if she was in another room.

As Edie turned her head to look at her friend, her vision dimmed, like a veil descending. She could just make out Dolly's white-blonde hair, catching and reflecting the sunlight like a halo . . .

'You'd best sit down, lass.' Big May's face swum hazily into view.

'I – I'm all right . . .' Edie turned to say, but no sooner were the words out than her knees buckled underneath her and she slid to the ground.

***

She woke up coughing and spluttering. Something foul and pungent was burning her nose and throat, making her eyes stream. She fought to sit up, but several pairs of hands came out of nowhere, pushing her back down again.

'That's enough of the *sal volatile*, Beattie,' she heard Big May saying. 'Stand back, girls, let her breathe.'

The hands retreated, until there was just Big May looking down at her, her broad face full of concern.

'How are you feeling, lass?' she asked.

Edie squinted around at the circle of concerned faces looking down at her. 'What happened?'

'You fainted,' Iris said. 'Passed clean out on the floor, you did.'

Suddenly it all came back to her. Edie struggled to sit up, still coughing from the smelling salts Beattie had wafted under her nose. 'I don't know what came over me. It must be the heat—'

'Aye,' Beattie said. 'That'll be it. Either that, or the baby in your belly.'

Edie looked at her sharply. Beattie looked back at her with a shrewd expression.

'I – I don't know what you mean—' Edie started to say, but Big May cut her off.

'Come on, ducks, we in't daft. We've had enough bains between us to know the signs. In't we, girls?'

Edie felt the heat rise in her face as she saw the knowing expressions on the other girls' faces.

'Might as well come clean,' Beattie said. 'Tell the truth and shame the devil.'

'How long have you known?' Edie said quietly.

'Ever since the day you first walked in here,' May said.

Edie flashed her a look. 'And you didn't say anything?'

'We didn't think it was our business.'

She had misjudged them all, she thought. All this time she had been keeping her secret, and they had been keeping it too.

'Why didn't you tell us you were expecting?' Iris asked.

Edie lowered her gaze. 'I wanted to, but I was worried you wouldn't give me the job. And I needed the money.'

'Aye, I daresay you did, with a bain on the way and no husband to look after you.' Big May looked grim. 'How far gone are you?'

'The baby's due in November.'

The women looked at each other in astonishment. 'You in't very big for five months,' Dolly said. 'I was the size of a house when I were pregnant with our George.'

'No wonder you managed to hide it.' Big May looked her up and down with a critical eye. 'Mind, you don't look well. Having a hard time of it, are you?' Edie nodded. 'Not eating properly either, I expect.'

'It makes me feel sick.'

'No wonder you've been fainting,' Beattie said. 'You've got to eat, lass, whether you feel like it or not. You're eating for two, don't forget.'

'That's what the midwife says.'

'Nurse Shepherd from Coltman Street, is it?' Dolly said. 'You want to listen to her. She knows what she's talking about.'

'Ginger biscuits are what you want,' Beattie said. 'They'll take away the sickness in no time. I'll make some for you, next time I get my rations.'

Edie looked around gratefully at the other women. They were all being so kind to her, she wished she had confided in them sooner.

Big May looked to the window at the sound of heavy horses' hooves clopping down the street below. There was a gruff cry of 'Whoa, Bertha,' followed by the creak of wheels and the loud jingle of a harness.

'About time, too,' May said. 'That'll be Pop, come to take you home.'

Panic assailed her. 'But I don't need to go. I'm feeling a lot better now—' Edie started to say, but May shook her head.

'Nonsense, I won't hear of it. You need to go home and rest.' Big May helped her to her feet. 'Now, do you think you can get down the stairs by yourself, or do you want Dolly and Iris to go with you?'

'I can manage by myself.' Edie swallowed hard to stop herself crying with disappointment. This was it. Her earning days were over. And just as she was beginning to get back on her feet, too. She lifted her chin. 'When do you want me to come in and collect my cards?'

Big May frowned. 'What are you on about, lass? Cards? What cards?' She looked towards the window, and realisation seemed to dawn. 'Oh, you think I'm giving you the sack?' She laughed. 'Bless you, of course not. What kind of a woman would I be to do that? Besides, we need all the help we can get!' She shook her head. 'No, you can carry on as long as you feel able.'

'And when the bain's born, I can get my Sam to build you a frame at home so you won't have to stop working if you don't want to,' Beattie added.

A bubble of hope rose inside Edie's chest. 'So I could carry on earning?'

Big May shrugged. 'I don't see why not. Although I'm not sure what Patience Huggins will have to say about you turning your house into a netting loft!' she added.

Edie grinned back at her. She was so happy and relieved, she couldn't have cared less what Patience Huggins thought at that moment.

'Does Patience know about the baby?' Beattie asked.

Edie gazed down at her belly. 'No,' she said. 'And I can't say I'm looking forward to telling her, either.'

'I don't blame you.' Beattie Scuttle cackled mischievously. 'Tell you what, I wouldn't mind being a fly on the wall when you do!'

'I don't know about that.' Big May looked rueful. 'Fly on the wall or not, I reckon when Patience Huggins finds out the whole of Jubilee Row will be able to hear her!'

Chapter Seventeen

Dear Mrs Sandacre
I hope this letter finds you well. I am writing to inform
you of a rather distressing matter that has come to my
attention, regarding your tenant, Mrs Edie Copeland, of
10 Jubilee Row . . .

On the other side of the room Horace cleared his throat,
making Patience jump. She watched him for a moment, but
he was too busy twiddling the knobs of his wretched wireless
to pay her any attention as she sat at the chenille-covered
table, writing her letter.

It has come to my attention that Mrs Copeland is five
months pregnant, a fact which she freely admits she kept
from you when she took on the tenancy. She also admits
that she was aware of the clause in the tenancy agreement
that forbids babies and infants under five years old from
occupying the house . . .

Edie was quite brazen about it when she confronted her with
the contract. She hardly batted an eyelid as Patience retrieved
her copy from the dresser drawer and waved it under her
nose.

'If I'd told her, she wouldn't have let me have the rooms,'
was all she could say.

She lied to you, Mrs Sandacre. She has deliberately flouted the terms of the agreement which you signed in good faith.

Horace shifted his weight, the springs of his ancient armchair creaking under him. He looked round and caught Patience's eye with a smile.

'Who are you writing to?'

'Does it matter?' Patience snapped back, then checked herself. It was a harmless enough question. 'My cousin,' she said.

'The one in Preston? It must be years since you've spoken to her.'

'Yes, well, we have a lot to catch up on.' Patience sent him a wary look as she went back to her writing.

Horace would not approve of her letter. For some reason he didn't seem to share Patience's outrage over Edie's lies.

'Best not to get involved, love,' he said, when Patience told him. 'It in't our business.'

'Not our business?' Patience echoed in disbelief. 'How can you say such a thing? We have to live under the same roof as her. And I don't know about you, but I don't want to have to put up with a baby screaming night and day.'

'Oh, I don't know,' Horace said mildly. 'I like babies. And it might be nice to have a bain about the place. We've not had a little one in the house since our Joyce—' He stopped abruptly.

Once again, he had point-blank refused to go down to the rent office and speak to Mrs Sandacre.

'No, Patience. I'll not have anything to do with it. If you want to get a pregnant widow thrown out on the streets, then you'll have to see to it yourself. It'll be on your conscience, not mine.'

'But she lied—'

'And two wrongs don't make a right, do they?'

*As you are aware, my husband and I have been residing
at Jubilee Row for nearly 40 years. In all that time, I
consider we have been excellent tenants, and never given
you a moment's trouble. I hope, therefore, that you will take
our concerns into consideration when deciding what to do
about Mrs Copeland . . .*

It'll be on your conscience, not mine.

Patience's hand stilled as Horace's words came back to her.
Was that really what she wanted? She felt a pang as she tried
to imagine herself standing at the window, watching Edie
dragging her suitcase down the street, alone and pregnant
with nowhere to live.

But then another image came into her mind. Her back
yard full of buckets of dirty nappies soaking, lines full of
washing when she wanted to hang hers out, a pram parked
in her passageway, taking up all the room, sticky little hand
prints on her pristine paintwork.

This house was her whole world. She could control what
happened to her within these four walls. It had been hard
enough when Edie Copeland burst into it, causing all kinds of
change and chaos and disruption. The thought of her bringing
a baby into it too caused Patience's chest to tighten with anxiety. Her ribs squeezed so hard she could scarcely breathe.

*In my opinion, I do not feel we can go on living in the
same house as someone who makes such a mockery of her
tenancy agreement, aside from all the disruption of an
infant in the house. I trust, under the circumstances, you
will take appropriate action to remedy this distressing
situation.*

*Yours sincerely
Patience Mary Huggins (Mrs)*

'Finished?'

She didn't think Horace had been paying her any attention. It took her by surprise when he piped up as she folded up her letter and placed it inside the envelope.

He still had his back to her, his head close to the wireless, listening to all the various crackly voices and faint music, turning the dial this way and that.

'Yes. Yes, I have.'

'Leave it on the mantelpiece and I'll post it for you in the morning.'

Patience stared down at the address, carefully written on the envelope. As soon as Horace saw Mrs Sandacre's name he would know exactly what she was doing. He would have something to say about it, too. She couldn't even be sure he would agree to post it for her. Perhaps it might find its way into a bin before it ever reached the post box on the end of the road.

'Patience?' Horace was looking over his shoulder at her, his expression curious. 'Are you all right, love?'

'Quite all right, thank you.' Patience slipped the letter into her apron pocket and stood up. 'I'm going to the kitchen to put the kettle on,' she announced.

'I'll have a brew, if you're making one.'

Horace went back to his twiddling and Patience hurried from the room.

As she approached the kitchen, through the open back door she could already hear the raucous cries of the children playing up and down the ten foot beyond the back gate. Usually the noise would cause her endless vexation, but for once she was pleased to hear it. With a swift glance over her shoulder to make sure Horace hadn't followed her, she crossed the yard, not even bothering to change into her outdoor shoes, and opened the back gate.

The Maguire boys were playing one of their rowdy games, aiming a wooden ball at some tin cans. A skinny little girl with straggly pigtails was wailing at them, wanting to join in.

'You,' Patience called out to the boy nearest to her. 'Come here.'

The grubby, dark-haired little urchin took a step away from her, clutching the crumpled shirt-tail that had come loose from his trousers.

'I in't done anything!' he protested. 'I swear to you, Missus, I in't—'

'Never mind that,' Patience dismissed. 'How would you like to earn yourself a penny?'

The boy's eyes widened, then narrowed again.

'What do I have to do?' he asked cautiously.

'You know the red post box on the end of the road?' The boy nodded. Patience took the letter out of her apron pocket and held it out to him. 'Go and post this for me.'

The boy looked from her to the letter and back again. 'Is that it?'

'That's it. And the penny will be waiting for you when you come back.'

The boy turned to look back at the other boys. Then he snatched the letter out of Patience's hands and ran off down the ten foot, his cousins at his heels.

Chapter Eighteen

After weeks of escaping with nothing more than light air raids, the city got its first real battering in the early hours of a late August morning, when eight high explosives rained down on the east and west of the city, damaging buildings and killing six people.

Joyce could almost feel the tension in the air as she opened up the shop on Saturday morning. There was little pleasure in the warm summer day. People carried their gas masks again, and looked about them. On every street corner, they seemed to be discussing the bombing, and the tragedy of the lives lost. Rationing and blackouts and air-raid precautions were one thing, but this all seemed much more real. Even the bomb that had exploded at Saltend, shocking and terrible though it had been, had not touched them the way the loss of a young family did. It was as if the war had reached out its hand and touched the people of Hull.

Charlie was in a state of high nerves after spending the night in his mother's new air-raid shelter. He could not seem to settle to his work, starting and whimpering at every noise from the street outside. Reg had no patience with him, so Joyce asked if he could help her in the shop.

'I want to give the place a good spring clean this afternoon,' she said. 'He could help clear the shelves while I'm serving the customers.'

For once Reg did not argue. 'Do what you like, I'm not

bothered,' he shrugged. 'I could do with him out of the way, anyway. My pal Lenny's coming in and he reckons Charlie gives him the creeps.'

If anyone's creepy it's Lenny Maxwell, Joyce thought. He was one of Reg's cronies from the pub, a slimy, insinuating little weasel of a man, always involved in various shady deals. Joyce wished Reg would stay away from him, but of course he never listened to her.

'What does Lenny want?' she asked, then tensed as she saw Reg's expression darken. But luckily for her, he seemed to be in one of his better moods.

'He reckons he's got something I might be interested in,' he said.

Joyce hoped it wouldn't be more bacon, or butter or sugar, or anything else that came from under the counter. She felt so guilty about cheating on the rations that she could never eat anything Lenny provided, much to Reg's annoyance.

In the shop, she set Charlie to work.

'Take these boxes down from the top, like this, and put them down here out of the way,' she instructed. 'Then when we close up I'll give all the shelves a good scrub, ready to put them back on Monday morning. Here, I'll give you a hand while we're not busy.'

She reached up to take a box of locks and bolts down from the shelf and winced at the sudden, sharp pain in her ribs.

Charlie grabbed the box from her, his face a picture of concern.

'It's all right,' Joyce said. 'I've just pulled a muscle, that's all. You carry on, I'll be all right in a minute.'

Joyce caught the worried look Charlie sent her over his shoulder as he went about lifting the other boxes down from the shelves. She wondered if he had guessed the real reason for the agony she was in.

Reg had got better at hitting her where the bruises did not show, especially after the previous week when the swelling around her eye had taken so long to go down. Even the thickest layer of face powder had not been enough to hide the dark shadow along her cheekbone.

But the blow to her ribs last night had knocked the wind out of her. It still hurt to breathe too deeply, and Joyce worried that Reg might have cracked a bone. She had lain awake all night, too afraid to move because of the pain it would cause.

And as she lay in bed, listening to Reg snoring beside her, she had imagined what it would be like to leave him.

It was something she thought about a great deal, especially after she had taken a battering. She would picture her life, wonder what it would feel like to be free, not to have to account for her every movement, not to have to worry that her every remark might cause offence, or trigger a bout of violent rage.

But her thoughts always ended in despair. Where could she go? She had no money, Reg made sure of that. He held on to everything. If Joyce needed to go shopping, Reg would carefully count coins into her hand. And he would wait for the change when she returned. There was no housekeeping, no chance to put anything by for herself.

She had no friends, either. She was on friendly terms with lots of people. She could pass the time of day with other women in the greengrocer's queue, or make pleasant chit-chat with customers who came into the shop. But there was no one she could really confide in, no best friend she could trust with her secrets.

And as for family . . .

You've made you bed, now you must lie in it.

Her mother's final harsh words came back to her, as they so often did. At the time, they had meant little to Joyce. She was in love with a man who she truly believed loved her and would take care of her forever.

Looking back on it, she wondered how she could have been so wrong about him. But how could she have known any better? Her life had been so sheltered before Reg Shelby came into it. Her world was a narrow one, full of nothing but books and studying. The furthest she was ever allowed to go by herself was the library on Albion Street.

It was on her way home from a trip to the library that Reg swept her off her feet. Joyce had been crossing Hessle Road with her arms full of books, daydreaming as usual, when she heard an almighty clank and rattle of metal behind her, and a voice cried out, 'Get out of the way!'

Joyce turned round in time to see a curious-looking bicycle careering down the middle of the road towards her. It was so laden down with pots and pans, sharpening and grinding tools that she almost could not see the person cycling it. It swerved to avoid her, clipped the kerb and landed with a clatter against a lamp post.

'Are you all right?' Joyce dropped her books and rushed over to help, and found herself looking into a pair of angry grey eyes.

'What do you think?' A voice growled from under the heap of battered, twisted metal. 'Well, don't just stand there. Help me up!'

By the time she had helped to disentangle him from his bent bicycle frame, Reg Shelby had recovered some of his composure – and his charm.

'Nothing damaged, except my pride,' he said cheerfully. 'How about you?'

'I – I think I'm all right.' Joyce, staring at him, was at a loss for words. He looked like a romantic hero from one of her novels, with his black hair and rippling muscles.

She was overwhelmed when he insisted on carrying her books back to her house, although she was careful to part ways with him well before they reached the corner of Jubilee Row. When her mother questioned her later about why she had been late home, Joyce could scarcely stop herself blushing.

'I was nearly hit by a bicycle crossing the road.' She could not bring herself to lie to her mother, but she knew better than to tell her the whole truth.

After that, Joyce often saw Reg on her way home from the library, or the school where she worked as a pupil-teacher. At first she was surprised to find him waiting for her, then she started to look forward to seeing him standing on the street corner. He would tuck her books under his arm and fall into step beside her. At first Joyce was too shy to speak to him, but it did not seem to matter because Reg always had enough to say for both of them.

'Why do you wait for me?' she asked one day.

Reg grinned at her. 'Listen to you, fishing for compliments!' he said. 'I suppose you want me to tell you it's because you're the prettiest girl in Hessle Road, don't you?'

Joyce stared at him, genuinely perplexed. The thought had not occurred to her. She knew very well that she was nothing special to look at. But for some inexplicable reason Reg seemed utterly charmed by her.

'Do you ever go anywhere else but the library?' he asked her one afternoon, as they strolled down Coltman Street.

She frowned. 'I don't know what you mean.'

'You know. Dancing, the pictures and suchlike?' She shook her head. 'I could take you dancing, if you like?' he offered.

Joyce considered the suggestion, then shook her head. 'I don't think my mother would like it.'

'I don't want to go with your mother. I want to go with you.'

'I can't,' she said.

'Then I'll not stop asking until you say yes.'

He was as good as his word. And finally, after weeks of badgering and persuasion, Joyce agreed to ask her mother if she could go dancing with him the following Friday.

She already knew what the answer would be.

'The very idea!' her mother huffed. 'Honestly, Joyce, I'm surprised that you would even suggest such a thing. Dancing, indeed!'

'The other girls go dancing all the time,' Joyce said quietly. 'Florence Maguire's my age, and she's already courting—'

'You're not a Maguire, are you? You're a lady.' Her mouth curled. 'And who is this young man asking you to go dancing with him, anyway?'

'His name's Reg Shelby.'

'Shelby? I don't know anyone called Shelby. Where did you meet him? Is he a teacher at the school?'

Joyce shook her head. 'I met him on Hessle Road.'

'Then what does he do?' Patience put her hand to her chest. 'Please don't tell me he works on the fish docks?'

'He mends pots and pans. And he sharpens knives,' Joyce added, seeing her mother's face fall. 'But he's got big plans. He's going to own his own ironmonger's shop one day.'

But Patience wasn't listening. 'A pot mender?' she echoed faintly. 'You expect me to let you step out with a person who mends pots?'

She said the same thing to Reg Shelby when he came to call for her the following Friday. Joyce felt her insides wither with mortification as Patience faced him down on the doorstep.

'My Joyce is too good for the likes of you,' she said in her haughtiest voice. 'If you think I'd ever allow her to get herself mixed up with a common tinker, you'd best think again! Now be on your way.'

And then she slammed the door in his face. But not before Joyce caught the look of suppressed fury in Reg's eyes.

Sometimes, in her bleaker moments, Joyce wondered if it wasn't spite that made Reg Shelby so determined to win her after that. Joyce had never expected to see him again, especially as her mother refused to allow her out of her sight for several weeks afterwards. But eventually Patience decided that what she called Joyce's 'silly infatuation' was over, and she could be trusted to go out on her own again.

And the first time she returned from the library by herself, there was Reg, waiting on the street corner for her.

'I can't get over you, Joyce,' he clutched her hand, tears filling his grey eyes. 'I've been hanging about here for weeks, hiding in shop doorways, just to catch a glimpse of you. Promise me we can go on seeing each other? I'll go mad if I have to give you up.'

Joyce was overwhelmed. She had never felt like the centre of anyone's world until this moment. Her father spent most of his time at work, and her mother had always seemed chilly and distant. But here was someone who could not live without her. It was not hard to believe she was passionately in love with him. And infatuated as she was, within a few months she had agreed to his plan to elope.

'Your mother will never let us be together,' Reg had pleaded with her. 'But you're the only girl I'll ever love. Promise you'll marry me, even if we have to run away together to do it?'

He had made it sound as if it was the only way. But the moment the ring was on her finger, Joyce was racked with guilt and fear. She knew how much her father dreamed of the day when he would walk her down the aisle, and now she had taken that special moment away from him.

And as for her mother . . .

The idea of facing them made her feel sick to her stomach, but Reg insisted they should do it straight away.

'No sense in putting it off,' he said, as they emerged from the registry office. 'They've got to know some time, in't they?'

'Can't we enjoy the moment before my mother ruins it?' Joyce pleaded.

'She can't spoil anything,' Reg smirked. 'We're married and there's nowt she can do about it.'

There was something about the way he said it that made Joyce wary. She had planned to break the news to them alone, but Reg insisted on coming with her.

'We're husband and wife now, Joyce. My place is by your side,' he said.

'At least let me tell them,' Joyce begged.

But in the end Reg ended up blurting it out.

'I'm sorry, love. I couldn't help myself,' he told Joyce afterwards, but when she looked into his eyes, she couldn't help feeling he'd enjoyed it.

But she hadn't. Even now, nearly twenty years later, Joyce could hardly bring herself to think about that horrible night. It was the first time she had stood up to her mother, and it was every bit as awful and frightening as she had expected. Looking back on it, Joyce wished she had not let her anger get the better of her. But when Patience started to lay down the law, years of resentment and bitterness had come out in an ugly, gushing, venomous mess, which ended in Joyce smashing the plate in a fit of frustration.

As long as she lived, she would never forget the hurt on her mother's face. Until that moment, it had never occurred to Joyce that her mother could be hurt by anything, least of all her. That was what had cut her the deepest.

But before she had time to apologise for what she had

done, Patience turned on her and delivered her final, crushing blow.

Go and never come back, she had said. *If you leave this house with that man, I never want to see you again. You've made your bed, now you must lie in it.*

And Joyce had been doing just that ever since.

* * *

At noon, she closed up the shop, left Charlie taking down the last of the boxes from the shelves and hurried upstairs to prepare Reg's dinner. Last night's argument had started when she had been late with his tea, and Joyce wasn't going to make that mistake again.

But by the time his food was on the table, Reg had still not appeared. Perhaps he was still with Lenny, Joyce thought. Once the two of them got talking business they often lost track of time. She listened at the top of the stairs, but there were no voices coming from down in the workshop. Only the sound of her husband's tuneless whistling.

Finally, she summoned the courage to go downstairs and knock on the door to the workshop.

'Reg?' she called out softly. 'Your dinner's on the table.'

'I'll be there in a minute,' Reg called back. Then, as Joyce turned to go back upstairs, she heard Reg say, 'Come in here, I want to show you summat.'

When Joyce opened the workshop door, she found Reg standing in the middle of the workshop, beside the battered remains of a big bassinet pram. It was a sorry sight, its wheels all buckled and bent, the sides collapsed inwards as if the whole pram had been crushed in a giant fist. The black fabric hood hung in tattered shreds from a broken frame.

But Reg was gazing at it as if it was a thing of great beauty.

'What do you think?' he beamed. 'Lenny came up trumps, didn't he?'

'How did it get in such a state?' Joyce asked.

'Does it matter?' Reg ran his hand over the twisted chassis. 'I reckon I can beat out these dents, put some new wheels on it and repair the paintwork, and it'll be as good as new. Reckon we should be able to get a few quid for it.'

Unease crawled up Joyce's spine. 'Where did you get it?'

Reg frowned in irritation. 'I told you, Lenny brought it in.'

'And where did he get it?'

'He found it.' Reg looked defensive. 'He didn't steal it, if that's what you're thinking. Come and have a look.'

Joyce took a step towards the battered pram, then stopped. There was something about it that repulsed her.

'Where did he find it?' she asked.

'I don't know. T'other end of Hessle Road.' He had his back to her now, bending down to examine the wheels.

'The other end of Hessle Road?' In her mind, she heard the drone of a plane passing low overhead, the rattle of anti-aircraft fire, then a distant explosion. They had stood in the yard, she and Reg, and watched the thick plume of smoke rising into the air to the west.

'Not Carlton Street?' she whispered. Reg said nothing. 'Not that house that was bombed? Reg—'

'I don't know anything about it,' he cut her off bluntly. 'I don't ask questions and nor should you.'

'But that's looting!'

'Ruby Maguire would call it salvage,' Reg retorted. 'Besides, it in't as if they wanted it any more.'

Joyce stared at him, numb with horror. 'How can you say that? A baby died, Reg.'

'I told you, I don't know anything about it,' Reg repeated stubbornly.

Joyce averted her eyes from the pram. She couldn't even bear to look at it now she knew where it had come from.

'Get rid of it,' she said.

'I will, once I've finished doing it up.'

'No, I want it gone now. It's bad luck. No good can come of having that thing under this roof.'

Reg grinned. 'And I thought it was only us gypsies that were superstitious!'

'I mean it, Reg.'

'As if I give a damn what you think.' He turned his back on her, crouching down to examine the pram's bodywork.

As he bent down to examine the pram, Joyce eyed the hammer, lying on the worktop just within her reach. Her fingers inched towards it as her gaze fixed on the back of Reg's head, his thatch of oily black hair and thick, sunburnt neck . . .

The noise from the doorway made her jump. She looked up to see Charlie watching her, a box in his arms. His face was an expressionless mask.

'What are you staring at?' Reg demanded. Charlie kept his eyes fixed on Joyce.

'Go back in the shop, Charlie,' she said quietly.

Charlie hesitated for a moment, then he turned on his heel and went back into the shop, closing the door behind him.

'I'm going to have words with him,' Reg muttered. 'He should remember who pays his wages!'

Joyce stood motionless for a second, then withdrew her hand slowly. 'I'll put your dinner in the oven,' she said.

Chapter Nineteen

But she did not go back upstairs.

She didn't know how it happened; her head was telling her to return to the kitchen, even as she was shrugging on her coat and going out of the door.

It was a grey, muggy day, with a pall of heavy clouds overhead that seemed to press down on her, making her head ache. She walked fast down Anlaby Road towards the city, pain pulsing through her temples. She knew she would pay for it later on when Reg found out she was gone, but at that moment all she could think about was putting as much distance between herself and him as possible.

Joyce turned cold, thinking about what she might have done if Charlie Scuttle had not walked in when he did. *Was this what madness felt like?* she wondered.

She wasn't even thinking about the direction she was going in until she found herself on the wide thoroughfare of Ferensway, pushing open the double doors to the WVS centre.

The place was quite empty. There were no sewing machines whirring, no sound of chatter. Just a few women in green uniforms, milling about. They barely gave Joyce a glance as she stood marooned in the middle of the room, staring about her, suddenly at a loss.

'Joyce?'

She turned at the sound of Ruby Maguire's voice. She was walking towards her, a welcoming smile on her face.

'Have you come to join the knitting group? You're a bit early, they don't usually start until one o'clock.'

'I – I haven't come to knit,' Joyce whispered.

'Haven't you? Oh, well, I'm sure we can find something for you to do. I'm very pleased to see you, at any rate.' Ruby squeezed her arm gently. She really did look pleased, Joyce thought, still in a daze.

'I wasn't planning on stopping . . .' she started to say, but Ruby cut her off.

'Happen you could make a start on the tea?' she suggested brightly.

'I—' Joyce looked to the kitchen door. She hadn't meant to stay. She didn't even know what she was doing here. 'I suppose I could,' she heard herself saying uncertainly.

'Would you? Oh, that's such a great help.' Ruby was already propelling her towards the kitchen. 'You'll find everything out there in the kitchen. Best use the urn, not the kettle. We'll likely get busy later on, and our ladies love their tea!'

The kitchen was a surprisingly big room, with cupboards on all sides and a well-scrubbed wooden table in the middle. As Joyce set about filling the towering metal urn, Ruby said, 'Be careful with that, it's a temperamental beast when it wants to be. I hope there's some tea left in the caddy. Mrs Franklin might have used it all last night.'

'Last night?'

'She and some of the others were out making refreshments for the rescue workers in Carlton Street all last night.'

Joyce's hands shook as she took down the tea caddy from the shelf.

'Did you hear what happened?' Ruby went on. 'Such a bad business. When I think about that poor family . . . It's awful, in't it?'

Joyce thought about the pram, sitting in the middle of the workshop. 'It's terrible,' she murmured.

Ruby Maguire was right, the urn was temperamental. But Joyce was used to dealing with far worse tempers, and it wasn't long before she had managed to coax it into bubbling life.

As she was making the tea, the other women started to arrive. Joyce heard their voices as they greeted each other. It was hard to miss the strident tones of Big May Maguire. Joyce caught a glimpse of her formidable figure through the crack in the kitchen door, tiny Beattie Scuttle following, like the tug boat in the wake of an ocean liner. There was another woman with them. Joyce recognised her as Freda Powell from Strickland Street, who came into the shop every week to get her battery accumulator filled.

'It's just the three of us knitting today, our Ruby,' she heard Big May greeting her daughter-in-law in her booming voice.

'Is Mrs Oxton not coming?'

'Not today.' Big May lowered her voice a fraction. 'She's had some bad news.'

'Her son,' Beattie said, looking sombre.

'Oh.' Ruby's smile faded.

'She got the letter yesterday,' Big May said.

'Poor woman.' Ruby shook her head.

'It in't unexpected, he'd been missing for a few weeks,' Beattie said.

'But there's still hope, in't there?' Big May put in. 'While you still don't know for sure, I mean.'

The other women fell silent for a moment. Thinking of their own loved ones, Joyce guessed. She had a sudden picture of her boy Alan, so proud in his Army uniform. It was a man's uniform, but somehow it made him look even more like a little boy.

'I'll call in and see her later, in case she needs anything,' Ruby said.

'I went to see her this morning,' Freda Powell said. 'She said she was managing all right, but you only had to look at her to see she weren't.'

Joyce went back to her tea making, her heart heavy with sorrow for poor Mrs Oxton. But dreadful as it must be for her, at least she had people around her who cared.

Who would call on me if it happened to our Alan? she wondered. It was at times like this that she realised how truly alone she was.

Ruby Maguire must have told everyone Joyce was there because no one seemed surprised when she pushed the tea trolley round later.

'I hope you've made it nice and strong?' Big May beamed up at Joyce as she handed her a cup.

'I'm sorry,' Joyce looked anxiously at the watery-grey brew, 'there wasn't much tea left in the caddy. I could make you another cup, if you like?'

'Don't fret about it, lass, at least it's wet and warm.' Big May smiled back at her. 'To be honest, I've forgotten what a decent brew looks like since they put it on the ration.'

'Didn't expect to see you here,' Beattie said, looking up at her with those sharp little eyes of hers. 'Reg given you the day off, has he?'

'I—' Joyce had been so busy, she hadn't given Reg a second thought until now. Lost for words, she stared at the basket on the table, piled high with balls of yarn in various shades of dark blue and green.

'There's a spare pair of needles here, if you fancy making a start?' Big May changed the subject. 'Our Ruby's been telling us what a dab hand you are with knitting and sewing.'

'We're making jumpers for pilots,' Freda Powell said. 'Got a special order from the RAF.'

'We could always use another pair of hands,' Big May said. 'Especially with Olive Oxton not here.'

Joyce shook her head. 'I can't. I've got a bit of a headache.' She touched her temples where the pain still pulsed relentlessly.

'A cold compress is what you want,' Big May took a slurp of her tea, then set down the cup and went back to her knitting. 'My mother used to get terrible headaches,' she said, the stitches flying between her needles. 'She'd always soak a flannel in ice water and lie down with it over her eyes. Worked a treat, it did.'

'My mother swore by soaking her feet in hot water,' Beattie Scuttle said. 'She reckoned it was supposed to draw the bad blood out of her head.'

'Bad blood?' May turned on her scornfully. 'You do talk some rot, Beattie Scuttle!'

Freda Powell winked at Joyce. 'That's set them off,' she said. 'They're always arguing about something, these two.'

'No, no, you've got it wrong,' Big May was saying to Beattie. 'It's molasses you rub on your temples for a headache.'

'Well, I heard it was cow dung,' Beattie said.

Big May roared with laughter. 'I can just imagine you, Beattie Scuttle, rubbing dung on your face! No wonder the boys never wanted to know you.'

'That in't true, and you know it. I was very popular.' Beattie looked offended. 'Anyway, at least I never scared 'em, the way you did.' She turned to Joyce and Freda. 'D'you know, she used to arm wrestle the lads on West Dock Road?'

'And what's wrong with that?' May said. 'What's the point in courting a man if you're stronger than he is?'

'You'd never believe they're the best of pals, would you?' Freda Powell said.

Joyce left the three of them laughing and went to hand out tea to the women sorting through the clothes salvage. There were only two of them, and they didn't seem to be making a very good job of it. Joyce watched them conferring over what looked to her to be a perfectly good dress.

'This dart's coming unravelled,' one of them said. 'And look, there's a hole here, near the hem.'

'Chuck it out,' her partner nodded towards the pile behind her. 'There's nowt to be done with it.'

Joyce looked at the dress, lying on top of the pile. It seemed like a criminal waste to her. Darts could be restitched, and holes mended. At the very least, it could be cut down to make a little frock for a child . . .

'Is everything all right, Joyce?'

She started guiltily at the sound of Ruby Maguire's voice behind her.

'Yes, thank you.' Then a thought occurred to her and she blushed. 'Why? Has someone complained about the tea? I did my best, but I'm not sure that urn came to the boil . . .'

'You did a grand job with the tea,' Ruby reassured her. 'But I saw you looking at those clothes, and I know you're good with a needle. Do you have any ideas?'

Joyce glanced at the two women, who were now staring back at her. *Don't get involved,* a small voice whispered inside her head. *You don't know anything about it, no one needs you interfering . . .*

'I'm sure we'd all be very grateful if you could help out?'

'No!' The word came out too fast. Ruby looked startled. 'You don't need my help,' she whispered.

'I reckon we do!' One of the women spoke up. 'We don't have the first idea what we're doing. Do we, Wyn?' she turned to her friend.

'Not a clue!' the other woman shrugged helplessly.

'But I don't want to interfere . . .'

'You'd be helping us. That's what we do here, help each other out.' Wyn smiled at her encouragingly.

'Happen you could give them a hand when you've finished with the tea?' Ruby said.

It took a long time to sort through the salvage pile. Joyce got so absorbed in her task, she was dismayed when she looked up at the clock and realised it was gone three o'clock.

Reg will be furious.

But it had been worth it. She could not remember when she had enjoyed herself more.

Charlie was alone in the workshop when Joyce returned home.

'Where's Mr Shelby?' she asked.

Charlie jerked his head towards the ceiling. So Reg was up in the flat, waiting for her. That was not a good sign.

Joyce looked around the workshop. There was no sign of the pram. Her heart lifted. Perhaps Reg had listened to her after all? It would be worth a beating just for that.

But then she followed Charlie's gaze to the corner of the workshop. It was hidden in the shadows, covered with a tarpaulin shroud, but there was no mistaking the shape of it.

She took the stairs slowly, half dreading what was to come. In the kitchen, Reg's plate still sat on the kitchen table, untouched, the food a dried-out mess. Joyce knew a rebuke when she saw one.

She was clearing it away when she heard Reg's footsteps coming down the hall.

'Where have you been until this time?'

Joyce's nerves jolted, but she tried not to show it as she rinsed the plate in the sink. 'I had a headache so I went for a walk.'

'For two hours?'

'I wasn't walking all that time. I ended up going to the WVS.'

'Where?'

'The Women's Voluntary Service in Ferensway.' She picked up the tea towel to dry the plate. In the scrap of mirror over the sink she saw Reg's lip curl.

'Ruby Maguire's lot, you mean? Load of busybodies, they are.'

'Actually, they do a lot of good work.'

'Such as?'

'They looked after the rescue workers last night while they were digging those dead bodies out of the house in Carlton Street.'

She stared at his reflection, saw the twitch of guilt in his face.

He quickly recovered, his scowl back in place. 'Anyway, they don't need you,' he grunted.

'Ruby Maguire seems to think I'd be useful.'

Reg bared his teeth in a cruel smile. 'She doesn't know you then, does she?'

Joyce flinched inwardly at the insult but she kept her face calm and she put the plate away in the cupboard. 'Anyway, I think I'll be going down there again,' she said.

'Oh, you will, will you?' Reg snorted.

'Yes.' She turned to face him. 'Yes, I think I will.'

For a moment she thought he would go for her. But he must have seen something in her face because for once he was the one who looked away first.

'We'll have to see about that,' he muttered.

Yes, Joyce thought, allowing herself a small smile at her reflection. It felt like a victory. *We will, won't we*, she thought.

Chapter Twenty

'I hear you're expecting?'

Edie stared at Mrs Sandacre, sitting on the other side of the desk from her. She was a hard-faced woman in her late forties, with dyed red hair and iron-grey eyes. Her scarlet lipstick emphasised the thin, angry line of her mouth.

Edie's heart drummed in her chest but she wasn't surprised. Why else would Mrs Sandacre have summoned her to the rent office this morning? She had barely slept since she received her letter.

She knotted her hands in her lap. In her belly, her baby stirred and uncurled, as if trying to make its presence felt.

No use trying to hide me any more, it seemed to say.

'I suppose Mrs Huggins told you?' Patience had been standing there in the doorway when Edie picked up Mrs Sandacre's letter from the hallstand a few days earlier. She had scarcely been able to keep the self-satisfied look off her face.

'Never mind how I know. Is it true?'

Inside her, the baby shifted again. Edie lowered her gaze from the landlady's angry face. 'Yes,' she said quietly. 'Yes, it's true.'

Mrs Sandacre sat back in her chair and let out a long, slow breath. 'And you didn't think to tell me when you took on the tenancy?'

'Would you have let me have it if I had?'

'Don't get cheeky with me, lass! You're in no position.' Mrs Sandacre picked up the tenancy contract that lay on the desk between them. 'The agreement says no children. It's written here in black and white, couldn't be clearer. And you signed it.' She tapped the piece of paper where Edie's signature was scrawled beside hers. 'You signed it, knowing you were expecting.'

Edie could hardly swallow, a painful lump of fear in her throat. 'Yes,' she whispered.

'So you lied to me?'

Edie stared down at her hands and nodded.

'And how long did you think you could keep it from me? Did you not think I'd notice a bain in my house?'

'I – I wasn't thinking. I was desperate.'

As soon as she said the word she wished she hadn't. Mrs Sandacre's gaze sharpened.

'Desperate? Why?'

'I didn't know what I was doing. I'd only just found out I was pregnant when Rob was – when I lost him. I was trying to cope with it all, and I had to find somewhere to live, and I just – panicked,' she said.

Mrs Sandacre was silent for a long time, her hard gaze fixed on Edie.

'You come from York, don't you?'

'That's right.'

'And you've got family there?'

'My father and my stepmother.'

'Couldn't you stay with them?'

Edie didn't blame her for wondering. Anyone would have the same thought. Families were supposed to stick together, after all. They were supposed to help each other out in a crisis.

And surely a young, pregnant woman who had just lost her

husband would need her family around her? It was exactly the time a girl would need her mother.

But Rose had only ever been a mother in name. She had never wanted Edie as her daughter, although she made a good show of it before she married Edie's father.

She remembered when her father first brought Rose to their house. Edie was eight years old, and dazzled by the pretty young woman with her yellow hair and high-heeled shoes, who wore carnation-pink lipstick and smelt of roses.

'White Rose. Like my name, see?' she had said, with a smile that showed off her pearly teeth. 'I always wear it. I'll buy you a bottle so we can be the same, shall I?'

That was only one of the many promises she made to Edie. She promised to curl Edie's hair, and to buy her a new dress.

'I have two little boys, but I've always wanted a girl,' she said, hugging her fiercely. 'My Cyril and Kenny would love a big sister, too.'

Edie hadn't really taken in what Rose meant until later, when her father was putting her to bed.

'What did you think of Rose?' he asked.

'She was very pretty,' Edie replied.

'Did you like her?'

Edie paused. 'She was quite nice,' she said, then added, 'but Bella didn't care for her.'

Bella was her mother's rag doll, that she had passed on to Edie when she was born. After thirty years of loving, she was showing her age. Her clothes and most of her wool hair had gone, her features were faded and her stuffing poked out of a hole in her side where her stitching had come unravelled.

Rose had laughed when she saw her.

'What's this?' she had asked, holding the doll up by her pink-painted fingertips. 'You poor mite, I don't know what your father's thinking, leaving you with such a wretched thing to play with.'

Edie watched Bella dangling from Rose's fingers, her heart in her mouth. 'Please don't drop her,' she had begged.

'Drop her? She belongs on the bonfire.' Rose smiled at her. 'Don't worry, my little pet. You shall have a beautiful new doll, I'll see to that.' She leaned closer, so that Edie could see that her face wasn't really that pretty at all, just a mask of artfully applied powder and paint.

'I don't want a new doll, I want to keep Bella. She was my mother's and now she's mine.'

Rose had only smiled at that, a tight little smile. But Edie had the idea that she had said something wrong.

Now, as he tucked in the blankets around her, her father smiled and said, 'I'm not asking Bella, I'm asking you.' He looked at Edie. 'Would you like her to be your mother?'

Edie had gazed back at him and knew that if she said no, then that would be the end of it. But she also saw the longing in his eyes. Her mother had been gone for five years, and in all that time it had been just the two of them. He was a good father, but he was lonely and tired. It was about time he had someone to love and look after him, too.

'I would like that very much,' she had said.

That brought a smile of relief to his face. He hugged her tightly, something he did not often do. 'I'm glad,' he said, his voice muffled against her shoulder. 'You'll see, we'll all be one big happy family.'

It's your choice, John. Either she goes, or I do.

She faced Mrs Sandacre across the desk. 'We're not close,' she said shortly.

'Why not?'

The older woman looked curious. Perhaps if Edie tried to

explain the kind of woman Rose was, and the life she had led her over the past twelve years, then Mrs Sandacre might have some sympathy for her. But she had already said too much. She had not come here for pity.

She stood up, took her keys out of her pocket and set them down on the desk in front of her.

Mrs Sandacre stared down at them. 'What's all this?'

'Your keys. Look, we both know you're going to evict me anyway, so why don't I save us both a lot of trouble? I can be out of the house by Friday.'

'Where will you go?'

In truth she had no idea. 'I'm sure I'll find somewhere. It's no concern of yours.'

The landlady's pencilled brows rose. 'I'll thank you not to take that tone with me! You're very sharp, considering.'

'Considering what?' Edie turned on her. 'You said yourself, I've lied to you and broken the terms of our contract. And Mrs Huggins wants me out, so—' She stopped, tears clogging her throat. She would not cry, she told herself. She did not have much pride left, but she would not allow herself to be even more humiliated.

'Sit down, lass.' Mrs Sandacre's tone was softer. 'Sit down,' she said again, when Edie hesitated. 'Happen we can sort this out, if you stop flying off the handle for five minutes?'

The baby bucked and twisted inside her. Edie sank into the seat. 'I'm sorry,' she mumbled.

'That's better.' The landlady sent her a considering look. 'Your husband was killed at Dunkirk, wasn't he?' Edie nodded. 'And now you're left to bring up a bain all by yourself?'

'Yes.'

Mrs Sandacre was silent for a long time. 'I lost my husband to the Spanish 'flu, just after the war,' she said finally. 'I was left with a two year old daughter.'

Edie's heart went out to the hard-faced woman. 'I'm sorry.'

'Oh, I was lucky. We had a bit of money put by. I took over his business, and the houses he owned. But I don't know what I would have done if I'd had nothing.' She leaned back in her chair and steepled her fingers in front of her. 'The way I see it, you're going to have a hard enough time coping on your own, without me adding to your burden.'

Edie blinked at her. 'You mean I can stay in Jubilee Row?'

'You can stay,' Mrs Sandacre said, 'as long as I don't get complaints from Mrs Huggins every five minutes. I just can't be doing with it.' Her mouth pursed. 'You'll have to make more effort to get on with her. I know she can be a bit – difficult,' she said. 'But she's a good tenant and I don't want her upset.' She eyed Edie severely. 'Get her on your side, or I really will have to reconsider your tenancy.'

'I'll do my best,' Edie promised.

* * *

Edie knew she was being watched as soon as she let herself in through the front door. Patience Huggins was nowhere to be seen, but Edie could feel her presence loitering nearby.

'Hello, Mrs Huggins,' she called out into the empty air.

At that, the door to the parlour opened and the woman herself appeared, taking off her apron. She did a poor job of feigning surprise at the sight of Edie.

'Oh, Mrs Copeland. I thought I heard your voice.' It was the first time Edie had ever been greeted with more than a scowl. In fact, if Edie looked really closely she could almost see the hint of a smile tugging at the corners of Mrs Huggins' thin mouth.

'You look very smart,' she commented. 'Been somewhere nice, have you?'

'As a matter of fact, I've been to see Mrs Sandacre.'

Mrs Huggins' mouth twitched. 'Oh? What was that about?'

As if you didn't know. 'She found out I was expecting.'

'Well, I suppose she was bound to find out sometime.' Patience Huggins looked away, rubbing an invisible speck of dust on the hallstand with her finger. 'So I suppose you'll be moving out?'

'Actually, she said I could stay.'

Patience swung round, her face aghast. 'But – you can't! The tenancy agreement clearly states no babies—'

'I know,' Edie said. 'Like you, I expected her to evict me, but she was very nice about it.' She reached out and patted the other woman's arm. 'Oh, Mrs Huggins, I can't tell you how relieved I am. I don't mind admitting, I was absolutely dreading seeing her this morning. But it's such a relief to have everything out in the open at last. I don't know how she found out, but I reckon whoever told her did me a big favour.'

Patience Huggins stared down at Edie's hand resting on her arm, and her eyes boggled behind her horn-rimmed spectacles. Her mouth opened and closed but no sound came out.

Edie tried not to smile. She mustn't crow too much, she told herself. But it was difficult when Patience Huggins was so nonplussed.

Tomorrow she would start making an effort to get on with her, she thought. But today she was going to savour her rare moment of triumph.

Then she turned and saw the letter lying on the hallstand. She snatched it up and stared down at the familiar handwriting.

'When did this arrive?'

'It came in the second post,' Patience Huggins replied

absently, her thoughts clearly elsewhere. 'I hope it wasn't important.'

Edie did not reply. She could only look down at the letter she had sent her father, the name and address crossed out and three words written in Rose's unmistakable scrawl:

Return To Sender.

Chapter Twenty-one

'What's keeping her, I wonder?'

Iris looked up from her digging. Dolly had been walking back and forth between the outhouse and the back door for at least half an hour.

'You'll not make her come any quicker by pacing up and down,' she said.

'But she said she'd come and let us know as soon as she heard.'

'Aye, I daresay she will.'

'Yes, but she should be back from seeing Mrs Sandacre by now.' Dolly reached the battered wooden door of the out-house and turned around to make her way back across the small square of yard. 'It's bad news, I know it is.'

'You don't know that.' Iris stuck her spade into the newly dug earth and wiped the perspiration from her brow. It was a warm, muggy day, too hot for September. Iris gazed mourn-fully at the tiny patch of ground she had spent hours weeding and turning over. She was beginning to wish she had left digging this vegetable bed for Pop after all.

'Why else would it be taking her this long?' Dolly twisted a blonde curl around her finger. 'I bet she's over there now, packing her bags. I've a good mind to go over there myself, give Patience Huggins what for!'

'I can't believe she had the cheek to give that letter to your George to post,' Iris said.

'I know! He deserves a clip round the ear for taking it.'

'It in't his fault. He was only trying to be helpful, like you've always taught him.'

'Since when has that boy ever listened to anything I've taught him?' Dolly looked rueful. 'But I made him give that penny back. I handed it to Horace Huggins myself, when I saw him in the corner shop.'

'What did he say?'

'He was a bit lost for words. I don't think he knew what she was up to until I told him. He's such a nice old man, I feel sorry for him.' She stopped her pacing and peered at Iris. 'You've got dirt all over your face.'

'Have I?' Iris wiped her cheek with her shirt sleeve. 'Is that better?'

'Not really. You do look a sight, Iris Fletcher. Are those Arthur's trousers you're wearing?'

Iris shook her head. 'They belong to our Jimmy. I borrowed them off Ruby. I got rid of all Arthur's clothes, remember?' She could not bear to have them in the house after he'd gone. 'Anyway,' she said, 'what does it matter what I look like? I'm digging the garden, not taking part in a fashion parade.'

'You wouldn't catch me doing it.' Dolly examined her carefully manicured fingernails.

'Oh no, you're far too glamorous.'

'And you're far too independent.'

'And what's that supposed to mean?'

'Nothing.' Dolly directed her gaze to the ground at Iris' feet. 'Should your Kitty be eating worms?'

'Kitty, no!'

Iris was in the kitchen rinsing soil from her baby's mouth when Edie let herself in. One look at her pale, distracted face told Iris all she needed to know.

'Oh love, what's happened? It's bad news, in't it?' Dolly pounced on her straight away.

'Give the poor lass a minute. Here, take Kitty and I'll make us a brew.' Iris dumped the baby in Dolly's arms and headed for the kettle.

'What did she say?' Dolly wanted to know. Then, before Edie could speak, she went on, 'I bet that old bat Patience Huggins is pleased with herself. Well, she needn't think anyone on the street will talk to her after this!'

'Dolly Maguire, will you shut up a minute and give the girl a chance?'

'It's all right,' Edie said. She sounded weary, her warm hazel eyes dull with exhaustion. 'It went well,' she told Dolly. 'Mrs Sandacre said I could stay on.'

Dolly and Iris looked at each other. 'Well, that's a relief,' Dolly said. 'Good old Mrs Sandacre. I knew she had a heart.'

Edie said nothing. She looked distracted, Iris thought as she made the tea.

'It must be a weight off your mind?' she said.

Edie ran her finger around the rim of the teacup Iris had just put down in front of her. 'Yes,' she said. 'Yes, it's the best news I could have had.'

'So why do you still look as if you've lost a penny and found a farthing?' Dolly asked.

'Do I?' Edie sat up straighter, pulling herself together. 'Sorry.'

Iris sat down at the kitchen table and pulled her own cup towards her. 'What's happened?' she asked.

'It's nothing.' Edie picked up her teacup, then put it down again. 'I just got a letter today.'

'Who from?'

'My father. Well, not him, exactly . . .'

Once again, Iris and Dolly exchanged glances.

144

'Blimey, lass, you don't half talk in riddles sometimes!' Dolly said.

Edie's mouth twisted. 'Sorry. Take no notice of me, I'm just being daft.' She pushed her cup away from her. 'I'd better go,' she said.

'Already? You've only just got here.'

'I know, but I – I'm not feeling well. I haven't been sleeping, what with everything going on, and—'

'You go home and get some rest, lass.' Iris smiled at her. 'We'll see you later, won't we, Doll?'

She looked at Dolly, silently warning her not to argue.

No sooner had Edie gone out of the front than the back door flew open and Iris' four year old daughter Lucy burst in, red-faced and sobbing.

'Our Archie's run away from me again!' she cried. 'I tried to go after him but I fell over.'

'Let's have a look at you.' Iris sat her up on the scrubbed wooden draining board to examine her. Under her thin cotton dress, her knees were grubby and grazed. Iris spat on her hand and briskly wiped away the dirt. 'There, you'll live. Now let's go and sort this out, shall we?'

She stood at the back door and called out, 'Archie Fletcher! What have I told you about leaving your sister behind? You come back here this minute!'

There was no reply. Rolling up her oversized shirtsleeves, Iris stomped across the yard. 'I'm warning you, Archie. If I have to come out there—'

She threw open the back gate and found herself nose to nose with Sam Scuttle.

'You're wasting your breath,' he grinned. 'Last time I saw him, he was running hell for leather towards West Dock Road with his cousins.'

Iris sighed. 'I'll skin him when he comes home.'

'Happen you could skin these instead?'

He held up a brace of rabbits dangling from each hand.

'Is one of those for me?'

'As many as you want.'

'We'll have a couple, since you're offering. I daresay Mum will want one. And Dolly too, I expect. What do you say, Doll?' She led the way into the kitchen, Sam following.

'So what's with the get-up?' he asked as he dumped the rabbits on the draining board. They lay there, staring glassy-eyed up at the ceiling.

'Do you like it?' Iris did a comical twirl.

He looked her up and down. 'You're no Vesta Tilley, that's for sure.' He leaned closer. 'And you've got dirt all over your face.'

'Still? I thought I'd wiped it off . . .'

Iris went to rub her cheek but Sam said, 'No, you're making it worse. Let me.'

Holding her chin with one hand, he licked the end of his other thumb and very gently stroked it down the side of her face. He was so close, Iris could see his tanned, weather-beaten skin and the gingery lashes that fringed his sea-green eyes.

'There, that's done it.' Iris hadn't realised she had been holding her breath until Sam released her. She looked round to see Dolly watching them, an odd expression on her face.

'So I'll leave you a couple of these, shall I?' He nodded towards the rabbits on the draining board.

'Thanks. Mum will be delighted. I expect she'll cook them into one of her pies. Or a nice, tasty stew.'

'Let me know, and I might invite myself round,' Sam said.

'You know you're always welcome, Sam.'

As she closed the back door, she heard Dolly sigh behind her.

'When are you going to put the poor man out of his misery?' she said.

Iris looked over her shoulder at her. 'What are you talking about?'

'Sam. He likes you.'

'Don't be daft.'

'It's true. You only have to see the way he looks at you—'

'Sam looks at all the girls like that.'

'Not the way he looks at you.'

Iris laughed. 'Have you seen the state of me?' She looked down at herself, her hair scraped back under a faded headscarf, her brother's baggy trousers tucked into her old gumboots. One sleeve of her shapeless old shirt had come unrolled, swallowing her hand. 'I in't exactly Lana Turner, am I?'

'Sam don't seem to mind,' Dolly shrugged. 'Anyway, I'm not the only one that thinks it,' she said. 'Mum says the same, and the other girls in the netting loft. Even Beattie Scuttle thinks—' She trailed off as Iris's eyes narrowed.

'You mean you've all been talking about me?' she snapped.

'No.' It was a blatant lie; Dolly's deep blush said as much. 'We only want the best for you,' she wheedled.

'Then you should all just mind your own business!'

'But we want to see you happy.'

'I *am* happy.' As she said it, Iris' gaze strayed reluctantly to Arthur's photograph on the kitchen mantelpiece. She could hardly bear to look at it, but she kept it there for the sake of the children. They needed to be able to remember their father, especially little Kitty, who was so tiny when he passed away. They needed to keep his face in their minds, even if seeing it every day did cause Iris unbearable pain.

'He's gone, ducks,' Dolly said softly. 'He in't coming back. And you're only thirty. That's a long time to be on your own.'

'It suits me,' Iris said shortly.

'Does it?' Their eyes met and held. 'I know you've always said you'd never want another man after Arthur, but—'

'And I mean it,' Iris said firmly. 'Now, I want to finish that garden before teatime, so unless you're going to put on a pair of our Jack's trousers and help me—'

'No thanks!' Dolly shuddered. 'I'll come round later and set your hair for you. I reckon it could do with it!' As she reached up to tuck one of Iris' lank locks back inside her headscarf, Iris caught her eye and saw her expression soften.

'Don't forget what I said, will you?' Dolly said kindly. 'We all want what's best for you . . .'

'See you, Dolly.' Iris took her friend by the shoulders, turned her round and propelled her towards the back door.

Alone again, Iris went outside to carry on digging while Kitty and Lucy dug their own little patch with a spoon in the corner of the yard. Lucy seemed to have forgotten about following her brother, thank goodness, and at least she could stop her little sister picking more worms out of the soil to eat.

She's got it wrong. We're just friends.

She glanced over towards the fence that separated her garden from the Scuttles'. Over the top, she could see the hump of bare earth covering the new Anderson shelter.

Dolly's comments were nothing new. For six months after Arthur's death no one had said a word. But then, gradually, it began. Just the odd hint, a slight nudge here and there. She was no age to be a widow. The children needed a father, Arthur wouldn't want her to be on her own forever. Surely she didn't want that either, did she?

Iris looked around Arthur's garden, once his pride and joy. Actually, she did want to be on her own. After Arthur had gone, she had made a vow to herself that she would never allow another man into her life, her heart, her bed . . .

A fleeting memory came into her mind, of Sam's thumb stroking her cheek, the warmth of his breath fanning her face. She pushed it away, turning her gaze up to the muggy grey sky, tears running down her face as she thought of her husband somewhere up there, beyond the clouds. Was he looking down on her?, she wondered. And if he was, what was he thinking?

Oh, Arthur, she called up to him silently, *what did you do to me?*

Chapter Twenty-two

'What can we do with this?'

Joyce looked up from the pile of clothes she was sorting through to see Wyn Johnson holding up a voluminous flannel nightgown. It was so vast she nearly disappeared behind it.

'Dusters,' Maggie Cornell declared as she rummaged around in the pile looking for a companion to the sock she held in her hand.

'That's a bit of a waste, isn't it?' Wyn said. 'I mean, there's a lot of material in it . . .'

'I suppose we could send it to the Navy to use as a sail,' Maggie said.

'Let's have a look.' Joyce took the nightgown from Wyn and examined it carefully. 'You're right, there is a lot of cloth in it. I think if we unpicked the seams we could cut it down and make a nice little child's nightgown, or some pyjamas. It's so big, there might even be enough left over for a couple of cot blankets.'

'I would never have thought of that.' Wyn looked at the garment in her hands.

'That's because you in't got Joyce's knack,' Maggie said. 'Where you and I might look at summat and see nowt worth saving, she can see all sorts.'

Joyce looked away, blushing at the compliment. The truth was, she had been making do and mending long before the government came up with the idea. It was the only way to manage when Reg counted every penny she spent.

'All right,' Maggie said. 'Come on, then, Joyce, tell us what you see in these—'

She held up a gigantic pair of bloomers. Joyce pretended to examine them.

'A barrage balloon?' she suggested finally. Wyn and Maggie laughed, and Joyce laughed with them, her heart lifting with happiness.

After just a couple of weeks, she was already beginning to feel at home here. She managed two afternoons a week, on Wednesdays and Saturdays when it was half-day closing at the shop. On the mornings she knew she was coming she would wake up with a real feeling of joy, looking forward to the day ahead. It wasn't just the sense of purpose it gave her, although she liked the thought that she was doing her bit. She also enjoyed the camaraderie of the other women. Joyce had been shy at first, then everyone had been so warm and welcoming that it wasn't long before she really felt she belonged.

She would have come every day if she could, but of course Reg would not hear of it. He sulked enough when she did go.

'You spend more time at that place than you do here,' he would grumble every time. 'You should be here, looking after me and helping with the business.'

But even though he was bad-tempered every time she left the house, and even worse when she returned, Reg did not try to stop her going. Joyce had expected much worse from him, and she was ready for it. But it was almost as if he had sensed her determination and realised that even he could not stand against it.

It was a revelation to her. Perhaps, Joyce thought, if she

had put her foot down earlier on in their marriage things would not be as bad as they were now?

As always, the session was over far too soon. Joyce was putting the rest of the salvaged clothes into bags to put them away until next time when Ruby came over.

'Can I have a word with you, please, Joyce?' she said.

A torrent of panicky thoughts surged through her mind. She must have done something dreadful, she thought. Ruby was going to ask her to leave and never come back . . .

'Is something wrong?'

'No, far from it.' Ruby smiled. 'I just wanted to thank you for everything you've done. You've been a real inspiration to the other women with all your ideas and tips.'

Joyce stared down at her shoes. 'It's nothing,' she mumbled.

'You're too modest, Joyce. You have a real talent.' Ruby paused. 'I wonder if you'd like to give a talk to the other women? Maybe show them some basic sewing skills?'

Hot colour flooded her face. 'Oh no, I couldn't. Who'd want to listen to me?'

'You'd be surprised. Will you think about it, at least?'

'Yes,' Joyce mumbled, but she had already made up her mind to say no.

She turned away to finish packing up the clothes but Ruby said, 'I have another favour to ask you.'

Joyce picked up a skirt and shook out the pleats. 'Oh yes? What's that?'

'It's personal, nothing to do with the WVS.' Ruby hesitated. 'I wondered if you would help with our Ada's wedding dress? She's got the material, but she's still dithering over what she wants, and time's getting on. The wedding's only six weeks away!' She looked at Joyce. 'I'm not asking you to make it, I know you're very busy with the shop and everything. But I thought if you could come round and give her a few ideas . . . ?'

'I'd love to help – if I can,' Joyce said. 'I could help her sketch out a pattern if she tells me what she wants.'

'Would you? I'd be so grateful.'

'I could even make it up for her, if it wasn't too complicated.'

Ruby stared at her, hope dawning in her green eyes. 'Would you? I was hoping you'd offer. I'd gladly pay you for your trouble—'

'I wouldn't hear of it,' Joyce said. 'But I'll need to get some measurements and find out what she wants first.'

'Come round tonight,' Ruby said eagerly. 'Ada's on an early shift at the hospital, so she'll be home by teatime.'

Joyce did some quick calculations in her head. Reg went out to the pub with his cronies on a Saturday night, so he wouldn't be home until seven at the earliest.

'Tonight would suit me very well,' she said.

'Thank you,' Ruby said. 'This is such a weight off my mind.' She laid her hand on Joyce's shoulder. 'You're a real friend.'

Joyce smiled. She couldn't remember the last time anyone had called her that.

* * *

Joyce reached the top of Jubilee Row and stopped dead. In all her eagerness to help Ruby and Ada, she hadn't thought about what visiting the Maguires' house would mean to her. Now she stood outside Pearce's corner shop and stared down the narrow, cobbled terrace, afraid her feet wouldn't carry her another step.

She hadn't set foot in the street since she had fled twenty years ago, vowing never to return. Now, seeing it again brought all the memories flooding back. She saw herself as a small girl, running up to the corner shop with a threepenny bit held tightly in her palm, off to buy tobacco for her father's pipe. She remembered sauntering off to school every morning, her shoes polished, her hair in tight pigtails tied up with white ribbon. She would reach the top of the street and then turn, and her mother would always be there, standing on the doorstep, waving goodbye to her.

She was always there . . .

She watched the children, running to and fro across the cobbles. They were playing a wild game of tag, their excited shrieks filling the air. Joyce had never been allowed to join in with such games as a child. She could only watch from the window as she practised her handwriting or reading under her mother's ever-watchful eye.

'You'll thank me one day,' was all Patience would say. 'When you're a schoolteacher and they're chopping off fish heads down the docks.'

At the time, Joyce had felt like a prisoner. Patience Huggins was not like the other mothers in Jubilee Row. While they shouted and scolded and hugged their children fiercely, Patience had held herself aloof and rigid, never showing the slightest shred of affection. As a child, Joyce had often wondered if she loved her at all.

But now, seeing the mean little terraced street, she felt as if she understood. Patience had shown her love by wanting better for her. Not with kisses and cuddles, but with polished shoes and carefully fastened plaits, and dreams of a life where she did not have to come home bent and weary and reeking of fish.

Joyce glanced over at number ten. Her mother could be lurking at her window now, watching her. She waited for a tell-tale twitch of the thick lace curtains, but nothing happened.

Chapter Twenty-three

Ruby lived at the far end of the street, opposite Big May's house. Joyce could hear raised voices coming from inside even before Ada opened the door.

'Hello, Mrs Shelby,' Ada greeted her politely. She was a pretty girl of twenty-two, dark-haired like the rest of the Maguires. 'Mum said you'd be calling.'

'I don't know what you're smiling about, young lady,' Ruby's voice drifted from the far end of the passageway. 'You should be thoroughly ashamed of yourself.'

'I don't see why,' Sybil's voice came back. 'I've done nowt wrong.'

'Nowt wrong? Have you heard yourself?'

Joyce hesitated. 'I could come back another time, if it's more convenient?' she said, but Ada shook her head.

'Oh, take no notice of them,' she said cheerfully. 'Our Sybil's always in trouble for something.' She stepped aside to let Joyce in. 'Go through to the parlour, will you? We might get some peace in there.'

As Joyce followed her into the front room, she could hear Sybil saying, 'You're acting like it's me that got arrested. He was the one that broke the law, not me!'

'It's only a matter of time, the way you carry on!' came her mother's grim reply.

But Ada seemed unconcerned as she ushered Joyce to the moquette couch. 'Here's the material,' she said, pulling a brown paper-wrapped parcel out from behind the couch. 'As you can see, it's quite heavy . . .'

Joyce fingered the thick white satin Ada was showing her and tried her best not to listen to the argument that was still raging in the kitchen. But intriguing little snippets kept drifting up the passageway.

'He wouldn't even be in trouble if he could speak English!'

'You're lucky your father's still at sea, or he'd have something to say about it.'

'I've got some pictures I've cut out, of things I like . . .' Ada dumped a scrapbook on her lap. 'I like lace, but I think it might be too much. What do you think, Mrs Shelby?'

Joyce opened her mouth to speak when the front door slammed, making her jump. A moment later, Ruby came in, calm and smiling as if nothing had happened.

'Hello, Joyce. I see our Ada's already got you thinking of ideas.' She beamed at her daughter.

Joyce stared at her.

'Has Syb gone out?' Ada asked.

'Flounced out, more like.' Ruby rolled her eyes at Joyce. 'She went dancing with a Norwegian sailor last week, and he was picked up for breaking his curfew. Now he's been fined and Sybil says she knew nothing about it.'

'I wouldn't be surprised if she egged him on to do it,' Ada said.

'Nothing surprises me about that girl.' Ruby turned to Joyce. 'You should be glad you've got a son. Boys are far less trouble. Except for you, Ada,' she added, as her daughter pulled a face.

She sat down in the armchair and smoothed her red curls back from her face. 'I'm sorry, Joyce,' she smiled wearily. 'You must think you've walked into a madhouse!'

'Actually, I was thinking how nice it is to have a bit of life and noise about the place,' Joyce looked around her. 'Our flat has been so quiet these past few months with Alan gone.'

'I can imagine.' Ruby's green eyes were full of sympathy. 'He finishes training soon, doesn't he?'

'Next week. He's coming home for a couple of days before he gets posted.'

'I'll bet you can't wait to see him, can you?'

'No,' Joyce said. 'No, I can't.'

'Mind,' Ruby went on, smiling, 'it can get a bit too lively here sometimes, with my lot!'

They spent the next hour or so discussing wedding dresses. Joyce tried to interpret Ruby and Ada's ideas in a drawing, but it was difficult because as fast as she got them down on paper, Ada came up with a new thought. One minute she wanted her sleeves long and fitted, then loose and gathered in at the wrist, then she didn't care for sleeves at all.

Finally, Joyce managed to sketch out something that everyone was happy with.

'Will you stay for your tea, Joyce?' Ruby asked, as she took Ada's measurements. 'It's only fish pie, but there should be plenty to go round, now our Sybil's taken herself off in a huff.'

'That's very kind, but I'd best be getting back for my Reg.'

'I thought you said he was out?'

'He is, but he'll still be expecting his tea waiting for him when he gets home.' Joyce shrugged on her coat. 'I'll take the material home and get it cut out this week,' she said.

'Will you be able to manage without a pattern?'

'Oh, I'll make one up myself.'

Ruby turned to her mother-in-law with a smile. 'I told you she was clever, didn't I?'

Once again, Joyce felt herself blushing. 'I wouldn't say that,' she mumbled, embarrassed.

As Ruby saw her to the door she said, 'I can't thank you enough for helping us like this. You've made our Ada's day.' She lowered her voice. 'Between you and me, she's been so worried about this wedding. You can't blame her, I suppose. She had such big plans before this wretched war ruined everything.'

'At least her dress will be beautiful,' Joyce promised. 'I'll make a start on it and perhaps I could call in a couple of weeks to fit it properly?'

'That would be grand, thank you. But don't forget, you're always welcome to call round,' Ruby called after her as she started up the street.

You're always welcome to call round. Joyce wondered what it must be like to live in such a happy, busy, chaotic home. She had never lived in a place where people were free to come and go. Her mother liked everything very orderly, and would not tolerate unexpected visitors. And Reg didn't like visitors at all. Until now, it had never struck Joyce how lonely she had been, trapped inside four walls, never seeing anyone.

She looked across at number ten, the windows already blacked out in the gathering dusk. Suddenly she ached to cross the road and knock on the front door. What would her mother do, she wondered. Would she welcome her, or turn her away?

You've made your bed, now you must lie in it.

Patience Huggins' harsh words were like a slap in the face, bringing her back to her senses. She didn't know why she was asking herself the question, since she already knew what her mother's response would be. Once her mind was made up, Patience was as rigid and unbending as steel.

Joyce averted her gaze, gripped her shopping basket tighter in her fist, and hurried home.

* * *

Joyce was busy cutting out the pieces of fabric when Reg came home. She heard the clumsy scrape of his key in the lock, a sure sign he had been drinking.

'Your tea's in the oven,' she called out to him from the parlour, her head down, snipping away with her scissors.

She expected him to go straight through to the kitchen, and jumped when she heard him say, 'What's all this?'

She looked up sharply. Reg leaned against the doorway to the sitting room, watching her. He nodded towards the fabric spread out on the parlour table. 'Well? Answer me, woman!'

'Ruby's asked me to help with Ada's wedding dress.' Joyce's voice turned to a whisper in her throat.

'Has she now? And how much are you charging her for that?'

'Nothing. I'm doing it as a favour for a friend.'

'A favour for a friend!' Reg mimicked, his voice slurring. 'Funny how these people always decide they're your friends when they want summat, in't it?'

'It in't like that,' Joyce said quietly.

Reg shook his head. 'You're too naive, Joyce, that's your trouble. You can't see when people are taking advantage of you.'

Joyce looked down at the slippery white satin between her fingers. She knew Reg wasn't right, but some of her joy had still ebbed away.

'My tea's in the oven, did you say?' Reg said.

'Yes.'

'Then you'd best go and fetch it for me.'

Joyce hesitated, then set down her scissors.

'By the way,' Reg called after her as she headed down the passage towards the kitchen, 'I've finished fettling that pram.

I'll be putting it on sale tomorrow morning, if anyone asks. Reckon it'll fetch at least a quid, two if we're lucky.'

Joyce looked over her shoulder at him. He was looking for a fight, she thought. She could see it in his florid face, his fists balled at his sides. The slightest excuse and he would lash out at her.

She kept silent as she picked up a cloth and carefully took his dinner plate from the oven.

Reg was wrong, she thought. She knew exactly when people were taking advantage of her.

Chapter Twenty-four

'Good morning, Mrs Copeland!'

Edie scarcely recognised the cheery voice that sang out as she stood inside the doorway of Shelby's ironmonger's on a wet Wednesday morning.

'Nasty day, isn't it? Chilly, too. I reckon autumn is finally on its way, don't you think?'

Edie paused as she shook the rain off her umbrella. Was that really Joyce Shelby speaking? Edie had never known her say more than three words, and then only in a whisper.

Joyce Shelby looked up from her knitting with a bright smile as Edie approached the counter. There was something different about her, she thought.

'You've done something to your hair,' she said at last.

Joyce patted her light brown curls. 'Do you like it? Wyn Johnson at the WVS did it for me. It's only a wash and set, but I think it's rather nice.'

'It looks lovely,' Edie said. But it wasn't just Joyce's hair that had changed. There was a radiance about her that had not been there before. Her pale blue eyes sparkled, roses bloomed in her cheeks – even the way she held herself was different. Her shoulders had lost their hunched, apologetic look, her chin was lifted and she looked at Edie with a warm, direct gaze.

'I wanted to look nice for our Alan. He's due home the day after tomorrow.' Joyce set down her knitting on the counter and stood up, smoothing down her brown apron. 'Now, what can I do for you?'

'I need a hinge, and some screws,' Edie said. 'I bought a cupboard second-hand and one of the doors is hanging off.'

Joyce looked impressed. 'And you're fixing it yourself? Good for you, ducks. I wouldn't know where to start.'

'Neither do I,' Edie admitted cheerfully. 'But I've got to have a go. And Mr Huggins has said he'll help me, so—' She saw Joyce's face fall and immediately realised what she had said. 'I've got a lot to get ready before the baby arrives, anyway,' she mumbled.

'I'm sure you have.' Joyce's smile was back in place. 'How long have you got to go now?'

'Just over two months.'

'You must be looking forward to it?'

Edie hesitated, unsure how to answer her. Of course she was looking forward to meeting her precious baby, but at the same time the prospect filled her with utter terror.

She looked into Joyce's warm blue eyes and before she knew what she was saying she had blurted out, 'Truth be told, I'm a bit frightened.'

'Oh, love . . .' Joyce's expression softened.

'I don't know what's going to happen to me, what to expect—' The words came tumbling out, falling over each other. 'I've talked to the midwife and she's tried to explain it all to me, but I couldn't take it in . . .' She lowered her gaze, ashamed of her own naivety. Here she was, a couple of months from becoming a mother, and she still didn't really understand how babies came to be born.

'I know. It's a lot to think about, isn't it?' Joyce's hand rested lightly on her arm. 'I was exactly the same when I had our Alan. I had no idea what to expect, either. And I had to go through it on my own, too. I mean, at least I had Reg, but at times like that you really need—'

Her voice trailed off, the sentence hanging unfinished in the air. But Edie saw her wistful face and understood what she was going to say, even without her saying it.

'I wish my mother was here, too,' she said.

Joyce's hand slid slowly from her arm. 'How big a hinge did you say you wanted?' she asked, her smile fixed.

'About this big?' Edie measured out the space between her fingers.

'I'm not sure if we've got any that size. I haven't seen them on the shelves.' Joyce searched about her, her gaze moving along the rows of brown cardboard boxes. 'They might be in the cellar. Wait a minute, and I'll go and look.'

As Joyce disappeared through the door that led down to the cellar, Edie wandered around the shop. She was idly turning the handle of a mangle when she spotted the pram, tucked behind a display of washtubs.

Edie went over to take a closer look. It was second-hand, she could see that straight away. It had taken a battering in its time, too; when she ran her hand over the chassis she could feel the dents and scratches under its gleaming fresh paintwork. But the frame and wheels looked new, and it seemed sound enough otherwise.

Edie gripped the handlebar and rocked it back and forth. She pictured herself walking down the street, pushing her own baby in the pram . . .

'Don't touch that!'

Edie swung round in surprise. Joyce Shelby was standing at the top of the cellar steps, watching her. She was no longer smiling.

'How much do you want for it?' Edie asked.

'It's not for sale.'

Edie frowned. 'What's it doing here, then?'

Joyce did not reply. 'Your hinge,' she said, slapping it down on the counter. 'I think that's the size you wanted?'

Edie went on rocking the pram. The chassis bounced gently on its springs. 'I'll give you two pounds for it,' she said.

'I told you—'

'Two pounds ten. I can't afford more than that.'

Joyce sighed. 'No.'

'Where's Mr Shelby? I'll have a word with him—'

'You really don't want it.' There was a pleading note in her voice. 'Believe me, love. You're better off trying some of the pawnbrokers on Hessle Road. They often have prams for sale—'

'Now then, Joyce, what are you thinking? You don't stay in business by sending your custom elsewhere.'

Reg emerged from the workshop, his avid gaze fixed on Edie. 'Interested, are you? It's a beauty, in't it? I renovated it myself.' He ran his hand over the bodywork. 'You wouldn't believe the care and love that's gone into this. Two pounds ten, you said?'

Edie glanced at Joyce, standing rigid behind the counter, a look of mute fear in her eyes. In an instant, she seemed to have shrunk in on herself again, her bloom gone under an ashen pall. Her tongue flicked out, licking dry lips.

She looked back at Reg. He was smiling, but it was as if a sudden chill had descended over the shop.

'I've changed my mind,' she said. 'I don't think it's what I'm looking for.'

She saw Reg's jaw tighten, a muscle twitching in his cheek.

'That's a shame,' he said. But he was staring straight at his wife as he said it.

* * *

'But why didn't she want to sell it to you?' Big May asked, as she stood at the stove, stirring a stew pot.

'I don't know,' Edie said. 'I can't fathom it out.'

She sat at May's frame by the fireplace, finishing off a net for her. Her braiding was still slow and clumsy, and she could tell it was all Big May could do not to snatch the needles from her hands and do it herself. But Edie was grateful for the practice and the extra money.

'I daresay Reg Shelby wasn't too happy,' Dolly remarked. She and Iris stood side by side at the sink as usual, peeling potatoes.

'No, he wasn't.' All day Edie had been haunted by the sight of Joyce's stricken face. It was the last thing she had seen before Reg closed the shop door on her. 'I hope she's all right.'

The back gate creaked, and a moment later the children started shouting in the yard.

'Who's that?' May craned her neck. 'Pop in't home yet, surely?'

Dolly lifted her gaze to look out of the window. 'It's Sam.'

A moment later Sam Scuttle came in, ducking his head through the back door. A trail of children followed him, like the Pied Piper.

'Now then, Sam,' Big May greeted him.

'Afternoon, Mrs Maguire. Edie, Dolly, Iris.' He greeted them each in turn. Edie noticed how his gaze lingered on Iris, as usual. She did not look up from her peeling.

It was Dolly who turned away from the sink, wiping her hands on her apron. 'What can we do for you, Sam?'

'One of the fire-watchers from Maybury Road brought this in and I thought your lads might like it?'

Archie, George and Freddie crowded round as he reached into his pocket and pulled out a charred and battered-looking metal cylinder. Little Lucy peered between the boys' legs, trying to get a glimpse of the object.

May squinted at it. 'And what's that when it's at home?'

'It's an incendiary device,' Archie said, his eyes round as saucers.

'Is it real?' Freddie wanted to know.

'Aye. Lucky it didn't get a chance to do any damage.'

'Don't you recognise it, Mum?' Dolly said. 'It's like the one Harry Pearce and our Florence had at their demonstration a while back.'

'So it is.' Big May eyed it nervously. 'It in't going to burst into flames like that one, is it?'

'No, Mrs Maguire. It's quite safe,' Sam said.

'Can we really have it?' George said.

'Aye.'

As Sam went to hand it to them, Iris suddenly said, 'No, you can't have it. We don't want it in the house.'

There was a howl of protest from the boys. 'Why, Mum?' Archie whined.

'Honestly, it's harmless—' Sam started to say, but Iris stopped him.

'I don't care. Those things drop out of the sky to cause fires and destroy people's houses. I reckon it'd be inviting bad luck to have it under our roof.'

'But Mum—'

'I don't want to hear it, Archie. There's enough misery in the world at the moment, without wishing more on ourselves.'

Edie looked at Sam. He was staring down at the device in his hands, a crestfallen expression on his face.

Dolly stepped in. 'We'll have it, Sam,' she said. 'I'm sure the lads would like to take it to school and show it off.' She shot a look at her friend as she said it. But Iris had turned her back on them. Her knuckles were white as she gripped the edge of the stone sink.

Sam handed the incendiary to George. He and Freddie examined it, while Archie looked on. From the way he was biting his lip, Edie could tell he was trying his best not to cry.

'It in't fair!' he blurted out. 'Sam brought it for all of us!'

'Archie!' Iris scolded him, but he had already fled, running across the yard and through the back gate into the ten foot.

'Go after him, you two,' May said to Freddie and George. 'And let him share that thing if he wants.'

As the boys ran off, Iris snapped at Sam, 'You see what you've done? That wretched thing's only been in the house five minutes and it's already causing trouble.'

'I'm sorry,' Sam muttered. 'I just thought they might like it—'

'It was very good of you to think of us, Sam,' Big May said firmly, glaring at Iris. 'I was just about to put the kettle on, if you'd like to stay for a brew?'

'No, thank you. I'd best be off. My mother will have my tea on the table.' With another quick, embarrassed glance at Iris, he left.

'And what was that about?' Big May wanted to know, as soon as the door had closed behind him.

'I don't want it in my house,' Iris repeated stubbornly.

'He was only trying to be nice,' Dolly said. 'He meant well.'

'I hope you're still saying that when your house blows up,' Iris snapped.

'He said it was harmless.'

'It's bad luck.'

'Since when have you been so superstitious, Iris Fletcher?'

Iris picked up her knife and went back to her peeling, her face unrepentant.

'He only did it to impress you,' Dolly said.

'Well, it didn't work, did it?'

Edie saw the helpless look that passed between Dolly and Big May. They were in on it together, she thought, colluding to try to push Iris and Sam together. All the girls at the netting loft knew about it, too, even Sam's mother Beattie.

The only one who didn't want it to happen, it seemed, was Iris.

Chapter Twenty-five

Joyce carefully placed another piece of crystallised fruit on top of her cake and stepped back to admire her handiwork. It was a recipe she'd got from *Kitchen Front*, and certainly not the finest creation she had ever baked. But it was the best she could manage under the circumstances.

She could feel Reg watching her as she put the finishing touches to the decoration.

'You never usually bake any more,' he said. He made it sound like an accusation.

'Yes, well, it's not so easy when everything's on ration.'

'You've managed it today.'

'It's a special occasion, isn't it?'

'So I see.' Reg's expression was sour as he gazed at the plates of daintily cut sandwiches laid out on the kitchen table. 'Anyone would think King George himself was coming to tea.'

'I wanted to make it nice for our Alan. He's been away for such a long time, he's bound to have missed his home comforts.'

'As long as I in't had to miss mine,' Reg muttered.

'I don't know what you mean.'

'I mean I hope you in't used any of my rations to make this spread for him? Only, I don't want to think I've gone without.'

As if you'd ever let that happen, Joyce thought. 'You haven't gone short of anything,' she said. 'It's my sugar and butter rations I've been saving.'

'That's all right, then.'

Joyce glanced at her husband. Reg had always been jealous of Alan, right from when he was a baby. He seemed to resent every bit of time and attention Joyce gave to their son.

She wished he could have been a bit more generous, that he had loved Alan as much as she did. Things might have been so different for all of them.

She started at the sharp rap on the door below. 'He's here!' She hurried to the mirror to check her reflection.

'Making yourself look beautiful for your son?' Reg's voice dripped with sarcasm.

'If you must know, I was making sure the bruises haven't shown through.'

Reg winced at that, as well he might. He had been so angry after that business with Edie Copeland and the pram that for once he had forgotten to be careful.

'Ma? Are you up there?'

Alan's voice came from the bottom of the stairs. Charlie must have let him in. Joyce's hands fumbled with her apron strings.

'You won't spoil this, will you?' she pleaded with Reg. 'He's only here for one day, and I don't know when I'll see him again.'

'Spoil it?' Reg snorted. 'How am I going to spoil it?'

I don't know, Joyce thought. But if she knew her husband, he would find a way somehow.

* * *

Three months away had turned Alan into a man. His lanky height had filled out into lean strength, and his regulation Army haircut framed a face that had lost any trace of boyishness.

Joyce found herself studying him avidly across the table as she poured his tea, searching for traces of her baby in his manly features.

'Another sandwich? Or a piece of cake?' She offered him the plate.

'No thanks, Ma. I'm full.'

'But you must have cake. I made it specially—'

'For heaven's sake, woman, you heard the lad. Now stop mithering him! You haven't stopped fussing over him since he got here.'

Joyce was mortified, but Alan laughed it off.

'Leave her be, Dad, I don't mind,' he shrugged. 'It makes a change to be spoilt after three months living in an Army camp!'

'You're spoilt all right,' Reg muttered. 'I daresay I would have been making do with bread and dripping if you hadn't been here. It's what your mother usually gives me when she's off gallivanting with her WVS cronies.'

'I only go out two afternoons a week, and I always make sure your tea's on the table,' Joyce corrected him quietly. The only time he'd had to make do with bread and dripping was the night he returned late from the pub and his tea was ruined.

Reg ignored her. 'I'm surprised she in't there now,' he said to Alan. 'Those knitting sessions are life and death to her.'

'I sort clothes for salvage,' Joyce murmured. 'And I enjoy it.'

'Well, it suits you, whatever you're doing.' Alan helped himself to another sandwich from the plate. 'I've never seen you looking so well, Ma. Since when did you start wearing lipstick?'

'One of the girls at the WVS lent it to me.' Joyce blushed deeply. 'Is it too much, do you think?'

'Not at all. You look a picture.'

Reg snorted and cut himself a big helping of cake.

'So they're sending you up to Scotland, are they?' he changed the subject.

'That's right. We're being put on coastal watch.'

'Not exactly the front line, is it?'

Alan bristled. 'That's hardly my fault, Dad. I have to go where I'm sent.'

'Of course you do,' Joyce stepped in swiftly. 'Anyway, I'm pleased you're not being posted abroad,' she said. 'I'll sleep better at night, knowing you're safe.'

'Safe!' Reg's mouth curled. 'He didn't join the Army to be safe, did he? He joined to fight for his country.'

'Happen I might be doing just that, if the Germans decide to invade,' Alan said.

'They won't invade now winter's coming.'

'How do you know that?' Alan said. 'As I recall, you don't have much of a military record?'

Joyce tensed, seeing Reg's eyes narrow. When they were courting, he'd bragged about how he'd managed to dodge enlistment by pretending to have a weak chest. Over the years, he'd tried to play down his act of cowardice.

'Tell me more about your training,' she urged, waving the plate of sandwiches under her son's nose again. 'What were the other boys like? Did you make any friends?'

'For God's sake, woman. It wasn't a Boy Scout jamboree!' Reg snarled at her. But Joyce did not mind. While he was snapping at her he wasn't ruining Alan's last few precious hours at home.

When tea was over, Alan insisted on helping her to clear away the dishes. Reg hung about in the kitchen, looking sullen.

'I was thinking,' he said, 'how would you like to go to the picture house tonight?'

Joyce stared at him. 'Me?'

'Why not? I looked in the paper and they're showing *Untamed* at the Cecil. It's meant to be good, so I've heard.'

'You don't want to be taking your mother to the pictures!' Reg laughed. 'Isn't there some local girl you could go with instead?'

'I'd rather take Ma,' Alan said gallantly.

'More fool you, then! If I was a young soldier, I know how I'd like to spend my last night of freedom.'

'Reg!'

'For God's sake, Joyce, I know you like to think he's still a bain, but he's a man now. And I daresay he's heard worse talk than that in the barrack room. Eh, lad?' Reg grinned at his son. Alan gave him a tight little smile in return.

'Yes, well, he in't in the barrack room now,' Joyce said.

'Well, I in't going to no picture house,' Reg muttered. 'I've got better things to do with my time. And so has your mother.'

He glared at Joyce, as if daring her to argue with him.

'What do you say, Ma?'

Joyce looked from one to the other, caught between them. She longed to spend time with Alan while she still could, but she feared what Reg might do if she defied him.

'It's such a long time since I've been to the cinema,' she ventured cautiously. She looked at Reg, silently pleading for his understanding. But he turned away from her, an expression of stone cold rage on his face.

'Right, that's settled, then.' Alan rubbed his hands together. 'Go and get your glad rags on, Ma. We're going to the pictures!'

* * *

'What did you think, Ma?' The house lights went up and Alan was grinning at her. 'It was a good film, wasn't it?'

The truth was, Joyce had barely taken in a moment from when the lights dimmed and the red velvet curtains opened. All she could think about was Reg, and how angry he would be.

But she couldn't tell that to Alan. He was so pleased with himself, thinking he had given her a rare treat.

'Yes,' she said. 'Thank you, son. I thoroughly enjoyed it.'

They walked down Anlaby Road in the blackout. The darkness usually terrified Joyce, but she felt safe holding tightly on to Alan's arm. He kept the dim beam of his torch angled towards the pavement, lighting their way.

'Are you sure you don't mind walking me home?' Joyce said. 'It seems silly for you to come all this way out to the shop when you've only got to turn round and go back to the station afterwards.'

'I don't mind, honestly.' Alan patted her hand in the crook of his arm. 'I'm only sorry I couldn't stay the night.'

'You can't miss that overnight train up to Scotland. I'm just grateful you found time to come and visit us.'

'I couldn't leave without saying goodbye, Ma.'

They walked on, and Alan chatted about the film, and about the books he had read while he'd been away. Joyce listened, enjoying the flow of her son's conversation, but at the same time dread lurked in the pit of her stomach, knowing it would be a long time before she heard his voice again.

'Are you sure you're all right, Ma?' Alan's question came out of the blue, startling her.

'Yes,' she said. 'Why shouldn't I be?'

He sent her a sideways look. 'I think we both know the answer to that, don't you?'

Joyce was glad the darkness hid her shocked face. Beside her, she heard Alan sigh.

'Ma, I'm not a bain any more. You don't have to go on pretending. I know what Dad's like.'

Do you? Joyce thought. She hoped to God he did not. 'I – I don't know what you mean. Your father's a good man, he's worked hard over the years to provide for us, to make a good home—' The words spilled from her lips almost automatically.

'If you say so,' Alan replied sullenly. 'But as far as I'm concerned, the only one who's kept our home together is you.' He stopped, turning to face her. 'I know what you've put up with over the years for my sake,' he said.

Joyce could not bring herself to look at him. She wondered how much her son had witnessed over the years, in spite of her trying to protect him. Alan was not daft, he had eyes and ears. Shame washed over her at the thought of what he might know. Please God he didn't think her weak and foolish.

'But you don't have to do it any more,' Alan went on. 'I'm a grown man now, Ma. I can make my own way in the world. And it's time for you to do the same.' He paused, and Joyce could feel his steady gaze on her. 'You could leave him,' he said.

'And where would I go, a woman of my age?' She forced a smile into her voice. 'I'm nearly forty, Alan. I've got no money, no real skills. All I've ever done is mind the shop and look after our home. I'm not good for anything, really.'

She thought of her mother, standing over her as she studied night after night. Patience had constantly drilled into her the importance of having a career – 'something to fall back on', as she called it. Joyce had not understood at the time, but now she realised her mother had been preparing her for just such a time as she faced now.

And she hadn't listened.

You've made your bed, now you must lie in it.

'That's not true!' Alan's face was urgent. 'You've got to believe in yourself, Ma.'

'I do.' Or at least, she was starting to. Her work at the WVS had given her confidence, made her believe she was more capable than she had ever imagined. But not enough to make her think she could manage on her own.

'I could help you,' Alan said. 'I'll send all my money home, if that's what you need—'

'I don't need help, love,' Joyce said. 'I'll be all right, honestly.' She tapped her hand against his chest. There were muscles there now that had not been there before. 'If you really want to help me, then you should try to get through this wretched war in one piece!'

Alan smiled back, but his eyes were still sad in the darkness. 'I'll do my best,' he promised.

There were no lights on in the flat above the shop. Reg must have gone to bed, Joyce thought. Or to the pub.

Alan bent down and kissed her on the cheek. 'I'll come back for another visit as soon as I can get some leave,' he promised. 'Or happen you could come up to Scotland and visit me?'

'That would be lovely,' Joyce smiled, but she already knew Reg would never allow it.

'Promise me you'll keep going to the WVS, won't you? Whatever Dad says about it. It does you good to get out of the house, away from the shop, and—'

'I will,' Joyce said. 'You're right, it does do me good.' She felt like a different woman, stronger and more confident.

Not confident enough to walk away from her husband, but at least it helped her to cope better with Reg's moods and tempers.

'I wish I could see you off on the train,' she said. 'Get back to the station safely, won't you?'

Alan laughed. 'Ma, I'm a soldier in the British Army. I don't need my mother to make sure I get on a train!'

No, Joyce thought sadly. *Soon you won't need your mother at all.* She watched him trudging off back in the direction of the city, straining her eyes to catch one last sight of him as the blackout swallowed him up.

Having Alan was the only thing that gave her sorry life any meaning, and soon she was going to lose him.

Weariness overcame her as she made her way up the stairs to the flat. She hoped Reg would not give her a hard time, she was too tired to cope with it.

'Reg?' she called out into the darkness. There was no answer. He was at the pub, she thought. At least that gave her an hour or two's respite until closing time. And then . . .

She pushed the thought from her mind. Hopefully his cronies would have put him in a good mood.

As she pushed open the bedroom door, the dim light from the landing behind her fell on a figure stretched across the bed, ghostly white and streaked in blood.

Joyce screamed and backed away, her heart crashing against her ribs. She scrabbled for the light switch, almost afraid to turn it on in case of what she might see.

Light flooded the room and Joyce took in the scene in front of her. Her legs buckled and she fell to her knees, the scream dying in her throat.

'Oh Reg,' she whispered, 'what have you done?'

Chapter Twenty-six

'I'm so sorry.'

Joyce could hardly bear to look at Ruby Maguire as she spoke. She had lain awake all night dreading this moment, and it was just as awful as she had imagined it would be.

'But I don't understand.' Ruby was more bewildered than angry. 'How did it happen?'

'I – don't know. I wasn't thinking, and I made a mistake and cut the pattern pieces out wrong. Now the whole thing's ruined ...'

All around them, the WVS centre was stirring into action. Women were arriving, greeting each other, shrugging off coats, putting the kettle on to boil and clattering teacups.

Usually Joyce would have been with them, catching up on all the news. But instead she had to face Ruby Maguire.

Poor Ruby. She had looked so surprised and happy to see Joyce when she walked in that morning.

'What are you doing here? You don't usually come in on a Thursday morning—' Then her smile dropped. 'Oh Joyce, whatever is it, love?' she had said. 'Sit down and let me make you a cup of tea – you look awful.'

Her concern had made Joyce feel even more wretched and guilty. And now it was Ruby who looked as if she might faint as she stood before Joyce.

'And there's nothing you can do to put it right?' she said.

Joyce pictured the tattered remnants of what had once

been a beautiful wedding dress, ripped to shreds and streaked with black grease.

'No.' She shook her head. 'I'm sorry, I really am.'

She had repeated the words so many times in the past few minutes, she hardly knew what she was saying any more. And every time she said them they seemed more and more inadequate.

She forced herself to look into Ruby's face. The poor woman had gone very pale. Her sprinkling of freckles stood out starkly against her milky skin.

'Our Ada will be so upset,' she said.

'I know.' Joyce glanced away. 'I'll pay for the ruined material, of course.'

She didn't know how, but she was determined to find a way. Even if she had to pawn everything she had to do it.

'But she'd set her heart on that dress,' Ruby said. 'She was so looking forward to seeing it finished . . .'

'What's all this?' Joyce's heart sank as she saw May Maguire bustling towards them. Why did she have to be here, Joyce wondered. It was bad enough having to break the news to Ruby, without having to deal with the wrath of Big May too.

'What's going on?' May looked from one to the other.

'It don't look like our Ada's going to get her dress after all,' Ruby said.

Joyce stared down at her feet as Ruby explained to her mother-in-law what had happened, repeating the same story Joyce had told her. The same story she had made up on the way to the WVS centre that morning.

'But I don't understand – why can't you just make a new one?' May turned to Joyce with a frown. 'Surely if we get some more material—'

'I can't,' Joyce said. 'It was too much for me to take on. I – I should never have agreed to do it in the first place. It's all my fault.'

That was what Reg had said to her the previous night when he had come home from the pub, reeking of beer.

'You see what you've made me do?' he'd spat at her. 'This is your fault!'

At first she hadn't been able to speak. All she could do was stare at the ravaged dress laid out on the bed. It was so badly damaged, she could barely make it out. Reg must have been in a real frenzy to rip it to shreds like that. And those black, greasy handprints smeared all over it that she had thought were blood . . .

'Oh Reg,' was all she could say, over and over again. 'What have you done?'

'You drove me to it. If you hadn't got me all upset . . .' He jabbed his finger in her face. 'You're never here any more. You're always too busy gallivanting off here and there.'

'I went out to the pictures with our son. You could have come with us.'

'Don't answer me back, woman!' Reg had lashed out, catching her with the back of his hand. 'You've been too full of yourself since you started up at that place. But I won't have it, d'you hear? I won't have it!'

'Happen you should have thought of that before you took it on,' May interrupted her thoughts. She stared at Joyce, stony-faced.

'I'm sorry.'

'Aye, it's all very well saying that, now you've let Ruby and our Ada down. But what's she going to do for a wedding dress, eh?'

'I—'

'Now, Mum, don't take on,' Ruby said. 'I was the one who

asked Joyce to help in the first place. She was only trying to do me a favour.'

'Some favour!' Big May looked scornful.

A hush had fallen over the room. Out of the corner of her eye, she could see the other women stopping in their tracks, curious looks coming their way.

'Happen I put too much on her,' Ruby said, but Big May was having none of it.

'She should have said no then, shouldn't she? She's got a tongue in her head.'

'Mum!'

'Oh, don't worry. I've said all I've got to say on the matter.' Big May glared at Joyce. 'For now,' she added ominously.

'Take no notice of her,' Ruby said, as May stomped off. 'She'll calm down soon. She's got a temper on her, but she don't mean anything by it.'

'She's disappointed.'

'Aye. We all are.' Ruby smiled bravely. 'But I'm sure we'll sort summat out.'

Joyce felt tears pricking her eyes. She could cope with Big May's rage, but Ruby's smiling optimism broke her heart.

'I'd best go,' she said.

'Won't you stop for a cup of tea? Mrs Franklin's just filling up the urn—'

Joyce looked across at the women on the other side of the hall. They had gathered in a circle around May Maguire. From the dark looks they were throwing her way, Joyce guessed she was telling them the whole story.

'It'll be all right,' Ruby said reassuringly. 'They'll have summat else to gossip about soon. We've just had some new salvage in, if you want to stay and sort it?'

But Joyce was already hurrying away. She kept her head down as she passed the women, but she could feel them all scowling at her. Whatever Ruby said about it, she was sure none of them would forget what she had done. Big May would see to that.

And Joyce didn't blame her for it. She deserved every bit of their scorn and outrage.

* * *

'How did you get on?'

Joyce had done her best not to face Reg when she returned to the shop. She had shut herself away in the cellar, sorting through the stock and only emerging when she heard the tinkle of the bell over the shop door.

But then she heard his voice, shouting down the cellar steps.

'When are you going to bring me a brew? I'm parched.'

Joyce could not bring herself to look at Reg as she carried the tea tray into the workshop. He was at the bench, hammering a dent out of a bicycle frame. She set the tray down on the other end of the bench, but just as she reached the door Reg called out, 'In't you going to pour it out for me?'

Joyce took a deep, steadying breath. He was smiling at her, actually smiling, as if the previous night had not happened.

'How did you get on?' he repeated his question. 'Did you see Ruby Maguire?' Joyce nodded. 'What did she say? I daresay she wasn't too pleased, was she?'

'She was – disappointed.' Her throat was so dry, she could hardly get the words out.

'Furious, more like.' Reg did not even try to keep the smirk off his face. 'Oh well, accidents happen, don't they?'

He picked up his cup and slurped it noisily. Joyce caught Charlie watching her from the corner of the workshop, where he was putting a bicycle back together.

Reg turned to him. 'Did you hear what happened, Charlie boy? That wedding dress Joyce was making for Ada Maguire got ruined.'

It didn't get ruined, Joyce wanted to scream. *You ruined it. You hacked it to pieces because you're jealous and you couldn't bear for me to have anything nice in my life.*

Her gaze fell on the battered can of oil sitting on the work bench. A vision of ugly black handprints smeared on to pristine white satin came into her mind.

She had thought it was blood. Reg's blood. Now she almost wished it had been.

He was watching her carefully over the rim of his cup. Waiting for her to break down, Joyce thought. Well, she wouldn't give him the satisfaction.

'Anyway,' Reg said, putting down his cup. 'I expect they will have forgotten all about it by the time you go back.'

Joyce looked at the ground. 'I don't think I'll be going back,' she whispered.

'Whatever do you mean?' Reg feigned surprise.

She thought about Big May and the other women, the black glares that had followed her out of the WVS centre. 'I don't think I'd be very welcome.'

'Happen you're right.' Reg shrugged, picking up his hammer. 'It's a shame, though. You enjoyed going there, didn't you? But I suppose all good things must come to an end, eh?'

Joyce caught Charlie's look of mute sympathy from the other side of the workshop.

'I suppose they must,' she agreed.

Chapter Twenty-seven

On a dull Saturday morning at the end of September, Edie went down to Hessle Road to look for her pram. Dolly offered to go with her, but Iris wanted to stay at home because, she said, Lucy had a cold coming.

'She never seems to want to go out these days,' Dolly said as she tripped along beside Edie, her high heels tapping on the pavement. 'All she ever does is stay at home and look after her bains.'

'And what's wrong with that?' Edie said, as they went into yet another shop, called Schultz Brothers.

'Nowt, I suppose. But she used to be a right laugh.' Dolly paused. 'If you ask me, she needs a man.'

'She's already told you she doesn't.'

'Yes, but she doesn't know what's good for her, does she?'

'And you do?'

'Yes, as a matter of fact. I know exactly who would put a smile on her face.'

Edie sighed. 'You're not still going on about Sam Scuttle? She's already said she in't interested.'

'I told you, she don't know what's good for her,' Dolly shrugged. 'And between you and me, I haven't given up on getting the two of them together.'

'I reckon you're best leaving well alone,' Edie said.

'But she's my friend.' Dolly's blue eyes were wide and innocent. 'I want to see her happy.'

'Happen she's still grieving for her husband?' Edie looked around the cramped interior of the shop. It was a tiny warren, full of glass cabinets stuffed with jewellery, cigarette cases, spectacles and old scraps of lace, clothes rails hung with men's suits and shirts, and bright ladies' dresses, and a dresser full of old china ornaments and oddments of dinner sets.

'But it's been nearly a year!' Dolly looked exasperated.

'A year isn't a long time to get over someone. Sometimes it takes a lifetime.' She could never imagine finding anyone to take Rob's place.

'I suppose you're right,' Dolly sighed. She took down a box from the shelf, opened it and let out a scream.

'What is it?' Edie peered inside and recoiled at the sight of half a dozen sets of false teeth grinning back at her. 'Ugh, that's horrible! Who would pawn their false teeth?'

'I wouldn't put anything past the folk round here!' Dolly said.

'So what was Iris' husband like?' Edie asked, as they made their way down the road to the next shop on their list.

'Arthur? Oh, he was handsome. The best-looking man in Hessle Road – except for my Jack, of course!' she grinned. 'Always laughing and joking, he was. Everyone loved him.' She sighed. 'Iris was a lucky girl.'

'He sounds like my Rob,' Edie said.

Dolly sent her a sympathetic look. 'Poor lass. It should be him here, looking for a pram with you, eh?' Dolly's arm went through Edie's, linking them together. 'Come on, let's go and find you a bargain.'

But even though they searched every pawnbroker's along the length of Hessle Road, they still could not find a pram.

'I've a good mind to go back to Shelby's,' Edie said, when the final shop proved empty.

'That pram's probably gone by now. Anyway, the pawn-brokers round here know you're looking out for one now, so they're bound to find something.'

'I hope so.' Edie was glad Dolly was there to keep her flagging spirits up. If it hadn't been for her making her laugh, Edie knew she would have been utterly despondent.

'Tell you what,' Dolly said as they left the shop. 'Why don't we go down to the Gainsborough café for a nice cup of tea and a bun? My treat.'

But Edie was not listening. Her attention had been caught by a box of odd bits of china, stacked up by the shop door.

'Edie? What are you after now?'

'Just a minute, I'm sure I saw – here it is.' Edie rooted in the box and produced the item that had caught her eye a second before.

'An old plate?' Dolly frowned at it. 'What do you want that old thing for?'

'It's not for me,' Edie said, dusting it off with her sleeve.

* * *

'Blackout violation? What blackout violation?'

Patience faced Florence Maguire angrily across her door-step. Florence might think she was important, bustling about in her ARP uniform, but Patience was not one to be impressed by a tin helmet.

'I saw it myself, Mrs Huggins,' Florence said. 'There was a crack of light showing at the front upstairs window just before dawn this morning.'

'Well, that's nothing to do with us, is it? It's her upstairs you need to be talking to.'

Florence looked irritated. 'That's why I knocked, Mrs

Huggins, but your husband says Edie in't in. I just wondered if you could pass on the message?'

'Surely that's your job, not ours—' Patience started to say, but Horace interrupted her.

'We'll have a word with her,' he promised.

'Thank you, Mr Huggins,' Florence said gratefully. 'I should really report it, but I'm keeping it as a friendly warning this time, as she's a neighbour. But next time she does it there'll be a fine.'

'We'll let her know, don't worry.'

'I don't see why we should—'

Horace closed the door on Florence as Patience was drawing breath to give her another mouthful. She stared at him. 'I hadn't finished,' she said.

'I reckon you've said more than enough already.'

'She's got a cheek, coming here and disturbing us when we've done nothing wrong,' Patience said, following him down the passage to the kitchen.

'She's only doing her job, love.'

'She isn't though, is she? She's having a go at us when it's her she should be talking to.' She pointed towards the ceiling. 'Where is she, anyway?'

'You'd probably know that better than me, since you keep such a close eye on her comings and goings.' Horace sat down at the kitchen table and picked up the newspaper.

'I most certainly do not!' Patience said. 'I've got better things to do with my time, thank you very much.' She went to the stove, banging pots and pans about in her temper. 'Anyway, even if I did, I'd never be able to keep up with her, since she's in and out all the time. It's like Paragon Station in here sometimes, with her coming and going. This used to be such a quiet, peaceful house until she arrived. I told you, didn't I? I said she would cause chaos, and she has.' She shook her head. 'And now she's brought the ARP warden knocking on our door. I might have known she'd be the type not to follow the rules . . . Horace, are you listening to me?'

She looked round at her husband. Horace was bent over, rubbing his belly. 'Gracious, what's wrong with you? Is it that pain again?'

'Aye.' Horace grimaced. 'It's getting worse, I reckon.'

'You'll feel better when you've eaten.' Patience set his plate down in front of him.

'I don't think I can manage it, love. I in't very hungry.'

'But it's rissoles. You like rissoles.'

'I know, but I've not got much appetite at the moment.'

Patience peered at him across the table. His face was ashen. 'You do look a bit peaky,' she admitted. 'You should have a spoonful of syrup of figs. That'll sort you out.'

'Aye, I'm sure you're right.'

Just then Patience heard the sound of the front door opening. She set down her knife and fork and jumped to her feet.

'Where are you going?' Horace asked.

'To have a word with her, what do you think?'

'Give the lass a chance to get in the door before you start on her. Finish your tea first.'

'I can't,' Patience said. 'I won't be able to eat a thing until—'

There was a knock on the kitchen door. They stared at each other across the table.

'It's her!' Patience hissed. 'What does she want?'

'Only one way to find out . . .' Horace went to the door, Patience at his heels.

Edie Copeland stood before them, all smiles, her hands behind her back.

'Sorry,' she said, 'I hope I in't disturbing you?' Her gaze drifted past them to the neatly laid table. 'I see you're having your tea. I can come back later?'

'You stay where you are,' Patience said. 'We want a word with you.'

'Oh!' Edie looked startled. 'What about?'

'Never mind that for now,' Horace interrupted. 'What can we do for you first?'

Edie held out her hands, proffering a flat package wrapped in newspaper to Patience. 'I bought this for you,' she said.

Patience took it reluctantly, feeling the weight of it in her hands. 'What is it?'

'Open it and see.'

Patience could feel Edie watching her eagerly as she carefully peeled back the layers of rumpled newspaper to reveal . . .

'It's to make up for the one that got broken,' Edie explained. 'I think it matches the rest of the set, but I couldn't quite remember—'

'It's perfect,' Horace said. 'Where did you find it?'

'Isadore Turner's, on Hessle Road. I went there to look for a pram, and I spotted it in a box of oddments by the shop's front door.' Edie looked pleased with herself. 'It was a lucky find, wasn't it?'

'Yes, it was,' Horace said.

Patience did not reply. She could only stare at the blue and white Wedgewood plate in her hands.

'It seemed such a shame not to finish off your lovely set,' Edie said.

'That was very thoughtful of you,' Horace said. 'Wasn't it, Patience?'

Patience went on staring at the plate, turning it around in her hands. 'Yes,' she murmured. 'Very thoughtful.'

'I'm glad you like it,' Edie said. 'Well, I'll leave you to have your tea—' She turned to go, then looked back again. 'Oh, I nearly forgot. What did you want to speak to me about?'

'What?' Patience said.

'You said you wanted a word with me?'

Patience glanced at Horace, then back at the plate in her hands. 'It's not important,' she mumbled.

* * *

'Well,' said Horace as he closed the door. 'What do you say to that?'

Patience did not reply. She could only stare at the plate in her hands.

'I'll take it to the parlour and put it up with the rest—'

'No.' Patience held on to it tightly.

Horace sighed. 'It's time things were put right, Patience.'

Their eyes met for a long time. Slowly, reluctantly, Patience let go of the plate.

She sat back down at the table as Horace went off to the parlour. She picked up her knife and fork, then laid them down again and stared down at the food congealing on the plate in front of her. Her throat was so dry, she couldn't have swallowed a mouthful of food, even if she had wanted it.

She could hear the boards creaking overhead, and the faint sound of singing, but for once Patience didn't rush for her broom handle to bang on the ceiling.

She stood up and gathered up the plates. She could keep Horace's warm for him in case he fancied it later. But as for hers . . .

She looked back up at the ceiling, then down at the food. Should she take it up to her?, she wondered. She looked like a wraith, and Patience was certain she could not be eating properly.

What's this? Are you going soft, Patience Huggins? Patience frowned at the thought. There was nothing soft about it. She

190

was just being practical, that was all. Waste not, want not, as the Ministry of Food was always telling them.

She started towards the door, then stopped. What if she refused it? What if she slammed the door in her face? Patience hesitated, the plate still in her hands. Then she set it down on the draining board and stood staring at it for a long time.

She would get Horace to take it up to her, she decided. Edie liked him, she wouldn't turn him away. Although he was bound to think it was more than it was – an olive branch, or some such nonsense . . .

'Patience?' She heard him call out her name from the parlour. His voice sounded weak, uncertain.

She hurried up the passageway. 'What is it?' she said, pushing open the door. 'I hope you haven't—'

She stopped dead, the words dying in her throat at the sight of her husband sprawled on the parlour floor.

Chapter Twenty-eight

Edie was gazing into her empty kitchen cupboard, trying to summon up the energy to find herself something to eat, when she heard Patience Huggins cry out in alarm.

She forgot all about food and rushed downstairs. The parlour door was open and she could hear Patience and Horace's voices coming from inside.

'Don't fret yourself,' she heard Horace say. 'I'm quite all right, really I am.'

Edie looked in at the door. 'Whatever has happened—' she started to say, then stopped. Horace was sprawled on the floor and Patience was pulling on one of his arms, trying to drag him to his feet. She was huffing and puffing with effort, but he was a big man and she was hardly equal to the task.

'Nothing to worry about, lass,' Horace's voice was a hoarse croak of pain. 'I've just had a funny turn, that's all.'

He was trying to make light of it, but Edie could see the perspiration standing out on his brow.

'Let me help you.' She hurried forward to get hold of Horace's other arm.

'Leave me be, lass. You can't be lifting in your condition,' Horace said, but Edie ignored him.

'We'll get him into the chair,' she said to Patience, and together the two of them hauled him to his feet. Horace landed heavily in the armchair, with a grimace of pain.

'What's wrong with him?' she asked Patience.

'He's been complaining of stomach pains since this morning.'

'It's just indigestion, honestly—' Horace Huggins bent double, his hand on his abdomen. His face was ashen and bathed in sweat.

'I'm going to fetch Ada Maguire,' Edie said.

'I'm sure we don't need—' Patience Huggins started to say, then she glanced back at her husband and seemed to change her mind. 'You'd best fetch her,' she said shortly.

Luckily Ada had just finished her shift at the Infirmary when Edie called at the Maguires' house. By the time they returned to number ten, Patience was kneeling beside Horace, mopping his brow with a cool, damp cloth. As soon as she saw Ada, she got to her feet and stepped out of the way.

Ada examined Horace, asking him all kinds of questions about the pain and how long he had had it.

'It came on this morning,' Patience replied from where she stood in the corner, behind Edie. 'Although he wasn't right last night, either.'

'Any vomiting?'

'Once or twice this afternoon. It's probably summat I ate,' Horace said. 'I'll be right as rain by tomorrow—'

'I don't know about that, Mr Huggins.' Ada turned to Edie. 'I reckon we'd best call the doctor,' she said quietly.

Edie heard Patience's hiss of indrawn breath behind her. 'What is it?' Edie asked.

'I'm not sure, but I think it might be appendicitis.' Ada looked past Edie at Patience. 'Could you pack him a bag, just in case he has to go to hospital?'

Edie glanced over her shoulder at Patience Huggins. Her face was a mask, white and expressionless. Then, without a word, she turned on her heel and hurried out of the room.

Ada left to fetch the doctor, while Edie wrung out the

flannel in an enamel bowl and gently mopped Horace's perspiring brow.

'Will you do me a favour, lass?' he asked.

'What's that?' Edie asked.

'If they send me to hospital, can you keep an eye on my Patience for me?'

Edie dipped the corner of the cloth in the cool water. 'Don't worry about her, Mr Huggins. You've got to think about getting yourself better.'

'I'll feel a lot better if I know someone's looking after her. I know you two haven't exactly seen eye to eye, but she don't mean anything by it. She's wary of people, it's just her way. She needs someone around her,' he said quietly. 'She in't nearly as tough as she likes to make out.'

Edie looked into the old man's worried eyes. 'Of course I'll keep an eye on her, if it will make you feel better,' she promised.

Horace settled back in his chair. 'Thank you, lass. I can rest easy now. You'll have to be the one to offer, mind. She'll need help, but she'll never ask for it.'

At that moment Patience came bustling back in, carrying a small and very battered-looking leather suitcase.

'This is all a lot of fuss about nothing,' she murmured, dumping it down beside Horace's chair. 'I should have fetched you that syrup of figs, then we wouldn't have had any of this nonsense.'

'Aye,' Horace agreed amiably. 'I daresay you're right, love.'

But the doctor had other ideas. He took one look at Horace and summoned an ambulance to take him straight to hospital.

Edie waited by the front door, shivering in the late September chill and watching the pitch black street for the ambulance to arrive. Beattie Scuttle's cat wound its way round her legs in the darkness and she yelped in fright.

At last the ambulance arrived. As Horace was helped into it, he turned to Edie and said, 'You won't forget what I said, will you?'

'I won't,' Edie promised.

They watched him go together, Edie and Patience Huggins standing shoulder to shoulder. Edie could almost feel the tension radiating from Patience's stiff little body.

'He'll be all right, you know,' Edie said.

'Yes, of course he will,' Patience snapped back. Her lips were taut and bloodless.

As Edie closed the front door, Patience was already striding down the passage towards her kitchen.

Edie followed her. 'I'll sit with you, if you like?' she offered.

'There's really no need.' Patience bustled about, clearing the table. 'I shall be keeping myself busy. I have all the brass to clean.'

Edie watched her in disbelief as she spread out a sheet of newspaper on the table. Horace Huggins was wrong about his wife, she thought. Patience was utterly heartless. Her husband had just been taken to hospital, and all she could think about was polishing her brass!

Then she remembered what Horace had said.

She'll need help, but she'll never ask for it.

'Happen I could give you a hand?' she said.

Patience looked up at her, startled. 'You? What do you know about cleaning brass?'

'I had to do it every week at home.'

'Did you?' Patience paused for a moment, then she shook her head. 'I daresay you don't know how to do it properly.'

You don't know my stepmother, Edie thought. Rose would

crack the poker over her knuckles if she found any smears or smudges.

'Anyway,' Patience went on, 'I prefer to do it myself.'

Edie sighed. Mr Huggins was right, there was no helping her. 'I'll go back upstairs, then,' she said. 'Let me know if you need anything—'

'Do you like rissoles?'

Edie turned back to look at her. 'Rissoles?'

'Yes, rissoles. Do you like them?' Patience's voice had an edge of irritation.

'Yes, why?'

'I've got some leftovers. I could warm them up for you, if you like?' Patience looked away, almost as if she was annoyed with herself for asking. 'You could eat them while I polished.'

Edie stared at Patience's turned back. Her spine was rigid under her perfectly starched blouse.

Once again, Horace's words came back to her.

She in't nearly as tough as she likes to make out.

She smiled. 'Thank you, Mrs Huggins,' she replied. 'That would be very nice.'

Chapter Twenty-nine

She ate as if she hadn't seen food in months.

Patience watched Edie Copeland across the table, ploughing through the plate of rissoles as if her life depended on it.

She was very thin, Patience thought. Her belly was rounded and heavy, but her limbs were painfully slender and her face was all sharp angles.

Edie must have realised she was being watched, because she looked up with an apologetic smile and said, 'Sorry, Mrs Huggins, but I can't seem to stop eating, it's so delicious. Aren't you having any?'

Patience glanced at her plate, untouched on the draining board. 'I might have it later,' she said. But she couldn't imagine when she would ever feel like eating again. Her stomach was a knot of anxiety.

She couldn't stop thinking about poor Horace. She tried to keep the thoughts away, but they kept straying back to that awful picture of him doubled up in pain on the parlour rug.

'He'll be all right, you know.'

Patience looked up sharply, meeting Edie's sympathetic gaze across the table. 'What?'

'I spoke to Ada,' Edie went on, putting down her fork. 'She reckons there's no reason why Mr Huggins shouldn't make a full recovery. Even if they have to operate, he'll probably be home in a couple of weeks—'

'More potatoes?' Patience cut her off, holding out her hand for Edie's plate.

'Yes, please.' She could feel the girl looking at her curiously as she passed it over. But the truth was, Patience couldn't bear to think about her husband being away from her. They had barely been separated from each other since the end of the previous war.

But it was more than that. Nowadays, Horace was her only link with the outside world. It terrified her to imagine how she would cope without him, even for a few days, let alone if he were to . . .

She caught Edie's eye and dragged her mind sharply back to the present. She quickly doled a spoonful of mashed potatoes on to the plate and handed it back, careful to manage her features into a neutral expression.

If Edie noticed her shaky moment, she did not comment on it. Instead she picked up her knife and fork and said, 'Thank you for this, Mrs Huggins. It's like something you'd get in a restaurant. Where did you learn to cook?'

Patience blushed at the unexpected compliment. 'I went into service when I was scarcely more than a child. I grew up in a kitchen as a scullery maid, learning from the cook.'

'That must have been hard for you, leaving home so young?'

Patience had a sudden picture of herself, shivering and sobbing in the back of a lurching cart, a thin blanket pulled around her shoulders to keep out the chill of the early dawn.

'Stop snivelling,' her mother had said, thrusting a handkerchief into Patience's hands. 'You'll thank me for this one day.'

'Were you ever a cook yourself?' Edie's voice brought her out of her reverie.

Patience shook her head. 'I worked my way up to kitchen maid, and then moved to house parlour maid. You don't often get maids moving out of the kitchen, but the housekeeper said I had nice manners.'

How jealous the other kitchen maids had been when she was moved up. And the other parlour maids weren't very welcoming, either. For a long time Patience had felt very isolated and friendless, belonging neither upstairs nor down.

And then she had met Horace Huggins, the smiling under-gardener who everyone loved and who insisted on being her friend, in spite of all her efforts to put him off. It was against every rule for the two of them to even speak to each other, but that didn't seem to matter to Horace.

Patience swallowed hard. Why did all her thoughts keep straying back to him?

'You worked at the prison, didn't you?' Once again, Edie's voice broke into her thoughts.

Patience looked at her sharply. 'How did you know that?'

'I think Mr Huggins might have mentioned it once.'

'Did he now?' Patience pursed her mouth. She would have to have words with Horace, telling everyone their business.

Then her heart sank and she wondered why it even mattered. Nothing really mattered any more, not with her husband lying in a hospital bed.

'That was after we were married,' she said. 'He found a job as a prison warder and I became housekeeper to the Governor and his family.'

She smiled at the memory. What happy times they had been! The Governor's wife and her children had been so warm and welcoming, Patience had almost felt as if she was part of the family. She had run that house like clockwork for seven years, until their Joyce was born.

'It must have been nice for you when you came to Jubilee Row,' Edie said.

Patience frowned. 'What makes you say that?'

'Well – I mean, finally having your own place and not having to wait on other people any more?'

'I wasn't waiting on other people!' Patience said sharply. 'The Governor's wife trusted me, she treated me more like a friend than a servant. I helped her organise the most wonderful dinners and parties. And I liked the house, too. All those big, airy rooms, filled with such beautiful things . . .'

And then they had moved to Jubilee Row, cramming all their belongings into three cramped little rooms surrounded by dirt and ugliness, where children ran around the cobbled streets with no boots on, and the air stank of fish. The first time Joyce came home from school crawling with lice, Patience had cried and cried, longing for the elegance of their old lives.

She remembered what Joyce had said to her, the night she left. Perhaps she had let her resentment show more than she had thought? But she had never ever blamed her daughter. She would have gladly given up the world for Joyce . . .

Her outburst seemed to surprise Edie, who went back to eating in silence. When she had finished, she picked up her empty plate and took it to the sink, but Patience said, 'Don't worry about washing up, Mr Huggins will—' She stopped herself, biting her lip.

'I don't mind, honestly,' Edie's voice was gentle. 'I'd like to help out.'

Patience watched her standing at the sink. It made her skin prickle, seeing someone else washing up. What if she didn't rinse the dishes properly? Or what if she used the same cloth for the pans and the plates? Patience liked the dishes washed just so, and it had taken a long time before she could even trust Horace to do them properly.

She wanted to tell her to go, but at the same time she was terrified of being on her own.

'Do you want me to send for Joyce?' Edie said suddenly.

Patience stiffened at the mention of her daughter's name. 'Why?'

'I thought you might want her to keep you company?'

'Joyce? I hardly think so!'

'All the same, she should be told,' Edie said. 'I'd want to know, if my father was taken ill ...' Her voice trailed off for a moment. She concentrated on her scrubbing and Patience thought about the letter that had come back to her with *Return To Sender* scrawled across it.

'Anyway,' Edie went on, 'she might want to help.'

'Why would she want to help me?'

Edie turned to look at her, and Patience was annoyed by the pity she saw in her eyes.

'I suppose you're right,' she said briskly. 'She should be told. But don't you dare ask her for help on my account,' she added sharply.

'If that's what you want.' Edie put the last pan on the draining board and reached for a towel to dry her hands. 'Anyway, I'll be off now, unless you've changed your mind about me staying?' Patience shook her head. 'I can do some shopping for you tomorrow, if you give me a list of what you need?'

It was all Patience could do to hide her relief. 'Thank you,' she said stiffly. 'That would be very helpful.'

At the door, Edie stopped and said, 'I was thinking, happen I could make tea for us both tomorrow night?'

Patience stared at her, taken aback. 'You want me to come up to your flat?'

'Why not? I don't often bother for myself, so it would be nice to make something for both of us. I can't promise it will be as good as your cooking, though!' she smiled wryly.

Patience looked up at the ceiling, struggling with her thoughts.

She wanted to refuse. She wanted to close her door and keep everyone out. If she wasn't careful the outside world would start seeping through. She did not want people, least of all Edie Copeland, to think that she needed help from anyone.

But at the same time she was afraid, so very afraid, to be alone.

'Thank you,' she said. 'I think I would like that.'

Chapter Thirty

'I just thought you ought to know.'

Joyce stood frozen, her mind blank with shock. Dirty water dripped from the scrubbing brush she held in her hand. She had been washing down the shelves when Edie walked in.

'Appendicitis?' she repeated the word.

Edie nodded. 'I telephoned the hospital first thing this morning and they're going to operate today.'

'Operate?' The scrubbing brush landed with a noisy splash in the bucket at Joyce's feet, but she barely noticed. All she could think about was her father lying in a hospital bed. He had always been such a tough, capable man, the rock everyone depended on. She had never known him suffer a day's illness in his life.

'It's not as bad as it sounds,' Edie reassured her. 'Ada Maguire reckons there's no sign of the appendix rupturing, which is good news. And he's very strong for his age.'

For his age. It came as a shock to Joyce to remember he was in his late sixties now. All those years had passed, years when she should have been with him, watching him grow old.

Instead she had held him at arm's length, their relationship measured out in occasional snatched visits.

'It's your mother I'm really worried about,' Edie interrupted her racing thoughts. 'She's lost without your father.'

Joyce automatically glanced behind her towards the

workshop door, even though she knew Reg had gone out to collect a pulley system that a customer had ordered.

'I can't imagine my mother being lost,' she said.

'You'd be surprised.'

'Would I? I doubt it.'

'I was hoping you might think about going to see her—'

Joyce was shaking her head before Edie had finished speaking. 'No, I couldn't. She wouldn't want me there, anyway.'

'I'm sure she would—'

'How do you know? Has she asked for me?'

'Well—' Edie's face was all the answer she needed.

'I thought not.' Joyce hated herself for the sinking disappointment she felt. She picked her brush out of the water and turned away to carry on with her scrubbing.

'It's been twenty years,' Edie said. 'Surely you can find it in your hearts to forgive each other after all this time?'

'It's her you should be asking, not me.' Joyce turned on her. 'Look, I know you're trying to be helpful, but you really don't know my mother. When she turns against someone, there's no forgiveness, no second chances. She cut me out of her life twenty years ago, and there's no going back.'

You've made your bed, now you must lie in it.

Joyce went back to her scrubbing again. 'Thank you for coming and letting me know about my father,' she said. 'I'll go and visit him as soon as I can.'

She waited for Edie to argue. But a moment later she heard the bell over the shop door ring as it closed behind her.

She spent the rest of the morning cleaning. But all the time her conversation with Edie played through her head.

Her father needed her. Her mother needed her. What if this was just the chance they both needed to patch things up? Should she swallow her pride, and would her mother welcome her if she did?

She was still pondering over it when Reg came home from collecting the pulley. Joyce went to see him in his workshop and told him about her father.

'Appendicitis, eh?' Reg dumped the heavy metal pulley on the floor and straightened up, scratching his head. 'Poor old devil.'

'I'm going to see him on Saturday afternoon, when he's had a chance to recover a bit.'

'Don't you go to that WVS place on a Saturday afternoon?'

He was taunting her. Joyce could see it on his face.

'You know I stopped going there,' she reminded him quietly.

'So you did.'

He crossed the workshop to check the paintwork on a bicycle he had been working on that morning.

Joyce cleared her throat. 'I was thinking of going to see my mother, too,' she said.

Reg swung round to face her. 'Why would you want to do that?'

'Edie Copeland thinks she needs help. You know how she depends on Dad—'

'Then let Edie Copeland help her.'

'But I'm her daughter.'

'That in't what she said twenty years ago! Don't you remember? She said you were no child of hers and she never wanted to see you again.'

'Those weren't her exact words,' Joyce tried to argue. 'And besides, she was angry . . .'

'Seems like you're in the mood to forgive her,' Reg turned away from her.

'I didn't say that,' Joyce said. 'I just think a lot of time has gone past, and—'

'I don't care how much time has gone past, I'll never

205

forgive her for what she said to me!' Reg snapped. 'I'll never forget the way she looked at me, neither, like I were a piece of dirt on her shoe.' He turned to Joyce, his eyes cold. 'You must do as you please,' he muttered. 'If you want to take your mother's side against mine, then I in't going to stop you. But just remember who's stood by you all these years, who's kept a roof over your head.'

'That's not fair—' Joyce pleaded, but he had already turned his back on her again, shutting her out. 'All right,' she said. 'I won't go.'

'As I said, you must do as you please.'

Joyce stared at his turned back, hunched over his work.

I stopped doing that a long time ago, she thought.

Chapter Thirty-one

Patience waited at the bottom of the stairs until the grand-father clock in the hall struck five before she went up and knocked on Edie Copeland's kitchen door.

'Come in,' Edie's voice came from inside.

Patience frowned. The polite thing to do would be to open the door and greet a guest, but Edie clearly had no breeding.

She opened the door and looked inside. The kitchen was in chaos, with peelings on the draining board, dishes piled in the sink and an array of bubbling pans on top of the stove.

And in the middle of it was Edie, smiling away as if nothing at all was amiss.

'Hello,' she said cheerfully. 'I wasn't expecting you so early.'

'You did say five o'clock.' The last chimes of the grandfather clock echoed from the hall below.

'So I did.' Edie looked amused, for some reason Patience could not fathom. 'You'll have to excuse the mess. I'm afraid I've got a bit behind.'

Patience looked around at the kitchen and fought the urge to grab a cloth and start cleaning it.

'Happen you'd be more comfortable waiting in the other room, till tea's ready?' Edie suggested.

Patience's gaze skimmed the room again. Edie would never do in service, she decided. And as for using all those gas rings – well, it was simply wasteful. The girl had no home management skills at all, from what she could tell.

'I think I will,' she said.

The other room had certainly changed since the last time Patience had seen it. The faded, yellowing wallpaper was gone, replaced by a very pleasant shade of sky blue. The heavy, dark-wood furniture had been painted cream, and there were new flowery curtains up at the windows. Even with the blackout fabric over the glass and the lamps lit, the room was still bright and cheerful. The lingering damp smell had gone, too, replaced by the scent of beeswax and lavender and fresh air.

Patience was grudgingly impressed. Miss Hodges, the previous tenant, might have been refined, but her age and poor eyesight meant she didn't always notice the dirt and dust.

Not that everything was perfect. The room might be clean, but it was still too messy for Patience's liking. There were pieces of fabric spread out on the bed, as if someone had taken a dress apart and was trying to put it back together. A pair of scissors lay abandoned on the pillow.

Patience bent to pick up the reel of thread that had fallen on the floor, just as the door opened and Edie came in.

'Tea won't be too long,' she announced breathlessly.

I should think not. Patience held back the comment. She had been invited for five o'clock, and tea should have been served promptly at that time.

But even though it had been a long time since she had been anyone's guest, Patience Huggins still knew how to behave, so she held her tongue.

'I see you've made quite a few changes,' she said, looking around the room.

'Yes, I have.' Edie's chin lifted proudly. 'Do you like it?'

Patience disliked change of any kind. She found it all too unnerving. But for once this seemed to be a change for the better.

'Yes,' she said. 'Yes, I do.'

'Do you really?' Edie looked so pleased, it nearly touched Patience's heart. She turned away quickly.

'And what's all this in aid of?' she asked, pointing to the fabric pieces strewn across the bed.

Edie grimaced. 'I need a dress for Ada Maguire's wedding. I was trying to let one of my old dresses out at the seams, but it's all gone wrong and now I can't seem to get it back together again.'

'May I look?' Patience picked up one of the pieces and examined it. 'You haven't got nearly enough to let out. The seams won't hold even if you do manage to get them back together.' She placed it back on the bed, smoothing it out carefully. 'And the material is too delicate to be hacking about at it, anyway. I'm surprised it hasn't fallen apart.'

'So what should I do?'

Throw it away and start again, Patience was about to say, then she saw the doleful look on the girl's face.

'I suppose you could put in another panel of fabric. Do you have another dress? Something old, that you don't wear any more?'

Edie shook her head. *Don't get involved,* the voice in Patience's head whispered. *This is her problem, not yours. Let her sort it out for herself.*

'I might have something,' she heard herself saying instead. 'I'll fetch my scraps box after tea and we'll have a look.'

The meal consisted of sausages, mashed potatoes and carrots – plain, but at least it was edible. All the way through the meal, Patience was conscious of Edie watching her nervously across the table.

Of course, there was a lot she could have said about it – the sausages were too dry, and there wasn't nearly enough salt in the potatoes – but Patience remembered her manners, and complimented Edie on the carrots.

'Pop Maguire gave them to me,' Edie said, looking pleased. 'They're from his allotment.'

'They're very – fresh.' Patience surreptitiously scraped off a piece of dirt and left it on the side of her plate.

'I meant to tell you, I telephoned the hospital this afternoon,' Edie said.

'And?' Patience tensed.

'And the operation was a complete success. The ward sister said Mr Huggins had just come round from the anaesthetic when I called.'

'Oh, thank God,' Patience whispered. She took out her handkerchief and pretended to blow her nose so Edie would not see the emotion on her face.

'He can have visitors on Saturday,' Edie said. 'I thought we could catch the tram to the Infirmary,' she suggested.

Patience stared across the table at her. 'Catch – a tram?' she echoed faintly. 'Me?'

'Or we could walk, if you'd prefer? It depends on the weather—'

'I won't be going to see him.'

Edie frowned. 'Why not?'

'You know perfectly well why.' Patience felt the heat rising in her face.

'I know you don't like to go out,' Edie said. 'But I would have thought you'd make the effort for your own husband. And I'm sure it would do Mr Huggins good to see you,' she added.

Patience glared at her. 'Don't you think I know that?' Anger made the words spill out unguarded. 'Don't you think I want to see him, to make sure he's all right?'

'Then come with me,' Edie said.

'I can't.' Patience lowered her gaze. 'It's out of the question.'

'Why? What are you afraid of?'

Everything. Everything and nothing.

But how could she explain that to this young woman? Edie Copeland was fearless enough to pick up the pieces of her life after so much tragedy, to move to a new city and start again. Patience couldn't even walk to the corner shop without her inner demons mocking her and taunting her and putting unknown terrors in her head.

'It might do you good,' Edie was saying.

Patience pursed her lips. 'I'll be the judge of what's good for me, thank you very much.'

'Promise me you'll think about it, anyway?'

Patience sighed. The wretched girl was obviously not going to shut up about it until she did. 'Very well,' she said. 'I will think about it.'

But she already knew what her answer would be.

After tea, while Edie cleared the table and washed the dishes, Patience went downstairs to fetch her mending box from the back of the wardrobe.

'Here you are.' She carried it into the parlour and dumped it at Edie's feet. 'Have a look through there and see if there's anything that catches your eye.'

Edie peered into the box. 'What are they?'

'Just a few things I don't wear any more. I keep meaning to sort through them but I haven't had time. I know they're not modern,' she said, 'but at least we could use the material.'

It felt strange, watching Edie picking through the clothes. Each garment held a special memory, which was why Patience could never bring herself to get rid of them.

'I like this,' Edie held up an eau de nil blouse. 'And the blue would go perfectly with the dress. But this is so pretty, too . . .' She held up a silk skirt in a deep-rose pink.

'Yes, it's beautiful, isn't it?' Patience took the skirt from her, running her hands over the rich folds of fabric. 'There's a matching bodice somewhere, too. I wore it for the Governor's Christmas ball the year before Queen Victoria died. The first Christmas of the new century.'

Edie stared at her. 'You went to a ball?'

'The Governor and his wife invited me every year,' Patience replied primly. And what a night it was. All of society was there, and for one night Patience Huggins could be among them, eating fine dainty foods, sipping champagne from the finest crystal and dancing in Horace's arms under the glittering chandeliers while the orchestra played.

The look of astonishment on Edie's face made her smile. 'You don't have to look so surprised,' Patience said. 'I wasn't always this old, you know. I used to quite enjoy a waltz.'

'Did you?' Edie still looked disbelieving.

'As a matter of fact there was one time—' Patience started to say, then remembered herself. 'But it doesn't matter.' She turned her attention back to the skirt in her hands. 'You're right, the blouse would do for making panels in the dress you've got,' she said. 'But there's enough material in this skirt to make a whole new dress, if you like? Especially if we could find that bodice . . .' She started to rummage through the box.

'Really?' Edie looked from the skirt to Patience and back again. 'No, I couldn't,' she said. 'It's too precious. All your memories . . .'

'I'll still have my memories,' Patience dismissed. 'Besides, what use is it doing in the bottom of a box? I'm hardly likely to wear it again, am I?' She could scarcely believe she had ever worn such a bright, frivolous garment in the first place. Now she lived her life in drab browns and greys and thick, practical fabrics that never wore out.

'I suppose not.' Edie looked longingly at the skirt. 'If you're sure?'

'I wouldn't have said it otherwise, would I?' Patience said briskly. 'Now pass me those scissors, and we'll make a start on those panels. Then I'll measure you up for the dress . . .'

They worked steadily for the next two hours, cutting and pinning and stitching. Patience, who had spent all day watching the clock and worrying about Horace, was surprised to find she scarcely noticed the time flying by.

That was partly because it took all her concentration to stop Edie making a mistake. Left to her own devices, the girl was completely hopeless with a needle.

'No, no, no, that's not the way to do it,' she scolded when Edie sewed the wrong seam yet again. 'Check your work first, before you start stitching. Why do you have to rush headlong into everything without a thought?'

'I don't know,' Edie said. 'It's just the way I am.'

There was something about the way she said it that made Patience look up from unpicking the stitches. Edie's expression was strangely wistful as she rethreaded her needle.

They carried on working in silence until the grandfather clock in the hall struck nine o'clock.

'Is it that time?' Patience laid down her work and rubbed her eyes.

'There's been no air raid tonight,' Edie said. 'That's a blessing.' She looked towards the blacked-out windows. 'Happen they've given up on us at last?'

'Let's hope so.'

No sooner had she said the words than the all too familiar drone of the siren filled the air.

'Looks like we spoke too soon.' Edie put her work aside with a sigh. She stood up and stretched.

Patience felt a sudden pang of anxiety for Horace, lying

in his hospital bed. What if the Infirmary was hit? Her one comfort during the air raids was that if the Germans ever did drop a bomb on them, they would go together, sheltering under the stairs with a pot of tea.

And now they were separated. She had never faced an air raid alone before. If Horace went without her saying goodbye, she would never forgive him, or herself.

Edie went to the window and listened. 'I can't hear any planes yet,' she said. 'Perhaps it won't be too bad tonight—'

'I will come to the hospital with you,' Patience blurted out the words.

'Will you?' Edie turned to face her, smiling. 'I'm sure Mr Huggins will appreciate it,' she said.

Patience looked down at her hands, already trembling in her lap at the thought of venturing outside.

I hope so, she thought.

Chapter Thirty-two

'I love you, Geoff. There's nothing I can do about it. I just love you . . .'

Jean Arthur gazed deep into Cary Grant's eyes, their faces inches apart. He swept her up into his arms, and the audience held their breaths, knowing it was only a matter of moments before their lips met in a passionate kiss . . .

And then the message flashed across the cinema screen, telling everyone that an air-raid warning had just been sounded.

'Right, that's it.' Iris wriggled in her seat, shrugging on her coat. All around them, the rows of people were beginning to stir, but Dolly did not move.

'I'm not going anywhere,' she said.

'But you saw the message. There's an air raid . . .'

'All the more reason to stay put then.' Dolly lit up a cigarette. The tip glowed bright in the darkness of the cinema. 'We're as safe here as we are out there. Safer, probably. And I want to see the end of the film.'

'But—'

'Iris Fletcher, it's taken me a month of Sundays to get you to come out for the night. Besides, we've paid a shilling for our tickets. I don't know about you, but I want to get my money's worth.'

Iris slumped back in her seat beside Dolly and stared at the screen, where Cary Grant and Jean Arthur's passionate embrace had been rudely interrupted by Thomas Mitchell. But she could hardly concentrate on what was happening in the film. All she could think about was her children, back at home in Jubilee Row with her mother.

The sound of plane engines on the screen made her heart beat faster, thinking they were passing overhead.

As if she understood what her friend was thinking, Dolly reached out and patted her arm.

'They'll be safe with Mum,' she whispered in the darkness. 'Besides, it won't be a bad one tonight. There's no moon.'

The All Clear had sounded by the time they emerged from the cinema into the deserted street. It felt as if they were the only people in the whole world.

'You see? I told you there was nowt to worry about.' Dolly pointed up at the sky. 'No moon, see?'

No moon also meant no light to guide them home. Iris fumbled in her bag for her torch and switched it on. Its dim beam barely pierced the all-enveloping blackness.

'I hate the blackout,' she muttered.

'Don't we all?' Dolly put her arm through Iris'. 'Buck up, lass. We're only five minutes from home.'

As they were making their way up Hessle Road the drone of the air-raid siren filled the air again, shattering the silence.

'Not again!' Iris looked up at the sky. From far away came the drone of a distant plane, drowned out a moment later by the sharp retort of anti-aircraft fire.

'They'll see it off, whatever it is,' Dolly said. But Iris noticed her friend had quickened her pace as they neared Gillett Street.

It was a relief to turn the corner into Jubilee Row. As they hurried past Pearce's corner shop, Dolly pointed and said, 'Is that light coming from Beattie Scuttle's window? I hope our Florence doesn't see it, or she'll have something to say.'

Iris turned to look. It was only the thinnest sliver of light showing through the downstairs window, but it stood out bright as a beacon in the blackness.

'Beattie can't have closed her blackout curtains properly,' she said. 'I daresay she was in a rush to get Charlie to the shelter. Here, you take the torch. I'll call in and let her know.'

'In't you coming with me?' Dolly asked, taking the torch from her.

'I'll be there in a minute. Or happen Beattie will let me share her fancy Anderson shelter?' Iris grinned. 'Tell our Archie to look after his sisters,' she called back over her shoulder as she crossed the road. 'And tell him I'll know about it if he plays up!'

'I will.' The sound of Dolly's high heels receded down the street, the faint glow of the torch bobbing ahead of her. Iris missed its light as she stumbled on the cobbles, still slippery under her feet from the recent rain.

She went straight down the narrow alleyway that ran down the side of the Scuttles' house, into the ten foot that ran the length of the street, then through the back gate into their yard.

A plane droned above her, and Iris flinched. But it was one of theirs, thank God, sent to chase the Germans out of the sky.

'Beattie?' she called. 'Beattie, are you in there? You've left your light on, love.'

As she went to knock on the metal door of the shelter, it swung open, revealing nothing but darkness inside.

'Beattie?' Iris picked her way up the path and tapped softly on the back door. Still no reply.

She hesitated, looking around her in the darkness. Her sister Florence would be doing her rounds soon. There would be hell to pay if she saw the faintest chink of light.

She knew the back door would be unlocked. No one in Jubilee Row ever locked their doors, except for Patience Huggins at number ten.

The scullery was in darkness as Iris let herself in through the back door, but there was a chink of light coming from beyond the curtain that separated the scullery from the kitchen.

She swished aside the curtain – and screamed at the sight of Sam Scuttle sitting in a tin bath in front of the fire.

'What the—' Sam let out a yell and started to get up, then thought better of it and snatched a towel from the back of the chair. He clutched it to his broad chest like a maiden preserving her modesty. 'What are you doing here?'

'There was a light on.'

'What?'

'It was showing on the street. I came to close your blackouts.'

Iris turned her back as Sam let the towel drop a fraction. She caught a glimpse of a muscular torso gleaming like bronze in the firelight, water dripping off his hair and running in rivulets over powerful shoulders . . .

'I'll wait outside,' she stammered, and fled.

She stood in the darkened scullery, her gaze fixed on the stone sink as she listened to the sound of splashing water and tried not to imagine what the rest of Sam's body looked like.

She jumped as the curtain swished aside, and automatically averted her gaze.

'It's all right.' Sam's voice was amused. 'I'm decent.'

Iris sent him a cautious look. He had put his trousers on and was buttoning up his shirt. Iris saw his scar, etched like silver across the right-hand side of his ribcage.

He'd got it the night Arthur died. Sam had dived into the icy waters to save him and Ted Weir, and ended up being swept underneath the boat.

He caught her staring and turned away.

'I've closed the blackouts in the front room,' he said. 'Thanks for letting me know. Mum would have had a fit if I'd landed her with a fine.'

'Where is she?'

'Gone to the public shelter, would you believe?' His face was rueful. 'All that trouble I went to, building that thing in the yard, and now she's decided she misses the company!'

'What about Charlie?'

Sam shook his head. 'He don't like it either. I reckon it reminds him too much of the tunnels he got buried in during the last war.'

The silence stretched between them.

'Sorry for bursting in like that,' Iris said. 'What must you have thought?'

'What must you have thought of *me*?' A faint blush rose in Sam's weather-beaten face. Iris could feel herself blushing, too.

'You're allowed to have a bath in your own home,' she mumbled.

'I've just finished my shift. I was about to turn in for the night.'

'Did you have a busy night?'

Sam shook his head. 'Very quiet.'

No sooner had he said it than a distant burst of anti-aircraft fire rattled the windows.

'You were saying?' Iris said.

They grinned awkwardly at each other. When did everything become so difficult between them?, Iris wondered. They used to laugh and joke for hours, but now she felt self-conscious about every word.

He likes you. You only have to see the way he looks at you.

He was looking at her now, his sea-green eyes fixed on hers.

'I should go,' she said.

'I was just about to put the kettle on, if you fancy a brew?'

'I thought you were going to bed?'

'I never sleep well after a shift. I'd welcome the company.' He paused. 'And there's something else,' he added. 'Something I've been meaning to say for a while now.'

Here it comes, Iris thought. Her breath stuck in her throat.

'I wanted to apologise.' His next words took her by surprise. 'About the incendiary.'

'The – incendiary?' It was so unexpected, it took Iris a moment to recollect.

'You're right, I should never have given it to the lads. It was a daft present, thoughtless of me—'

'No, it's me who was being daft,' Iris said hastily. 'It was just something Dolly said—'

'What? What did Dolly say?'

Iris shook her head. 'It doesn't matter. It in't even worth repeating.'

Another strained silence. 'I'd best go,' Iris said. 'I want to make sure the bains are all right.'

'Are they with your mum?'

Iris nodded. 'I've been to the pictures with Dolly.'

'What did you see?'

'*Only Angels Have Wings.*'

A plane droned overhead. 'That in't true though, is it?' Sam said grimly.

Her hand was on the back door, ready to leave, when he suddenly said, 'Happen I could take you to the pictures one night?'

Iris looked down at her hand, resting on the back doorknob.

She was glad she had her back turned so he couldn't see her face.

'No,' she said.

He laughed in surprise. 'Don't you even want to think about it?'

'I can't, Sam. It wouldn't be fair.' She looked over her shoulder at him. 'I wouldn't want to give you any ideas.'

'Iris, I'm only asking you to go to the pictures, I'm not proposing marriage!'

'I know, but—' She knew how it would go. One night at the pictures would lead to another, and then they would go dancing, and then . . .

She could see it, all too clearly. And that was the trouble.

'You know how people talk. I wouldn't want them to read more into it than there is,' she said.

'I don't give a damn what people think.'

'I do.'

'Is it because of Arthur?' he said quietly.

Iris looked at him. His gentle gaze was full of understanding.

'I thought so,' he said. 'You loved him very much, didn't you?' Iris nodded, lost for words. 'And now you don't want another man?'

'I'm sorry, Sam.'

'Don't be. At least I know where I stand now.' He smiled bracingly. 'I'll just have to try and find myself a girl who loves me as much as you loved your Arthur.'

The All Clear sounded as Iris stepped out into the back yard. She could feel Sam watching her as she picked her way down to the back gate and let herself out.

She had done the right thing, she told herself. It was for the best.

She only wished it felt like it.

Chapter Thirty-three

'How are you?' Edie asked yet again.

'I do wish you'd stop asking me that. I'm quite all right, thank you,' Patience snapped, even though her heart was beating so wildly in her chest, she was surprised Edie couldn't hear it.

She wished Horace was there with her, but of course he was still in hospital. Which was why she and Edie were venturing out on a chilly Saturday afternoon in October.

She had been awake since the early hours, worrying about it. She had scrubbed every room from top to bottom, dusted and polished every surface she could find, but nothing seemed to settle her racing mind or the dread in the pit of her stomach.

It had taken every shred of willpower she possessed to step out of the front door and out into the street. Leaving her house made her feel horribly exposed, as if everyone was looking at her.

As it happened, there was hardly anyone about on Jubilee Row, much to Patience's relief. The cold weather had driven May Maguire and Beattie Scuttle indoors to braid their nets, and the few children larking about outside scarcely paid her any attention.

She hadn't realised she had been gripping Edie's arm so tightly until she said, 'We can always go home if you want to?'

'Nonsense, we're out here now,' Patience said briskly. 'Let's just get on with it, shall we?'

Everything felt strange. The hard, uneven cobbles under her feet, the smell of factory smoke, the damp chill of the October fog against her face. It was as if she had been stripped of a layer of skin, so every sensation felt unbearably vivid.

Harry Pearce was putting up a sign in the window of the corner shop, announcing that they had a limited supply of lemons for sale. He lifted his hand in greeting but Patience could only stare back. When did young Harry become a grown man? She felt as if she had woken up from a long sleep and stepped back into a world where everyone had aged except her. For her, time had stood still.

It was only sheer bloody-mindedness that forced her up the length of Coltman Street to Anlaby Road, where they caught the tram to the Infirmary.

Patience stared out of the window at the people, houses and shops trundling past. She found herself avidly searching the faces of the other passengers, taking in their unfamiliar features, her nose wrinkling at the pungent aroma of un-washed bodies.

And then there was the city centre. It seemed so over-whelming, the broad streets and enormous buildings. So much had changed, and yet it all seemed so familiar to her. She recognised the tower of the Prudential building, and the new Hammonds department store in Paragon Square. Not so new any more, of course, but she remembered the grand opening during the last war.

She mentioned it to Edie, who told her they had opened a ballroom on the top floor a few years earlier.

'No! A ballroom, you say?'

Edie nodded. 'Ruby Maguire's girls often go dancing there. And they have a special staircase that moves by itself. All you have to do is stand there. It's called an escalator.'

'Well, I don't like the sound of that!' Patience declared, tight-lipped.

'They have commissionaires standing at the top and bottom to help people on and off.'

'I'm not surprised. I can't think why anyone would want such a thing.'

Patience shook her head. The world had changed so much, it was utterly terrifying. Even the staircases moved faster these days.

It was a relief to get to the Infirmary. Although that was another overwhelming experience, with its wide, sweeping staircases, long corridors and endless amounts of doors. But Patience felt curiously calmed by the sense of order; the highly polished floors, the scent of disinfectant and the nurses in their starched uniforms that crackled as they walked.

Visiting time had already begun, much to her dismay. Years in service had instilled in her a strong need for punctuality.

'We're only a quarter of an hour late,' Edie said, as they hurried up the flight of stairs in the direction the porter had told them.

'A quarter of an hour is a long time,' Patience replied sternly. 'I dread to think what would have happened if the food had been served a quarter of an hour late at one of the Governor's dinner parties.'

'Yes, well, we're not serving at a dinner party now, are we? Ah, here we are—' Edie pushed open a glass-panelled door that led to the ward.

The vast, high-ceilinged ward was already full of visitors. The thin October sunlight streamed through the tall windows, illuminating the long rows of beds down each side of the room. Each bed seemed surrounded by a throng of anxious wives and mothers.

A junior nurse in a striped uniform took their names at the door.

'We're here to visit Horace Huggins,' Edie said, as Patience struggled to find her voice.

'Oh yes, Mr Huggins.' The young nurse consulted her list. 'But I'm afraid one of you will have to wait outside. Only two visitors are allowed per bed, and Mr Huggins already has his daughter with him.'

His daughter.

Even in the crowded ward, Patience's gaze found her straight away. She was sitting beside his bed at the far end, holding Horace's hand. She looked older, of course, but somehow she was still the young girl Patience remembered.

She flashed an accusing look at Edie. 'Did you know she'd be here?'

'No,' Edie said, but she was blushing as she said it.

Patience looked back at her daughter. She was smiling, but her smile didn't reach her eyes. Even from a distance, Patience could see the tension in the lines of her body, the tendons in her neck as taut as tent ropes, the way she held her shoulders hunched . . .

As if she knew she was being watched, Joyce suddenly looked up and their eyes met.

She let go of her father's hand and shot to her feet. Horace followed her gaze.

'Patience?' he stared at her in shock.

For a moment no one spoke. Then Edie said, 'I'll wait outside.'

'It's all right, I'm going now.' Joyce was fussing around, gathering up her coat and bag with anxious, jerky movements.

'You don't have to go,' Edie said. 'It will be nice for Mr Huggins to have all his family around him.'

Joyce was watching Patience warily, like a cornered animal

watching its hunter. It seemed as if she was waiting for Patience to speak.

Patience wanted to speak. She knew that the next words she uttered might change everything, and she wanted to get them right.

She opened her mouth but no sound came out.

Joyce's gaze dropped. 'Honestly, I think it would be better if I left,' she said quietly. She leaned in and gave Horace a peck on his cheek. 'Goodbye, Dad. I'll try to come in and see you next week.'

'I'll look forward to it, love.'

She gave Patience a quick, nervous smile and then left.

'Well,' Horace said, when Joyce had gone. 'Fancy you being here. This is a sight I never thought I'd see again, I must say.'

Patience did not reply. Her gaze was still avidly following her daughter as she walked away from her.

'I know what you mean,' she murmured.

* * *

Joyce fled from the hospital in a state of nervous confusion.

Seeing her mother again had sent a charge of electricity through her body. She could still feel it fizzing through her veins, making her want to run.

If only she had known she was coming, she might have been prepared for it. She might have been able to smile, to speak. But shock had robbed her of all her senses.

God knows what her mother had thought of her.

Now all she wanted to do was get away, to put as much distance between herself and her humiliation as she could. She was in such a state, she ran straight into a nurse coming into the hospital building and nearly knocked her flying.

'I'm sorry,' she muttered, her head down.

'Mrs Shelby?'

Joyce looked up sharply to see Ada Maguire standing before her. Her tall, slender figure was shrouded in a navy-blue heavy wool cape, her dark hair hidden under a starched cap.

Joyce felt another sizzle of panic through her veins. She hadn't seen the Maguires at all since Reg destroyed the wedding dress.

'Hello, Ada,' she said warily.

She could scarcely bring herself to meet the girl's eye, but she seemed to be smiling.

'Been to see your father, have you?' Joyce nodded. 'I've been keeping an eye on him, since he's on my ward. He's doing very well. The doctors are really pleased with him.'

'So he said. Thank you for taking such good care of him.'

'He's a very easy patient, unlike some of them!' The silence lengthened between them, then Ada said, 'Anyway, I'd best be going. I'm due on duty in ten minutes.'

As she started to walk away, Joyce plucked up her courage and said, 'Ada?'

The girl stopped. 'Yes?'

'I wanted to apologise. About the dress . . .'

'Oh.' Ada's smile faltered slightly.

'I spoke to your mother about it, but I just wanted to tell you how sorry I am that I let you down. I know how disappointed you must have felt—'

'It's all right, Mrs Shelby.' Ada laid her hand on Joyce's arm. 'I'll admit I was upset about it at the time, but it's turned out all right now.'

'Has it?'

'Oh, yes. Better than all right, I'd say. One of the other nurses has lent me her dress, and it's much nicer than anything I could afford. She got it from Elsie Battle on Prospect

Street. That's where all the society brides go,' she said proudly.

'Oh. Well, that's – that's marvellous news.'

'Isn't it? It fits perfectly and I'm thrilled with it.' Her dark eyes were alight with joy. 'Gran always says things work out for a reason, and I reckon she's not wrong!'

'Yes. Yes, I'm sure that's true.' Joyce smiled with relief. 'Anyway, I'm pleased you found something you like. I'm sure you'll look beautiful.'

'I hope so. Anyway, you'll see it for yourself when you come to the wedding. You are still coming, in't you?'

Joyce looked away. 'I wasn't sure if I was still invited, after what happened.'

'Of course you're still invited! It's my wedding day, I want everyone there to enjoy it with me.' Ada smiled. 'As Pop always says, we've all got to get on in this world. It doesn't do to hold on to grudges, does it?'

'No,' Joyce said quietly, looking back at the hospital building. 'No, I suppose not.'

Chapter Thirty-four

In the middle of October, the day after a German bomber dumped four high explosives down the length of Stoneferry Road, Edie walked up from St Andrew's Dock to Schultz Brothers' pawnshop on Hessle Road after work and paid the last instalment on her pram.

She had been very lucky. Just a week after she had visited the shop with Dolly, the proprietor had sent her a note saying that they had a pram come in if she still wanted it.

Edie had hurried straight down there and paid the first instalment, and she had been paying it off ever since.

And now it was all hers. Edie felt very proud, pushing it up the length of Hessle Road. Even though the pawnbroker had wondered at her wanting to collect it so early – 'Most mothers like to leave it until after the bain is born,' he had said – Edie could hardly wait.

This made it all real, she thought. In a few weeks she would have a baby of her own. She looked into the empty pram and tried to imagine herself gazing down at her baby. Who would he look like?, she wondered. Would he have her dark hair and hazel eyes, or Rob's light colouring? Her heart ached at the bittersweet thought of seeing her darling Rob's twinkling eyes and crooked, endearing smile reflected in her child every day. It would be a constant, painful reminder, and yet she wouldn't want it any other way.

She left the pram outside Pearce's corner shop while she

went in to collect Patience Huggins' rations. Viv Pearce was behind the counter, serving a customer and talking nine-teen to the dozen, as usual. This time she was relaying the news that two people had been hit by a bomb the previous night.

'Two young girls, just out for a walk, so I heard,' she was saying. 'One was killed straight away, and the other one's in the Infirmary.' She shook her head. 'Can you imagine it? One minute you're walking along the street, having a lovely chat with your friend, and then—' She gestured into the air. 'Is that everything, Mrs Marsh?' she went on, without pausing for breath. 'Only we've got a few tins of stewing steak put by in the back for our regular customers, if you're interested?'

Mrs Marsh paid for her shopping and left, and then it was Edie's turn. Viv Pearce greeted her with a broad smile.

'How's Mr Huggins?' she asked as she clipped the ration book.

'He's doing well, thank you.'

'I'm glad to hear it. We're short on bacon, so it's only half rations today.' She pushed the ration book back to Edie. 'Any idea when he'll be coming home?'

'Not for a few more weeks.'

'Yes, well, I daresay he'll need time to recover. It's a good thing Mrs Huggins has got you to help her out, or I don't know what she'd do.' Her voice rose over the sound of the bacon slicer. 'Although Harry reckoned he saw the two of you out and about the other day. I told him he was imagining things. I mean, the old dear hasn't set foot out of the door in years.'

'Actually, I took her to see Mr Huggins in hospital.'

'Is that right?' Viv turned to look at her, the slices of bacon in her hand. 'Well, that's a surprise, I must say. You must be a good influence on her.' She smiled. 'Happen she'll look in here next time? It would be nice to see her.'

'I'll be sure to let her know,' Edie said.

'Happen she might find time to call in on her daughter, too?' Viv said.

Edie smiled blandly back at her across the counter and changed the subject. 'Did I hear you say you had stewing steak?'

Viv looked put out. 'Aye, we do.' As she went to fetch it, she looked out of the shop window and said, 'Is that your tansad outside?'

Edie lifted her chin. 'Yes, it is.'

'It's a beauty. Got it from Schultz's, did you?'

Edie frowned. Was there anything Viv Pearce did not know? 'That's right.'

'You in't taking it home, I hope?'

'Why not?'

'Don't you know it's bad luck to bring a tansad into the house before the bain's born?'

Edie glanced at the pram parked outside. No wonder the pawnbroker had been so surprised.

'No,' she said. 'I didn't know.'

'You'd best find somewhere else to keep it,' Viv said.

'It's just an old wives' tale,' Edie shrugged. 'I don't believe in it anyway.'

'You might say that,' Viv said darkly. 'But there's plenty of women around here that will tell you different. And with these air raids and everything going on around here, I don't reckon I'd like to take any chances.'

Viv's warning stayed with Edie as she left the shop and turned down the narrow passage that led to the ten foot. She did not believe in superstition. But she didn't want to attract any more bad luck, either.

Iris's and Dolly's boys were gathered in a tight circle outside the back gate, playing marbles. Little Lucy stood watching as usual, her round face hungry with longing. She looked up, her face brightening at the sight of Edie approaching with the pram.

'Is that your bain, Missus?' she asked, hurrying towards her.

'Don't be daft, Lucy,' George sneered as the boys scrambled to their feet. 'It in't come yet.'

'Yeah, don't be daft,' Archie joined in with his cousin's taunting. 'You don't know owt, Lucy.'

They gathered around the pram. 'It'd make a champion cart,' George declared, running his hand over the wheels.

'I daresay it would, but you in't having it.' Edie cocked her head to listen. The back gate was open and she could hear raised voices coming from the house.

'I'm only saying—'

'Well, don't.'

'I'm only saying you should go and see him. As a friend, that's all.'

'Say another word about it and I shall walk out of this house, Dolly Maguire!'

Edie looked down at Lucy, who stood beside her, her eyes solemn.

'Mum and Auntie Dolly are arguing again,' she said.

Edie pushed the pram through the open gateway into the yard and, after warning George, Freddy and Archie to keep their hands off it, she went inside the house.

Dolly was at the kitchen table sawing thick slices of bread while Iris sat opposite, spreading jam on them and looking thoroughly fed up.

Her expression lifted when she saw Edie. 'Thank the Lord,' she muttered. 'Now happen we can talk about something else.'

Edie looked from one to the other. 'I heard you shouting from outside.'

'She was the one shouting,' Dolly pointed at Iris. 'I was only talking.'

'The problem is, you never know when to shut up,' Iris said.

Dolly ignored her, turning to Edie. 'We were talking about Sam Scuttle,' she explained.

'What about him?'

'Don't ask,' Iris groaned.

'He's been injured,' Dolly said. 'Last night, in a fire.'

'Is he badly hurt?'

'No,' Iris said. 'But you'd think he was at death's door, the way she's carrying on.'

'He's got a couple of burns on his hand and arm,' Dolly said. 'But he was lucky – it could have been much worse,' she added, shooting an accusing look at Iris. 'I was just saying as how Iris should go and see him.'

'He's got his mother fussing over him, he doesn't need me,' Iris said.

'I'm sure he'd be glad to see you. You are supposed to be his friend, after all.'

'That's enough!' Iris threw down her knife. 'I'll go and visit him, all right? But only to shut you up.'

'Thank you. That's all I wanted to hear.' Dolly gave a self-satisfied smile.

Since she was clearly in a good mood, Edie decided to ask her a favour.

'I've just collected my pram and I wondered if I could keep it here until the baby's born? I know it's just superstitious nonsense, and I don't believe in it, but—'

'It's not nonsense at all,' Dolly said seriously.

'Everyone knows it's bad luck,' Iris nodded. At least they were agreed on something at last, Edie thought.

'Of course you must keep it here,' Dolly said. 'Where is it?'

'It's outside. In the yard.'

'Let's have a look.' Iris got to her feet and went outside, Edie and Dolly following.

Edie watched proudly as they oohed and aahed over it. 'It's grand,' Dolly said, rocking it back and forth.

'It still needs a touch-up of paint to cover the scratches,' Edie said. 'And I'll have to make a new mattress, if I can get hold of some offcuts. But Mrs Huggins has promised to help me make the bedding.'

'Has she now?' Edie caught the knowing look that passed between Iris and Dolly. 'You two are thick as thieves these days, in't you?' Iris said.

'I'm only helping her out while her husband's in hospital.'

'You spend more time with her than you do with us,' Iris said.

'We're beginning to feel left out,' Dolly joined in.

'It in't like that—' Edie started to say, then she saw the teasing smile on Dolly's face.

'We're only having a joke with you,' she grinned. 'Although I reckon you deserve a medal for putting up with her!'

'She in't that bad,' Edie said, and was surprised to find she meant it. Over the past week she had got to know Patience Huggins quite well. And she was beginning to suspect that under that brittle shell lurked a good heart.

'Have you thought about where you're going to have the baby now?' Iris said, changing the subject.

Edie frowned. 'What do you mean, "now"? I'm booked into Hedon Road Maternity Home.'

Iris glanced at Dolly. 'You mean you haven't heard?'

'Heard what?' Edie looked from one to the other. 'What are you talking about?'

Iris laid her hand on Edie's arm. 'You know you said you didn't believe in all that superstitious nonsense?' she said. 'Well, I'm sorry, but I reckon you might end up eating your words ...'

Chapter Thirty-five

Patience stood at the window, watching out for Edie. She was late for her tea.

It was too bad, Patience thought. She had gone to all the trouble of preparing it, and Edie couldn't even be bothered to get home on time. She was probably idling her time away with her friends again, she decided.

She didn't want to admit it but she missed Edie when she wasn't there. Even though her constant chatter and singing drove Patience quite mad, the house seemed very quiet without her.

But Edie was strangely silent when she finally came home twenty minutes later. There were none of her usual smiles or bright greetings. There was no titbit of news, either. Of course, Patience had no time for gossip, but she did quite like to hear what was happening on the terrace, and Edie was a lot better at finding things out than Horace.

'And where have you been?' Disappointment made Patience's voice sharp as she followed Edie into her kitchen.

'I called in to see Dolly and Iris.'

'I thought so!' Patience tutted. 'Never mind that I've got your tea on the table.'

'I'm sorry.' Edie dumped the basket down on the kitchen table. She looked so thoroughly downcast, Patience wondered what on earth had happened to her.

'I thought you were collecting your pram on the way home?' she said.

'I left it at Dolly's.'

Patience felt a stab of disappointment. She had been looking forward to seeing it.

'Good thing too,' she huffed as she searched through the grocery basket. 'I certainly don't want some monstrous thing cluttering up my hall . . . Where are the split peas?'

'I forgot them,' Edie mumbled. She took off her coat, her back to Patience.

Patience sighed. 'And how am I supposed to make pease pudding for tea tomorrow without them?'

'I'll get them next time.'

'That's no good, is it? They need to soak.' She rummaged through the basket. 'And what's this? Stewing steak? How much did this cost, I wonder? Half my points, I daresay—'

She looked round. Edie still had her back to her, but she could see the girl's shoulders shaking.

'Are you crying?' she demanded.

'No,' Edie mumbled, shaking her head. But no sooner had she said the word than she burst into noisy sobbing.

Patience stared at her, taken aback. 'What on earth is the matter?' she said, but Edie only sobbed harder. 'Look, I didn't mean it,' Patience's voice was lost over the sound of her weeping. 'It doesn't really matter about the peas . . .'

'It – it's not that.' Edie rummaged in her pocket and pulled out a handkerchief. 'I've just had some – bad news, that's all.'

Fear washed over her, rooting her to the spot. 'What news?'

'The maternity home on Hedon Road has been bombed.' Edie turned red-rimmed, watery eyes to meet Patience's. 'I've just been down to the clinic on Coltman Street to find out what's going on. The midwife says they've evacuated all the mothers and locked the doors.'

'Gracious, was anyone hurt?'

'No.'

'Then why are you crying about it?' Patience stared at her, bemused by her hysterics. 'Good heavens, the way you're carrying on, I thought it was something dreadful.'

'It *is* dreadful.' Edie blew her nose noisily. 'I can't have my baby there.'

'Then you'll just have to have it somewhere else, won't you?'

Those words were enough to bring on more sobbing. Patience pressed her fingers to her ears, wincing at the sound.

'I can't,' Edie wept. 'According to the midwife I'd have to pay to go to a private maternity home.'

'And what's wrong with that?'

'The only one I could possibly afford is in Malton, and that's miles away. And I'd have to book in two weeks before the birth. I haven't got the money for that.'

Patience looked across the kitchen at her. They never discussed money, but she had the impression Edie Copeland did not have much of it to spare. Whenever she ventured upstairs, she usually found Edie making a feverish list of scrawled household income and expenses, trying over and over again to make the figures balance.

'And there's nowhere else you can go?' she asked.

'The midwife says I could have the baby at home. But only if I have family around to look after me.'

Patience sighed with relief. 'Well, there you are, then. You'll just have to go back to York.'

'I can't,' Edie sniffed, through her tears. 'My stepmother would never allow it.'

'It isn't a matter of what she will and will not allow. You are family, and she must help you.'

Edie shook her head. 'You don't know Rose. She'd never

help me. She hates me. And she doesn't count me as family, either.'

'That's absurd,' Patience dismissed. 'Of course she's your family. She married your father—'

'But she doesn't think of herself as my mother,' Edie said. 'She told me that when they wed. She said her sons needed a father, but I wasn't to get any ideas about her.'

'And how old were you?'

'Eight.'

Patience flinched. What a cruel thing to say to a young motherless child.

She was surprised at the sudden urge to hug poor Edie, but she turned away and finished unpacking her shopping basket to give herself a chance to pull herself together.

'The way I see it, you really have no choice,' she said. 'If you can't afford to pay for a maternity home, then you'll have to—'

'I could have the baby here.'

Patience stared at her. 'What?'

'I might be able to persuade the midwife to let me have the baby here, as long as she thought I had someone to help me?'

She looked at Patience, her expression full of appeal. It took Patience a moment to understand what she was saying. 'You want – me to look after you?' she said slowly.

'You wouldn't have to do anything,' Edie said. 'I wouldn't expect you to help me. Just as long as I could tell the midwife. Please?' she begged. 'You're my only hope.'

Patience looked around her neat, scrubbed kitchen. Edie had helped her so much since Horace was taken ill. She didn't know what she would have done without her.

But even so, it was such a lot to ask. She had spent too many years avoiding messy, difficult emotional situations to allow herself to get involved.

239

'I'm not sure,' she murmured. 'It's a great deal to think about—'

'I know.' She could almost feel Edie's despair and disappointment from across the room. The poor girl looked utterly bereft.

'Are you sure you can't go home? Perhaps if you talked to your father—'

'He won't talk to me.'

Patience remembered the letter. *Return To Sender.* The message could not have been more clear.

What kind of a parent turns their back on their child? she wondered. And then she remembered.

'I'll get your tea,' she said quietly.

Chapter Thirty-six

There was nothing wrong with her visiting Sam, Iris told herself. She was his friend. It was only natural she should call in and see how he was.

As she let herself in through the Scuttles' back gate, she wondered why she was even making excuses to herself. It was all Dolly's fault, she decided. Her foolish talk had made Iris feel all self-conscious about even speaking to him.

And it wasn't as if she was leading him on, or anything. She had made her feelings perfectly clear to Sam that night he had asked her out.

Beattie Scuttle must have been watching from the scullery window. She flung open the back door as Iris picked her way around the hulking mound of the Anderson shelter.

'Right eyesore, in't it?' She nodded towards the shelter. 'I'm sorry I ever asked our Sam to build it.'

'I'm sure it'll come in useful one day.'

'I doubt it.' Beattie shuddered. 'Nasty dark, damp thing, reminds me of a tomb.' She turned to Iris. 'What can I do for you? Have you come about the sugar?'

'Sugar?' Iris echoed, then she remembered. Big May had asked all their friends and neighbours to contribute some of their rations towards making Ada's wedding cake. She wanted the poor girl to have something special, since she'd been so disappointed over her dress.

'Only I haven't had a chance to collect my rations yet,' Beattie went on. 'I've been that preoccupied, what with our Sam being injured.'

'How is he?' Iris asked.

No sooner had she uttered the words than she heard Sam's voice coming from beyond the scullery curtain, followed by the sound of laughter.

A woman's laughter.

'Oh, he's well on the mend, as you can tell,' Beattie said. 'Mind, I think his visitor has helped put a smile on his face.' She leaned in confidingly. 'A young lady,' she whispered. 'Her name's Gwendoline and she's ever so posh.'

'Oh.' Iris was still taking in what she had heard when the scullery curtain twitched aside, and there was Sam.

'Hello,' he said. 'I thought I heard voices.'

Their eyes met and held, and Iris glanced away.

'I heard you'd been hurt?' she said.

'Aye.' He looked down at his bandaged arm. 'It in't too bad, though. Nothing, really.'

'Bad enough for them to send you to hospital,' Beattie put in.

Sam sighed. 'I was only there for five minutes, Ma.'

'Anyway, I won't keep you from your visitor,' Iris said.

'Come and meet her, if you like?'

'No, I don't think—' she started to say, but Sam had already called out,

'Gwen? There's someone I'd like you to meet.'

'Don't bring her in the kitchen, Sam!' Beattie hissed, but it was too late because Gwendoline was already there.

She was young, blonde and very pretty, dressed in a smart dark-blue uniform, not a hair out of place. Iris was painfully aware of the contrast between them – she in her old pinny and scuffed shoes, her hair in need of a curl.

'This is Gwendoline,' he said. 'We work together at the Fire Service.'

'I work on the telephone switchboard,' Gwendoline said. She reminded Iris of Ruby, with her firm, no-nonsense manner. Iris imagined she would be very calm in a crisis.

'This is Iris,' Sam finished the introduction. 'She's – an old friend.'

'Iris.' Gwendoline looked her up and down thoughtfully. 'I think Sam's mentioned you.'

He's never mentioned you, Iris thought, looking from her to Sam and back again.

'Well, it was nice meeting you, Iris. Now, I'm afraid I'm going to have to love you and leave you,' Gwendoline broke the tense silence.

'Do you have to go?' Beattie looked disappointed. 'I was just going to make a fresh pot of tea.'

'I'm sorry, Mrs Scuttle, but I'm due on duty at four.' Gwendoline turned to Sam. 'When are you back on duty?'

'Not until ten.'

'Well, you be careful. I don't want to pick up the telephone and hear you've been injured again. It gave me quite a scare, I can tell you.' She reached up and kissed him on the cheek.

It was nothing more than a slight peck, but it jolted Iris as if she had had an electric shock.

'Well, don't just stand there looking gormless,' Beattie said to her son. 'See your guest out. Out of the front,' she added, as Sam headed for the scullery door. 'We don't want Gwendoline traipsing across the back yard, do we? What will she think of us?'

No sooner had Sam and Gwendoline gone than Beattie turned to Iris, her beady eyes gleaming.

'Well?' she said. 'What do you think?'

'Of what?' Iris stared at her blankly.

'Those two, of course. Don't they make a grand couple?'

Iris looked towards the kitchen door. 'I suppose so.'

'She seems like such a nice girl, don't you think? And so well spoken.' She chuckled to herself. 'Can you imagine, my Sam courting a girl from Kirk Ella? Wait till your mother hears about it!'

She looked over her shoulder at Iris. 'I'm so pleased he's found a nice lass at last. I in't seen him this happy in a long time. It's about time he found someone who'll give him the love he deserves.'

There was no mistaking the look she gave Iris as she said it.

'I'd best be going,' she mumbled.

As Iris stepped out into the yard, Beattie suddenly said, 'You will be glad for him, won't you?'

Once again, Iris caught the look in her eyes. She knew a warning when she saw one.

'I am glad for him,' she said. 'Very glad.'

Chapter Thirty-seven

'And what did you tell her?' Horace asked.

Patience stared at her husband, sitting up in his hospital bed, lighting his pipe. He must be better if he could face smoking that wretched thing, she thought.

'I said I'd think about it.'

'And are you?'

She had been thinking about little else since her conversation with Edie two days earlier. She was desperate to discuss it with Horace. With him in hospital, it made Patience realise how much she relied on his sound advice.

Even if she did choose to ignore it a great deal of the time.

She had fidgeted her way through the first half hour of their weekly hospital visit, desperate for Edie to leave them alone. Finally, thankfully, she had taken herself off for a walk to give them some time together.

'What do *you* think about it?' she asked.

'Well . . .' Her husband leaned back against the pillows and puffed on his pipe. 'To be honest, I'm surprised you're even considering it.'

'I'm not,' Patience replied, a little too quickly. 'Of course there's no question of her having this baby at our house. It's a dreadful idea.'

Horace said nothing, but he watched her thoughtfully through a cloud of pipe smoke.

'But something must be done,' Patience said. 'Her family

should be looking after her, not us. But Ed— Mrs Copeland – refuses to have anything to do with them.' She paused. 'I've a good mind to write to them myself,' she said.

'You haven't got their address.'

Patience looked down at her hands, folded neatly in her lap. 'A letter came, a couple of months ago,' she said. 'She had sent it to her father but it had been returned. I may have made a note of the address. But only because I thought we might need it,' she added quickly, seeing her husband's narrow-eyed look. 'And I was right, wasn't I?'

Horace shook his head. 'I wouldn't go doing anything hasty,' he said. 'You've said yourself, it's none of our business.'

'Which is precisely why we should tell them,' Patience said. 'Otherwise this will all end up on our shoulders.'

'But if Edie doesn't want them involved—'

'They are involved, whether they like it or not!'

Horace sent her a considering look. 'I'm surprised at you, Patience,' he said. 'I would have thought you were the last person to go interfering.'

'I'm not interfering!' Patience bristled. 'I just want to help, that's all. For my own sake, no one else's,' she added quickly.

Horace's mouth twisted. 'And there was me, thinking you had a soft spot for Edie Copeland.'

'I most certainly do not!'

The bell rang to mark the end of visiting time. As Patience stood up and began to gather her belongings, Horace reached for her hand and said, 'Promise me you won't write to Edie's family?'

'But—'

'Promise me, Patience.'

She looked down at his fingers laced in hers. 'I promise I won't write to them,' she said solemnly.

* * *

They were both quiet on the journey home. Patience spent most of her time gazing out of the window, deep in thought. Edie longed to ask her again about her giving birth at Jubilee Row, then decided against it. Patience Huggins was not the kind of woman to take kindly to being pushed.

Edie only hoped she would decide to help her. She was desperate. It was only a matter of weeks before her baby was due, and she had nowhere to give birth.

She had thought about lying to the midwife and telling her she could give birth at home, but she knew Nurse Shepherd would come round to check. Even if Patience Huggins agreed to help her, she wasn't sure if that would be good enough for the midwife, or if she would insist that it had to be kept in the family.

But she could never ask Rose. She couldn't face being rejected by her family all over again.

Besides, she had already made up her mind that she never wanted Rose anywhere near her baby. He or she would grow up surrounded by love, not resentment and jealousy.

When they arrived home, Edie headed for the stairs but Patience said, 'Wait. I have something for you.'

She left Edie in the hall and went into the bedroom, closing the door behind her. Moments later she returned holding a small parcel wrapped in yellowing tissue paper.

'Just some bits for the baby,' she said. 'They're a bit old, but they've never been worn. I've given them a wash, made sure the moths haven't got to them.'

Edie carefully peeled back the tissue paper. There, nestled within, was a set of the most exquisite hand-knitted baby clothes – a white lacy matinee jacket, rompers and tiny bootees trimmed with delicate white ribbon.

'They're beautiful,' she breathed.

'They were meant for my grandson.'

Edie looked at Patience. Her face was impassive, but there was no mistaking the emotion in her voice.

'Anyway, I thought you might as well have them,' she said briskly. 'They've been sitting in the top of the wardrobe, cluttering up the place for too long.'

'Thank you.' Edie smoothed her hand over the soft white wool. 'I'll take good care of them.'

As Patience went to close the door, Edie said, 'Why didn't you give them to your grandson?'

Patience blushed to the roots of her tightly drawn bun. 'I did,' she said. 'But they were returned.'

'Joyce gave them back to you?'

'No, she sent *him* to do it.' Patience's mouth tightened. 'He said she wanted nothing from me.'

'I'm sorry.'

'Don't be.' Patience's chin lifted. 'At least I knew where I stood.'

She closed the door on Edie before she could say another word.

Chapter Thirty-eight

As soon as May Maguire took down the blackouts from the window and saw the thick pall of fog shrouding the rooftops of the houses opposite, she understood exactly what it meant.

Her granddaughter knew it too. All morning, Ada kept a desperate, silent vigil by the window, her nose pressed against the glass, staring out at the fog.

'I think it's lifting,' she would say.

'It will be,' May would reply, but deep down she had her misgivings. All trawlermen's wives knew about the weather. Especially when their men were due home from sea. And this dense fog was not the kind to disappear easily. It blotted out the sun, smothering the docks in a thick, damp blanket. By early evening it was still there, hanging over the back yard in thick wisps.

May went to bed that night with a heavy heart. She lay awake most of the night, praying that the *Venus* would come home. Not just for Ada's sake. She couldn't bear to think of her sons stuck out there in the estuary. What if the fog lifted and the Germans launched another air raid? The *Venus* would be a sitting target, bobbing out there at anchor while bombers buzzed overhead.

Please let them come home, she prayed, her lips moving silently in the darkness. *Please let them be safe.*

Just before dawn on the morning of her wedding, Ada put on her coat and went down to the docks while May went across the road to wait for news with Ruby and the twins. As time went by, Beattie, Edie, Iris and Dolly joined them. Dolly looked especially anxious, as she was looking forward to seeing her husband Jack again.

As soon as she walked in the back door, May knew from Ada's distraught face that it was bad news.

'The *Venus* has missed the tide,' she said in a choked voice. 'He in't coming home.'

Straight away, they all rallied round to try to comfort her.

'I'm sorry, love,' May said. 'But it will be all right, I promise.'

'You can still get married. You'll just have to put it off, that's all,' Iris said.

'They'll be home by this evening,' Dolly added.

Iris nudged her sharply. 'What did you say that for? It'll be too late by then!'

'You're the one telling her she'll have to put it off!' Dolly hissed back.

All the while, Ada said nothing. There was an unnatural calm about her, as if she had shut down completely.

'She's in shock,' Beattie whispered. 'Hot sweet tea is what she needs.'

May made a pot of tea and added two spoons of saccharine to Ada's cup for good measure. But Ada did not touch it. She sat at the kitchen table, staring down at the engagement ring on her left hand.

'We should fetch the brandy,' her sister Sybil whispered, then added, 'Happen we should all have some, just to be on the safe side?'

'We're not all sitting here supping brandy in the middle of the day—' Ruby started to say, but then suddenly Ada stood up, scraping her chair back across the wooden floor.

'I'm going upstairs,' she announced.

'Good idea, love,' Ruby said. 'You go and have a lie down. You'll feel better for it.'

Ada trudged upstairs, and they all congregated around Ruby's kitchen table to talk about what was to be done.

Not that there was much that could be done. Trawlermen had always been slaves to the sea and the weather. Big May knew of several brides who had had their weddings postponed two or three times because their men had missed the tide.

'She's been up there a long time,' Ruby said anxiously, after an hour had passed. 'I hope she's all right.'

'She's probably having a good cry, poor thing,' Iris said.

'It must be awful for her,' Dolly said. 'What a thing to happen on your wedding day.'

'It's a shame,' Beattie agreed with a sigh. 'And after you've gone to so much trouble making that cake, Ruby.' She paused for the briefest second. 'What will happen to it, do you think?'

'Don't worry, Beattie, I daresay you'll get your share,' May snapped. Beattie's cheeks reddened.

'I'm sure I didn't mean—'

'Listen!' Ruby shushed her, looking up at the ceiling. 'I think I can hear her coming down the stairs.'

They all jostled around, trying to compose themselves, as the kitchen door opened and there stood Ada, a vision in her beautiful white wedding dress. Her dark hair fell in thick, glossy waves around her pale face.

'Well?' she said. 'How do I look?'

They all exchanged anxious looks. For a moment none of them spoke.

'Oh, Ada,' Iris managed at last. 'You look a picture, love.'

Ada gave them a tremulous smile. 'Is it really all right?'

'It's beautiful.'

'But what's it in aid of?' May asked the question no one else could bring themselves to utter.

Ada stared at her. 'I'm getting married, or have you forgotten that?'

May glanced at Ruby. She shook her head, puzzled.

'She's gone mad,' Beattie muttered. 'The shock has turned her brain.'

Ruby crossed the kitchen to her daughter, reaching for her hands. 'Don't you remember, ducks?' she said gently. 'Peter's ship—'

'—missed the tide. Yes, I know. I'm not daft. But I know my Peter. He won't let me down. He won't miss our wedding day.'

'Yes, but how can he get to shore when—'

'I don't know, do I?' Ada cut her off. 'I don't know how he'll do it, but I know he'll find a way. He'll be there, I know he will.' She looked around at the others, her face oddly calm.

They all fell silent. Perhaps Beattie was right, May thought. The shock had made Ada take leave of her senses.

'Happen we should have a think about this, lass—' she started to say, but Ada shook her head.

'I know what you're all thinking,' she said, looking round at them. 'But Peter won't let me down. He'll find a way, I'm sure of it.' She lifted her chin. 'And I'm going to be there waiting for him, even if I have to do it on my own.'

They all fell silent. May looked at her granddaughter, standing there so proud in her beautiful wedding dress, and tears pricked her eyes.

'You won't be on your own,' she said. 'We'll be there with you. We Maguires stick together, no matter what. In't that right?'

She looked around at the other women, daring them to disagree. No one did.

Chapter Thirty-nine

'You're still going to this wedding, then?' Reg said.

Joyce tucked a lock of hair behind her ear, fastening it in place with a pin. 'Yes,' she said. 'Why shouldn't I?'

'I'm just surprised you'd want to face the Maguires again, after what happened,' Reg muttered.

That wasn't my fault, was it? Joyce glanced at Reg in the mirror as she took out her compact to powder her face.

'Ada was all right about it when I spoke to her. She said she wanted me at the wedding.'

'And you believed her, did you?' Reg gave a pitying shake of his head. 'She was just being polite, Joyce. You're probably the last person she wants at her wedding. And as for the rest of the Maguires . . .' He smirked as he put on his collar, fiddling with the studs. 'I daresay Big May's made sure your name's mud at that WVS place.'

Joyce gazed back at her stricken reflection. Reg was probably right, she thought. She suddenly pictured herself approaching the church, seeing the sullen faces of the WVS women staring back at her, their whispers following her . . .

'We could always just forget all about this wedding and stay at home?' Reg's voice insinuated itself into her ear.

It would be so easy to stay at home. She could change her best dress for her comfortable overall and go downstairs to the shop. She was safe behind the counter, among the brooms and the washboards and the boxes of nails. It was where she belonged, and she was a fool for thinking it could ever be different.

And yet . . .

She remembered the laughter and the warmth of the women at the WVS centre. The way they had welcomed her, sought her advice, listened to her. For a while she had truly felt as if she belonged somewhere.

'I think I will go,' she said.

Reg's smile disappeared. He dropped a collar stud and cursed under his breath. 'If you must,' he muttered. 'Although I can't say I'm happy about shutting up the shop. Saturday morning's a busy time for us.'

'You don't have to come.'

'And what kind of a husband would I be if I let you go by yourself?' He shook his head. 'Oh, I'm coming, all right. Besides,' he grinned, 'I in't missing the chance to sup at someone else's expense. If Jimmy Maguire is fool enough to pay for my food and drink, then I in't going to be fool enough to miss out!'

He went off, laughing at his own joke. Joyce peered at her reflection. The thick powder only seemed to emphasise her pallid, tired face.

It was going to be a long day, she thought.

Joyce's nerve began to fail her as they approached the church and she saw the women from the WVS all gathered outside, their heads together.

'Just ignore them,' Reg whispered, linking his arm through hers. 'Walk straight past and don't say a word.'

Joyce took a deep breath, her legs suddenly unsteady. She did her best to lift her chin and keep her gaze fixed ahead, but as she went to walk past, one of them suddenly called out to her, 'Joyce?'

She turned around slowly. Wyn Johnson was standing with the other women, all staring at her.

'We didn't expect to see you here,' she said.

Joyce steeled herself. *Here it comes*, she thought.

Then, to her amazement, a smile spread across Wyn's face. 'It's grand to see you, Joyce.'

'We've missed you at the WVS,' her friend Maggie joined in. 'No one knows what to do with all those second-hand clothes without you there!'

Joyce looked from one to the other in amazement. All the women looked so pleased to see her.

'I – I've missed you all too,' she said, and felt Reg's hand tighten proprietorially on her arm.

'When are you coming back?' Wyn asked.

'I—' Joyce opened her mouth to speak but Reg got there before her.

'My wife has got better things to do with her time than sit around, drinking tea and gossiping,' he snapped.

An embarrassed silence fell. Joyce dropped her gaze, too mortified to look at the others.

Another woman, Alice Peachey, spoke up, changing the subject.

'I wonder what's keeping everyone?' she said.

'I'm surprised the Maguires aren't here yet.'

'Never mind them,' Wyn said. 'Where's the bridegroom?'

Maggie nodded past them, down the street. 'Here's Beattie Scuttle. Happen she knows something.'

They all turned round to see Beattie trundling up the street, wearing her old coat topped off by an extravagant feathered hat. Charlie loped along beside her in an ill-fitting Sunday-best suit. They made an odd pair, Charlie so tall and lanky beside his tiny, sparrow-like mother.

'Now then, Beattie,' Wyn greeted her. 'What's to do?'

'You might well ask.' Beattie's expression was grim. 'It doesn't look like there'll be a wedding today.'

They listened in horror as Beattie explained what had happened.

'So they're stuck out there in the estuary until the tide comes in?' Wyn said.

'They've got lifeboats, haven't they?' Maggie asked. 'They're small enough to get through the shallows. Can't they come in on one of them?'

They all looked at each other uneasily. 'And what will happen to the rest of the crew if there's an air raid while they're stuck out there?' Wyn voiced the thought that none of them wanted to utter. 'They daren't take the lifeboat.'

Beattie cleared her throat. 'Anyway, my Sam's gone down to the docks to see what can be done,' she said. 'But I shouldn't think he'll be able to help.'

'Poor Ada,' Joyce said. 'She must be in a terrible state.'

'Well, that's the funny thing,' Beattie replied. 'She's as calm as anything. She reckons she's getting married today, come what may.'

They all looked at each other. 'It'll be the shock,' Wyn said.

Beattie nodded. 'That's what I said.'

'Well, that's that, then,' Reg whispered to Joyce. 'We might as well go home.'

'May says we're to wait here,' Beattie said. 'She says Ada wants to come to church, and they're coming with her.'

'But what if she gets left standing at the altar?' Maggie looked horrified.

Beattie shrugged. 'It's what Ada wants, and May reckons we should all back her up.'

'In that case, I'm definitely staying,' Wyn looked around at the other women. They all nodded back.

'Well, we won't be staying,' Reg said. 'Come on, Joyce.'

She looked around at the other women. 'I'd like to stay, too, if that's all right?'

His eyes met hers, and Joyce saw his pupils shrink with anger.

'If that's what you want,' he said in a clipped voice. 'But it'll be a waste of time.'

Inside the church, the other women all headed down to the front pews, but Reg insisted on sitting at the back. His fingers closed painfully around her wrist like a vice.

'What do you think you're doing, showing me up in front of those women?' he snarled, dragging her into the seat behind him.

'I'm sorry, Reg.'

'Do it again and you will be!'

The church pews gradually filled up, but the front two pews on the bride's side remained conspicuously empty. All around them, people began to whisper and shift in their seats, wondering what was going to happen next. From time to time someone would get up and go outside, only to return a few minutes later with nothing to report.

Then suddenly, the church doors creaked open and some-one shouted, 'Here comes the bride!'

'But where's the groom?' someone else called back.

'He's all at sea!' another said, and everyone laughed.

But the laughter stopped when Big May Maguire strode in, followed by her husband and the rest of the family, all dressed in their finery. Ruby Maguire followed her mother-in-law, with Florence, Iris and Dolly bringing up the rear. Dolly and Iris were both dressed to the nines, their hair fashionably rolled and faces made up. One of them pushed a pram down the aisle, while the other ushered a small army of noisy children. Edie Copeland was with them, heavily pregnant in a pink dress. There was something familiar about that dress, Joyce thought. But she couldn't imagine where she might have seen it before.

May took her seat in the front pew, looking around her with an expression of pride and defiance, her dark eyes flashing, daring anyone to challenge her.

Pop Maguire made his way to the front of the church and turned around to address the congregation.

'Ladies and gentlemen, thank you for coming,' his voice rattled around the high rafters of the church. 'As you probably know, we've had a bit of a mishap—'

'Time and tide wait for no man!' someone called out from the congregation.

Pop grinned and said, 'You're right there. Anyway, we seem to be missing a bridegroom at the moment, but the bride has decided she wants to wait for him, so if you wouldn't mind waiting a while—'

'To think I shut up shop for this,' Reg said loudly.

May swung round and aimed a dirty look at him. 'You can go home whenever you want, Reg Shelby!'

'I've a good mind to do just that!'

Joyce closed her eyes. *Please make him stop,* she prayed. *Don't let him humiliate me.*

At that moment the church doors opened again and a cheery voice called out, 'Sorry we're late!'

Two men stood in the doorway, dressed in shabby fishermen's jerseys and thick oilskin trousers. A grinning Jimmy Maguire stood beside a nervous-looking young man who Joyce guessed must be Ada's intended, Peter.

Joyce watched as Jimmy Maguire made his way to the front of the church where Ruby was waiting for him. She saw the affectionate smile that passed between them, the way their hands touched, and her heart ached. What must it be like to know a love like that, she wondered.

'How did you get here?' Pop asked.

'And where's my Sam?' Beattie said, looking around.

'He'll be along shortly, Mrs Scuttle. He's just getting changed,' Jimmy grinned at her. 'We thought we'd best come straight here. Don't want to keep our Ada waiting any longer than we already have, do we?'

There was a hurried conference between the Maguires, then Pop returned to the front of the church and announced, 'Well, I'm pleased to say the groom and the bride's father have both turned up, so if you'll all take your seats, the bride is waiting outside. And I don't know about you, but I'm looking forward to a well-earned pint when all this is over!'

'Hear, hear!' someone called out.

'Thank the Lord,' Joyce whispered, as the organ struck up with the opening bars of 'Here Comes The Bride' and everyone got to their feet.

Reg glared at her but said nothing.

Chapter Forty

Jubilee Row was deserted when Patience set off that morning. She had watched from her window as the neighbours set off for Ada Maguire's wedding, followed finally by a parade of the Maguire family, all in their finery, and the bride herself, sitting atop her grandfather's rully. Even the old cart horse was dressed up, its mane plaited with colourful ribbon.

'You could come with me?' Edie had offered as she straightened her hat in the hall mirror.

'But I haven't been invited,' Patience said.

'That doesn't matter. I'm sure the Maguires wouldn't mind.'

Patience bristled at the impropriety of it all. To her mind, invitations were formal, with copperplate engraving and thick vellum envelopes. They were delivered by the butler on a silver tray every morning, displayed on the mantelpiece and taken very seriously indeed. All this free-for-all, come-as-you-are business did not sit well with her at all.

She shook her head. 'I have other plans,' she said.

Edie looked over her shoulder at her. 'What kind of plans? Are you going somewhere?'

'I might,' Patience said. 'I haven't decided yet.'

Edie looked pleased. 'I'm glad you're getting out and about.'

Patience sent her a sideways glance. Edie might not be so pleased if she knew where she was going, she thought.

She had promised Horace she would not write to Rose,

and she had kept to it. But he hadn't said anything to her about not visiting her in person.

She had lain awake for several nights, wondering if she was doing the right thing. Horace was wrong, she thought; it was their business. Edie had made it her business when she asked for her help. And unless she could convince Edie's stepmother to do the right thing and take on the responsibility, it would continue to weigh on Patience's mind.

But when the time came for her to leave, Patience began to have doubts. What was she thinking, imagining she could go all the way to York on her own? Going on the tram into Hull a couple of times with Edie was one thing, but finding her way to the station and catching a train all the way to York was quite another. It would be a big undertaking for anyone, let alone someone who had never ventured further than her own back yard for twenty years.

Every time she pictured herself at the crowded station, being jostled about by a seething mass of people, she felt sick.

She tried to push her doubts from her mind as she prepared to leave. But as she opened the front door the cold November air hit her in the face, stopping her in her tracks.

She couldn't do it. She couldn't.

She paused for a moment, looking up into the sky. The fog was beginning to lift, but the sky was still heavy and dark as lead. It might even rain later. Damp weather always made her bones ache. What if it brought on her lumbago? What if she caught a chill?

And what if there was an air raid while she was away, and she got caught? She wouldn't know where to go, or what to do. She wouldn't be able to find her way to a shelter. She would be stuck, at the mercy of strangers. She might panic, have one of her turns . . .

What if. What if. What if.

She dithered on the front step. Why should she put herself through all this misery, anyway? It wasn't really her problem where Edie had her baby. She certainly didn't have to get involved. She was far better off staying indoors, where it was warm and safe and comfortable . . .

She stepped outside and slammed the front door behind her before she had a chance to think any more about it.

On the tram, Patience sat staring out of the window, her face averted from the other passengers, clutching her gas mask in its cardboard case to her chest. She missed Edie's calming presence beside her, chattering away as she usually did.

Go home, the voice in her head whispered. *Stay indoors, where you're safe.*

'Oh, be quiet!' Patience hadn't realised she had spoken the words out loud until she saw the look of dismay on the faces of the two women gossiping opposite.

Paragon Station was as busy as she had feared it would be. For a moment, she could only stand rooted to the spot, overwhelmed by the sights, sounds and smells. Belching black steam, the acrid smell of burning coal, the shriek of a guard's whistle, the soldiers gathered around a WVS mobile canteen, the endless people hurrying past, nearly knocking her off her feet.

She finally forced herself to walk to the ticket office and buy a ticket. The train was already waiting at the platform, and Patience got into the first carriage without thinking. It was full of soldiers, smoking and laughing and larking about, as if they didn't have a care in the world. The carriage was filled with the smell of their cigarettes and damp wool uniforms. They were just boys, Patience thought, watching them.

'It's nice to see 'em having fun, eh?' the woman opposite

looked up from her knitting and smiled. 'They've not had a lot to laugh about lately, I daresay.'

'No,' Patience said. 'No, I suppose not.'

She turned her face towards the window, but the woman seemed to want to make conversation.

'It's a scarf, for my son. He's away on the minesweepers up in the Arctic Circle.' She held up her knitting for Patience to admire.

'Oh. It – it's very nice.' Patience was not sure she approved of knitting in public, but everyone seemed to do it these days, she had noticed.

'Do you have any lads serving?'

Patience opened her mouth to say no, then she remembered Alan.

'I have a grandson.' It felt strange to say the word aloud.

'How old is he?'

'Eighteen.'

'In the Navy, is he?'

'The Army.'

'You must be very proud of him.'

Patience looked down at her hands in her lap, not sure how to answer her. How could she be proud of a young man she had never met?

York was bathed in wintry sunshine. Patience had not visited the city since she was a young woman, and she had forgotten how beautiful it was. She gazed out of the taxi window as they skirted the city wall, admiring the ancient gates with their impressive crests and portcullises and statues, giving way to narrow, cobbled streets beyond. And then there was the majestic Minster towering over it all, its windows glittering in the light.

The taxi headed out of the city, and soon in the distance Patience could see the Rowntrees works. It was like a small town in itself, with a wide, tree-lined avenue leading from the main gates to a cluster of large red-brick buildings. Edie had told her she worked at the Card Box Mill, fashioning fancy boxes for chocolates and trimming them with various ribbons and tassels. Until the Army took it over at the start of the war for a supply depot, and she was moved to filling fuses in the gum block extension.

Patience smiled to herself, surprised at how much she knew about Edie Copeland. Who would ever have believed, when Edie arrived five months ago, that Patience would ever give her the time of day, let alone find herself travelling alone to a strange city for her sake?

She could scarcely credit it herself and yet here she was, in the back of a taxi, going off to meet a woman she had never even seen before. Life was full of surprises, she thought.

But she reminded herself she wasn't doing this for Edie's sake; she was doing it for her own. She had no doubt that this Rose was a sensible woman, and that once Patience had sat down and had a proper conversation with her, she would see sense and make peace with her stepdaughter. She was family, after all.

And what about you making peace with your own daughter? a small voice whispered in the back of her mind. Patience pushed the thought away determinedly.

The taxi turned into White Cross Road and Patience asked the driver to stop on the corner. She didn't want Rose to get the wrong idea, seeing her swanning up in a cab. Besides, she wanted some time to gather her thoughts before they came face to face.

Her first impressions of the street were very favourable. It was a well-kept terrace of respectable houses, with neat front gardens and bay windows. Rose's house was particularly impressive, with fresh paintwork and spotless net curtains.

Patience nodded with approval. She could tell she and Rose had similar standards, which was a good sign.

The young man who answered the door was also very well turned out. He was about fifteen years old, tall and fair-haired.

'Yes?' He smiled politely at her. Such a well-spoken boy, she thought. And such clean hands, too.

'May I speak to your mother?'

'Who is it?' A voice came from inside the house. A moment later a woman appeared.

Patience's first thought was that she was far too young to be Edie's stepmother, or the boy's mother for that matter. She was no older than mid thirties, attractive in a brittle kind of way, although none of her beauty seemed natural. Her lips were painted, her cheeks were rouged and those stiff platinum blonde waves could only have come from a bottle.

'What do you want?' Her rough accent was nowhere near as well-spoken as her son's. 'If you're collecting for charity we in't interested—'

'I haven't come collecting,' Patience said quickly. 'It's about your daughter.'

Rose's face hardened. 'You've got the wrong house, Missus. I in't got a daughter.'

She started to close the door but Patience put a hand out to stop her. 'Your stepdaughter. Edie?'

Rose looked Patience up and down with hostile eyes.

'She's nowt to do with me.'

'I share a house with her, and—'

'Well, that's your bad luck, in't it?'

The door slammed in her face. Patience stood on the doorstep, staring at her shocked reflection in the polished brass knocker. She had thought about this meeting endlessly, picturing it over and over in her mind, but never once had she imagined that this would happen.

She knocked on the door again. There was no answer.

'Mrs Russell, I want to talk to you,' she called through the door.

'Well, I don't want to talk to you,' came the muffled voice from inside.

'But I've come all the way from Hull ...'

'And you can go straight back there.'

Patience blinked. She had never had a door slammed in her face before, and she did not care for it at all. As far as she was concerned, it was the height of bad manners.

She rapped on the door again, louder this time. There was no reply.

She bent down and lifted the letterbox to peer through. The passage was empty. Patience straightened up and adjusted her hat, squaring it up on her head.

'Mrs Russell, I've come a long way and I have no intention of going home until I've said my piece,' she called through. 'Now, you can either open the door and we'll discuss it, or I'll stand out here and shout your business for all to hear ...'

Footsteps thudded down the hall and the door suddenly flew open. Rose stood there, bristling with rage.

'All right, what's she done now?' she demanded.

'If I could come in—' Patience started to say, but Rose held up her hand.

'We'll talk here,' she said flatly. 'So come on, then. What's she done that's so terrible it's brought you all this way?'

'What makes you think she's done anything?' Patience asked.

'Because she's wicked. She's got bad blood, I could see that right from the minute I laid eyes on her. Sneaky, devious little cow.'

Patience stared at Rose, shocked. She had the coldest blue

eyes she had ever seen. 'What a horrible thing to say about a child.'

'You don't know her, do you?' Rose folded her arms across her chest. 'Go on, then. I'm listening. But I'm warning you now, whatever trouble she's in, it's no concern of mine. I told her that the last time I saw her.'

'Was that when you threw her out of the house?'

Rose's face twitched. 'She told you that, did she? I daresay she was giving you some old sob story, trying to make you feel sorry for her. She's good at turning things round, making out she's so hard done by. God knows, she tried it with her father often enough. Had him twisted right round her finger until I put a stop to it.' She lifted her chin. 'Well, I won't deny it. But I did it for my family.'

'She is your family—'

'She's no family of mine! Look, this is a decent house. My sons are brought up well, they go to the grammar school, they've got nice friends. Do you think I'm going to ruin all our lives by bringing a little bastard in here?' She shook her head. 'As I said to her father, it's best for everyone if she just gets rid of it. But no, she had to do things her way as usual, never mind how much trouble she causes—'

But Patience was no longer listening.

'I – I don't understand,' she said. 'How can the baby be a—' She stopped herself, unable to say the word. 'She was married. Her husband was killed at Dunkirk . . .'

'Is that what she told you?' A slow, malicious smile spread across Rose's face. 'Happen you'd best come in after all, Missus,' she said. 'Then I can tell you the whole story . . .'

267

Chapter Forty-one

'Well,' Dolly laughed, 'I don't think anyone in 'Road is going to forget this wedding in a hurry, do you?'

'I reckon you're right, Doll,' Iris agreed.

The reception was in full swing at the Somerset Street Social Club. Her sister-in-law Ruby had somehow managed to put on a full spread of sandwiches and sausage rolls, with a proper fruit cake as the centrepiece, albeit decorated with chocolate and crystallised fruit rather than white icing. Typically, her brother Jimmy seemed to have invited the whole of the fish docks to celebrate his daughter's wedding, and the hall was filled with music, laughter and dancing.

But all anyone could really talk about was Sam Scuttle, and how he had rowed out into the foggy estuary to rescue the stranded bridegroom and save Ada's wedding. Everyone was hailing him as a hero and buying him drinks, especially Jimmy Maguire, who had also hitched a lift in the rowing boat.

'Mind, I in't happy about him leaving my Jack behind,' Dolly went on, as she and Iris sat beside the dance floor with Edie Copeland, nursing their drinks and watching the dancing couples spinning past them. Iris had one hand on Kitty's pram, which she rocked back and forth as she sat. The boys and Lucy were outside, playing in the street.

'He's the skipper,' Iris reminded her. 'He couldn't very well leave his own vessel, could he?'

'I suppose not.' Dolly sighed. 'Still, he would have loved this. My Jack always enjoys a good party.'

'I'm sure he'll be here as soon as he can,' Iris said.

'I know.' Dolly sent her a wry smile. 'Look at us, a pair of proper wallflowers. I remember a time when you couldn't keep us off the dance floor.'

'It's all I can do to walk these days, let alone dance!' Edie said, rubbing her swollen belly.

Iris looked at her sympathetically. 'Playing you up, is he?'

'It's my back that's playing me up. Been killing me all day, it has.'

'Sounds as if it won't be too long now,' Dolly said.

Edie shook her head. 'He in't due for another three weeks.'

Iris caught the knowing look Dolly sent her. After five children between them, they both knew better than to take any notice of due dates and calendars.

'He'll come when he's ready,' Dolly said. 'In't that right, Iris?'

Just at that moment Sam Scuttle came dancing past with Gwendoline in his arms. She was smiling up at him adoringly, her fair hair flying as he swung her round.

'Have you seen that?' Dolly nudged Iris sharply in the ribs. 'Who's she, I wonder?'

'Her name's Gwendoline,' Iris said. 'They work together.'

Dolly gawped at her. 'How do you know that?'

'I met her a while ago.'

'You never said.'

'Didn't I? Happen it slipped my mind.'

Iris ignored the glance that passed between Dolly and Edie. She knew exactly what her friend was thinking, and she wanted none of it.

'I thought he only had eyes for you,' Dolly said.

Iris had just opened her mouth to reply when the music

stopped and Sam and Gwendoline came over, arm in arm. Gwendoline looked even prettier in her party dress than she did in uniform, her face flushed from dancing.

'Your ears must be burning, Sam Scuttle,' Dolly said. 'We were just talking about you. Weren't we, Iris?'

Once again, Iris ignored her friend's pointed gaze.

'All good, I hope?' Sam said.

'We were saying what a hero you were, saving the wedding,' Dolly said.

Gwendoline simpered. 'Everyone keeps telling him that. He'll get a big head if he's not careful!' She stroked his arm.

'Well, I think he was a fool,' Iris said.

They all turned to look at her. Gwendoline's smile faded.

'Iris!' Dolly scolded. 'Don't be like that.'

'I'm just speaking as I find. I think he was daft to risk his life going out there in the fog.'

'I wasn't risking my life,' Sam said. 'I know every inch of that estuary blindfold.'

'You could have been killed.'

'I didn't know you cared.'

For a moment they stared at each other. Iris could feel the others shifting awkwardly around her, but she couldn't seem to tear her eyes away from Sam's.

'Is this your baby?' Gwendoline broke the spell, looking into the pram. 'She's adorable. What's her name?'

'Kitty.'

'How old is she?'

'Just turned a year.'

'I love babies,' Gwendoline sighed. 'I'd like a big family one day. Do you like children, Sam?'

'Aye.'

'He's been very good with Iris' bains since their father died,' Dolly put in. 'In't that right, Sam?'

270

'Oh!' Gwendoline turned to Iris. 'I didn't realise you were a widow.'

'Her husband's been dead nearly a year,' Dolly answered for her.

'I'm sorry to hear that.' Gwendoline looked from Iris to Sam and back again. 'Sam didn't say.'

There was an awkward silence. Then Sam stirred himself and said, 'Do you fancy another dance, Gwen?'

'Why not?' Gwendoline smiled up at him, but her smile was not quite as warm as it had been. She looked quite thoughtful as Sam led her back on to the dance floor.

'She seems like a nice girl,' Edie commented as they watched her go.

'She is,' Iris said. 'Very nice.'

Dolly turned on her. 'I hope you're happy with yourself, Iris Fletcher!'

Iris stared at her blankly. 'What are you on about?'

'Him!' Dolly jabbed her finger towards the dance floor. 'That could have been you, if you'd played your cards right.'

Iris sighed. 'Don't start that again—'

'I mean it. Sam Scuttle is a good man, one of the best. And he was yours for the taking, if only you'd had the good sense to snap him up while you had the chance. But no, you didn't, did you? You had to go moping around, making out you weren't interested!'

'I'm not—'

'Don't give me that! I'm your best friend, I know when you're lying.'

Do you? Iris bit back the retort. 'You don't know how I feel,' she muttered.

'I don't think this is the time or the place—' Edie started to say, but Dolly was having none of it.

'You like Sam,' Dolly said. 'You've always liked him, you

just won't admit it to yourself because you're frightened you might be betraying your Arthur if you're happy again.'

'Don't,' Iris warned.

'Dolly, please,' Edie begged. 'You don't understand what it's like to lose someone—'

'I know grieving and being miserable won't bring him back,' Dolly said.

Iris looked at her friend and something inside her snapped. Dolly was so sure of herself, thought she had all the answers. But she knew nothing about it. She knew nothing about the secret heartache she had kept to herself for all these years.

'You think that's what I want?' she said. 'To bring him back?' She laughed, a harsh, bitter sound. 'You think no man will ever match up to Arthur Fletcher?'

Dolly shot a worried look at Edie. 'I – I don't understand—'

'No, you don't,' Iris said. She knew she should keep silent, but somehow she could not hold back the words any more. 'You don't understand anything about me, Dolly Maguire. You think I don't want to marry again because I might not find a man like my Arthur? Well, I'll tell you something, shall I? The real reason I don't want to marry is because I'm scared I *will* end up with someone exactly like him. And believe me, the last thing I need is another lying, cheating swine like Arthur Fletcher!'

Chapter Forty-two

'I always knew he was a charmer,' Iris said. 'That's what caught my eye in the first place. You know what he was like, the way he could be,' she turned to Dolly.

Her friend nodded. 'He was a flirt, that's for sure. But you were the one who tamed him.'

'That's what I thought, too,' Iris said sadly.

She knew she was the envy of the Hessle Road girls when she wed Arthur Fletcher. He was a popular young man among the lasses on the docks, in the netting lofts and the filleting sheds. Even on her wedding day, her mother had said to her, 'You'd do well to keep your eye on that one.'

At the time, Iris had laughed off her mother's advice. She knew Arthur's reputation with the girls, but she was the one he had chosen to marry. She was the one he truly loved.

Or so she had believed.

'I'm sure he thought he could change,' she said to Edie and Dolly. 'I like to think when he stood in that church and made his vows before God, he meant to keep them. And he did, at first. We set up home, and then Archie was born, and I thought I must be the luckiest girl on earth.'

'And then what happened?' Dolly asked.

Iris turned to look at her. 'And then I found out he'd fathered a child by another woman.'

Dolly gasped. Edie stared at her, eyes wide with horror.

'How did you find out?' Dolly wanted to know.

'She came and told me. She reckoned it was only right I should know what my husband had been doing.'

'But how did you know she was telling the truth?'

'Oh, I knew all right.'

It was just after their son Archie was born. Arthur was so proud and pleased with his new son at first, but the novelty of being a father soon wore off as Iris became lost in a haze of broken nights, feeding and caring for her new baby. Arthur was restless, jealous and bored. He complained that Iris was giving all her attention to their son and there was nothing left for him.

'If you're not careful I'll start looking elsewhere,' he would say.

Or perhaps he was just looking for an excuse? Iris could never be sure. But when this woman turned up at her back door several months later with a baby in her arms, she only had to look at his face to know that he was Arthur's child.

'Who was it?' Dolly asked.

Iris hesitated a moment. 'I can't say,' she said. 'I promised I'd keep it a secret.'

'Are you having me on?' Dolly's eyes blazed. 'Listen, if this woman did that to you, then you don't owe her anything. Go on, you can tell me,' she coaxed. 'Do I know her? You can tell me that, at least . . .'

'Bessie Weir.'

Edie uttered the name quietly. Iris wasn't sure she had even heard her at first.

'How did you know?'

'I saw the way you looked at her. I could tell straight away you didn't like her.'

'No!' Dolly's hand flew to her mouth. 'You mean little Ronnie's—'

'Arthur's bain,' Iris finished for her.

Dolly looked stunned. 'I had no idea . . .'

'No,' Iris said. 'You wouldn't. We agreed not to tell anyone. She didn't want it to get out, any more than I did. She had too much to lose.'

'Then why did she do it?' Edie asked quietly.

'She said she was in love with him.' Iris closed her eyes, thinking of that moment. She could still picture it as clear as day, Bessie standing there in her kitchen, telling her everything. Iris had stood at the open back door, scarcely listening as her own life unravelled in front of her. She would have run away if it hadn't been for Archie, sleeping peacefully in his cot upstairs. 'It turned out they'd been – together – before we got married. She said she'd never got over him. "Unfinished business", she called it. So when her and Ted were having troubles, and Arthur told her we weren't getting on either . . .' Her voice trailed off. Even now, eight years later and a year after Arthur was dead and buried, she still couldn't bear to think about what had happened.

'But Ted Weir was his best friend!' Dolly said.

'And I was his wife!' Iris said. 'But that's what Arthur was like. He didn't care who he hurt, as long as he got what he wanted.'

Dolly shook her head. 'I can't get over it,' she said. 'Bessie Weir . . . And I used to think so much of her, too.' Her mouth curled in disgust. 'Honest to God, what kind of a woman would do something like that?'

'Happen she thought Arthur loved her, too?' Edie murmured.

'She was wrong if she did,' Iris said. 'She was just a bit of fun when he was feeling bored and left out at home. He said as much when I confronted him about it. After he'd stopped denying it, of course. The way he talked about her – it made me feel sorry for her, in a way.'

'I know how I'd feel about her!' Dolly said. 'And I wouldn't feel sorry for her, I can tell you that.'

Iris shook her head. 'It wasn't all her fault,' she said. 'She believed him when he said that it was over between us, that I meant nothing to him. She thought he was going to leave me, to be with her and their son. She must have been so hurt when he panicked and ran a mile.'

She looked at Edie. The poor girl's back must be playing up, because she had gone quite pale.

'So why did she decide to come to you?' Dolly said, looking furious. 'Just to make trouble, I suppose?'

'That's what Arthur said. He blamed her for everything, said she was the one who had started it all, she had chased him. He said she was trying to come between us, to part us so he would have no choice but to be with her.'

'Do you think he was telling the truth?' Edie asked.

'I don't think Arthur would have known the truth if it had bitten him,' Iris said bitterly. Bessie hadn't come to make trouble for her. As she had explained to Iris, she had already decided her best course of action was to stay with Ted and never tell him the truth of what had happened. But she had seen Arthur Fletcher for what he really was, and she wanted Iris to see it too. Iris believed that Bessie had been trying to help her in her own way.

And like a fool she had ignored the other woman's warning, just as she had ignored her mother's wise words on her wedding day.

'What happened then?' Dolly asked.

'I wanted to leave him,' Iris said. 'I should have left him, but he begged me to stay, for Archie's sake. He broke down, said he had been a fool, swore he loved me and it would never happen again. But it did.'

'How many . . . ?'

276

'I don't know. I stopped counting after a while.' Just as she had stopped confronting him about it. She had grown too used to the pleas, the tears, the promises that this would be the last time. Iris tried to believe him, but she knew he didn't mean it. She knew it would only take a pretty face, a smile or a wink, and his head would be turned again.

It was as if by forgiving him over Bessie, she had somehow given him permission to hurt her again and again.

'I wanted to leave him,' she said again. 'I told myself that next time it happened, I would. But I couldn't bring myself to do it. I kept thinking about what everyone would say, the way they'd talk. And I had the bains to think about. How could I leave their father?'

Tears filled Dolly's blue eyes. 'I wish you'd told me,' she said in a choked voice. 'I'm supposed to be your friend. I should have known . . .'

'I didn't want to tell anyone,' Iris said. 'I didn't want it to be true. I thought if I kept it quiet, then I wouldn't have to face what was happening. And besides, I was ashamed,' she admitted quietly.

'Ashamed?'

'That my own husband didn't love me. That I wasn't enough for him.'

She looked at Edie. The poor girl looked so upset.

'I'm sorry it happened to you, love.' Dolly put her arm around Iris' shoulders. 'And I used to think such a lot of Arthur, too. You always seemed so happy together, you and him and the children—'

'Appearances can be deceptive,' Iris said. She had certainly put a brave face on for many years.

'But I don't see what this has got to do with Sam,' Dolly said.

Iris pursed her lips. 'He was Arthur's friend.'

Dolly looked shocked. 'Do you think he knew what was going on?'

'I don't know. I wouldn't be surprised. But it's got nowt to do with that. I just don't want another man in my life. I made up my mind after Arthur died that I was never going to let anyone hurt me, ever again.'

'Sam would never do that. He worships you.'

So did Arthur, thought Iris. 'We'll never know, will we?' she said.

'We all have to take chances sometimes,' Dolly said. 'Otherwise, how can we hope for a better life?'

'I'm quite happy with my life as it is, thank you very much.'

'Are you?' Dolly gave her a sceptical look. 'I saw the way you were watching Sam when he was dancing with Gwendoline. You certainly didn't look happy to me.'

Iris slid her gaze away. 'I'm pleased he's found someone nice at last,' she murmured. 'He deserves it.'

'He deserves you,' Dolly said. 'He loves you. And you love him.'

Iris opened her mouth to deny it, but the words wouldn't come.

'If you let him go, then you're a bigger fool than I ever thought you were, Iris Fletcher,' Dolly declared. 'You've been given another chance at finding love, and I reckon you should grab it with both hands before it slips away forever.' She laid her hand on Iris' arm. 'I know you're scared after what happened with Arthur, and I can't tell you how it will turn out with Sam. But I think you should take a chance to be happy while you can. Lord knows, the way things are going, we could all be blown up or invaded by tomorrow!'

Iris was watching Sam on the dance floor, Gwendoline in his arms. They looked so good together, her blonde head resting against his burly shoulder as they twirled slowly.

'Look at her,' she said quietly. 'She's so clever and beautiful, and she adores him. What have I got to offer him compared to that?'

'Nothing, if you put it like that!' Dolly let out a heavy sigh. 'Just talk to him,' she pleaded. 'Tell him how you feel. If he prefers Gwendoline, then at least you've lost nothing.'

'Except my pride!' Iris said.

'It's a small price to pay, I reckon. What do you say, Edie?'

They both turned to her. She was staring at the dance floor, a faraway look on her face.

'Look at her. She's away with the fairies!' Dolly grinned. She turned back to Iris. 'Honestly, go and talk to him,' she urged.

Iris stared back at her in horror. 'What – *now*?'

'Why not? There's no time like the present. As I said, we don't know where we'll be tomorrow.' She nudged her. 'Go on. I'll take the bains home with me, give you a bit of time. If my Jack arrives, tell him I'm at home waiting for him.'

Iris looked back towards the dance floor. Sam was smiling down at Gwendoline, his eyes full of love. She felt her stomach sink.

'I can't do it,' she whispered. 'I can't talk to him.'

'You can.' Dolly seized her by the shoulders and shoved her towards the dance floor. 'Go on, before it's too late and Gwendoline snaps him up. And don't even think of speaking to me again before you do!'

Chapter Forty-three

Joyce wanted to leave after the ceremony, but Reg would not hear of it.

'You wanted to come here, so now I'm going to enjoy it,' he said.

Joyce watched him staggering across to the barrel to refill his glass yet again. It was still early evening but he was already unsteady on his feet. What would he be like later on, she wondered nervously. With any luck he would be too drunk to remember his anger.

But if he wasn't – the thought filled her with dread.

'Your Reg certainly knows how to enjoy himself, don't he?' Beattie commented acidly. 'Look at him, he can barely stand!'

'Never mind him,' Big May dismissed. 'Why don't you come over and sit with us, love?' she said to Joyce.

Joyce hesitated, glancing back at Reg. His glass now full, he had shouldered in to join a conversation between Jimmy and Pop Maguire.

'He'll be all right,' Big May tugged on her arm. 'Come on, you can't spend all night standing here on your own.'

Joyce followed Big May over to the corner, where the other WVS girls were already sitting. Edie Copeland was with them, but Joyce could see from the girl's face that she was not really present. She nursed a glass of lemonade, a faraway expression in her eyes.

'Where's Dolly and Iris?' Beattie asked.

'I left them talking over there.' Edie nodded to a corner of the room.

Big May's eyes narrowed. 'You in't fallen out, have you?'

'Oh, no. I just needed to sit down. I'm not feeling too well.'

'I hope the bain in't on its way?' Beattie laughed. 'That would really make this a wedding to remember.'

'As if it in't already!' Wyn said.

'Well, our Ada wanted her wedding written up in the newspaper,' Big May said. 'I daresay it will be after this!'

'Aye,' Maggie said. 'I can see it in the *Hull Daily Mail* now. "The bride wore white and the groom wore oilskins"!'

'At least he got here,' Big May looked grim. 'And we've got your Sam to thank for that,' she said to Beattie. 'He's the hero of the day, all right.'

Beattie looked pleased with herself. 'He's a good lad, I'll say that for him.'

'I see he's got himself a young lady?' Wyn nodded towards the dance floor.

'Aye, and I hope it lasts. It's about time one of my boys got themselves wed.'

'So it's serious, is it?'

'He seems to like the lass. And she likes him, too.'

'Now you've just got to get your Charlie off your hands!' Maggie giggled.

Beattie bristled. 'And what makes you think I want to get him off my hands?'

'Charlie's a fine man,' Joyce said quickly. 'Any woman would be lucky to have him.'

'He is.' Beattie shot her a quick, grateful look.

Reg's loud laughter carried across the room. Joyce tensed at the sound of it. When she risked a glance, Reg was slapping Jimmy Maguire on the shoulder. He did not look very amused, she thought.

The music changed tempo and Big May clapped her hands.

'"The Beer Barrel Polka"!' she cried out in delight. 'Now this is more my style.' She threw back her head and crooned, '*Roll out the barrel, let's have a barrel of fun . . .*'

'You could have warned us you were going to start singing!' Beattie put her hands over her ears. 'Shut up, for God's sake. Folk'll think there's a seagull got loose in here!'

Joyce felt a tap on her shoulder. She turned around and there was Charlie Scuttle looking down at her. It was strange to see him in a suit instead of his work overalls, but somehow he still managed to look rumpled.

'All right, Charlie?' She smiled up at him.

Charlie nodded. He pointed to her, then to the dance floor.

'I think he wants to ask you to dance!' Wyn smirked.

'Oh!' Joyce glanced across at Reg. 'I'm sorry, I don't really dance—'

'Especially not with Charlie Scuttle!' Maggie whispered loudly.

Charlie's lopsided smile faltered and he turned red with mortification. What must it have taken for him to walk across the dance floor and ask her, Joyce thought.

Before she knew what she was doing, she was on her feet.

'Actually, I will have that dance,' she said. 'But I'm warning you, it's years since I took a turn on the dance floor.'

Charlie grinned back. *Me too,* his expression seemed to say.

He was no dancer, that was for sure. But at least he was enthusiastic. It was all Joyce could do to cling on to him as he lolloped around the floor, his arms and legs flailing.

'Stop, you're making me dizzy!' she laughed helplessly, but Charlie only went on whirling her around in his arms, the room spinning around her.

And then she saw Reg storming towards her, pushing his way through the crowd towards them.

'What do you think you're doing?' he demanded.

Joyce glanced around her. Everyone had stopped dancing and were watching them. 'Reg, please—'

'Reg, please!' He mimicked her voice. 'How dare you make a fool of me. Flaunting yourself in front of everyone.'

'I wasn't—'

'And with him, of all people! You couldn't even choose a real man. You had to pick this – this imbecile! If anyone's dancing with you, it's going to be me.'

'But I don't want to dance.'

'I don't care what you want!'

Reg went to grab Joyce's arm but Charlie stepped between them, blocking her with his body. For all he was as thin as a whip, he was still a head taller than Reg.

Reg sneered up at him. 'Take me on, would you? I wouldn't try it, pal, or I'll knock you flat.'

'Touch my brother and I'll knock you even flatter.'

Sam Scuttle stood behind them, his arms folded across his broad chest.

'Stop it, Reg,' Joyce pleaded in a whisper. 'I'll dance with you, all right? Just don't spoil everything.'

The band stopped playing, and an uneasy silence fell.

'You want to fight, do you? I'll give you a fight!' Reg squared up to Sam, his fists up. But he was so drunk he could barely stand still.

Sam sent him a pitying look. 'Go home, Reg,' he said wearily.

He took his brother's arm and was just turning away when Reg took a drunken swing at his jaw. Sam's hand flashed out and caught him by the wrist, twisting his arm up behind his back.

Joyce screamed as Reg fell to his knees, yelling in pain and outrage.

Jimmy Maguire pushed his way through the gathering crowd of onlookers.

'Sam's right,' he said. 'It's time you went home, Reg.'

Joyce tried to help him to his feet but Reg shook her off angrily.

'I in't going anywhere!' he roared.

'Want to bet?'

Jimmy and Sam faced him, a wall of implacable muscle. Reg staggered about, his fists swinging for a moment. Then the fight seemed to go out of him.

'I don't want to stay here anyway,' he muttered, pulling himself up to his full height. 'Come on, Joyce, we're going.'

'She in't going anywhere.'

Big May's voice came from behind her. Joyce turned round. May, Beattie and the other women had closed ranks behind her. They looked even more formidable than the men.

Reg sneered. 'What's this? A mothers' meeting?'

'Aye,' Jimmy said grimly. 'And it's our mothers, so mind you think on before you open your mouth.'

'It's all right, son, I can fight my own battles.' Big May turned to Joyce. 'You don't have to go with him,' she said in a low voice. 'You don't have to do anything he says.'

'She'll do as she's told!' Reg took a step towards May but Jimmy blocked his way.

'Leave it, Jimmy. He might strike the fear of God into his wife, but he don't frighten me.'

Big May looked him up and down, her eyes full of contempt. Joyce stared at her, then back at the other women.

They knew.

All this time she had thought she had been so clever, hiding the truth from everyone under a veil of powder. But all the time they knew.

She flinched from the pity she saw in their faces. What little pride she still had shrivelled to nothing inside her.

'Are you coming, Joyce?' It wasn't a question. Reg was glaring at her, daring her to disagree.

She looked back at the other women. Big May was watching her intently, silently imploring her.

You don't have to go.

But how could she stay when she was so full of shame?

'I'll fetch my coat,' she said quietly.

Chapter Forty-four

Patience arrived back at Paragon Station that evening, still in a state of shock. This time she barely cared about the crowds that jostled her on the platform, or even the fact that darkness had fallen and the streets were an eerie, pitch black.

All she could think about was how Edie had lied to her.

And Rose had taken the greatest delight in telling her, too.

Rose had not offered her a cup of tea – 'We don't share our rations with strangers' – but she had grudgingly given her a glass of water. Patience was glad of it; her throat was as dry as sand by the time she had heard what Rose had to say.

'She's wearing a wedding ring now, is she? I wouldn't let that fool you. I know for a fact that she can't be married, because the lad who got her pregnant already has a wife.' Rose looked mockingly at her. 'I'll bet she didn't tell you that, did she?'

'No,' Patience said faintly. 'No, she didn't.'

'Took up with a pilot from Church Fenton,' Rose went on. 'Of course, we all know what these lads are like. All they want is a bit of fun. I tried to warn her, but of course she wouldn't listen. Stupid lass thought it was the love affair of the century.' Rose's mouth twisted.

'Did she know he was married?'

'How should I know? She said she didn't, but you can never believe a word that comes out of that girl's mouth. It probably wouldn't have made any difference to her anyway, knowing her. Little hussy!'

Patience stared into her glass, lost for words. But she didn't need to say anything, because Rose was already going on.

'Of course, it was only a matter of time before she fell pregnant. She was such a fool about it, too. She kept saying how much he loved her, how he was going to leave his wife and come home to her when the war was over.' Her lips thinned. 'If you ask me, it was a mercy he was killed, otherwise she might have gone on waiting forever.'

She poured herself another cup of tea from the pot in front of her. 'Of course, we couldn't let her stay here. This is a respectable house, I have my sons to think about. She would have dragged us all down with her.'

Patience looked around at the tidy room. The polished surface of the table in front of her was littered with lace doilies. Embroidered antimacassars were draped over the backs of the sofa and armchairs.

Rose was obviously a woman who liked covering things up, concealing what lay beneath to keep everything looking nice.

'She tried to get round her father, begging and pleading and putting on the tears,' Rose went on. 'She's very good at that, the sly minx. She nearly managed to convince him to take her side.'

'But you talked him out of it?'

'I made him choose between us. I told him, if she stayed under this roof then I'd have no choice but to go and take Cyril and Kenny with me.'

'And he chose you?'

'He didn't have to. She'd already made up her mind to go by then, thank God. She had some fanciful idea about moving away. She wanted to feel closer to him, she said. Pathetic, if you ask me.' Rose's face was full of contempt. 'I'm surprised she hasn't made a nuisance of herself with his family. I really wouldn't put anything past her.' She smoothed her skirt over her knees. 'To be honest, I'm just glad to be rid of her. As long as she's not making trouble for us any more, coming between me and my husband, I don't really care what she does.'

She's jealous, Patience thought. She could see it in Rose's wary, narrowed eyes. She must have jumped at the chance to get rid of Edie.

'So why are you here?' Rose asked. 'You still haven't said.'

You haven't given me a chance, Patience thought. 'I've come to try to sort things out.'

'Then you're wasting your time.'

'The girl is about to have her baby.' Patience set down her glass. 'She should be with her family—'

A slow smile spread across Rose's sharp face. 'Oh, I see it all now. You're sick and tired of her too, so you're trying to palm her off on to us again.'

'That's not true—'

'If she's that much of a bother you can tell her to go to an unmarried mothers' home. That's where she belongs. Or she can go to hell for all I care, as long as I never have to see her again.'

At that moment the door opened and Rose's son walked in. She immediately jumped to her feet to fuss over him, offering him her chair and a cup of tea.

'This is Cyril, my eldest,' she announced proudly. 'He's at the grammar school. Top of his class.' She beamed at him.

'When is our tea going to be ready?' Cyril demanded, ignoring Patience. 'Kenny is home from chess club, and we're hungry.'

Patience scowled at his rudeness, but Rose said, 'I'll make a start on it straight away, love.' She turned to Patience. 'You're going to have to go,' she said. 'My husband will be home from work soon and I've got a lot to do.'

'Yes, of course.' Patience rose stiffly. 'Thank you for your time.'

'I hope you've heard enough.'

'Oh yes. More than enough.'

As she ushered her to the front door, Rose said, 'We did our best for her, whatever she might have told you. I know it might seem heartless to you, me telling her to get rid of the baby, but I did it for her sake. What kind of life could she give it? She barely has a penny to her name, and not the first idea about looking after a child. You must know how hopeless she is, or you wouldn't have come here.'

Patience thought about Edie, singing to herself as she painted and stitched curtains and put up shelves. She never gave up, never stopped trying, even when the odds were stacked against her.

'I wonder why you wouldn't try to help her more, if she was that hopeless?' she said.

Rose's face hardened. 'She made her bed, now she must lie in it,' she bit out.

Before Patience could respond, the front door opened and a man came in. He was in his forties but looked much older, with his hunched shoulders and worn-down expression.

'Hello, love, I – oh!' He stopped when he saw Patience. 'Sorry, I didn't realise you had a visitor.'

'She's just leaving.' Rose was already ushering her towards the door, but Patience stood her ground.

'I've come about Edie,' Patience said. Rose glared at her.

The man's expression changed. 'Is everything all right? How is she?'

'She's fine,' Rose answered for her.

'And the baby?'

Patience looked into John Russell's stricken face. She could see the yearning in his eyes, even if his wife could not.

'It won't be long now,' she said. 'Actually, that's why—'

'Anyway, don't let us keep you,' Rose gave her a little shove in the small of her back. 'I daresay you've got a train to catch. There's a bus at the end of the road you can catch back into the city. Ask the conductor and he'll let you off at the station.'

'I'll walk you to the bus stop—' her husband offered, but Rose said:

'She'll be all right on her own, John. Besides, tea will be ready in a minute.'

The door closed quickly on the man's sorrowful expression before Patience could say another word.

She caught the train back to York with her mind in a whirl.

Rose Russell was a cruel, jealous bully, there was no doubt of that. Patience could only imagine the terrible life she had led Edie.

But at the same time, Edie had lied. Terrible, shocking lies, playing on her sympathy and making herself out to be something she definitely wasn't.

Patience rubbed at her temples, trying to ease the headache that was building there. Things used to be a lot easier for her, when she saw life in black and white. Things were either right or they were wrong, there was nothing in between. But more and more these days, she found herself unable to make up her mind, seeing different sides to the same story. It was all very confusing.

It took a long time to get back to Hessle Road. Patience had never been out in the blackout before, and she was terrified at how much the engulfing blackness disorientated her. Some people had dim torches they angled at the pavement to help them see their way, but Patience could only shuffle along as best she could, still clutching her gas mask. Luckily the fog had lifted and the moon was full in the clear sky, which offered some kind of silvery light.

'Look at that,' a man at the tram stop nodded towards the sky. 'A bomber's moon. They'll be coming over before long.'

'I hope not!' Patience gazed up fearfully.

The man grinned. 'Don't worry, Missus. They've missed us so far!'

At least the trams were still running, but they were all blacked out and it was hard to see when one was coming or where it was going. Patience gazed fearfully out into the darkness and prayed she would get home before the air-raid siren sounded.

Finally, thankfully, she arrived at Jubilee Row. She took off her coat, put away her gas mask and put up the blackout curtains before she switched on the light.

She listened carefully. She could not hear Edie upstairs. She must still be at Ada Maguire's wedding.

She smiled to herself, remembering what a picture she had looked in that pink dress. How she had stood in front of the mirror, smoothing the folds of silky fabric over her distended belly. She had thanked Patience so profusely, in the end she had been quite embarrassed.

Then she remembered what Rose had told her, and the smile vanished from her face. The girl was a liar, and she did not know whether she could ever look her in the face again.

But then she remembered her kindness, running errands for Patience and taking her to the hospital to see Horace every week, even when the tram journey seemed to exhaust her . . .

'I do wish you were here, Horace,' Patience said aloud as she filled the kettle. 'You'd know what to do, what to think.'

She was halfway across the kitchen to the stove when she heard the scream from above her. The kettle fell from her hands with a crash.

'What the—'

Another scream, louder this time. Before she even knew what she was doing, Patience was halfway up the stairs.

Chapter Forty-five

They walked home through the deserted docks in silence. The fog had lifted, and the wide expanse of the Humber looked almost beautiful, streaked with silver from the bright moon. Seagulls wheeled overhead, their harsh cries breaking the silence.

Reg weaved unsteadily ahead of her.

'I hope you're pleased with yourself,' he threw back over his shoulder.

'I'm sorry.' She had said it so many times, but Reg was too drunk and too angry to listen.

'Showing me up like that, making doe eyes at Charlie Scuttle, of all people. I don't know what you were thinking.'

Neither do I, Joyce thought. It seemed like such a long time ago that she had been laughing and dancing, and all her cares had seemed miles away.

'I was having a good time, until you ruined it all,' Reg muttered.

'You were the one who tried to punch Sam.'

Joyce thought of Reg, wheeling about on the dance floor, his fists drunkenly flailing, and felt sick with mortification.

'And what was I supposed to do, eh? What kind of a man would I be if I'd stood by and let you make a fool of me?'

'You made a fool of yourself, Reg.'

As soon as she'd said the words she knew she had made a mistake. Reg stopped dead in front of her.

293

'What did you say?' The blackout hid his face but Joyce could hear the taut fury in his voice.

'Nothing.' She tried to walk past him but Reg grabbed her hair, yanking her head backwards and pulling her off balance.

'Stop it! You're hurting me.' Joyce tried to twist from his grasp but he only gripped tighter, shaking her like a rat.

'You don't speak to me like that! You don't answer me back and you don't walk away from me. Understand?'

He drove his fist into the pit of her stomach, knocking the breath out of her. Joyce fell to the ground, dazed.

'Reg, please. I'm sorry,' she gasped.

'You will be.'

Joyce instinctively curled into a ball as he drove his boot into her again and again, sending bolts of white-hot pain through her body. He was savage, grunting like an animal with each blow.

And then, suddenly, it was over, and he was standing over her, panting with effort.

'Bitch,' he hissed. 'I've a good mind to put an end to you here and now.'

Do it, Joyce thought. She didn't care any more. All she wanted was the pain to end.

She lay still, not daring to move, to open her eyes.

'I could do it, you know. I could dump your body in the Humber and the tide would carry you out before anyone knew about it. It's not like you'd be missed, is it?'

She could feel a warm trickle of blood from her temple, cooling on her cheek in the cold night air.

'Even your precious son wouldn't care. He's gone at last, thank God. Another couple of months and he'll have forgotten all about you.'

She flinched as Reg's steps drew nearer. Then she felt his breath fanning her face, hot and reeking of alcohol.

'Did you hear what I said?' Flecks of spittle hit her face. 'No one cares about you, Joyce. I'm the only one you've got, so you'd better think about being nicer to me.'

He was walking away from her again, his boots ringing on the cobbles. Joyce uncurled herself, gingerly testing her limbs, bracing for the pain.

You don't have to go. You don't have to do anything he says.

As she struggled to sit up, dazed and bleeding, Big May's words came back to her.

She saw the women standing behind her, their arms folded, grim looks on their faces. It wasn't pity she saw in their eyes, she realised. It was sympathy. They had been standing with her, ready to pit themselves against Reg if she needed them.

'You're wrong,' she whispered.

The footsteps stopped. 'What did you say?'

If she was going to die here, then she had nothing to lose. He had already taken everything from her.

'People care about me.' Her words came out as a hoarse whisper. 'They were all there tonight. They saw how you treated me.'

She staggered to her feet, like a prize fighter who had beaten the count. Pain blossomed deep inside her with every move, but nothing seemed to be broken.

'They saw you making a fool of me—'

'They saw what you really are. A vicious thug.' She took a deep breath and her ribs sang with pain. 'Tinker Reg,' she said quietly.

Suddenly he was there in front of her, towering over her, his face livid. 'What did you call me?'

'You heard.'

She saw the surprise in his eyes. His fist went back and she fought the urge to flinch.

'Go on, then, hit me, if it makes you feel like more of a

man,' she could hardly get the words out for the pain. 'But you'll have to look me in the eye while you're doing it. I'll never cower in front of you again.'

She held herself very still, forcing herself to stare at him.

For a moment she braced herself. Then Reg lowered his fist, his gaze dropping from hers.

'You in't worth it,' he muttered.

As he stepped away from her, Joyce let out the breath she had been holding.

'I'll deal with you at home.' He turned and started to walk away but Joyce did not move.

'I'm not coming home with you, Reg.' She hadn't realised what she was going to say until the words were out of her mouth.

'You bloody well are!'

'I'm not.'

'And where will you go?' he sneered.

'I don't know and I don't care.'

She turned and started to walk away from him. Her legs were so unsteady they could barely hold her up but still she kept on walking.

'I'll pack your bags for you, shall I?' Reg called after her.

Joyce kept walking.

'You'll be back,' Reg shouted, but there was a note of uncertainty in his voice. 'You'll come crawling once you've realised you've nowhere else to go!'

Chapter Forty-six

Iris never imagined she would ever have reason to be grateful to Reg Shelby. But she was relieved when she saw him arguing with Jimmy Maguire and Sam Scuttle in the middle of the dance floor. At least he stopped her making a terrible fool of herself.

She swerved away from the tussle and hurried outside. The fog had lifted, leaving a cold November night, brilliant with stars and illuminated by a full moon. Iris paused for a moment, looking up into the speckled sky. Was it her imagination, or did there seem to be more stars in the sky since the blackout began?

She thought about her brother Jack, still out on the mine-sweeper. He should be on his way in now, she thought. She hoped there wouldn't be an air raid while he was on his way into dock.

'They used to sing love songs about the moon, didn't they?' She jumped at the sound of Sam's voice behind her. 'Now when we see one, we only ever think of bombs coming down.'

'You might have a busy night at work tonight,' she said.

'I daresay I will.'

Iris looked over her shoulder at him. She could barely see him in the darkness, but she could feel his presence.

'What happened to Reg Shelby?'

'He decided to go home.' Sam's voice was low and grim.

'Just as well,' Iris said. 'You looked as if you were about to have a fight with him.'

'Reg Shelby only takes on people who can't fight back, like our Charlie.'

'And his wife,' Iris said.

'Aye, poor woman. I don't know how she puts up with him.'

Iris turned her face back up to the sky. 'She in't the only woman who's ever put up with a man who treats her badly.'

'No,' Sam said.

Iris glanced back at him. He was closer now, and she could see his face, etched in moonlight. Did he know about Arthur's secret? She had often wondered. Trawlermen stuck together, she knew that from her brothers.

She shivered and drew her arms around herself, hugging herself to keep warm. She wished she had worn more than a flimsy summer dress for the wedding. It might have looked nice in the church, but it was freezing now.

She heard the strike of a match as Sam lit up a cigarette. 'Where are the bains?' he asked.

'Dolly took them home, so I could—' she stopped herself.

'What?'

'It doesn't matter. Anyway, it's getting late. I'd best be getting home myself.'

'Can I walk you back?'

'What about Gwendoline? Shouldn't you stay with her?'

'Would you believe, she was the one who sent me to find you?'

'Why?'

'Can't you guess?'

Iris stared at him, lost for words. She was glad the blackness of the night hid her flaming face.

'She said she could see it the minute she saw us together,'

298

Sam went on. 'She knew then that she didn't stand a chance with me.'

She heard him take a step towards her and blundered backwards.

'But she's such a lovely girl,' she murmured.

'Aye, she is. And I tried to fall for her, I really did. But I couldn't do it.' He sighed. 'Ma will probably give me hell over it. She already loves her.'

'But you don't?'

'How can I, when I'm in love with you?'

She turned away sharply, panic tightening her chest. 'Don't say that,' she begged.

'Why not? It's true, and you know it. I've always loved you, right from when we were kids, larking out in the street together with your Jack and the other bains. I knew then that you were the only girl for me.'

The night air felt suddenly icy against the heat in her face. Iris looked about her, feeling trapped. She wanted to run, to put as much distance as she could between herself and Sam.

But she could never run away from her feelings. God knows, she had tried hard enough. Now it was time to turn around and face them.

'Gwendoline reckons you might like me, too?' Sam said quietly. 'She says she's seen the way you look at me, and she can tell. She reckons I'm a fool for not noticing myself.' He took a step towards her and this time Iris did not back away. 'Well?' he said. 'Is she right?'

Iris stared down at her feet, willing them to move. But they were rooted to the spot. 'I – I can't—'

Sam sighed. 'I know you loved Arthur. But he wouldn't have wanted you to mourn him forever. He would have wanted you to be happy—'

'The last thing Arthur ever cared about was my happiness!'

The words burst out of her, hanging in the cold night air.

She saw the stricken look that crossed Sam's face before he could manage to hide it. 'You knew, didn't you?' she said. 'About Arthur's other women?'

'I wanted to tell you,' he said.

'But you were too loyal to Arthur.'

'Loyal? Is that what you think?' Sam's voice was harsh in the silence of the night. 'You think I enjoyed watching him make a fool of you?' He shook his head. 'You don't know me at all, do you? I only kept quiet for your sake, because I didn't want to hurt you. But if you want the truth of it, Arthur Fletcher was no friend of mine.'

He turned away from her. Iris stared at his broad back.

'I hated him for what he did to you,' Sam said. 'I told him so, too. I begged him not to carry on the way he did. I told him I'd tell you, or your brothers. But he knew I wouldn't, because I didn't want to hurt you.' His face was bitter. 'He knew how I felt about you, and he never missed a chance to taunt me about it.' His hands balled into fists at his sides. 'I can't tell you how many times I've wanted to break his jaw, or worse—'

'Did Ted Weir kill him?' Iris blurted out.

Sam stared at her. 'Ted?'

'I've often wondered if he might have found out – about Bessie and Arthur, I mean. That night they both went overboard, I wasn't sure if it was really an accident ...'

Sam shook his head. 'It was an accident, all right,' he said. 'I was there, I saw what happened. The steam-pipes had frozen up and Arthur and Ted were trying to thaw them with burning paraffin rags when the ship hit floating ice and they were knocked overboard. They didn't stand a chance out there, in that sea with a black fog all around. I tried to save them, but they must have perished the moment they hit the water.' He took a deep breath. 'I wanted to save him,' he said. 'I couldn't have lived with myself if I hadn't tried, at least. Not for his sake. All I could think about was having to break the news to you and the bains . . .'

His face was bleak, and Iris understood his sorrow. She had still mourned Arthur and felt deep grief when she found out that he was dead, no matter what he had done to her.

'I'm sorry he hurt you,' Sam said.

'I knew what he was like when I married him.'

'I wish you'd married me.'

'You never asked.'

Sam smiled ruefully. 'Ma always says I'm too backward in coming forward.' He looked at her. 'But it in't too late, is it? I mean, if I was to ask you now—'

Iris shook her head. 'I don't know, Sam. Being married to Arthur changed me, it made me bitter. I'm not the girl I used to be.'

'You're still the girl I love.'

He reached for her hands and held them in his. For once she did not pull away.

'Give me a chance,' he said. 'Let me show you that all men in't like Arthur Fletcher.'

Iris looked down at their entwined fingers. 'I want to,' she said. 'But I'm not sure I'm ready . . .'

'Then we'll take it slowly,' Sam promised. 'God knows, I've waited for you all these years, I reckon I can wait a bit longer!'

Iris looked up into his eyes and knew he was going to kiss her. Time seemed to slow down and she was aware of everything happening second by endless second as his mouth came towards hers . . .

The moan of the air-raid siren filled the air, making her jump backwards in fright.

Sam cursed under his breath. 'Talk about bad timing!' He checked his watch. 'They're early tonight.'

'They're making up for not being able to come over last night,' Iris said.

The distant drone of approaching planes filled the air, followed by the sharp retort of the anti-aircraft guns.

'We'd best get everyone down to the shelter,' Sam said.

'They're already on their way.' Iris looked past him to where the others were beginning to spill out on to the street, ushered by her sister Florence.

'All right, all right, no need to shove me,' she heard her mother saying crossly. 'You in't got your tin hat on yet, our Flo!'

At that moment Beattie appeared and called out to him: 'Sam! Come and see to your brother. He's got himself in a right old state and he won't come out.'

Sam looked at his mother, then back at Iris.

'Go,' she said. 'Charlie needs you.'

He took a couple of steps away from her, then looked back. 'You will get yourself to safety, won't you?'

'I'll follow Florence.' She pointed to where her sister was herding a gaggle of guests down the street, all still dressed in their finery. Ada brought up the rear, holding hands with her new husband, her white wedding dress glowing eerily in the gloom.

Sam hesitated a moment, then before Iris knew what was happening he had leaned forward and impulsively planted a kiss on her lips.

'I'll see you later,' he grinned.

Iris smiled as she watched him go. She pressed her fingers to her lips, feeling the imprint of his mouth on hers.

Perhaps it might be worth taking a chance on him after all, she thought.

Chapter Forty-seven

The air-raid siren wailed outside the window, but all Patience could think about was Edie on her hands and knees on the floor in front of her, sobbing with pain.

'How long have you been like this?' she asked.

'I – I don't know. I came home from the wedding early because I wasn't feeling right. I thought I might have a bath, but then something happened, and—' Her next words were lost in another sob.

'It's all right,' Patience said. 'Don't try to talk.'

'But – but I don't understand. Why does it hurt – like this? Some – something's wrong, I know it is!' She turned pleading, tear-filled eyes to Patience.

'Nothing's wrong. The baby's on its way, that's all.'

'But what – what shall I do?'

Her next cry was drowned out by the sound of a plane passing over, so low it made the glass shake in the window frames. A moment later came a volley of anti-aircraft fire, followed by the rattle of falling shrapnel.

Patience pressed her hands to her ears and tried to think. 'We need to fetch the midwife,' she said.

'But how—'

'Let me worry about that. Let's get you downstairs. Can you manage to walk, do you think?'

'I – I'm not sure . . .'

Patience staggered under Edie's weight as she helped her to

her feet. Together, they managed to make it out of the room and halfway along the landing. But they had barely reached the top of the stairs before Edie had to stop, doubling over in pain.

'I – I can't,' she wept. 'It hurts too much.'

'You've got to,' Patience insisted, as another plane swooped overhead. She glanced nervously at the light fitting, rattling above their heads.

Edie seemed to read her thoughts. 'Are we going to get bombed?'

'Let's not worry about that now.' Patience held on to her tighter. 'We've got this baby to think about first. We'll go downstairs and make you comfortable, then I'll go and fetch the midwife—'

'No!' Edie clutched Patience's arm, her fingers biting into the flesh. 'You – you can't leave me. I'm frightened – aaah!'

She gasped with pain as another contraction swept over her. Patience listened to the ponderous ticking of the grandfather clock downstairs. She couldn't tell how much time had passed, but the contractions seemed to be very close together.

'Let's get you downstairs,' she said, pulling Edie to her feet again.

It took them a long time to edge their way down the stairs. Once they reached the bottom, Edie sank down, exhausted. Even though the house was quite chilly, her hair clung in damp tendrils to her perspiring face.

'I can't go any further.' Her voice came in little gasps of pain.

'You'd be better off in the bedroom—'

A huge explosion outside shook the house, throwing Patience against the hall dresser. Edie grabbed the bannister rail, her face white with fear.

'What was that?' she whispered.

'I don't know.' Patience glanced towards the front door. 'But it sounded close.'

'You can't go,' Edie said again. 'You'll be killed if you go out there, I know you will.'

'But the midwife—' Patience started to say. Then she saw the terror on Edie's face and decided against it. 'Try to get under the stairs, if you can,' she said. 'I'm going to the kitchen to put the kettle on.'

Edie started to protest, but another contraction overcame her. She fell to her hands and knees on the tiled floor.

Patience left her sobbing and hurried into the kitchen. She filled the kettle and lit the gas under it, then turned off the kitchen light and cautiously opened the back door to look out into the yard.

At first she thought it must be snowing. She held her hand out, then realised it was thick dust drifting down. There was a distant glow of red in the night sky, coming from the direction of the docks. The air reeked of cordite and burning wood.

She closed the door and leaned back against it, closing her eyes.

Think, Patience. Think!

Edie's scream ripped through the air, shattering her nerves. It was all Patience could do not to cry out, too.

This would not do. She had to stay calm. That was the most important thing. She would be no use to anyone if she allowed herself to crumble.

Think, Patience.

Boiling water, she thought. That's what was needed. And plenty of it, too. She found her biggest saucepan under the sink and filled that, too, then put it on the gas to heat.

And towels. And fresh sheets for the bed. And newspaper.

Patience looked around. Typical, all the newspaper had gone for salvage the day before.

'Mrs Huggins!' Edie called out from the hall.

'I'm coming.' Patience did another quick scan around the room, then hurried to the linen cupboard. A satisfyingly clean aroma of starch and lavender water greeted her as she threw open the wooden doors, but for once Patience scarcely noticed it as she began pulling at the orderly piles of ironed sheets and pillowcases and towels, grabbing anything she could possibly carry.

She could barely see over the teetering pile of linens in her arms. 'Right,' she said briskly, 'let's see what we can do, shall we—' She peered over the pile at Edie and stopped dead.

There was a ghost in her hall, a pale wraith with blood trickling down her face.

'Hello, Mother,' said Joyce.

* * *

Joyce thought she had prepared herself for anything as she walked down Hessle Road to Jubilee Row. But she was not expecting the sight that greeted her as she let herself in through the front door of number ten.

She was on the doorstep, dithering about whether she should knock when she heard Edie's terrified scream from inside. Without thinking, Joyce reached for her key, still on her key ring after twenty years.

She had barely had time to take in the sight of Edie Copeland, sprawled on the floor and yelling in agony, when her mother appeared, staggering under the weight of an enormous pile of towels.

Joyce did not think she had ever seen her so dishevelled. Her blouse had come untucked from her skirt and her hair had escaped its tightly pinned bun and was hanging loose around her flushed face.

But the biggest surprise was when Patience said, 'Thank heavens you're here,' and dumped the pile of linen into Joyce's arms. 'We need to fetch the midwife.'

'We can't,' Joyce said. 'There's a bomb dropped near the docks, and all the roads are closed.' She glanced at Edie. 'And I don't think she'd get here in time, anyway.'

Edie let out another wail of pain. Joyce glanced at the clock. The contractions looked to be coming thick and fast.

'What shall we do?' asked Patience.

Joyce stared at her mother. She had never seen her looking so helpless and terrified.

'We'll just have to sort it out for ourselves.' She dumped the towels back into her mother's arms and rolled up her sleeves. 'Do you have any hot water?'

'The kettle's boiling now.'

'Good. You make up the bed, and I'll wash my hands. Then we'll see what's to be done, shall we?' She smiled brightly at Edie, hoping her nerves did not show.

By the time Joyce had scrubbed her hands with red carbolic soap and filled a couple of bowls with hot water, Patience had the bed made up. Between them, they managed to man-handle Edie into the bedroom.

'But I can't move,' she kept complaining. 'I can't walk. It – hurts too much . . .'

'You've got to try, love.' Joyce's bruised limbs screamed in protest under Edie's weight, but she could not allow herself to give in.

They got Edie into bed, and Joyce braced herself to examine her.

'Let's have a look at you,' she said. She did not have the

first idea what she should be looking for, but it was evident as soon as she lifted Edie's nightie.

'I can see the head!' she cried.

'Saints preserve us.' Her mother crossed to the fireplace and began to furiously rearrange the ornaments on the mantelpiece.

'What are you doing?' Joyce looked over her shoulder at her. 'This is no time for dusting. Make up the fire, if you want to make yourself useful. It's cold in here.'

Outside, another plane swooped low overhead, followed by a distant explosion. A Staffordshire dog fell from the mantelpiece and smashed on the hearth.

Patience stared at the fragments for a few moments, dumbfounded. 'I'll fetch some coal,' she mumbled, and hurried off.

Things happened very quickly after that. Patience was still in the kitchen when Edie's baby slithered into the world, so fast it was all Joyce could do to catch it. She was still staring at the tiny, blood-smeared, greyish-pink body in her hands, when her mother came back into the room with a bucketful of coal.

Joyce looked at her mother. 'It's a baby boy,' she said, but her voice was drowned out by the rattle of anti-aircraft fire.

Poor little bain, Joyce thought, coming into the world to the sound of guns going off.

'Is he all right?' Edie's panicked voice came from the bed. 'Why isn't he crying? He is all right, in't he?'

Planes wheeled overhead, guns firing. Joyce didn't know what was happening, but it sounded as if their boys were fighting back at last, driving the Germans away. But there, inside the bedroom, it felt as if they were all suspended in a bubble where time had slowed to a standstill. Just her, Edie, her mother – and the lifeless little body she held in her arms.

'My baby,' Edie sobbed. 'I want my baby!'

Suddenly Patience was there, beside Joyce, holding out her arms.

'Give him to me,' she said.

Joyce handed over the baby and watched as her mother grabbed a towel and began briskly rubbing him with it.

'Careful,' Joyce cried out. 'You'll—'

Her words were lost as a thin, reedy cry rose into the air.

'You did it.' Joyce looked at her mother. Patience held the baby in her arms, as still as a statue but for the single tear running down her cheek.

'I did, didn't I?' she said.

And then another welcome wail filled the air. It was the sound of the All Clear.

Chapter Forty-eight

The first thing Iris saw when she opened her eyes was the blurred vision of a young woman in a white dress and veil standing over her.

'Ada?' she murmured. Then the mist began to clear and she realised that what she had thought was a wedding dress and veil was actually a nurse's white cap and apron.

'She's awake,' the nurse said. Her voice seemed distant, even though she was leaning right over Iris.

'Oh, thank God!' Iris heard her mother say.

She blinked, trying to take in her surroundings. A brightly lit room, the smell of antiseptic and fresh linen, the weight of bedclothes on her body. She tried to turn her head to look around, but there was something trapping her, some kind of frame or cage that seemed to wrap around her, cold metal and stiff bandages holding her in place . . .

'Mum!' she cried out in panic.

'I'm here, love.' A moment later her mother's face appeared in view above her. She was smiling, but Iris could see the fear and sorrow in her brown eyes. Pop was behind her, his face etched with exhaustion and anxiety. Iris could see them but their voices seemed faint, far away.

'I'll fetch Sister,' she heard the nurse say. 'She'll want to know she's awake at last.'

Was she really awake?, Iris wondered. Everything felt

curious and dream-like, as if she was trapped inside someone else's rigid, unmoving body.

'What happened?' she asked.

Her mother grasped her hand, clinging on to it for dear life. It was her father who spoke.

'There was a bomb went off, near the docks. We weren't hit, but it was close enough.'

His words unlocked a door in her brain, and suddenly all kinds of broken fragments of memory came tumbling out.

She was walking. She could see her family coming out of the social club with Florence. She was walking towards them, putting one foot in front of the other, getting closer and closer until suddenly—

Nothing. Until this moment, opening her eyes and finding herself here, in a strange place, with her mother standing over her, tears filling her eyes . . .

Her mother never cried.

Panic ripped through her. She struggled to sit up, but the metal frame pinned her to the bed.

'Is everyone all right?' she said.

'Shh. Don't upset yourself,' Pop said. He looked around the room. 'Where's that Sister got to, I wonder?'

Iris looked from his face to her mother's and she knew there was something neither of them was telling her.

'Someone's dead,' she said.

'Now you've got to try to stay calm,' her father said. 'It in't going to do you any good, upsetting yourself.'

But Iris had already seen the alarm flare in her mother's face and she knew the truth.

'Who is it?' she wanted to know.

'Iris—'

'I want to know, Pop!' She pushed his hand away. 'I'm right, in't I? Someone's dead?'

Somewhere in the distance she heard a door open and a woman speaking. Iris turned desperately to her mother, saw her lip trembling, a tear spilling down her cheek. 'Mum?' Her voice rose, cracked and hoarse. 'Mum! For pity's sake, tell me, please!'

* * *

Patience took down the blackout curtains and watched the dawn rise from the kitchen window while she waited for the kettle to boil. Such a lot had happened in a few short hours, she could scarcely take it all in.

She had barely slept. She and Joyce had spent the night running up and down the stairs, stripping beds and changing linens, bathing Edie and getting her into fresh nightclothes and back into her own bed. They also had to empty a drawer for the baby to sleep in, since the pram was at Dolly's and Edie had not yet finished paying for the cot.

At the time, Patience had been so busy, she had hardly stopped to think what she was doing. Now she found herself shaking with the delayed reaction of it all.

She heard a sound behind her. Looking up, she saw Joyce's reflection in the window.

'I was going to make Edie a cup of tea,' Patience said, glancing at the stove.

'I've just put the kettle on.' It was odd how they had worked so easily together in the night, but this morning they were stiff and formal with each other, like strangers again.

'How is she?' Patience asked.

'A bit sore and shocked, but very happy, I think.' Joyce smiled, and Patience found herself smiling back, before she remembered herself and turned away.

'I'll walk up to Coltman Street and fetch the midwife once it gets properly light,' Joyce said.

Patience nodded. 'Good idea. You can call in on your way home.'

'Yes.' Joyce's voice was flat.

Patience forced herself to say nothing about it as she set about making the pot of tea. For once she was determined to tread lightly.

'Would you like a cup of tea?' she asked.

'Yes, please.' Joyce sat down at the kitchen table and rubbed her eyes.

'You must be exhausted,' Patience said. 'Did you get any sleep on that couch?'

'Not really. But I wasn't tired anyway. How about you?'

'I may have slept a little.'

'I suppose it's hardly surprising to feel awake after all that excitement.'

'I suppose not.' But it wasn't the excitement of the birth that had keep Patience staring at the ceiling into the early hours. How could she even think of sleep, when all she could think about was her daughter in the next room?

'You saved his life,' Joyce said. 'How did you know what to do?'

Patience risked a smile. 'I saw your father do it once with a puppy that had nearly drowned in a well.'

It was when she saw Huggins the under-gardener nursing the poor shivering little creature back to life that she made up her mind she would step out with him after all.

She set the cup down in front of her daughter. Joyce stared down at it, twirling the teaspoon between her fingers. It was then that Patience noticed the bruises on her wrist.

'You're hurt,' she said.

'I fell over in the blackout.' Joyce slid her cuff down to cover the marks.

Patience remembered the blood drying on her face. 'It

must have been a nasty fall,' she said. 'Those cobbles can be treacherous in the dark.'

'Yes.'

The silence stretched between them. Patience busied herself at the sink but she could not stop stealing glances at her daughter. There was so much she wanted to say, but she was too afraid of speaking out of turn.

'It feels so strange, being back under this roof,' Joyce said at last.

'You said you'd never set foot in here again.'

'You said I wouldn't be welcome here.'

Patience opened her mouth to argue, then closed it again.

'I think we can agree we've both said things we regret,' she said quietly.

'Yes. Yes, I think we can.'

A milk cart rattled down the street outside. From upstairs came a baby's wail.

'Someone's awake,' Joyce smiled.

'I'll make Edie some breakfast.'

She felt Joyce watching her as she took the remains of yesterday's loaf out of the bread bin and cut two thick slices.

'I wish you'd been there when Alan was born,' she said. 'It would have been nice to have someone fussing over me.'

'I wish you'd sent for me.'

'I didn't think you'd come.'

'Of course I would have come. I would have always come.'

Their eyes met and held.

'You didn't, though, did you?' Joyce sounded hurt. 'I waited for you, I thought surely you would want to see your grandson, even if you didn't want to see me. I thought it would help to heal things between us.'

'So did I,' Patience said. 'That's why I sent you those clothes, as a peace offering—'

'What clothes?'

'The baby clothes I knitted for Alan. You sent them back.'

Joyce looked blankly back at her. 'I don't know anything about any baby clothes,' she said. 'I never saw them.'

'But he said—'

Patience stopped. She and Joyce looked at each other across the length of the kitchen.

'I'm sorry,' Joyce said. 'I didn't know.'

'It doesn't matter.' Patience shook her head. 'You're right, I should have come to you anyway. But I was too proud.'

Joyce gave a small smile. 'I think we've both been too proud, don't you?'

A smell of burning filled the air, and Patience jumped up. 'The toast!'

She snatched the pieces of scorched bread from under the grill and dropped them on to a plate. She was scraping off the worst of the burnt bits over the sink when Joyce said:

'You were right, you know. About Reg.'

'Oh?'

Patience went on scraping and waited for Joyce to speak again, but she didn't. She glanced over her shoulder at her. Her daughter's silence, and the desolate look on her face, spoke volumes.

She held back the acid comment that immediately sprang to her lips.

'I wonder that you stayed with him, in that case,' was all she said.

'I didn't want to admit I'd made a mistake. And besides, I had nowhere else to go.'

'You could have come home.'

'Could I?'

Joyce looked up at her, her face full of appeal. Suddenly all the years melted away and she was a young girl again, in need of her mother's love and reassurance.

And this time Patience would not let her down.

'You can always come home,' she said quietly.

* * *

'Did you hear about the bomb on 'Road last night? Terrible business, it was. I heard they took a few to hospital.'

'Aye,' Horace said grimly. 'I heard that too.'

He had woken up to the nurses talking about the high explosives that had come down just north of Hessle Road, at the western end near St Andrew's Dock.

'Three casualties, so I heard,' the taxi driver continued. 'And a bain, one of them.' He shook his head. 'It's a bad business. I hope they pull through.'

One was already dead. Horace had heard that from the nurses, too. And only one of the other two was expected to survive their injuries.

'They were from round your way, too,' the taxi driver said.

Horace stared grimly out at Anlaby Road. Shopkeepers were taking down their shutters and opening up their doors, while housewives started to queue and workers cycled towards the city.

'Why do you think I'm going home?' he muttered.

There had been a big fuss on the ward when he decided to discharge himself. The nurse had fetched the Sister, who had berated him for his foolishness and sent for the doctor to berate him even more. But Horace remained calmly adamant.

'I have to go home,' he insisted. 'My wife needs me.'

He couldn't imagine the state Patience would be in. Jubilee Row hadn't been hit, but it had been close enough to the blast to feel it, he was certain.

316

He paid the driver and carried his bags down the length of the cobbled terrace towards number ten. The street was in silence, curtains still drawn. Yesterday had been Ada Maguire's wedding, and most of the street had been out celebrating in Somerset Street when the bomb came down close by.

Horace scanned the row of blank houses. Behind one of those closed doors, a family would be grieving. But which one, he wondered.

He opened the door to number ten, full of apprehension.

'Hello?' he called out. 'Patience?'

'Horace?' Patience emerged from the bedroom, a bundle of washing in her arms. 'Gracious, what are you doing here? I thought you were supposed to stay in hospital for another week at least?'

'I wanted to make sure you were all right.' Horace caught sight of the sheets in his wife's arms. They were streaked with blood. 'Patience, what's happened? Why are those—' he started to say, when suddenly his daughter appeared in the kitchen doorway, a tea towel in her hands.

'Hello, Dad.' She smiled shyly at him. 'What are you doing here?'

'Your father's decided to come home, against doctor's orders, I daresay,' Patience sniffed.

'I thought you might need me . . .' Horace looked from one to the other, still struggling to take in what he saw. 'What's going on?' he asked.

As if in answer to his question, the thin sound of a baby crying drifted down from upstairs.

Joyce and Patience looked at each other.

'You'd best come and sit down, Dad,' Joyce smiled. 'We've got a lot to tell you . . .'

Chapter Forty-nine

Edie looked down at the baby in her arms, marvelling at his tiny limbs, the fine fair hair, the little starfish hands. She had carried him inside her for so long, but now he was finally here she could scarcely believe he was real.

He seemed so unbelievably precious, so fragile. And yet the midwife had pronounced him a very healthy, strong little boy.

'He's bonny, all right,' Beattie Scuttle said when she came to visit later that morning. 'Have you got a name for him yet?'

'I'm going to call him Robert, after his father. Bobby, for short.' Edie stroked his cheek and smiled as his little rosebud mouth pursed. 'He looks like a Bobby, I think.'

'Does he take after your husband?'

'Yes. Very much.' So much, it nearly broke her heart to look at him.

And yet at the same time she was glad, because it meant she would always remember Rob whenever she looked at him. And she was sure there would come a time one day when she could think about him without feeling that tightness in her throat and the terrible ache in her chest.

'It's a shame your husband in't here to see him,' Beattie said.

'Yes. Yes, it is.'

There was a loud clatter as Patience, who was kneeling by the hearth making up the fire, dropped the poker.

'Sorry,' she muttered, snatching it up.

'This war, I don't know.' Beattie looked down at the knitted bootees that lay in her lap. She had brought them as a gift for the baby. 'It's a dreadful business, it really is. So many people gone, so many wasted lives . . .'

She stopped speaking so abruptly, Edie looked at her. 'Are you all right, Mrs Scuttle?' she asked.

Beattie smiled wearily. 'Just tired, that's all, ducks. I didn't get a lot of sleep last night.'

'The air raid was bad, wasn't it? Not that I remember much about it!' Edie looked rueful. 'I was too busy with this little one.'

She planted a kiss on Bobby's soft forehead. How many babies could say they were born in an air raid, she wondered.

When she looked up, Beattie was staring at her with an unreadable expression on her face.

'Are you sure you're all right, Mrs Scuttle?' Edie asked.

'Yes.' Beattie got to her feet. 'I'd best go,' she said.

'But you've only just arrived—'

'I only popped in to wish you well and give you these . . .' She laid the ribbon-trimmed bootees on the bed. 'I'll come again in a couple of days, if I'm feeling up to it.'

Edie frowned at her. Why shouldn't she feel up to it? It seemed like a strange thing to say.

'Are you ill, Mrs Scuttle?' she asked.

Beattie shook her head. 'Ill, me? No, I just—' She allowed her voice to trail away. 'I'll come back and see you soon, anyway.'

'And tell Iris and Dolly to come, too,' Edie called after her. But Beattie had already closed the door on her.

'Well,' Edie said to Patience. 'I don't know what to make of that, do you?'

'It's none of my business, I'm sure.' Patience jabbed at the coals with the poker. 'You'll spoil that baby, if you keep picking him up like that,' she changed the subject abruptly.

'I don't care,' Edie said, smiling down at the sleeping infant in her arms. 'I want to hold him and hug him forever. And I will, too.'

And no one could stop her, because he was hers. A tiny person of her very own to love, that no one could take away from her.

And to think, this time yesterday he hadn't been here. It felt as if he had been in her life forever. How could anyone be so overwhelmed with love in such a short time?, she wondered.

It terrified her how much she loved him. After all, she had loved Rob once, and she had lost him.

You won't lose Bobby. The midwife had pronounced him safe and strong, even if he did seem like such a fragile little scrap.

New fears assailed her. What if she couldn't be a good mother to him? What if Rose was right and she couldn't manage on her own? She had made so many mistakes in the past . . .

'There. All done.' Patience set the poker down and paused for a moment, watching the fire blaze. The flames reflected flickering red on her gaunt features.

'You're so good at making fires,' Edie said admiringly. 'It takes me ages, and I never manage to get it going like you do.'

'Yes, well, I've had years of practice.' Patience stood up and brushed the ash from her apron. 'I'm going to post a letter. Do you need anything while I'm out?'

'You could post something for me, too?' Edie said. 'It's over there, on the dressing table.'

Patience picked up the package. 'Mrs Mary Copeland,' she read the name aloud. 'A relation of yours, is she?'

'Of Rob's,' Edie said quietly.

She had made up her mind the previous night to send Rob's pocket watch to his wife.

It was Iris who had convinced her to do it, even though she did not know it. Seeing the pain on her friend's face, her heartache over her husband's betrayal, had made Edie think of Mary.

She didn't know Rob was married when she fell for him. If she had, she would never have answered that first letter, let alone fallen in love with him. It was only after she found out she was pregnant that he confessed the truth.

She had believed he would do the right thing by her. They were so in love, it was only a matter of time before they got engaged anyway. It had never, ever occurred to her that he would not make her his wife, until he told her he had been married for six years.

'Do you love her?' Edie had asked, her voice thick with tears.

'I – I don't know. I thought I did – until I met you. I didn't mean to hurt anyone,' he insisted. 'I was lonely when I was first posted here. I thought we could be friends . . .'

'Friends?' Edie spat the word back at him. 'Someone to pass the time with before you went back to your wife, you mean?'

'Perhaps – at first.' Rob didn't even try to deny it, and that hurt. 'But then I fell in love with you. I mean it, Edie. I love you, I really do.'

But they were just empty words to her now. He could tell her he loved her forever, but that would not make up for the fact that he had betrayed her, or for the desperate situation she found herself in.

Rob tried to write to her after that, but she tore up his

letters. But no matter how much she tried to push him out of her life and her thoughts, she still had the baby growing in her belly to worry about. She would lie awake at night, trying to think of some way out of this terrible mess. And all the while there was Rob, still in her thoughts, even though he deserved no place there. Sometimes she hated him, sometimes she wept because she missed him so much, but either way she could not forget him.

And then one night there he was, waiting at the factory gates after she had finished her shift.

'I need to talk to you,' he had said.

'I've nothing to say.'

'Then don't say anything. Just listen to me.'

'To more of your lies? I don't need to, thank you very much.'

As she had walked away he had stood in the street behind her and shouted, 'I want to marry you, Edie Russell!'

That had stopped all the other factory girls in their tracks, but not Edie. 'Have you forgotten, you've already got a wife?' she had shouted back.

That was when Rob had told her he couldn't go back. He loved Mary and he had never wanted to hurt her, but he knew his future was with Edie and their baby.

'How can I stay with her when my heart belongs to you?' he had said. 'I know I've given you no reason to trust me, but give me a chance to make it up to you, please.'

He was going to tell Mary it was all over, he said. He was being posted down south, but when he was next on leave he promised he would go to see her.

'I want to tell her face to face,' he had said. 'She deserves better than that after six years.'

He had given Edie a ring just before he left. It was only an old bit of brass, but he promised her a proper one on their

322

wedding day. She promised him she would never take it off, and she hadn't.

Edie had never really thought about Mary until she saw the pain on Iris' face the previous night. Up until then she had been so caught up in her own misery that it had not occurred to her there was another woman somewhere, grieving the loss of her husband.

Was Rob like Arthur Fletcher? Edie did not to believe it, but that did not stop the doubts creeping in. Rob had made promises to her and her baby. He had told her he loved her.

But Bessie Weir had thought Arthur loved her, too. And she had believed him when he made promises to take care of her and their son . . .

Edie would never know for sure. But with Rob gone, at least she could go on believing in the perfect future he had promised her, without ever having to find out if he meant to keep that promise.

* * *

She stared at Patience, the parcel still in her hands.

'You know, don't you?' Edie said.

'I don't know what you mean,' Patience said. But the unguarded look on her face had already given her away.

'How did you find out?'

'I have no idea what you're talking about. And I don't wish to know, either,' Patience added, as Edie opened her mouth to speak. 'As you know, I prefer to leave gossip to the likes of Mrs Scuttle.'

Edie looked at her searchingly, but Patience's composed expression was back in place as she put the parcel in her shopping basket. 'This should catch the morning post, if I hurry,' she said.

Edie smiled at her. 'Thank you.'

'Oh, I was going to the post office anyway.'

'You know what I mean.'

Patience looked back at her, and for the first time there was a warmth in her pale blue eyes. 'For what it's worth, I think you're doing the right thing,' she said. 'If the past couple of days has taught me anything, it's that it does no good to dwell on past mistakes. It's far better to look to the future.'

'You're right.' Edie looked down at her baby. Let Mary have her husband's watch, she thought. She had all the memories she could ever need, right here in her arms.

Chapter Fifty

The shop was locked up when Joyce returned home the following morning. But she could hear Reg banging about in his workshop as she climbed the stairs to their flat.

She was relieved he was not upstairs waiting for her. She needed time to gather her thoughts before she came face to face with him again.

Being in the flat again unsettled her. Each room seemed to resonate with the echoes of another fight, a past argument. Here was where Reg had blacked her eyes, where he had cracked her rib and left her sobbing on the floor. This morning she had woken up with a new-found confidence, but being here again, she could feel her nerve failing her.

She pressed her hand to her side, still sore and bruised from last night's beating. It was going to be the last time Reg ever laid a hand on her, she told herself.

She went into the bedroom. The bed had not been slept in. Joyce went to the chest of drawers and began to pull out what she needed, laying it all out on the quilt.

'What do you think you're doing, you useless article?'

She jumped at the sound of Reg's roaring voice, before she realised he was yelling at Charlie Scuttle.

Poor Charlie. What must he be going through? Joyce thought. Without her there, Reg would be taking out all his rage on him.

She was dragging the suitcase from under the bed in Alan's

room when she heard Reg's heavy tread coming up the stairs. She froze, her heart racing.

Don't look back, Joyce, she warned herself. If she allowed herself to weaken, it would be the end of her.

She went back to the bedroom and carried on unpacking clothes from the chest of drawers.

'Well, look who it is.' She could feel Reg behind her, watching her from the doorway. 'I said you'd be back, didn't I? What's the matter? Couldn't you find anyone to take you in?'

Her hands trembled as she folded a vest, but she did her best to ignore him.

'So that's how it is, is it? You're giving me the silent treatment?' There was a sneer in his voice. 'I should be the one sulking, after you walked out on me like that. Are you listening to me?'

She flinched as he snatched the vest from her hands and tossed it to the floor.

'Look at me when I'm talking to you!' He grabbed her roughly by the shoulders and swung her round to face him. His face was a blazing mask of fury. 'You stay out all night, and then you come home and act as if nothing's happened! Aren't you even going to apologise?'

'Take your hands off me.'

Her voice rose, coming out of nowhere, like a volcano in her chest, surprising even herself.

She saw the confusion in Reg's eyes. He was so surprised he released her without a word. Joyce sidestepped out of his grasp and bent to pick the vest up from the floor. Inside she was shaking, but on the outside, at least, she was composed.

'Where have you been?' Reg demanded.

'I spent the night at my mother's.'

'Your mother's?' There was uncertainty in his voice.

'That's right.'

'And since when did you start speaking to your mother?'

'Since last night.'

She added the vest to the pile on the bed, then took another from the drawer. Reg stood in the doorway but there was an awkwardness about him, as if he did not quite know what to say or do next.

'Go down and open up the shop and we'll say no more about it,' he managed finally. 'We've already lost enough custom for today, thanks to you.' He shambled off down the landing. 'And I'll be expecting a cup of tea when—' He broke off suddenly. 'What's this?'

Joyce looked out of the bedroom door. Reg was standing on the landing, staring down at the suitcase she had left there.

'What does it look like?'

Reg narrowed his eyes. 'Don't get smart with me! What's it doing here?'

'Isn't it obvious?'

'You're leaving me?' Once again Reg was in the bedroom doorway, blocking her way. 'You can't. I won't let you!'

Joyce sent him a pitying look. 'Do you really think I'm still afraid of you, Reg?'

For a moment they stared at each other. Reg's hands balled into fists, but he didn't strike her.

Joyce turned her back on him, something she had never dared before. 'I'm not going anywhere,' she said.

'Then why have you—' Reg looked from the suitcase to the pile of clothes on the bed.

His clothes.

He laughed harshly. 'Me, leave? That's a good one!' He shook his head, wiping tears from his eyes. 'Have you taken leave of your senses, woman?'

Joyce said nothing. She was surprised at how calm she felt as she carried on with her packing.

His packing.

'Talk to me!'

'I don't think we've got anything to say to each other.'

He was breathing heavily, snorting through his nose like an angry bull. He stomped off down the landing, only to return a moment later with the suitcase.

'Here's what I think of that idea!' He threw open the window and hurled it out. 'Now then,' he said, facing her. 'What do you think of that?'

Joyce looked from him to the window. Then she did something she never imagined she would do in Reg's presence.

She laughed in his face.

She was still laughing as she went downstairs. Reg followed her.

'You're mad,' he declared. 'Listen to yourself, cackling like a witch. That proves you've taken leave of your senses.'

'Actually, I think I've finally come to them.'

Reg glared at her, his eyes bulging. 'Well, I in't going anywhere,' he said. 'You can leave if you like, but this is my shop—'

'I think you'll find it's Joyce's shop, Reg.'

Joyce smiled at her father. He was waiting in the shop, just as they had planned. 'Hello, Dad.'

'Everything all right, love?'

'Reg threw the suitcase out of the window.'

'Aye, I saw that.'

They both looked indulgently at Reg, as if he was a child having a temper tantrum.

'Let's try again, shall we?' Horace went outside and fetched the suitcase. As he dragged it back inside, Joyce caught a glimpse of Charlie, watching them through the half-open workshop door.

'What are you looking at?' Reg roared at him. 'Get back to work, you lazy, good-for-nothing—'

'Don't talk to him like that,' Joyce said.

'I can talk to him how I want!'

'Not any more,' Joyce said firmly. 'You don't give the orders around here any more, Reg. I do.'

Reg's eyes darted from her to Horace. He looked like a trapped animal.

'It's my shop,' he insisted. 'It's my name above the door—'

'But it's my daughter's name on the deeds.' Horace's voice was quiet but firm. 'Don't you remember, Reg? When I came to see you, just after you were married? I wanted to make sure you were all right,' he said to Joyce, even though he had already explained everything to her earlier that morning. 'Your husband here told me all about his grand plans to open a shop and I agreed to set him up. In't that right, Reg?'

'But you never told me that,' Joyce said. 'You made it seem as if you'd got the money yourself. You were always reminding me how you were the one who'd put a roof over my head, and how grateful I should be. And all the time the shop was in my name. You never told me that either, did you, Reg?'

Her father shook his head. 'No wonder you wanted our agreement to stay a secret,' he said. 'I only went along with it because I wanted you to save face. Let the lad have a bit of pride, I thought. But it was nothing to do with pride, was it?'

'It is my shop!' Reg grunted. 'He might have put up the money but I was the one who put in all the hard work to make this place a success. And as for that stupid agreement—' he turned on Horace. 'Who cares if the deeds are in her name? It's my shop and no one's going to tell me different!'

'Happen we'll have to let the court decide that, eh?' Horace said. 'Don't worry, you'll not be cheated out of what's rightfully yours. We'll see you get any money you think you're owed. But in the meantime, I want you out of here and out of my daughter's life.'

For a moment Joyce almost felt sorry for Reg. He looked lost and confused, his whole life unravelling in front of him.

He let out an angry roar and suddenly he was coming towards her, charging like a bull. His hands closed round her throat and she fell backwards as his face filled her vision, so close she could see the veins pulsing in his temples.

And then he was high above her, dangling in the air and screeching in pain and outrage.

'That's the last time you lay a hand on my daughter, do you hear me?' Horace said.

'Let me go!' Reg struggled to free himself, but her father held him fast.

'Don't bother, lad,' he growled. 'I was a prison warder for twenty years. I've held down bigger and more frightening men than you, believe me.' He leaned forward, pressing his mouth to Reg's ear. 'Now, are you going to go quietly, or do I have to throw you out into the street for all the neighbours to see?'

Reg shook his head, defeated. Her father released him and he tumbled to the floor. He picked himself up quickly, brushing down his apron.

'You've got five minutes to pack what you need,' Horace said. 'We'll send on the rest.'

'You in't heard the last of this,' Reg turned to Joyce, his face twisted with spite. 'I've got mates, you know. I'll burn this place down before I let you have it.'

Horace looked amused. 'And I've got mates, too,' he said. 'Old lags and prison guards who wouldn't think twice about taking on someone like you. And if you even think about causing trouble, believe me, they'll come and find you.'

Joyce looked at her father. For all he was old and sick,

330

Horace was still a tough old swine when he wanted to be. And she had no doubt he meant every word he said.

'It's all right, Dad.' Her voice rose again. 'Reg won't do anything. He's all talk.' She turned to face her husband. Finally she could see him for the pathetic, weak bully he really was. How had she ever been afraid of him for so long?

Reg's expression changed, becoming wheedling and contrite. 'Joyce love,' he appealed to her. 'You can't leave me with nothing. I've got to make a living, in't I?'

'You're right.' Joyce turned to Charlie, who was still lingering in the doorway. 'Charlie, fetch Mr Shelby a bicycle, and one of those knife grinders from the stockroom.' She glanced back at Reg. 'I'm sure he remembers what to do with it,' she said.

Chapter Fifty-one

Edie had just finished changing the baby when she heard the knock on the front door.

She went downstairs to answer it, hoping it might be Dolly and Iris come to visit at last. But there was only Ruby Maguire, standing on the doorstep with a cloth bundle in her arms.

She looked surprised to see Edie.

'Oh, I didn't think you'd be up and about? Where's Mrs Huggins?'

'She's gone to post a letter. She won't be long, if you want to wait for her?'

'No, it was you I wanted. I just came to give you these.' Ruby handed her the bundle. 'Just a few second-hand baby clothes from the WVS. I thought you might like them.'

'Thank you, that's very kind. Do you want to come in for a minute?'

'No, I won't keep you ...'

Ruby turned to go, but Edie called after her, 'Wait. Don't you want to see the baby?'

Ruby looked back, biting her lip. 'I don't want to trouble you,' she said. 'You'll be wanting to rest, I daresay.'

'I've been resting all morning,' Edie grinned. 'And I'm sure you'd like to meet little Bobby, wouldn't you?'

If she did, she was doing a good job of not showing it. 'All right,' she said reluctantly. 'Just for a minute.'

'I'm surprised I haven't had more visitors,' Edie said as she led the way up the stairs. 'I thought Dolly and Iris would be here first thing. It's just through here—' She pushed open the door to the bedroom. Thank heavens Patience had tidied up that morning, she thought. But she was still embarrassed about Bobby's makeshift drawer cot.

'He arrived so suddenly, we just had to make do,' she said. 'But Mr Huggins says he'll go down Hessle Road and collect the crib later. I wondered if Pop might be able to take the rully and help him—'

'No.' Ruby's sharp reply surprised Edie. 'I think Pop's busy today,' she added quickly.

'Oh. Oh well, it doesn't matter. It was just a thought. Well?' Edie prompted. 'What do you think of little Bobby?'

'He's beautiful.'

Edie beamed with pride. 'You can hold him, if you like?' she offered. 'I'll put the kettle on while you have a cuddle—'

'I won't, if you don't mind.' Ruby was already backing towards the door. 'I'll call again another time. I've got a lot to get on with today.'

'I understand.' Edie tried to hide her disappointment. She was longing to share her excitement, but so far none of her friends seemed interested. 'I know you must have a lot on your mind, after last night.'

'Last night?' Ruby shot her a sharp look. 'What about last night?'

'The air raid? I suppose the WVS will be helping out, won't they?'

Big May always joked that wherever a bomb dropped there was Ruby, with a cup of tea and a sack of spare clothes.

'Yes. Yes, that's right.' Ruby looked distracted.

'Mr Huggins says the docks got hit. That's a bit close for

333

comfort, in't it? I'm surprised no one from round here was hurt . . .' She looked at Ruby. 'Are you all right?'

'I'm fine,' Ruby mumbled.

'I can see you're not. What's wrong?'

'I told you, I'm fine!' Ruby's smile was strained.

Edie folded her arms across her chest. 'You're not leaving here until you tell me what's going on,' she said.

Ruby's smile faltered, her gaze sliding away. 'I was told not to say anything,' she said. 'No one wants to upset you, since you've just had a baby.'

'Upset me about what?' A prickle of unease travelled up the back of Edie's neck. 'I'm worried enough now, anyway, so you might as well tell me!'

Ruby sank down on the edge of the bed and patted the mattress beside her.

'You'd best sit down,' she said. 'I've got some bad news . . .'

Chapter Fifty-two

Edie smoothed down the folds of her black dress. It clung tightly around her still swollen belly.

'No one expects you to go, you know,' Patience said from the doorway. 'Not so soon after you've had the baby—'

'I want to be there.'

Patience's mouth pursed. She obviously did not approve, but at least she did not try to argue.

'Are you sure you're all right to look after Bobby while I'm gone?' Edie asked.

'I suppose I'll have to be, won't I?'

'Take no notice of her,' Horace called up the stairs. 'She's been looking forward to having the bain to herself for days!'

'I won't be gone long.' Edie gazed down at baby Bobby, warm and sleepy in his new cot after his feed. She had never been apart from him in the week since he had been born, and it made her heart ache to think of leaving him now. 'I'll be back in time for his next feed.'

'Your mother fusses too much,' Patience said to Bobby. 'Anyone would think I'd never taken care of a baby before.' But as Edie leaned over, tucking in his blankets, she thought she noticed the beginnings of a smile on the older woman's face.

'Are you sure you don't want to come with us?' Edie asked as they made their way downstairs, where Horace was waiting.

'I—' Patience's hand went nervously to her throat.

'I don't think you're ready for that, eh love?' Horace said gently. He was right, Edie thought. Patience had done wonders over the past few weeks, venturing out and about. But this was bound to be too much for her.

'Besides,' Horace said to Edie, 'she was your friend.'

'I still can't believe she's gone.'

* * *

No one else could believe it either, it seemed. Edie gazed at the rows of shocked faces that filled the tiny church. Everyone seemed to be thinking the same thing.

How could someone as vibrant and full of life as Dolly Maguire just disappear from the world? It seemed so wrong, so unfair. It was impossible to think that Edie would never again hear her laughter, or see her blonde curls bobbing as she strutted down Jubilee Row.

Dolly was gone, and she had taken some of the life out of the street with her.

Now all her friends and neighbours had come to say goodbye. The Maguires filled the front rows, just as they had a week before for Ada's wedding. Ada herself sat clutching her new husband's hand, surrounded by her parents and her sisters.

Poor lass, Edie thought, *what must she be thinking?*

Edie tried to catch Big May's eye as she passed, but she was staring straight ahead of her, her eyes fixed on the altar, and the two coffins that stood side by side in front of it.

One big, one small.

In her arms, Big May held baby Kitty. Archie sat white-faced beside her, next to Dolly's sons, George and Freddie. The three boys looked so small and stiff in their shirts and ties, their hair slicked back off their scrubbed faces.

Beyond them was a dark-haired man Edie had never seen before. This must be Dolly's husband Jack, she thought.

Edie and Horace slid along the pew opposite, behind Beattie Scuttle and her sons. Charlie stared straight ahead of him, but Sam kept his head bowed, as if he could not bear to look.

The vicar climbed the steps to his pulpit.

'We are gathered here to say farewell to Dorothy Maguire and Lucy Fletcher, and to commit them into the hands of God . . .'

Freddie whimpered and his brother nudged him to be quiet, but the dark-haired man did not seem to notice either of them.

What must be going through his mind, Edie wondered. This was not the homecoming he had expected. Ruby had told her how he had been trying to dock the boat when the bombing started, how he and the rest of the crew had stood on deck and watched the explosion from out in the estuary, never imagining that his own wife had perished.

And then there was Iris . . .

At least Jack knew the worst of it. But Iris was still in the Infirmary, with no idea her little girl was dead.

'The doctors have said she's not strong enough yet to take the news,' Ruby had said to Edie. 'But how do you tell a mother something like that?'

It was a miracle any of the children had survived. The blast had sent baby Kitty's pram tumbling down the street, until it had come to rest upside down against a lamp post. The metal carapace had shielded her from the worst of the explosion.

'Just a few scratches and bruises,' Ruby had said. 'I don't suppose she'll remember a thing about it.'

Unlike her brother. Edie looked across the church at little

Archie's pale, haunted expression as he sat beside his grandmother. He had been running on ahead, trying to get away from Lucy, as usual, when the bomb hit.

Ruby had told Edie about his nightmares, how he woke up screaming in terror, fighting his way through imaginary flames to get to his little sister.

After the service, they all filed out of the church into the grey November afternoon. It was only three o'clock, but the sky was already darkening.

Ruby approached Edie. 'We're all going back to my house for a funeral tea,' she said. 'It's just family and a few close friends. Mum says you're welcome to come, if you like?'

Edie shook her head. 'Tell her thank you, but I'd best get back to Bobby.'

'Of course. The bain needs his mum.' Ruby's gaze strayed to Archie, George and Freddie as she said it.

'How is Iris?' Edie asked. 'Any news?'

'She's improving slowly.'

'I'd like to go and see her—' Edie began, but Ruby was already shaking her head.

'She in't up to seeing anyone yet. Mum and Pop are the only ones who are allowed to visit.'

Edie nodded. 'Let me know when she's well enough, won't you?'

'I will.'

As Ruby turned to go, Edie called after her. 'She will be all right, won't she?'

Ruby smiled bracingly. 'She's a Maguire,' she said. 'She'll get through this. We always do, in the end.'

When Edie and Horace returned home, Patience was already waiting for them in the hall.

'How did it go?' she asked.

'It was horrible,' Edie said, shrugging off her coat.

'I daresay it was.' She seemed slightly distracted as she said it.

'Has Bobby been all right?'

'As good as gold. He was still asleep when I looked in on him five minutes ago.'

'He should be ready for his feed soon.' After so much sadness, all Edie wanted to do was to hold her precious baby in her arms and breathe in his powdery smell. But as she headed for the stairs, Patience said:

'You've got a visitor.'

Edie looked at Horace. His face was blank too. 'Who is it?'

'You'd best see for yourself. I've told him to wait in our parlour.'

'Him?' As Edie turned to hang up her coat, she suddenly spotted the familiar coat and hat already hanging there, at the same time as she heard the voice from the doorway behind her.

'Hello, lass,' said her father.

* * *

He looked so out of place, for a moment she could only stare at him.

'What are you doing here?' she whispered.

'I wrote to him,' Patience said.

Horace turned on her. 'What did I tell you about interfering?'

'I thought it was only right he knew he had a grandchild.' Patience's expression was unrepentant.

Edie glared at her. She didn't know whether to laugh or cry.

'You've come at a bad time,' she said shortly. 'I've just been to a funeral.'

'I know. Mrs Huggins told me.' Her father looked crest-fallen. 'I'm sorry. Perhaps I should come back another time—'

'Nonsense, you're here now,' Patience cut in, before Edie could speak. 'And you've come such a long way.' She sent Edie a hard look.

Edie looked into her father's pleading eyes. She wanted to turn him away, to hurt him the way she had been hurt. But she couldn't do it.

'You'd best come upstairs,' she said, glaring back at Patience. 'We can talk in private.'

'Does Rose know you're here?' she asked as she led the way up the stairs.

'No.'

She looked over her shoulder at him, expecting him to say more, but he did not.

She felt very self-conscious as she showed him into her room.

'This is nice,' he said, looking around. 'Very cheerful. I like the colour.'

'Blue was Rob's favourite.'

Her father nodded, but did not comment. 'Who helped you paint it?'

'No one. I did it all myself.'

His brows rose. 'While you were pregnant?'

'I didn't have much choice.' She saw her father wince and she knew her barb had hit home.

A faint gurgle from the cot made him turn around. 'Is this my grandson? May I see him?'

He crept towards the cot and peered inside. Edie saw his face light up. 'Oh, Edie, love.' His voice was choked. 'He's a pet, isn't he?'

'You can hold him, if you like?' She hadn't meant to offer, but the words slipped out of her.

'I don't want to disturb him . . .' He gazed longingly back into the cot.

'I need to wake him for his feed anyway.' Edie carefully lifted Bobby from his warm nest and placed him in her father's arms.

John Russell looked down at the baby in his arms, his face trembling with emotion.

'I remember holding you for the first time when you were a baby,' he said. 'I didn't think I could ever love anything as much as I loved you at that moment. I told myself then I'd do anything in the world to protect you—' He looked up, and Edie saw the tears shimmering in his eyes. 'I didn't though, did I? I let you down.'

All the resentment she had felt for him seemed to fade away. 'Oh, Dad,' she said. 'It in't your fault.'

'Then whose fault is it?' His voice was rough with emotion. 'I thought I was doing the right thing when I married Rose. I wanted you to have a mother . . .'

'She was never a mother to me.'

'I know that now. But I didn't see it until it was too late. Or perhaps I didn't want to see it?' He looked down at the sleeping baby in his arms. 'I should have kept my promise,' he said. 'I should have protected you, and I didn't. When you came to us and told us you were expecting—' He took a deep breath. 'I should never have let you go.'

'You couldn't help it. She made you choose,' Edie said.

'I should have chosen you! You're my daughter, my flesh and blood. You needed my help, and I let you down.'

He started to sob, his big shoulders shaking. Edie had only seen him cry once before, on the day her mother died.

'I would have gone anyway, Dad.' She laid her hand on his arm, trying to console him. 'I couldn't stay under the same roof as her, not any more. Besides, you needed her more than you needed me.'

'That's not true—'

'It is, Dad. You were so lost after Mum died, you needed someone to look after you. And for all her faults, Rose has been a good wife to you.'

'But she's driven you away.'

'It was time for me to go.'

He looked up at her, his eyes red with tears. 'Come back with me,' he said. 'Back to York, where you belong.'

'What about Rose?'

'She doesn't have to know. I could find you a place to live, I'd even pay your rent for you—'

'Rose would never allow it—'

'Damn Rose!' her father snapped. 'I don't care what she thinks any more. You're my daughter. I want you to come home.'

'I *am* home, Dad.'

She hadn't realised it until she said the words. When she had first arrived in Jubilee Row she had been a stranger walking into a strange, hostile place. But somehow, almost without her noticing, the street had become her home. And the people who lived there, the Maguires and the Scuttles and most of all Patience and Horace Huggins, were her family.

Her father nodded. He looked defeated, the fight gone out of him.

He placed the baby carefully back into Edie's arms and reached into the inside pocket of his coat. 'This is for you,' he said, pulling out a piece of paper.

Edie saw the cheque and immediately started shaking her head. 'I don't want your money,' she said.

'It's *your* money,' he said. 'I've been putting it aside for years, since you were a girl. It was meant to pay for your wedding, but I reckon you could make better use of it now.'

Edie looked down at the baby in her arms. 'I certainly don't think I'll be needing it to buy a big white wedding dress, do you?' she smiled wryly.

Her father smiled back. 'I don't suppose you will,' he said. 'So will you take it? For little Bobby, if not for yourself?'

Edie took the cheque reluctantly. She couldn't deny the money would be useful.

But at the same time, she wanted more than money from her father.

As if he knew what she was thinking, he said, 'I'd like to see you and the baby sometimes, if you could manage it?' He looked down at Bobby. 'I want him to know his grandfather, if nothing else.'

'What about—' Edie stopped herself. She made up her mind there and then that she would never say that woman's name again, if she could help it. 'I'm sure we can sort something out,' she promised.

John Russell looked at her for a moment, then suddenly pulled her into his arms and embraced her and the baby fiercely.

'You will be all right, won't you, lass?' His voice was muffled as he pressed his face into her hair.

'I'll be fine, Dad.' And for the first time in a very long time, she truly meant it.

Acknowledgements

First and foremost, my thanks go to my editor Katie Brown for giving me the opportunity to create this series. From the moment we first discussed the idea to the final draft, she has been endlessly enthusiastic, encouraging and positive about the whole project. Also, she brings chocolate and doughnuts to meetings, which means she can do no wrong in my eyes.

I'd also like to thank the rest of 'Team Donna', especially marketing and social media supremo Katie Moss, press guru Alainna Hadjigeorgiou and all the sales team for their amazing efforts to get the books out there. Thanks too, to Isabelle Everington and the production team for dealing with some hair-raising deadlines without flinching (at least, not that I saw). And to the design team, who worked so hard to create such wonderful covers. And as ever, I must also thank my agent Caroline Sheldon, for her extreme patience and good sense when I was lacking in both.

Getting to know wartime Hull was a mammoth task, and I was helped on the way by some wonderful people. Thank you so much to Alan Brigham and the Hull People's Memorial for putting me in touch with local historians, who gave me great advice on where to start my quest. I haven't even begun to test the depths of their collective knowledge yet, but I will! Huge thanks also to Martin Taylor and his team at the Hull History Centre. What an amazing place! Every day I visited I seemed to uncover something more fascinating, whether it was a diary, a set of personal letters, or heartbreaking personal accounts of children living through the Blitz. Those records allowed me an insight into the city and its residents, and I hope I've managed to convey some of their fighting spirit in the book.

Last but not least, thank you to my family for their support and encouragement. Especially my daughter Harriet, my first reader and my sternest critic, and my husband Ken, who puts up with more artistic tantrums than is reasonable. I love you all.